THE CHESTNUT TREE

The summer of 1939, and the residents of the village of Boxham are preparing for war. Beautiful Judy Melton, social butterfly Meggie Gore-Stewart, demure Mathilda Eastcott, and tomboy Rusty Todd are determined to play an active role while their husbands and brothers, fathers and lovers are away fighting. However, it is not just the young women who are determined to find new roles—so are their mothers. In this manner the little Sussex port, facing as it does the coatline of Nazi-invaded France, finds its closely sewn social fabric beginning to unstitch, inch by inch. The women meet under the chestnut tree to look back on a landscape that has changed irrevocably. None of them is the same as before, and yet, as the men return from war, they are expected to slip back into their roles of mother, daughter, grandmother. Only the chestnut tree continues to flourish in the accepted fashion, becoming the uniting symbol of all that has passed forever.

THE CHESTNUT TREE

Charlotte Bingham

CHIVERS PRESS
BATH

First published 2002
by
Bantam
This Large Print edition published by
Chivers Press
by arrangement with
Transworld Publishers Ltd
2002

ISBN 0 7540 1825 3

All the characters in this book are fictitious, and any resemblance to actual persons, living or dead, is purely coincidental.

British Library Cataloguing in Publication Data available

Printed and bound in Great Britain by
BOOKCRAFT, Midsomer Norton, Somerset

To those women who lost their lives in the cause of Victory, 1939–1945, and whose courage remains unrewarded, their exploits unsung—but who are remembered always by those who loved them.

‘One sees great things from the valley,
only small things from the peak’

G. K. Chesterton

'One sees great things from the valley; only small things from the peak.'

G. K. Chesterton

Prologue

Everyone in the village loved the chestnut tree. It had become a part of their lives, something for the boys to climb, and for the girls to sit under on summer evenings pretending to talk, while all the time watching the boys watching them.

Over half a century's growth had seen the tree reach a height sufficient to dominate the green sward that lay in front of so many of Bexham's houses and cottages. On fine days, weekends, and, naturally, bank holidays, the older people would sit themselves in deck chairs under its now thick branches and wait for a cricket match to start, leaving it only to stroll across the green to the pub for much needed liquid refreshment.

Inevitably, initials were carved all over the trunk of the tree, hearts circling a good many of them, hope and romance entwined for ever in the rough but still shining bark. Many of the younger owners of those initials must have been completely ignorant of the circumstances of the tree's origin—that it had been, and still was, such a potent symbol to those who had planted it.

'We have known it since it was hardly more than a conker,' the older women liked to joke, stroking it, and often one or other of them would start to sing the old wartime song: 'Under the spreading chestnut *tree*, Neville Chamberlain said to *me*, if you want to get your gas mask *free*—join the blinking AR *Pee*!'

Originally, the singing of that song would often have stopped just as suddenly as it had begun, to be replaced by the sound of a siren, and the village green would have hurriedly emptied, mothers catching their children's hands and heading for the shelter, far ahead of the older people, who always seemed more concerned with the whereabouts of their library books and their umbrellas before falling in at the end of the orderly queue that led to the reinforced basement under the cricket pavilion. Nowadays that same pavilion echoed not to the wail of a siren but to applause for Bexham's cricket team, to the sound of talk and laughter, to those particular feelings of ease and contentment that are known, collectively, as peace.

AUGUST 1939

CHAPTER ONE

The sudden hush was eerie, a blanket of silence so complete it seemed as if even the pigeons and the London sparrows had decided to fall into line, ceasing all activity. From Chelsea Town Hall all the way back up the King's Road to Sloane Square people were stilled, such was the power of the electrifying wail that filled the air. For a moment, as the siren finally fell silent, it seemed that all that could be heard was the gentle rhythmic flap of a newspaper lying in the gutter, and the faint and distant mewing of a cat somewhere. It was an odd scene, made doubly so by the absence of children, all of them already safely despatched, together with pet dogs, to the country. No one moved, or spoke. For a second it was as if they were frozen into immobility, until on cue, everyone began to make for the places to which they had been instructed to go. The customers from Peter Jones department store, the shoppers in the King's Road, the passers-by in the side streets and the people who had been standing at bus stops, all heading for their designated roped-off refuge stations in strict and orderly fashion.

Yet still there was no panic. It was as if everyone had been waiting for this particular moment, which indeed many people had, and for months now. At the sound of the warning, every car had slowed and pulled to one side in order to allow past the ambulances and fire engines which had, of a sudden, appeared on the streets, their bells clanging noisily as they sped to perform their duties, coping with the anticipated high explosive bombs, putting out fires, attending the wounded, and digging the dead out of the rubble.

* * *

'Oh God, I wish I had put on more comfy undies,' Meggie sighed, staring up at a little patch of sky just in front of Peter Jones. 'My brassiere's killing me. By the way, what are you doing after this show's over, Judy?' She turned her head sideways and stared at her friend, who was lying beside her.

'I was meant to be driving down to meet Walter's family. But if the balloon's really gone up, I daresay his leave will be cancelled.'

'I'll bet it hasn't.' Meggie put her hands behind her blond-haired head and rested on them with a contented sigh as if they were an exceptionally comfortable and much loved pillow. 'I mean the balloon's having gone up, not Walter's leave. How long's he been in uniform? Not that long, surely?'

'Three months now. And anyway, length of service is nothing to do with it. Not if the balloon's gone up.'

'I always wonder where that phrase comes from? The balloon going up.'

'No idea, I'm afraid. Something to do with the Great War, I expect.'

'I say, Judy, what do you think they'll call this one when it's over—the Little War?'

Judy sighed and closed her eyes, blotting out the brilliant summer day. Despite everything, the coming war, her fears for everyone, despite all that, all she could think about was Walter. He had a weekend's leave coming up, and if this emergency presaged the real thing, then this might be the last chance they had of seeing each other for quite some time.

Or even ever. Somehow, before today, the implication of Walter's being in military uniform had not quite sunk in. His volunteering for the Senior Service had simply seemed rather dashing and heroic. But now as she and Meggie lay on the hard London pavement waiting to be attended by some of the multitude of nurses who were now converging on Sloane Square, while all around them the air raid wardens scoured the skies for signs of enemy aircraft, Walter's joining the Navy became a reality.

Her thoughts were interrupted by the sound of Meggie giggling.

'Oh, my *God*!' Meggie exploded, pulling a face and nodding her head in the direction of a body of women advancing on them. 'Just don't look—or, rather, just *do*!'

Judy closed her eyes in disbelief, before opening them again and starting to shake with suppressed laughter. The women ARP wardens had obviously not had the benefit of a fitting for their uniforms, the result being that the seats of their newly issued trousers reached down to their knees, a sight that was made all the more hilarious when they bent down over the bodies lying about Sloane Square.

'Well, this is one person who will not be joining the ARP and wearing those little numbers, darling . . .'

Meggie rolled her eyes in mock horror, and they both laughed.

Even the announcement that followed on the

loudspeakers, warning everyone of the imminent arrival of enemy bombers in eight minutes' time, only added to Meggie's amusement.

'Oh, for goodness' sake, that is just *too* much! How on earth do they know they'll be arriving in eight minutes? Why not six? Or even two?'

'Making trouble as usual, Miss Gore-Stewart?'

'Heavens above! Dobsie!'

Meggie half sat up again, flicking back her hair from her eyes and staring up in unaffected delight at a tall, well-upholstered warden who was smiling down at her from under her tin hat.

'Miss Gore-Stewart. How are you, dear?'

'Miss Dobbs was my old piano teacher, Judy. Dobsie, this is Judy Melton, a friend of mine. We were having such a giggle, Dobsie, I mean to say, those trousers, have you ever seen anything less modish?'

'This isn't a *garden* party, you know, this is very serious,' Miss Dobbs told Meggie, responding to a frowning look from another warden. 'So if you wouldn't mind resuming your recumbent position, Miss Gore-Stewart, while I find a nurse to attend to your wounds.' She stared momentarily at the blood on Meggie's long, elegant legs.

'Sorry, Dobsie.' Meggie lay back down. 'Didn't mean to get you into hot water. It's just *so* good to see you, but really—takes me back a bit, I can tell you.'

'There's been a slight misunderstanding. These wounds are so bad, surely this young woman should be taken to the ambulance?'

But perhaps because of Meggie's carefree demeanour Miss Dobbs's question fell on deaf ears, and Meggie was left firmly where she was, despite her obviously bloody wounds.

'So you're a *warden* now, Dobsie,' Meggie said, settling herself once more on the pavement. 'I was thinking of doing something like that, as a matter of fact. I was thinking of being a warden. Or driving something. Someone I know is driving a taxi with a trailer pump—you know, for the fire service.'

'I can't see you doing that, Meggie.'

'No.' Miss Dobbs nodded in agreement with Judy as she signalled in vain for someone to start bandaging Meggie. 'Not the sort of thing you're cut out for at all, Miss Gore-Stewart.'

'I don't know. You could hardly say Henrietta Clive was exactly cut out for it either. Up till now, the only thing she's really driven before last week was her fiancé dotty. Anyway, I rather fancy the fire service as it happens. According to Henrietta it's giving all the men a purple fit, having girls join. And the best thing of all—you'll never guess. The head of the fire service is called Mr *Firebrace*.'

'I just hope if you do join you don't get called out to *me*, dear.' Miss Dobbs prepared to go in search of a nurse. 'We're going to have our hands quite full enough without running after the likes of you.'

Meggie smiled at no one in particular, and then gave a contented sigh.

'Good old Dobsie. She was so cantankerous teaching me the piano. Used to threaten to drop the lid on my hands when I got a scale wrong. There's always something very Nazi about music teachers, don't you find, Judy?'

Miss Dobbs was back as quickly as she had gone, busy instructing the young nurse as to the extent of Meggie's and Judy's injuries.

'This one is an artery,' she said, pointing to Meggie's leg. 'Femoral, obviously. And the other casualty is a fracture—hence the bone sticking out of the lower leg.'

'*Ugh.*' Judy pulled a face.

'Double ugh,' Meggie agreed. 'And very painful, you bet.'

'I hate pain.'

With a mutual sigh the two young women lay back while the nurse began to see to their imaginary wounds; as she did so, despite the whole exercise being only, as Dobsie had just said, *a dress rehearsal for the real thing*, Meggie and Judy found they had both stopped believing England was still at peace.

* * *

Perhaps because of this, as they tidied themselves up later at Meggie's flat in Wilbraham Place and Judy got ready to drive down to Walter's parents in Sussex, the jokes seemed to have stopped.

Washing off her wounds in the bathroom Meggie said, 'God, I hate the sight of b for blood, really I do. It's just so—*bloody*.'

'It was only an exercise.' Judy sat back to examine her newly applied lipstick in the looking glass. 'And—you know, Meggie—I mean *who* knows? We *are* still at peace, after all. I mean, we are not yet at war, are we?'

'Meaning as in it may never happen?' Meggie glanced at her friend as she brushed out her hair. 'Not now Hitler's repudiated Munich. I hardly think so, Judy, hardly think so. No, we are at war already, and we all know it. It's just a question of time before peace is finally knocked for six.'

'Maybe that's all the Germans want. You know, peace? Even after Czechoslovakia. That's what some people say. There is no harm in hoping, after all, is there?'

'As a matter of fact I think we've had it, actually.' Meggie put down her silver-backed hairbrush, giving her fair hair a final careful adjustment with her hand. 'Everyone thinks so, except for some politicians. You should hear my grandmother on the subject. She says the politicians should have stood up to Hitler years ago, and by heavens I absolutely agree. But anyway, here we are, and I suppose we've just got to make the best of it. I mean who knows? We could all be dead in a few weeks.'

'I wish you hadn't said that just before I see Walter again. I won't be able to think of anything else all weekend.'

'It's just how it is—we have to accept it.' But because her voice suddenly sounded flat Meggie gave a brilliant smile.

'It's just that I'd rather not think about it right at this moment. I don't want to think—you know, that this is the last time I might see Walter.'

'Of course not.' Meggie smiled at her friend and gave her a quick hug. 'Sorry. Tactless old me—and here.'

Judy turned back from the door to see Meggie holding out a square cardboard box.

'Don't forget your gas mask.'

* * *

As she headed south to Sussex and Bexham and

Walter's family home, it seemed to Judy that Chummy, as she called her little motor car, must be feeling as nervous as she was—judging from the way the little Austin 7 pinked and spluttered up the hills approaching the South Downs.

'Anyone would think you were a horse,' she muttered to her car as it gave a particularly dramatic start before suddenly speeding ahead. 'And I had bad hands and was hurting your mouth. Come on—don't break down on me now. Please, Chummy, don't break down on me now!'

'Probably something in the petrol,' Peter Sykes, the young local garage attendant said to her when she stopped for help on the outskirts of Bexham. 'Bit of dirt, I should say.'

'She normally never misses a beat. Must be feeling tense. Like us all, eh, Peter?'

Peter nodded, his expression sober. 'They say we'll be at war by the end of the month.'

'Then there will be petrol rationing, I suppose. And after that, heaven knows what.'

'Well, there's definitely going to be a war all right. I just got my call-up papers.'

Judy looked up suddenly as Peter carefully replaced the nozzle of the pump back in its holder, before wiping his hands down his overalls.

'I say—have you really, Peter?'

'Yes. Got 'em yesterday, matter of fact, Miss Judy. Aiming to be a mechanic in the RE. The Royal Engineers, although Dad thinks I'm destined for greater things.'

'That's fathers.'

Peter smiled at the pretty, dark-haired slim girl in her perky hat. Bexham being Bexham they had known each other by sight for as long as they could remember, although their paths had never really crossed until Judy's father had bought her a car for her eighteenth birthday. Since then Peter had seen a great deal more of Miss Melton, since she dropped in to his father's garage to fill up her Austin 7 every time she left Sussex to return to London; although up until today he had hardly dared exchange more than a few words with her, holding only brief conversations that usually centred around Judy's little car. Now, with the prospect of joining up, Peter's shyness seemed to have vanished.

'I hear young Mr Tate's already in uniform, Mr Walter Tate that is.'

'That's right. He's joined the Navy, quite a few months ago, actually.'

Peter took Judy's ten-shilling note in payment. 'The Senior Service. Bexham likes the Navy, doesn't it?'

'Yes. Must be something to do with being on the sea.' They both laughed, and Judy looked away suddenly, at the day that was already in its country uniform, at the soft Sussex colours, at everything that was familiar to her, and so dear.

'Someone's got to fight the wars the older ones get us into, haven't they?' Peter went on as Judy followed him into his tiny office. 'And we can hardly let you girls go doing it, eh? Fighting our battles for us. We can't have that, now, can we?'

'I don't see why not. As a matter of fact I've been thinking about joining up. Maybe going into the Wrens. One of my cousins is absolutely determined on it. And a friend of mine in London—she says she's going to join the fire service. We girls must do *something*. Do our bit.

Can't just stay at home and knit, I mean can we?'

Judy looked round the immaculately kept garage, and found herself smiling at its familiar neatness, its meticulous sense of order, its reassuring smell of oils and petrols, of machines and dirty overalls.

For his part Peter looked up at her as he sorted out her change.

'Let's just hope it doesn't come to that, Miss Judy. They was saying in the Three Tuns the other night that even if it does come to war, it'll all be over by Christmas.'

'They said the same thing the last time, apparently, Peter. You know, the Great War? they said that then, that it would all be over by Christmas. I think they say that to get people to join up, so they'll think it's only going to be just for a bit, don't you think?'

'Maybe, but this time we really will see to them, Miss Melton. Good 'n' proper. You wait. We'll kick the little Nazi in his behind, if you'll forgive me saying so, Miss Melton.' He gave her a wink as he handed her the change.

'I hope you're right, Peter. It just all seems so . . . unimaginable . . . war, on a perfect summer day like this.'

'Doesn't bear thinking about, I agree.' Peter followed her to the car, holding the door open for her while she carefully tucked her long skirts under her as she sat behind the steering wheel. 'So let's just not, shall we? Let's not think about it.'

'Good idea, Peter. Far too nice a day altogether.'

As he watched Judy's ruby-red Austin 7 disappearing in the direction of the village Peter was filled with the particular emotion that is inevitable when for a few seconds a young man tries to contemplate his whole world ending.

'Come on, Weasel,' he said finally to his lurcher dog who was lying stretched out in the summer sun, happily enjoying an untroubled sleep. 'Time to shut up shop and go for a walk.'

*   *   *

Rather than head straight for her destination, Judy took a brief detour to one of her favourite spots on the outskirts of the village, a woodland laced with silver birch and dominated by the great elm trees that had stood for centuries guarding the long walks which time and man had cut through the swathe of trees. In spring the woods were always covered in primroses and bluebells. Now in summer they were filled with the pure scents of every kind of wild flower, some of whose names, like the scents of the flowers themselves, came drifting back to Judy. But as she sat looking at the flowers instead of beauty all she could see were the grim images recalled from paintings that she had seen of the last war, young men with bandaged eyes, dead, limbless; and instead of birdsong all she could hear was the sound of the siren ringing out over Sloane Square and Meggie's voice joking with Miss Dobbs.

Finally, realising it didn't really bear thinking about, she stood up, and hurried out of the woodland back to where her car was parked. Without looking back, she fired Chummy's engine and set off as quickly as she could for the village that lay at the bottom of the hill.

* * *

Shelborne, the Tates' seaside house, had been built in 1922 by Hugh Tate as a birthday present for Loopy, his American wife, and named by him after her parents' house in Virginia. Together they had planned and planted what was now the beautifully cultivated garden which surrounded the small family house built in the Tudor style. The large and charming grounds led down to a private beach, and what with all the main living rooms and bedrooms overlooking the sea and its air of informality, Shelborne was every inch a family home.

Hugh had met his wife on a visit to America some six years before the outbreak of the Great War when J. Walter Dauncy, the American company for which he worked as European representative, had invited him over in order to promote him. Asked out to the company chairman's holiday home on Long Island shortly after his arrival Hugh had met and fallen instantly in love with the chairman's beautiful, high-spirited and athletic daughter Loretta, known to all in her circle as Loopy.

After a brief and passionate courtship, they married, and Hugh had brought Loopy to live in England, where in keeping with the pace of their relationship they quickly produced three boys, all named after their maternal grandfather's company: John, Walter, and Dauncy.

Hugh had served the full term of the Great War in the Royal Navy, and had managed, miraculously, to survive, in spite of being injured three times. Nothing seemed to impair his unquenchable high spirits and on his safe return to England he had re-entered the domestic and professional frays with the same abundant good humour and energy that he had displayed both before and during the conflict.

All three of Hugh and Loopy's boys had inherited their father's good looks and high spirits, most of all Walter, 'the meat in the filial sandwich' as he always called himself. Effortlessly charming, Walter was the delight of every eligible girl in his circle, yet he entertained no notions of getting married and settling down until, on leave from the Navy, he had been asked to make up the fourth man in a mixed party.

As soon as Walter danced with Judy Melton he knew he had met the love of his life. It was one of those moments that people are inclined to ascribe to fate, but which Walter described as *It*—since he knew that from the moment he had taken this quiet girl with the dark hair and eyes into his arms the meaning of his particular existence had all at once become perfectly obvious.

Walter stared at himself in the bathroom mirror. Unbelievably, that first dinner with Judy and their friends was still less than one month ago. He sighed suddenly and hugely, holding on not just to the thought, but to the moment. Downstairs he could hear his father playing the piano in his usual vivacious style. He was just coming to the end of his, and Walter's, favourite selections from *HMS Pinafore*.

Walter smiled as he listened. He could hardly ever remember his father playing anything *except* Gilbert and Sullivan on his beloved Blüthner baby grand. Whenever the family had driven down to Shelborne from London for the weekend, it was always, always Gilbert and Sullivan, because Hugh

Tate loved what he called 'a jolly good tune'. Something that they could all sing together.

'You seem a little on edge, my love,' Hugh said, once he had finished sailing with great satisfaction through the Captain's Song. 'Not like you to clock-watch.'

He put a fresh piece of music up in front of him, and prepared to play and sing once more, this time something from *Trial by Jury*, as Loopy glanced at the clock yet again.

'Has to be because this is the first time any of the boys has brought a girl home instead of taking them out, Hugh,' Loopy replied, lighting one of her favoured Turkish cigarettes. 'I have a real feeling that this might be the Real Thing, for Walter, I really do. Imagine.'

'Knowing Walt he's probably bringing her home because he's stony broke and can't afford to take her out dancing. Let's hope she's not stuffy like her parents.' Hugh pulled a face.

'I don't think so, somehow. Besides, you're forgetting. Walter is now in uniform. Uniforms have a habit of hurrying things along, Hugh, remember, the last time?'

'Walter's not the sort of chap to go getting hitched just because there's going to be a bit of a dust-up, darling. And as I said, they've only just met.'

'I seem to remember a certain young Englishman who proposed to a certain young American the day after he *met* her.'

'I've told you over and over, Loopy darling, I only proposed to you because I couldn't think of what else to say.' Hugh deserted his beloved piano and strolled across the sitting room to the drinks table. 'Your usual?' He held up the cut glass cocktail jug. 'Do you know, I think whoever invented the dry martini should be made a Knight of the Garter.'

'A Knight of the Shaker would be a little more appropriate, and you don't have to laugh at such a poor jest.' Loopy tapped the side of an ashtray nervously with her cigarette, before glancing at the clock on the mantelpiece. 'I just hope Miss Melton is going to be on time. You know how tetchy Cook gets when people are even five minutes late.'

'Well, she would. Daughter of a ship's cook.'

'*Naval time is five minutes before time!*' they chorused together, and Loopy smiled affectionately across at her husband.

'Naval time is five minutes before time!' Loopy repeated to herself, and shook her head before going on, 'That is engraved on my heart, for heaven's sakes.'

'Then there's the staff.'

'*Must get home to their families*,' they chorused again, before raising their glasses to each other.

Since the Tates generally only came down to Bexham at weekends and for their summer holidays their domestic staff—comprising two maids and a cook—lived out in the village itself. Although it was an old joke of theirs, quoting Hugh's father, whose favourite sayings as regards domestic staff these had been, nevertheless the Tates had always been particularly conscious of their employees' need to get back to look after their own families; and now they realised they had an even greater responsibility to make sure that whatever happened they did not keep them too late.

Once the staff had left Shelborne of an evening

the Tates knew that they would be hurrying off to evening class, learning how to cope with gas attacks, to dress wounds, equip shelters, make sandbag barricades. In fact they would spend the rest of the evening finding out about all kinds of things they would have to be prepared to do if and when war broke out, for the whole of Bexham was getting ready for that eventuality. Young and old, parents, grandparents, and children, were rehearsing their gas attack drill, helping to put up blackout blinds at their bedroom windows, constructing sandbag defences—more than essential in seaside Bexham—as well as digging bomb shelters in their gardens, not to mention the work that was being put into preparing arms in readiness for defence against the expected Nazi invasion.

Since Walter had built Shelborne for her, Loopy had come to understand that the little harbour village worked and thought as one. To be part of Bexham was to belong to something they all knew was very special. Most of the working womenfolk were only part-timers, like Loopy's own staff; other than that their lives were entirely domestic. Cook, for instance, was a married woman with three grown children, and the two girls who helped clean and serve still lived at home with their families, preparing to become nothing more exciting than good housewives and mothers.

The growing popularity of Bexham as a small sailing resort had meant that there had been a slow but steady growth of new houses built specifically for part-time occupation by the affluent, something which suited the women of Bexham admirably since it meant that, as a consequence, there was a steady demand for part-time cooks, daily cleaners and housemaids. The wages were fair and the hours mostly weekend and holiday only. Thanks to a sequence of what had seemed to be endlessly fine summers, since the Great War life in Bexham had been as close to ideal as possible, marred only by the growing anxiety about what was happening across the waters that lay beyond the mouth of the pretty estuary.

The village itself was made up of an array of thatched white-painted cottages—some of them dating back as far as Tudor times. For the most part the village was made up of small Queen Anne and Georgian houses with perfectly manicured gardens, and a couple of historic and architecturally fine public houses. The new homes, those built for the yachting fraternity, lay to the west of the village itself, along a winding road that followed the contours of the coastline. Most of them had been put up in the nineteen twenties on sites with uninterrupted views of the estuary and the tiny, busy harbour, now separated from them by long, lush green lawns and burgeoning herbaceous borders.

This ever-growing row of houses was perfectly situated for the yachting families who owned them, the direct access to the estuary meaning they all had private moorings, thereby keeping the small harbour free for the use of local fishermen and boatmen.

Not that the seafaring fraternity divided itself into amateurs and professionals. The path that ran along the shoreline all the way from the mouth of the estuary back to the harbour ensured that all returning sailors, a class well known for its thirst, inevitably made their way back to the Three Tuns, the ancient brick and flint public house that dominated the quays.

It was a harder walk in winter, of course, with the flood tides and the heavy rains which swept in from the Channel. Sometimes in the worst of weathers the pub was cut off from any frontal approach, the estuary waters whipping themselves against the ancient masonry, cascading up the front steps, sometimes even battering the ground-floor windows, which at these times were usually lined with villagers intent on watching the storm rage outside, while drinking their way slowly through their pints of beer and cider in the warmth and safety of the snug.

'I was talking to Mrs Marsh this morning, down by the war memorial,' Loopy said now, as Hugh searched for another sheet of music. 'You know who I mean by Mrs Marsh? Her brother used to do some gardening here. She lost both her sons and her husband in the Great War. We were saying—we were remarking on the fact that they've hardly finished carving the names on the memorial from the Great War. And now—now here we go again, or so it seems.'

'Oh, Mrs Marsh. Bless her, but she is such a gloom pot.' Hugh stared at the music in front of him, his reading glasses on the end of his nose. 'Time for another song. And shouldn't Walter be down by now?'

'You know Walter, Hugh. He's so relaxed he's probably fallen fast asleep getting dressed.'

Hugh smiled at that and began to play. Loopy lit another cigarette and she too smiled as she heard what her husband had selected.

Upstairs, far from being fast asleep, Walter was

wide awake putting the final touches to his bow tie while lending half an ear to the strains of G&S that were floating up from down below as his father resumed his piano recital. Satisfied that his tie was now perfect, Walter checked his wristwatch and glanced yet again out of his bedroom window in the hope of seeing Judy's little plum-coloured Austin turning into the drive.

Downstairs, probably by popular request from himself, his father had abandoned *Trial by Jury* and returned once more to *HMS Pinafore*.

'Oh, pity, pity me—our Captain's daughter she!'

The words floated up to Walter, more than ever filled with poignancy.

Except Judy was not a captain's daughter but the daughter of an admiral. This, among many, was one of the reasons why their two families had never socialised, even though they had both had houses in the same small village for what now seemed to Walter to be for ever and ever.

The problem was that Judy's family, the Meltons, were Old Bexham, a distinguished family who had lived in the fine manor house two miles west of the village for centuries, apparently, while the Tates were considered at the very least *nouveau*—certainly by the Meltons. The fact that Hugh's father had served in the Royal Navy was simply not a good enough reason to bring the two families together socially, since Judy's father, Sir Arthur, had not only retired as an admiral but had also been awarded a rare naval VC for his heroism during the Great War.

Yet even though Hugh Tate had also been decorated for gallantry, the Tates were considered to be not only *parvenus* but also visitors rather than residents, coming down as they did for the greater part only at the weekends. The Tates were therefore not thought to be quite good enough to be included on the Meltons' social list—something which, being the Tates, they had always accepted with wry good humour.

Now that Walter had fallen in love with Judy, however, things must, or rather should, change. Now the very least the Tates might perhaps expect would be a few words of greeting after matins at St Mary's Parish Church, Bexham, instead of just the formal nod that Sir Arthur had been bestowing on a fellow member of the Senior Service for the past ten years, on those many occasions when they had attended the same church service on Sundays. As for the outcome of their falling in love, Walter knew he would have to wait and see, just as he knew it most certainly was not going to be plain sailing.

'Just don't be late, Judy, there's a good girl,' he muttered to himself as he brushed the sleeves of his dinner jacket carefully with a camel-haired clothes brush. 'Please, please, don't be late, whatever else you are.'

To his vast relief as he turned to leave his bedroom he caught sight of Judy's car also turning, slowly and carefully, into their gateway. Breathing a silent word of thanks to the Almighty, Walter faced himself once more in his dressing mirror. His heart was now beating absurdly fast and he could feel the palms of his hands turning hot. Giving a deep sigh he did his best to pull himself together, putting his shoulders back and adopting his favourite expression of apparent nonchalance, before taking out his silver cigarette case and filling it from the open packet of Players on his chest of drawers. But although outwardly he now looked the unconcerned and debonair man about town everyone took him to be, knowing the controversy his attachment to Judy Melton was going to arouse, Walter was actually praying as hard as he could, for just about everything, but most of all for Judy and himself.

* * *

Hearing the voices in the hall as Gwen the housemaid greeted their visitor, Loopy quickly checked her lipstick in the glass of the small silver compact Hugh had given her last Christmas. Her expression relaxed suddenly, as if she had heard some favourite bird singing in the garden beyond the French windows, and with sudden shock she realised that what she was actually hearing was the pretty light voice of a girl in the hall outside. To a mother of sons, used as she was to hearing only the baritone sounds of men's voices around her house, it was, of a sudden, quite lovely.

'I do hope I'm not late,' Judy was saying as Gwen took her coat. 'I had a little spot of trouble with my car on the journey down.'

It was a nice light voice, Loopy decided as she straightened her perfectly cut jacket, not particularly patrician, not particularly anything really, just a nice, musical voice.

'Do I look OK?' she hissed at Hugh, who was busy draining his second martini fast and furiously.

'You look just fine, honey child,' Hugh returned in mock American. 'One million and two dollars. Anyway. You know how much I like that outfit.'

Loopy kissed her fingers to him in gratitude before giving herself one last check in the large mirror that hung over the fireplace. The glass reflected a tall, auburn-haired, slim woman, elegant in a smoking suit in white albene with short sleeves and wide, sailor-style trousers. Perfectly suited to an informal dinner at home, the whole was set off by an organza blouse printed with large flowers and a string of stylish large pink pearls at the neck.

'Miss Melton,' Loopy said by way of greeting, standing framed in the doorway of the sitting room. 'How do you do?'

Meeting properly for the first time the two women took to each other at once, much to their mutual surprise. Judy had been more than nervous at the thought of meeting Walter's mother, Judy's mother, Lady Melton, having always referred to her, most unkindly, as Mother New Money, implying that she must be brash and vulgar, whereas the woman welcoming Judy to her house was in fact the very opposite. Judy saw at once that Loopy was elegant, charming, classy and quite wonderfully easy going.

In her turn Loopy found herself pleasantly surprised by Judy Melton, faced not with the expected diffidence of someone from a family that considered itself to be socially superior, but with an obviously shy, nervous, but impeccably mannered young woman. She was also surprised by Judy's beauty, now that she had a chance to see it close to, rather than just glimpsing it distantly. Judy Melton was blessed with that perfect English complexion which requires little or no make-up, as well as thick dark hair, dark brown eyes, and a slim but rounded figure. She was, in fact, in appearance and manner the very opposite sort of woman to Loopy who, whatever she wore, always managed somehow to look like something straight out of *Vogue* and to sound like someone out of a light comedy. In contrast to Loopy's sophisticated ensemble Judy, having not had time to go home, had chosen to stop at a friend's house near the harbour and change into a long, printed silk dress that fell to her feet. Capped sleeves, a tie belt in the same material, and a decorous bodice caught at two points with tiny gold clasps completed the design. With one evening glove on and one held in the accepted way, she looked every inch the kind of young lady that any father would wish his son to ask to his house.

'I do hope I'm not late,' Judy pleaded again, having been introduced to her silver-haired host. 'As I was telling your maid, my car started to misbehave on the way down, and it was all very worrying, really.'

'You're on deck before our son,' Hugh remarked, preparing fresh cocktails with some vigour. 'He seems to have got himself lost at sea somewhere.'

'A relief to get out of London, I imagine,' Loopy said, lighting a cigarette. 'We've been down here since last weekend. I can't say I found being in town very comfortable. All those alarms and excursions, and around Peter Jones of all places, I hear.'

Judy quickly took up this point, describing the war rehearsal in Sloane Square and how her friend Meggie Gore-Stewart had been forced to lie back while her old piano teacher bandaged her mock wounds, all of which Hugh immediately found hilarious, saying over and over, 'I say, what a hoot! What a hoot!'

'My husband has an extremely warped sense of humour, Miss Melton,' Loopy said, smiling, while accepting a fresh drink from Hugh. 'Perhaps he'll let us in on what's just *so* funny.' She winked at Judy, and blew a perfect round O with the smoke from her cigarette.

'The idea of holding rehearsals for a war, that's what is so funny. You can't rehearse *war*.'

'You have drills in the Navy. I really don't see the difference.'

'The difference is we sailors are drilled to perform and behave in a certain way. You can't do that with civilians. Besides, the fact is you don't know what's going to hit 'em—as well as where or how.'

'But you can rehearse where people are meant to go, Captain Tate, in the event of an air raid, I mean. In order to sort of minimise the panic, as it were. I mean, the drill must have been jolly useful for the ambulance people as well, not to mention the fire service.'

'Well, of course you can practise. But it's just so terribly British, wouldn't you say? And none the worse for it, I might add.'

Loopy smiled at Judy.

While they all waited for Walter to come down, they pretended to discuss how best to prepare a country for war, with Judy sticking staunchly to her contention that being forewarned was to be forearmed, in spite of Hugh's remorseless teasing.

'They're not giving you too hard a time, I hope,' Walter remarked, casually, as he wandered into the elegant modern sitting room. 'The Tates are inclined to gang up on single girls, I must warn you.'

Loopy stared at her middle son as he greeted his girlfriend. *Oh my!* Her heart went out to him—love really was so utterly, utterly painful. She remembered how it had been when she had been taken to meet Hugh's mother, as if it were yesterday. Old Mrs Tate had been such a stickler for convention. Loopy could still remember the look in Hugh's eyes, the transparent hope that she, Loopy, would not put a foot wrong, let alone both feet. Somehow she had got through that awful experience—she still didn't know quite how—and had finally won the approval of her mother-in-law, against all the odds, yet even now the thought of it made the palms of her hands sweat. She would do anything in her power to prevent this young woman standing by her son's side from suffering the way she had been made to suffer, while Hugh's mother had forced her to jump through every conceivable hoop.

'I see from the luggage in the hall that you have brought your gas mask, Judy,' Walter noted, solemn-faced. 'Don't tell me war's broken out in London and they have forgotten to tell us down here?'

'I came more or less straight from this air raid rehearsal in Sloane Square. I was just telling your parents about it, as a matter of fact.'

'It's the latest thing in London, old man,' Hugh told his son, over-seriously. 'They're learning to stampede in orderly fashion.'

'Don't tell me you were rehearsing dressed like that—'

'Doesn't she look smart?' Loopy put in, quickly. 'I just love that colour on you. Goes so well with your hair.'

'Thank you. Actually I went home and changed, once the rehearsal was over. We ended up lying on the pavement pretending to be casualties, covered in fake blood from a theatrical costumier. And then I changed again when I arrived down, at a friend's house, because it was quicker.'

Judy smiled shyly and took a sip at her drink, taking the chance to sneak a look at the elegant but casual way Walter's mother had chosen to decorate the sitting room. Its cool, pure colours and fashionable square-shaped but comfortable-looking furniture were very different from the traditional chintzes and faded pastels of her own home, the manor house. Yet much as she liked the modern look, she was quite sure her mother most definitely would not approve of such up-to-date style, however suitable for an informal weekend seaside home.

'Would you like to see the gardens?' Walter touched Judy gently on the arm. 'That is, Mother—if we have time?'

'Of course you do, honey. Papa will give an extra loud bang on the gong when we're ready to eat.'

* * *

Walter gave Judy his arm as they strolled down the long lawns that led to the sea. It was a perfect summer evening with barely a breeze. The tide was running out, and the lightly rippling waters glinted in the evening sunshine. A line of ducks swam upstream, looking as serious as ducks somehow always seem to do when in convoy, while overhead a cloud of swallows swooped to pluck invisible insects out of the air. Yachts bobbed at their moorings with their sails neatly furled while on top of their gently swaying masts large and lugubrious-looking sea gulls watched for any sign of food either in or on the water. At the far end of the estuary a couple of large yachts waited for the tide to turn, and eastwards in the harbour some of the local fishing boats were preparing to leave on the last run of the tide, for a night's fishing in the Channel.

'Odd, isn't it?' Walter pondered, tapping a cigarette on his silver cigarette case. 'This is about exactly how it always is this time of day, this time of year on the river. How it's been for centuries, I imagine. And yet—only a matter of a hundred miles or so up and over the Straits of Dover there are guns pointing in our direction. Bombers ready for take-off. Troops ready to embark. It just doesn't seem real somehow, more like something in a film or a play.'

'Do you really think there will be an invasion, Walter?' Judy asked, holding on to his arm with both her hands. 'Everyone's talking about it as if it's just about to happen, as if it's bound to happen.' She paused, hope in her eyes. 'But, I mean, some people seem to think there's a possibility it can still be averted.'

'There's an outside chance war can be avoided, I suppose. The government definitely has not given up all hope, not entirely. But if push does come to shove and there is a war, Judy darling, I'm afraid there will be every chance of an invasion.'

'It's too horrible to think of, Nazis in Bexham. I just can't bear to think of it.'

'We have to face reality. We have to imagine the worst. To do anything else is madness.'

'I'd much rather not, not just for the minute anyway,' Judy replied, detaching herself from him to walk to the point where the gardens ended and the beach began.

Walter watched her for a moment, silhouetted against the evening sun. He was trying not to take his own advice about eventualities, preferring to remember this moment for what it was, rather than for what it might never be again.

Cling to it, he urged himself. *Print this moment for ever on your mind so that it will become as much part of you as your own heart.*

At first neither of them heard the distant gong summoning them back to the house, at least not until it was practically an echo on the slight summer breeze.

'Judy.'

But Judy had already turned away from her prospect to come back to his side and re-link arms.

'I love this place, Walter,' she said as they began to walk back towards the house. 'I should like to live somewhere just like this. Right on the water. Overlooking the estuary. Our house has no view of the water at all. Somewhere like that, just along the bank there, that would be an ideal spot.' She waved vaguely at some acres of scrubland situated just before the Point. 'The best of both worlds. A view of the sea that's not too exposed, and the protection of the hills by the Point. Be a splendid place for a house.'

'Absolutely ideal.'

Judy stared longingly at the site she had pointed out, imagining herself married to Walter, both of them living there happily for the rest of their days.

She dropped his arm to take hold of his hand,

holding it loosely, and walked up the lawn in his wake, trailing behind him just a little, as Loopy turned from the sitting-room window.

'Play some Cole Porter, Hughie,' she urged suddenly. 'Please. I feel like singing.'

Hugh immediately turned from *HMS Pinafore* to the introduction of *Anything Goes*. Loopy's lovely smoky contralto voice floated out across the lawns, summoning Walter and Judy in to dinner.

CHAPTER TWO

In the older part of Bexham, the *correct* part as Lady Melton preferred to think of it, there was no sound of any music and precious little of any conversation at Magnolia's, the house inhabited by Lionel and Maude Eastcott.

In fact about the only noise to be heard around the house at dinner time that evening was the sound of Lionel Eastcott's fork scratching the bottom of his dinner plate as he slowly raised slice after thinly sliced morsel of boiled chicken to his mustachioed mouth. When he finally cleared his plate and carefully placed his knife and fork to one side of it, he slowly wiped his mouth with an over-starched white napkin before staring with little interest down the dark oak dining table at his wife Maude, seated at the far end.

'And Mathilda is?' he asked, as he generally did every Friday night.

'I told you. Mathilda has gone to the cinema with the Morrison girl,' Maude replied irritably, giving a small shove to her Wedgwood plate, as if by pushing it away from her she could dismiss not only the tastelessness of the chicken but also this ever growing belief in an impending war, the very reason Cook had abruptly upped and departed back home to her family in Derbyshire, leaving them with only Dolly the housemaid to help out, duties which unfortunately included acting as substitute cook.

Maude Eastcott knew everything there might be to know about flower arrangement but not one thing about composing menus, let alone the art of cooking. Like almost every other woman of her social standing she had always considered such matters to be beneath her, relying on Cook to tell her what the week's meals should be. So now, when Dolly arrived in the morning room holding a notebook and looking not only forlorn but utterly blank, Maude had absolutely no idea of what to suggest for the coming week—other than kedgeree, or some roast meat or other, and after all even Maude knew those two dishes could hardly be eaten at every mealtime. She had therefore taken to ordering women's magazines to help her out with suggestions for Dolly. Nothing too difficult, just simple menus, but enough to satisfy her husband, she devoutly hoped.

Fortunately Lionel was no gourmet, actually preferring simple food, simply cooked. So although the question of household meals continued to irk Maude, the matter was really an academic one, until this very evening when her husband chose to pass a comment.

'That chicken was inexcusably dull, Maude,' he said, after washing the taste of it away with a good draught of water. 'One would have imagined it not to be beyond the bounds of possibility to have served some sort of sauce with it. And as for the potatoes. What *does* Cook think she's doing?'

'*Cook*, as you well know, Lionel, returned to the bosom of her family over a month ago now,' Maude replied with a deep sigh. 'Cook was one of the first of the deserters to leave Bexham, if you remember.'

'Ridiculous. If there's going to be a war, it's hardly going to confine itself to the Home Counties.'

'I will have another word with Dolly, but not tonight.' Maude gave another tiny sigh, as if to indicate how hard her times now were. 'Tonight would not be the right moment. Her sister is having a baby, and her mother apparently—as Dolly puts it—is under the doctor once more.'

Lionel now placed his knife and fork to the other side of his plate and stared at them, assessing their new position.

'Rather him than me is all I can say to that. Rather him than me. So what's next? Plums and custard, I'll be bound—with too much custard, no doubt.'

Maude resisted the temptation to sigh yet again and instead simply raised her eyebrows as pointedly as she could, which was a useless exercise since her husband was staring not back at her, but up at the ceiling.

'Were you to have preserved your soul in patience for once, Lionel,' she told him, 'you might have discovered without my having to tell you so that while there may be none of the custard you care to mock, there is cream with the plums this evening. Plenty of cream, as it happens. I managed to get some at the weekend, from the farm beside Owl Cottage. You know, where the old Miss Hardings used to live, before they passed on.'

There was indeed to be cream with the pudding, but that circumstance was due not to foresight, but to chance. Unusually for Maude she had happened to glance into the kitchen just before she and her husband had gone in to dinner, only to spot a cold carpet of ageing yellow custard in the sauceboat. Knowing full well the sort of repercussions that would follow should such an obscenity find its way to her husband's dining table, more in hope than in confidence she had raided the Frigidaire, where as good fortune had it she found the remains of a jug of clotted cream left over from dinner two nights earlier.

'Cream, Mr Eastcott, sir?' Dolly wondered miserably. 'Not that there's much.'

'Thank you, Dolly,' Maude said crisply, noticing a look of alarm spreading across her husband's face. 'Just serve the plums, please, without any running commentary. Lionel?'

'What's she doing with her gas mask? Maude—' Lionel stared at the government issue gas mask that was hanging by a string from the maid's waist. 'The war hasn't started yet, Dolly. Least not to my knowledge, anyway.'

'Mr Eastcott is right, Dolly. One hardly thinks you need such a thing in here. In the *dining room.*'

Maude emphasised the location as if she were referring to some exclusive London club, which it always seemed to her dining rooms everywhere rather resembled.

'We've been told to be prepared at all costs,' Dolly replied valiantly, as if to disobey would be treachery. 'They told us last evening—at the lecher.'

'Lect-*ure*, Dolly,' Maude corrected her. 'And that will be all, thank you.'

'It's all very well—'

Dolly's protest was cut short by her employer.

'I said that will be all, Dolly.'

'Hmmm,' Lionel grunted, after sampling his first spoonful of fruit. 'Sugar. These plums are practically inedible like this, Maude. Is there no sugar?'

'The sugar's in front of you. Sifter. Sugar. In front of you, Lionel.'

Maude sighed yet again and stared out of the window. She was so bored she found herself almost longing for the threatened war, anything to break the terrible monotony of what now passed for a life. As for this evening, how she wished that she could be somewhere like the cinema, with her daughter Mathilda. Mattie went to the cinema every Friday evening, lucky thing, but since rather than being Lionel's daughter Maude was, for her sins, Lionel's wife, such a treat was quite out of the question. They had been to the cinema together once in the last five years, on a rare joint visit to London, and even then it had really been only because it was Maude's birthday. In celebration of which Lionel had, very graciously, allowed Maude the treat of going to see the latest Marx Brothers film, an entertainment he himself had found completely without merit. The only good thing about Maude's present family life was the fact that at least her daughter still lived at home, because without the liveliness of young Mattie's company Maude seriously believed she might, long ago, have gone mad. Lionel had always been nothing short of dull even at the best of times, but at least most of those times he had been away from home on business. Now, having sold his business in order to enjoy a premature retirement, he was at home all the time that he wasn't out on the golf course, which was about as exciting for Maude as her WI jam making was for Lionel.

As she stared out at the beautiful summer's day that was now drawing to a close, somewhere on the air she thought she could hear a band playing. Hearing the melody she found herself smiling, as the tune was the one to which she seemed to have spent her entire youth dancing.

'Black bottom,' she sang to herself in her head.

Suddenly it seemed unbearable to think of how far they had come together, and yet how little they had actually grown together. It had not always been like this. The sound of the clock ticking, Maude's foot moving up and down, up and down, relentlessly, ceaselessly, under the table. Emboldened by the extra sherry she had managed to steal before dinner she looked down the table at her husband.

'Lionel?'

'What is it now, Maude?'

'Can you hear the music? That tune? Listen—' Maude cocked her head towards the half-open window.

'Some people have little or no thought for others,' Lionel sighed, getting up from his chair and going to close the window. 'If I've told the Harrisons once about their wireless—'

'I rather meant you to listen to what was playing. Or have you forgotten how we used to dance to that? How we used to love to dance, Lionel? I can't remember the last time we did.'

'I should think not. At our age. I don't know what you must be thinking.' Lionel sat back down and resumed eating his plums.

'Black bottom,' Maude sang in a remarkably pretty voice, at once earning a hard stare of disapproval.

'We are at table, Maude, if you don't mind.'

To the accompaniment of her husband's crunching his way through the last of his now well-sugared plums, Maude half closed her eyes and cast her mind back to the days when she was first married, a time when it seemed to her she had spent forever dancing and partying in sequined dresses with little feathers in her hair. Glancing down the table at her husband she found it almost impossible to believe that the stolid, taciturn grump now carefully wiping the ends of his greying moustache with his table napkin was the same person who used quite literally to sweep her off her feet on the dance floor, doing the Charleston and the Black Bottom until they were both fit to drop.

'I should just love to go dancing again, Lionel,' Maude said suddenly, almost in spite of herself. 'Why don't we go to the Pantiles on Saturday?'

'You seem to have forgotten we are on the very verge of a European war, Maude.'

'I have not indeed, Lionel. That was the whole point of my suggestion.'

'To go and disport ourselves on the dance floor? When any moment the world might go up in flames?'

'Eat, drink and be merry was all I was thinking, Lionel,' Maude said quietly, pushing her pudding plate to one side. 'I fail to see the harm in that.'

'I fail to see the good.' Lionel frowned down the table at her, unable as ever to fathom the contradictions of the female mind. Here they were almost certainly about to be plunged into another continental conflict and all his wife could think about was putting on her glad rags to go dancing. It really was too much. But then it was only to be expected. His mother had tried to warn him off marrying Maude.

She's a fast girl, just as her mother was, she had kept telling him, with tears in her eyes. *You'll regret it, Lionel. You're far too conventional to marry a girl like that.*

But in spite of his mother's advice he had gone ahead and married the vivacious Maude Alderman, attracted more by her unconventionality and her apparent fast ways than anything else. And just as predicted he had lived to regret it because nothing, it seemed, was ever enough for his bride. Whatever she was given, time, attention or gifts, was never enough. So Lionel had long ago given up the unequal struggle to satisfy his restless wife, and hidden himself within his cocoon of social orthodoxy.

'I am about to smoke a cigar now, Maude,' he said, in warning. 'So knowing how much you object to the aroma—'

He eyed her over the cigar he was preparing, cueing her exit. But Maude was not to be hurried away from the dining table, as she usually was. Aware that time might well be running out for all of them, she remained firmly seated to make one last plea that they should go dancing at the weekend.

'I fail to see how you can think about such frivolities, Maude,' Lionel replied, carefully disposing of the cut end of his cigar in a small silver ashtray. 'Europe is gearing itself up to meet possibly its greatest threat since goodness knows when, and all you can think about is enjoying yourself. You would be far better occupied checking your blackout arrangements, making absolutely sure we are properly prepared for any major contingency, instead of entertaining such totally unsuitable notions in that head of yours.'

'I'll have you remember that is precisely what I have already done, Lionel,' Maude answered hotly. 'I have stocked the cellar—'

'As I see. With a bountiful supply of marmalade, not to mention a near endless quantity of tinned sardines—and a vast number of shoelaces and boxes of matches, the sight of which I have to admit quite stumped me. Apart from being quite unable to fathom their use should the balloon go up, I must tell you it is the sort of behaviour of which Whitehall utterly disapproves. Not to mention the opinion of our neighbours, should the fact of your hoarding come to their notice.'

'Goodness gracious. I am not alone, in case you think I am. Everyone's stocking up on things, Lionel. You don't go to the shops, so you wouldn't know. You should have seen the free-for-all for groceries in Underwoods yesterday morning. If I hadn't got there early—'

'You are not to hoard, Maude,' Lionel interrupted. 'It is quite against all the government directives.'

'I don't see the use of directives, not personally.' Maude sighed, and she took out a powder compact from her handbag, which was quite against all the rules of etiquette, and powdered her nose. 'Not if and when it comes to war. It'll be every man for himself. And much good will your attitudes do you.'

'You would rather we just sat here and let the Nazis walk all over us?'

'Of course not, but what good can you and I do at this moment, except defend ourselves with croquet mallets and golf clubs? I mean really, the government has been, like so many of your sex, just a little slow, wouldn't you say?'

'We will defend ourselves with whatever is to hand, Maude,' Lionel sighed, over-patiently. 'Until the provision of arms proper, that is.'

'He'll huff and he'll puff and he'll blow our house down,' Maude replied, waving the cigar smoke away from her face with her hand. 'I've never heard of anything so ridiculous.'

'At least we're prepared to fight for our country,' Lionel said, with a glint in his eyes. 'Unlike that appeasing family of yours.'

'You know I do not see eye to eye with my family.'

'I should hope not, Maude. It is precisely because of people like your family that we are in the situation we are in now. The petite bourgeoisie, famous for burying their heads in the sand, not to mention the so-called aristocracy and certain members of our royal family who see only good in Mr Chamberlain's wretched policy of appeasement—they are all responsible for our present grave predicament. We should have been prepared for this conflict—properly prepared, I mean—we should have been ready for it years ago.

Instead of burying our heads in the sand.'

'Really?' Maude looked at him, a hard gleam in her own blue-shadowed eyes. 'And whose golf club was it that told the Auxiliary Fire Service when they arrived there for an exercise to run along and find somewhere else to play?'

Lionel ignored the jibe, although he had in fact been one of the officials responsible. Instead he contented himself with tossing the discarded match he had used to light his cigar into the ashtray, and avoiding his wife's eye as she at last rose to leave the table, allowing him to enjoy his smoke.

After Maude had swept out, Lionel rose and poured himself a large whisky from the decanter on the sideboard. It was at these times he had little or no idea either why he had married such an infernally stupid woman, or why he had stayed with her. The other mystery was how they had managed to produce a daughter like his beloved Mathilda, a young woman who was so entirely different from her mother it was sometimes impossible to see where Maude had entered the equation. Mattie was such a good and undemanding girl. Unlike most of her contemporaries, she was a model daughter, never giving her parents any trouble or causing them a moment's embarrassment or worry.

Lionel checked the time on his gold wristwatch. It was five minutes after nine o'clock, which meant that it would be about an hour before Mathilda would be home to tell him all about what she referred to as the *flick* she had just seen, rattling off the story in double time and acting out some of the more dramatic bits. Lionel, who professed to be a devout non-cinemagoer, feigned as little interest as possible during these charades, but it obviously never fooled his daughter since she always launched into her cabaret almost before she had taken her coat off. Seeing that he had possibly another hour yet to waste Lionel dallied as long as he could before finally consigning his cigar to the fireplace, draining his second whisky and taking himself reluctantly off to the drawing room to spend yet more slowly passing minutes in the company of his ever restless wife.

*   *   *

As the Tates prepared to go in to dinner Judy looked around the assembled company, thinking how different life at Shelborne was from her own domestic existence. Here were Walter and his father, relaxed in dinner jackets and chatting idly over cocktails while at home her parents would be sipping a formal sherry, her father in traditional tails, scorning the newer, racier fashion for dinner jackets when dining at home. Lady Melton was also expected to dress in a much more formal style. Beaded gowns from her trousseau, together with embroidered reticules and small diamond earrings, were still adhered to by the admiral's dutiful wife, so different from the charismatic and utterly modern Mrs Tate.

Nor would their pre-dinner conversation have been accompanied by the sound of someone playing the piano, let alone being heard to be singing lustily in a fine baritone voice as their guests arrived. Judy's parents had never made the slightest effort to move with the times, but never had this fact been brought home so sharply as it was on this sun-filled summer evening at

Shelborne. As if meeting Walter had not been sufficiently wonderful, there was tonight the originality of his warm-hearted and idiosyncratic family to add to the excitement, their numbers now boosted by the arrival of Walter's elder brother John.

'I thought Walter had told us all about you,' John said as he was introduced to Judy. 'But I see what we got was merely a sketch, although we did all meet once, I think, at a village fête. You won the tombola.'

Judy blushed, feeling shy at the compliment, accompanied as it was by wide-eyed appreciation. Whereas Walter was of medium build, with a debonair and seemingly careless manner, John was tall and, being more even of feature, appealed as being more handsome, although not in Judy's eyes, naturally. However, with a sportsman's physique, and an immediately discernibly different approach to life, he was definitely what Meggie Gore-Stewart would call 'a dish'.

And while Walter confessed to fearing boredom more than anything else, which explained his dragonfly manner, preferring as he did to hop quickly from subject to subject, it seemed to Judy that John was the very opposite sort of person, perhaps resolute possibly to the point of stubbornness, as well as serious to the point of solemnity, judging from the way that he was staring down at her.

In fact this was not the case at all, and had John been able to guess what Judy was thinking about him he would have hooted with laughter, a character trait his mother had long given up trying to cure.

Young men need a socially acceptable laugh just as much as young women do, John. If you bray like a mule you'll only attract lady mules in return.

All this usually fell on deaf ears, until this evening, when the normally garrulous John seemed suddenly silenced by meeting the girl with whom he knew his brother Walter was so in love.

Quite simply he could not remember when he had seen anyone with such pretty colouring as Judy. What with her dark eyes and her dark hair, plaited for evening around her head and knotted carefully into her neck, her face seemed to have picked up an extra glow from the evening sun. As he shook Judy's hand it seemed to John that, with her shy smile, she was some sort of vision sent down to Shelborne for the evening, destined to take flight again once the clock in the hall struck twelve. The elegance in the way she moved, the manner of her smile, her sweetly modulated voice, made her entirely different from anyone else he had ever met.

'Do you think Judy might have her hand back now, John?' Walter came to Judy's side. 'Anyone would think you'd been away at sea for the last ten years without sight of land, let alone a pretty girl.'

'Yes, yes, of course.'

John turned quickly away. Probably the eve of war, but he had never felt jealous of his younger brother before. Walter, the meat in the sandwich, or whatever he called himself. He must be the luckiest young man alive.

* * *

'Have you asked her yet?' Hugh Tate questioned

his middle son as they strolled round the gardens after dinner. The others had returned inside, Loopy and Judy finding the air turned chilly and John accompanying them on the pretence of good manners but really because he could not bear to be parted from Judy for a moment longer than necessary.

'Asked her what, Pops?' Walter countered as casually as he could, glancing back at the house now glowing with lights and alive with the sound of chatter and the dance music someone had just put on the gramophone.

'Asked her if the moon's made of cheese, you idiot.' Hugh rolled his eyes and puffed deeply on his pipe. 'Because if you don't ask her soon, that great lump of a brother of yours will. Sure as eggs are eggs.'

'It's rare enough for John to ask a girl to dance, let alone—let alone anything else, Pops.'

'Oh yes?'

Walter followed his father's look back to the house. Young Dauncy, who had come in from a day's sailing too late for dinner, was dancing under the good-humoured tutelage of his mother, while Judy was dancing with John, laughing at something he had just said, enjoying herself; but not too much, he hoped.

'I haven't even been to meet her parents yet, Pops,' Walter finally replied, still watching his brother with Judy. 'That isn't going to be easy. What with Sir Arthur being an admiral. And—well. You know, the Meltons being Old Bexham.'

'I know.' Hugh took his pipe out of his mouth and pretended to examine the contents of the bowl to conceal his exasperation.

'I was trying to think about what Sir Arthur would make of me. I've only just joined the Navy. He'll probably see me as a bit of a rookie, I am afraid. Sure to, in fact. Want me to wait until I've earned my stripes, and all that, before I ask Judy to marry me.'

'That's why you've been thinking of becoming a submariner. Good choice. Nothing like heroism to impress the old salts.'

Hugh stuck his pipe back in his mouth and gazed up at the stars above them, trying to make sense of the fact that if there was to be a war there had to be submariners, and that even though all submariners were after all somebody or other's sons, the job was there and had to be done. Hugh had no favourite son, of that he was quite sure—it was just that Walter, his middle boy, was the one who was most like him, so he always felt he knew just how he was feeling. Walter even had his father's eyes.

'To be perfectly serious, Pops, if you don't mind,' Walter insisted, 'I want to try to get permission to marry Judy before the show starts. If we're going to be able to get married it has to be now. Before it all gets serious.'

'Of course. Understood, dear boy. Absolutely. But there again it's not as if you've even asked the girl.'

'That is quite correct.'

'She might say no, old thing. You're not going to know where you are till you ask her. Whole thing could be just a lot of hot air. She certainly seems to be enjoying dancing with your brother.'

Walter followed his father's mischievous look. For a moment they both watched Judy and John dancing in what was, after all, perfect innocence.

'Yes,' Walter said, losing his poise and gulping suddenly. 'But I mean this is hardly the time or the place, Father.'

Hugh smiled to himself. He knew from the quite unmistakable look he had seen on Judy's face when she had first seen Walter that evening how much she was in love with his son yet, as always, he could not resist teasing the boy. His leg-pull was obviously working, judging from the deep frown now furrowing Walter's normally sunny brow. Walter knew he should have proposed to Judy already but he had been fighting shy of it, so nervous was he of actually making the proposal. He had kept rehearsing the words in his head, and then imagining himself opening his arms and kissing her passionately and joyfully when she said yes, but what had prevented him so far was the possibility that she might refuse him, and he would have made a terrible fool of himself. After all, whatever they felt for each other had so far remained more or less unspoken. Hugh knew that she could refuse Walter, if only for the very best of motives. A war that was now almost certain to break out was a good enough reason for a girl not to want to be married.

'Whatever you might be thinking now,' he said, seemingly quite out of the blue, 'it will be worth it. I know what it's like, old boy. I was exactly the same age as you when I joined up. And when I came to my senses and wondered what the heck I'd done, it was precisely this sort of thing—a summer evening just like this, surrounded by family, wondering whether I'd ever see any of them again, then walking with my father out in the evening air, out into our gardens.

'I remember the smell of stocks on the air as if it was yesterday. The sound of my mother singing at the piano. There we were, at perfect peace it seemed, and just like now, all hell was about to be let loose the other side of the Channel.' He stopped. 'But it was all that, a sense of what we were and I believe still are. One knew one had to fight for it, or it would be lost for ever. Despite the grey areas of why we were fighting in the Great War I still saw it as a grand privilege to join in. Thank God, there are no grey areas this time, dear boy. We know what it's all about. You know what you're going to fight for, I know. You're going to fight to save our world.'

Walter nodded, but he said nothing in reply, because all he could really think about was how to propose to Judy, and when.

* * *

'Sit still, will you?' Rusty scolded her younger brother Mickey, at the same time removing the illicit unlit cigarette from his fingers and putting it in her pocket. 'You're a right blooming fidget box.' She frowned and pulled Daisy, her West Highland terrier, closer to her, as if to get her out of the way of Mickey's unsettling influence.

'Should be home and in bed, that's where Mickey should be,' Tom, her older brother said, filching the cigarette back from his sister's pocket and quickly lighting it up. 'Way past his bedtime.'

'Very funny,' Mickey growled, hoping his deep frown looked as fierce as he intended. 'I'm allowed to stay up as long as the rest of you now.'

'Then put a sock in it,' Tom advised. 'You know

how voices will just carry and carry over water until you might as well be on the telephone.'

The three Todd offspring, Rusty and her two brothers, Tom and Mickey, were sitting in the shadows of their father's boathouse on the edge of the quays, hoping to catch sight of the return of Mr Kinnersley's yacht *Light Heart* from yet another mysterious cross-Channel trip. They were also keeping a weather eye out for their father who was still out fishing. If he should appear first, then it had been agreed between them they should vanish silently into the summer night and stick to their alibi, that they'd been out rabbiting. Their father would not take kindly to the notion of his children spying, least of all on Mr David Kinnersley, one of Bexham's most eminent gentlemen residents.

'Course we all knows why Rusty 'ere's come out tonight, don't we?' Tom teased, drawing on his Woodbine. ''Cos we all knows who's got a pash on our nobby Mr Kinnersley.'

'Shut up, you.' Rusty screwed up her face, making a grimace. 'Or I'll tell Mum about you giving Mickey cigarettes.'

'You goes red like a beetroot every time he looks at you, Rusty Todd,' Tom continued. 'Let alone when he smiles at you.'

'That right?' Rusty replied. 'What about you and that Virginia Morrison then? You just have to look at her to go the colour of a Red Duster.'

'Don't know what you're talking about.' Tom widened his eyes and tapped the ash of his smoke with his index finger. 'She's the one what does the blushing, not me.'

'Like heck,' Rusty scoffed, pushing Tom

playfully off his perch on the pile of upturned herring crates. 'I could toast a teacake on your cheeks, so I could.'

'Least she's the same age as me,' Tom replied, picking himself up and pinching the top of his sister's arm in return. 'She's not old enough to be my mum.'

'Shhhh!' They both looked round at Mickey who was pointing to a light in the estuary. 'Here's a boat!'

They watched the bobbing mast light as the craft made its way slowly towards them, the faint throb of the outboard becoming gradually louder.

'That's him,' Rusty said jubilantly. 'That's the *Light Heart* all right. I'd know that jib anywhere.'

'Quick! Down behind the crates! Quick!'

Tom led the way, jumping off his perch and slipping out of sight behind the pile of boxes. Rusty quickly followed, Daisy under her arm, her free hand clasped over the terrier's muzzle. Mickey followed suit, and from their hiding place the Todds were able to watch the slow arrival of the lone motor yacht as its skipper brought her safely into berth at the very top of the quays.

'I can see his passengers all right,' Rusty whispered. 'There's two at least down below and there's another come out on deck.'

'More of his fancy women, you reckon?' Mickey asked, sticking his head a bit higher over the crates to get a better look.

'Well I'll be,' Tom said, slowly, as he watched the figure on the deck come into view. 'That's no fancy woman. Unless I'm seeing things, that's a nun.'

They all stared, none harder than Rusty who was quite unable to believe her eyes as she watched two more nuns emerging from the cabin to be handed off the boat and up on to the quay by David Kinnersley, immaculate as ever in his white sailing trousers, old school cricketing sweater, and the faded blue nautical cap which he doffed politely as he saw each holy sister safely ashore. Rusty was so used to seeing nothing but glamorous women on board the *Light Heart* that she found herself to be secretly relieved by the type of passenger with whom David Kinnersley had for some reason chosen to sail into Bexham that evening, while wondering quite what could have prompted the most dashing and eligible man in Bexham to have devoted an evening's sailing to such a group of unlikely ladies.

'They're tall,' Mickey whispered, 'for nuns, specially foreign nuns.'

Tom scratched his nose thoughtfully as they continued to watch the nuns, now being ushered towards David Kinnersley's Bentley saloon which was parked and ready waiting for his return, as always, in the road leading to the harbour.

The Todds fell silent, watching enthralled as the car disappeared into the summer twilight, driven by their hero, and bearing its mysterious cargo away from Bexham.

* * *

'Mathilda?'

Mathilda smiled conspiratorially at her friend Virginia as they hung their coats up in the hall, putting one finger to her lips to remind Virginia of the need for discretion.

'Yes, Dad,' she called back to her father. 'It's

only me—and Virginia. We were wondering—'

'Can't hear you, dear! I'm in the study!'

Mathilda put her head round the study door and smiled.

'Sorry, Dad. We were just wondering if it would be OK for Virginia to spend the night.'

'OK indeed.' Lionel sighed heavily, looking up at his daughter over the top of his newspaper. 'I don't know why I bothered to have you educated.'

'We wondered if it would be *all right*,' Mathilda corrected herself.

'You'll have to ask your mother.'

'But it's all right with you, Dad?'

'As I said, you'll have to ask your mother.' Lionel turned the page in his paper and flapped it straight. 'Course it's all right with me. Or OK—if you'd rather.'

Lionel smiled the smile he reserved for his daughter when he considered they were secretly conspiring against Maude, to be rewarded in return by Mathilda's equally special 'for-Dad-only' smile.

'You're an ace, Dad,' she said, bending down to kiss her father's forehead. 'I'll go and find Mum and ask her, while Virginia rings her mother.'

'How was the film?'

'Super,' Mathilda replied, with a quick look at Virginia. 'Absolutely super.'

'What did you see?'

'What did we see?' Mathilda echoed quickly.

'*The Loving Way*,' Virginia said. 'It was *very* good.'

'Thought that was the one you saw last week?'

Mathilda exchanged another quick look with her co-conspirator, widening her eyes in query.

'No, Mr Eastcott,' Virginia assured him. 'We saw

Wuthering Heights last week. They're showing *The Loving Way* this week.'

'You probably got muddled, Dad. When we talked about the trailer probably. Come on, Virginia—you'd better telephone your mother. So she knows where you are.'

The two girls hurried out of the room, watched benevolently by Lionel, his face glowing with delight at the sight of his beloved daughter in her little navy blue blouse and floor length skirt with matching jacket. He could hardly bear to think what he would do without his darling little Mattie. The one and only thing it sometimes seemed to him that marriage to Maude had brought him was the supreme happiness of being a father to such a daughter. Mathilda was the delight of his life.

Having suggested that the girls make themselves a cup of cocoa before retiring, Lionel took the opportunity to mix himself a fresh whisky and soda, and much to his horror found himself humming the Black Bottom as he did so. He stopped the moment his daughter came back into the room with a tray of cocoa and a plate of biscuits.

'What was that tune you were humming, Dad?' Mathilda asked, sitting down as Virginia came into the room behind her. 'Sounded rather jazzy.'

'Bit before your time, poppet,' her father muttered, helping himself to one of the biscuits on offer. 'Something your mother used to dance to.'

'Mum used to love to go dancing. You should take her sometime, Dad.'

Lionel sighed the sigh of a married martyr, but said nothing. Usually there was no need, since Mathilda was invariably on his side. Not this time, for some reason.

'We could all go dancing one evening,' Mathilda suggested, surprisingly. 'At the Pantiles. Mum and you, Virginia and I.'

Behind her father's back Mathilda winked at Virginia, because far from going to the cinema that evening, the two girls had just come back from the village dance, something which they knew would give the Eastcotts a twin fit. But Lionel Eastcott's thoughts were miles away, now that he realised that the wretched tune that had been going round and round in his head was the result of Maude's lament earlier that evening that they never went dancing any more. He coloured slightly, and to cover this pretended to blow his nose. The Black Bottom indeed. Frightful dance. His mother had hated even the mention of it.

'Asked your mother about Virginia here staying, have you?' Lionel wondered, taking a good swig of his fresh drink. 'She won't be that keen, mind—now she's a bit short of domestics. You finding this a problem, Virginia? Staff taking themselves off home to prepare for the worst, yes? Driving poor Mrs Eastcott to distraction, I say. And no wonder. Haven't a thought in their heads for anyone but themselves—hoarding provisions as if it's the end of the world. Totally nonsensical behaviour, as well as being completely against government directives.'

'My grandparents still have their housemaid, Mr Eastcott,' Virginia offered. 'And their head gardener. Jim and Bob, the under gardeners, they've enlisted, and Cook's inclined to come and go whenever she has the time—'

'What I mean,' Lionel interrupted. 'Precisely. When it suits them. Driving Mrs Eastcott to distraction. So if she's a bit odd about you staying, it's only because of the shortage on the domestic front.'

There was little objection to Virginia's staying overnight, as it happened, due to the sympathy Maude had for her daughter's young friend. She did not particularly like Virginia, considering her to have taken after her mother, someone who, both Lionel and she remembered, had, in her day, been considered fast. But that did not prevent Maude from feeling sorry for the girl, cooped up as she was in her grandparents' house with no one of her own age to whom she could talk, thanks to her mother's apparently irreconcilable separation from Virginia's father. It was actually this split which had brought Virginia's mother back totally uninvited—or so the gossip had it—to live with her well-heeled parents in Bexham. Lionel had grown up with Virginia's mother, escorting her on a number of occasions to the monthly dances at the Yacht Club. She had, however, proved a little beyond his social capabilities, not only as a dancer, but also as a companion. Being one of those young men seemingly born old, in the effervescent and flirtatious company of the young Gloria Bishop it had to be said that Lionel had felt positively Neolithic.

A local girl herself, Maude had also known the young Gloria, which was why, even though she felt sorry for Gloria's daughter, deep down in her deepest heart Maude still felt that Virginia might not be exactly the ideal choice of friend for Mattie.

If she had but known it her fears were more than justified, since whenever the two young women decided to plot something which they knew to be forbidden, it was invariably at Virginia's and not

Mathilda's instigation. Pretending to have been at the cinema when in reality they had been dancing the evening away at the local hop had been Virginia's idea—although it had to be said that as usual Mathilda had taken little persuading. It was not the first time they had played hooky. The two girls had actually attended at least three of the weekly hops at the village hall, giving as their alibis films they had already seen earlier in the week.

In actual fact their first visit had been born out of less a need to deceive than desperation, supreme boredom having overtaken the two girls as the summer grew longer and hotter, and they had grown tired of talking about fashion, hair and the narrow attitudes of their elders and betters. Besides, the music was good, supplied as it was by a small local dance band, and the boys—once they had overcome their initial shyness at finding such really rather classy girls in their midst—were fun and friendly. Some of them were even excellent dancers. Two in particular stood out, the elder Todd boy who worked in the local boatyard, and Peter Sykes who worked for his father in the Bexham garage.

Innocent of the regular deception being visited on him by Mattie and Virginia, as he sipped his nightcap of whisky and soda Lionel suddenly announced, 'We must ask your mother round sometime, Virginia. For supper and bridge. We have regular bridge evenings, you know. I'll ask Mrs Eastcott to arrange it.'

Virginia appeared to give Lionel the sweetest of smiles, although it was in fact a smile more to herself than to him. Since returning to live in Bexham she knew exactly what her mother thought of Mr Eastcott, thanks to Gloria's constant reminders.

'Virginia dear,' she was fond of sighing, *'if you must know, I would have shot myself rather than marry stuffy old Lionel Eastcott. I could never have married him. Not if he was the last man on God's earth. Which if Mr Hitler has his way he may very well turn out to be. What a dreadful thought.'*

Upstairs in her bedroom, a room that she did not share with her husband, Maude listened to the voices below, and the sound of doors opening and shutting. She constantly worried until Mathilda returned home, most especially when she was with Virginia Morrison. She had always been aware of Lionel's infatuation with Virginia's mother. Rumour had it that he had once apparently even contemplated proposing to the silly fly-by-night. Not that Gloria Bishop would have done other than laugh at any proposal from Lionel. Having been born and brought up in the same vicinity Maude had known all about Lionel, even before he first asked her out. She was also, alas, acutely aware that when Lionel had proposed to her, she had jumped at his offer, despite his dull reputation.

Looking back on it now, with the benefit of hindsight, Maude realised that she had only wanted to marry Lionel in order to get away from her parents, who since she was the last daughter in a long line of children had been quite transparent in their determination that Maude was going to stay at home and look after both of them in their old age.

Marrying Lionel Eastcott had been infinitely more appealing than spending her life fetching and carrying for her parents. Yet life with the acknowledged local dullard had seemed vastly preferable to looking after her somewhat selfish and self-willed parents until, with an increasingly sinking heart, she had come to realise that she had simply swapped one form of slavery for another. It was now more than likely that instead of looking after her parents in their old age, she would be looking after her husband in *his* old age.

What a thought! Maude sighed as she closed her library book, marking the chapter-end with her ex-libris tag, a passage which she had greatly enjoyed as she had reached the moment in the love story where the hero had at last gathered the heroine into his arms preparatory to kissing her passionately. Maude wished she liked kissing Lionel, but alas she never had. Dancing with him—yes, that had been tolerable, albeit nothing to write home about, but kissing him, no. Like his conversation Lionel's kisses had been dull and dry, and had failed to excite or arouse her from the first, something—like so much in their marriage—that she hoped he had never noticed.

Now she must go downstairs and see what her daughter and her friend wanted, if anything. She sighed as she went, hoping that her Mattie would, one day, meet and marry someone a little more exciting than her own ineffably dull and pompous husband.

* * *

On Sunday morning at breakfast she reminded her husband and daughter that they were expected for drinks at the Meltons' after church. Since Virginia's one night stay had now turned into a weekend invitation, Maude said she would ring her hosts to ask them if it would be all right to bring her along as well, since Virginia's mother had also been asked.

That morning, rather to her own astonishment, Maude found herself hoping that Gloria *would* turn up at the drinks party. As she bathed and dressed herself, of a sudden she realised she did not care whether Gloria Bishop that was had been either dreadfully fast or abysmally slow, because the truth was she did not care much about anything any more, not even the idea of Gloria Morrison flirting anew with Lionel.

Must be the thought of a war coming, she told herself, as she carefully arranged her hair, finding herself inexplicably excited by the thought. If in fact there was to be a war, she determined, then and there, that rather than shoring herself up in Bexham she would find herself an occupation.

No more sitting around waiting to hear Lionel moan about the lack of plums for his custard, or sugar for his peaches, or anything else for that matter. No more wondering if there was going to be enough marmalade in the cellar to last them. Maude was going to be free. She was going to go to the front door and walk out, not to go to the hairdresser's, or the grocer's, or to buy some darning wool for Lionel's wretched socks, but to go to work.

I shall learn to drive, that's what I shall do! So what if Lionel laughs at me? I heard people saying only the other day in the ironmonger's that there could well be a shortage of drivers—and I've always wanted to learn. And since Lionel won't teach me I shall volunteer as a trainee! Lionel can laugh all he may, but I shall—I will—drive. And once I can drive,

I can go anywhere, without Lionel, without anyone, just me—myself, all by myself, no one to make fun of me any more, no one to pity me—as Mattie always pities me—for being older, for being more foolish, for being old-fashioned, for being behind the times, or anything else. It will just be me against the world. Me Maude, not Mummy Maude, not Maude My Wife, just me MAUDE!

Not surprisingly, as she rose from her dressing table Maude felt more than elated, she felt euphoric. Unused to making anything more than minor decisions, having taken a major one she now felt as if she had taken over a government, which indeed in many ways she had. She had taken over the government of herself.

And so what if she ended up getting killed in an air raid, or shot during the predicted invasion? At least she would die doing *something*.

Who knows? She gave herself one last look in her dressing mirror. *I might even have my hair tinted.*

CHAPTER THREE

Meggie stared out of the window disconsolately and cursed David Kinnersley and everything to do with him. He was about as constant as the English climate. Had he not promised hand on heart—well, practically—to take her dancing to the Savoy, and now where was he? Nowhere, and over an hour and a half late on top of it all.

Blow you anyway, Davey K, she thought as she put a cigarette in her long holder and lit it. *I should have said no, forgotten all about you and gone to the*

Savoy with Raymond St George when he asked me. He might be dull but he's a heck of a sight more dependable.

She blew a long stream of cigarette smoke out of the open window and thought enviously of Judy down at Bexham with the Tates. Judy had asked her if she would like to come and stay with her family that weekend if she had nothing better to do, but, remembering Judy had mentioned that she thought Walter might actually propose to her, rather than crowd her style Meggie had pretended that she had a firm date to go dancing with David Kinnersley when all the time it was only a possibility.

If I can, dearest girl, Davey had said on the telephone, as he had countless times before, *if it is at all possible I shall be there. Who could possibly resist yet another opportunity to spend an evening with you in his arms?*

Now left stranded high and dry, Meggie wished passionately that she had accepted her best friend's invitation to Bexham, for yet another glorious weekend by the seaside with all that marvellous food and fun, as well as the company of the three Tate boys, not to mention the dashing captain himself. She envied Judy not only for her way of life but also for the fact that it was an odds on certainty that Judy was about to marry into such an attractive family.

Of course Walter Tate still had to get past Judy's mother. But now that the war seemed inevitable, Meggie could not imagine anyone really objecting to their daughter's marrying him, particularly since he had already joined up. She had even discussed the subject with her divinely madcap grandmother, someone with whom Meggie had always liked to talk over everything in her young life.

It's only good sense, Meggie darlin', her grandmother had said. *For people not to marry in wartime, you see. Perfectly all right for them to wish to be together—for however brief a time—but when peace comes it causes emotional chaos, believe me. I have seen it. It is the reason why so many of my generation resorted to drugs and so on during the Twenties. The pain of it all, and then to be in pain and find yourself living your life with a stranger, or rather living a lie with a stranger. Unlike a martini cocktail, not a good mix, darling.*

It was only common sense, Meggie remembered, as she smoked her cigarette and watched London life passing her by below her window. War had so many repercussions. And so it would go on, doubtless, with women giving endless birth to an equally endless number of children, only to see their sons slaughtered in yet another war.

Meggie reached over and stubbed out her cigarette in a small round silver ashtray, her thoughts returning to her present predicament. It was now well past nine thirty and she had not even had a call from Davey to explain why he had failed to turn up. By the time she had helped herself to a large gin and Italian, Meggie was no longer feeling mildly irritated but practically murderous. She could not stand to be treated like this. Even if Mr David Kinnersley was her oldest friend, devastatingly handsome and mesmerising company, she, Meggie, simply would not stand for it, not for a single second. She was far too pretty and popular to be stood up by anyone. She would simply forget all about him and take herself out, go and join her crowd who she knew were dancing the night away at the Savoy, even if by doing so she would unbalance the numbers. Having made her decision, Meggie promptly rang for her Portuguese maid, and, bestowing on the poor woman the angry frown she had actually reserved for her errant escort, informed her that she was out for the evening and if anyone called—anyone at all—to say that she had no idea, at all, of where Miss Gore-Stewart could possibly be.

'Not even Mr Kinnersley, should he bother to call,' she announced, almost as an afterthought as she swept out of her apartment. 'Least of all Mr Kinnersley in fact.'

But having flagged down a taxi, Meggie found herself giving the cabbie her grandmother's address in Brook Street instead of the Savoy, a change of mood brought about she realised by the sight of the sandbag barricades in the streets and the black criss-crosses of tape on seemingly every windowpane she could see. The thought of war, even though it was very much to the forefront of her mind, had seemed until recently to be more of a possibility than a probability, particularly since the newspapers and the radio bulletins had been so generally optimistic about the Prime Minister's renewed attempts to secure a lasting peace. Now, however, seeing the increased activity in the preparations for civil defence, it came to Meggie, even in her furious state, that time was actually running out, for her, as it was for everyone. Hardly surprising therefore that all at once Meggie felt the need not to go dancing, but to visit an older member of the family, someone wiser who had been through it all before.

Her grandmother having always been the most loving and attentive relative in her young life, due to her parents' peripatetic existence in the Colonies, it was only natural that, when in doubt, it was to her that Meggie always turned. Most of all Meggie knew that whatever time of night or day she called she was always assured of a welcome, regardless of what else might be happening in her grandmother's elegant house in Mayfair. For Meggie the door was always wide open, the champagne chilled.

I shouldn't say this, her grandmother used to say, *but we're kindred spirits, you and I. You're such a little skylark, just as I was at your age. And you certainly don't get it from your papa, darlin'. Much as I am devoted to my son, sometimes I cannot see how he can be your father. He's such a stuffy person, but you, darlin' Meggie—you have the restless Gore-Stewart spirit.*

As a result of spending so much of her infant life with her grandmother while her parents were abroad on foreign postings, unsurprisingly Meggie had grown up feeling closer to her father's mother than she did to her own. Old Mrs Gore-Stewart had taught her little granddaughter everything that she thought might matter: how to speak French and German without an English accent, how to both waltz and Charleston, and not least how to mix a lethal cocktail that would wake the dead. The end result of this was that by the time she was sixteen Meggie Gore-Stewart was one of the most poised and socially precocious young ladies in Mayfair society.

The other consequence of so much exposure to her grandmother's sophisticated ways was that youngMeggie Gore-Stewart became the despair of her straitlaced parents, a fact which needless to say delighted her grandmother.

Just think what might have happened to you if you hadn't come here to live with me when you were little, darlin'. Meggie heard her grandmother's voice in her head as she paid the taxi off outside the deep red painted front door in Brook Street. *Your dear mama would probably have married you off to some frightful chump of an equerry. Or even worse, the governor of some tin-pot province in goodness-knows-where-land. Condemned to a life of sipping medium dry sherries and dancing endless valetas! My! My! Just think of it!*

Meggie found herself starting to smile in pleasant anticipation as she waited for Richards to open the front door to her. There was always something delightful about to happen, or already happening, in the Gore-Stewart house, despite the age of its owner. It was just a fact.

But not tonight apparently. As soon as her grandmother's butler opened the door Meggie could see from his face that something was wrong.

'Madame Gran is a mite upset *en ce moment*, Miss Meggie,' Richards sighed as he took Meggie's evening cloak. 'Bad news from abroad, it would seem. Madame Gran was expecting the arrival of more of our *musical* friends from abroad? But so far—no show. Come along upstairs even so, because if anyone can lift Madame Gran's spirits, we know who that is.'

With another small sigh, the portly but poker-faced Richards stood aside and bowed his head to indicate that Meggie was to precede him.

'I thought my grandmother's visitors arrived at

the weekend, Richards,' Meggie murmured over her shoulder, as they climbed the stairs. 'Least that's what she told me on the telephone.'

'Fresh lot, Miss Meggie. Bit of a *crisis*. Madame Gran was warned that they might be going to have a visit from a band of jackbooters. But we do not dwell on it, Miss Meggie. You know how Madame Gran is, she likes to keep her emotions hidden under her camisole, as it were. Or perhaps next to her *heart* is what I mean.'

Meggie nodded. And even though Richards purported to make a joke out of it they both knew not only that it was true, but why it was true.

Elinor Gore-Stewart had been famous not only for her blond patrician beauty but for her courage. Despite having a horror of sickrooms, and most of all blood, she had insisted on joining the Red Cross in the Great War and had driven ambulances behind the Front Line. Not that she ever referred to it once the war was over. It just was not done.

In fact it was from Richards that Meggie had learned how her grandmother had begged, borrowed or stolen a horse—Richards could never remember which—and ridden by herself behind the lines, to search out the worst casualties. From her devoted butler Meggie had learned how the young Elinor had talked the Normandy farmers into helping with the loan of barns and sometimes even cattle sheds for use as hospitals and shelters. How, often under fire, she had helped to bring the wounded back to those very shelters. And how Richards and she had met during one of those same forays.

'Very good with a bandage, Madame Grandmère is,' Richards would often murmur. 'She saved my leg when I ran away to the war. Under age, of course, but she saved my young leg, did Madame Gran.'

But now, seeing the expression in her grandmother's eyes, Meggie sensed suddenly that Madame Gran felt she was getting older, that she doubted she could cope as she had once done, that she was feeling her years at the idea of losing yet another generation of young people.

'Meggie, darling girl. Come in—come in at once—come and cheer me up. Where are you off to, darlin'? Going dancin'? How wonderful. Some nice young man, I so hope. Anyone we know? Richards—some champagne, I really think. Some champagne, and quickly now, before the bubbles burst and we all go flat.'

'There is some beside you, Madame Gran,' Richards replied, raising his big round eyes to heaven.

'More needed, Richards.' Elinor pointed at the bottle. 'You have finished it.' She gave Meggie a conspiratorial look.

'Fine thing indeed,' she whispered, offering Meggie a cigarette from a large old silver box. 'Fine thing when one is reduced to making merry with one's butler, indeed,' she went on, not meaning it, since she and Richards were inseparable. 'So where are you off to, my angel?'

'I was going to the Savoy, darling, but then—'

'But then?'

'I don't know.' Meggie lit her cigarette and tossed back her hair, the diamond star set in it catching the light. 'I thought I'd come and see you instead.'

'Good. I need cheering up. Need someone

young to invigorate me.'

'Don't we all, madame. Do not we all!'

'Oh dear, Richards and his glums. Any minute now his leg will start playing up.' Elinor raised her eyes to heaven. 'What a pretty dress. Is that new?'

'Hardly, darling. You bought it for me last year.'

'Even I recognised that dress, madame. You bought it for her birthday.'

Richards, having refused to leave the room in answer to a look from his mistress, was now dusting the grand piano with a handkerchief he had just produced like a conjuror from his top pocket.

'Something worrying you, Grandmother?' Meggie wondered, coming to sit beside her on the sofa. 'You look a teeny bit serious, *pour vous*.'

'Some guests one was expecting are just a little late. Tarsome indeed, when one is expecting them. And so urgently.'

'Maybe they've forgotten?'

'Oh, I don't think so, Meggie darling. The person who—the person they are staying with wouldn't allow that. No, they wouldn't have forgotten. Too important.'

'I should say,' Richards observed, sitting himself down at the piano.

'Champagne, Richards! I told you, more champagne before you start your cocktail piano routine. Please.'

With a pointed lift of his eyebrows, the butler rose slowly from the piano and went to get the wine.

'I do not know how I put up with him, Meggie. He is getting worse by the minute.'

'You put up with him because he makes you laugh.'

'You know what I mean, darlin'. Oh, where is Richards with the champagne?'

As Richards returned Elinor nodded to him to pour the wine, while she busied herself lighting another cigarette.

'Why don't you play me something, darlin'?' she pleaded. 'Something cheery. Some jazz. I do so love jazz. Yes, some jazz would be fine.'

'I'll play you something, darling, of course,' Meggie agreed, going over to the boudoir grand piano with her champagne glass. 'But I'm not sure I'm quite in the mood for jazz.'

She played a Ravel waltz instead, and the two of them became so involved in the haunting piece that neither of them noticed Richards leaving the room and reappearing at the door with a small crowd of people behind him.

'Bravo, Miss Gore-Stewart.' A tall, tanned man led the general applause a few seconds after Meggie had finished. 'Quite beautifully played.'

'David,' Elinor said, almost reprovingly, as she opened her eyes and saw her surprise visitor. 'David, I had almost given you up for dead.'

Meggie rose from the piano stool.

'Forgive me, both of you,' David Kinnersley said, his smile at its most charming, the apologetic look in his eyes directed at Meggie. 'Bit of an emergency.'

'I didn't even notice,' Meggie lied, while eyeing the oddly dressed figures still standing behind him. 'Emergency, was it?'

'Quite correct, Meggie darling,' Elinor said, now on her feet and going towards her guests, her hands outstretched. 'An emergency all right. I should have said earlier, really, but I thought if I mentioned it I should only bring bad luck. Now then, David, where are your manners? Introduce us to your friends, please.'

'Of course.'

David stood aside at the door and ushered in the three people still hidden in the half-light. Once they were in the drawing room it was all both Meggie and her grandmother could do to contain their amusement and not burst out laughing.

'And what particular order are the sisters from?' Elinor asked as she found herself staring at three really rather broad-shouldered nuns. 'The order of the Holy Sporting Saints?'

'They are from the order of *Thank the Lord we're safely out of there*, Elinor—and they don't speak a word of English.'

David turned and said something in German to the three nuns who then smiled shyly at their hostess, taking off their large winged headpieces to reveal three very male haircuts.

At first Meggie tried not to stare at them, afraid of having a fit of giggles at the incongruous sight they made.

'I am sure our guests are hungry, David, after their journey,' Elinor said, nodding to Richards. 'Perhaps if you would like to ask them to follow Richards down to the kitchen he will give them dinner and wine. They must be ravenous.'

The sisters of *Thank the Lord we're safely out of there* obviously could not wait to disappear below stairs. Having made their bows, Richards shooed them before him as if they were chickens being taken to the laying barn.

'I really don't know how you do it, David,' Elinor Gore-Stewart said, pouring him a large whisky.

'But you always do come up with something, bless you.'

'I know, my ingenuity is terrifying, isn't it?' David took the proffered drink and lit a cigarette. 'We were nearly becalmed off the German coast on the way back, which wasn't really very good news since my passengers were convinced that, prior to arrival at Bexham, someone, probably someone who had already been arrested, had informed the authorities. So you can imagine. Three very tall, very frightened nunny wunnies.'

'Who can blame them? And as for you—'

David looked at Meggie.

'Truth to tell I think I am still rigid with fright.' He pulled on his cigarette and laughed. 'It was being becalmed that was the worst thing. When one's moving, when you're under sail, you know you're in with a chance, but just sitting there like a—well, like a sitting duck, well, you know. I swear I shall never go duck shooting again, not even when this show is over, really I won't.'

He laughed again, but shortly, and shook his head as if mystified at the change that he already saw in himself.

'You're a hero, Davey. Isn't he, Grandmother? Whatever he says, he is a hero.'

'Hear, hear, Meggie darling.' Elinor took both their hands and led them over to the sofa, sitting them down on either side of her like children.

'I'm afraid that will be the last jolly for some little while, Mrs Gore-Stewart.' David sat back against the sofa, stretching out his long legs. 'It's getting a bit *très chaud* over there. A mite too *très chaud pour* comfort. From the looks of what was going on in *das Vaterland* I should say we could expect a rather large and very unfriendly landing party here in the not too distant.'

'*Pas devant*, Davey, *pas devant*,' Elinor scolded teasingly with a nod to Meggie on her other side. 'We don't want the child having bad dreams.'

'Silly, isn't it?' Meggie said, ignoring them both. 'Only when was it? Only this morning it was like a game—my friend Judy Melton and I having to pretend to be bomb victims. It was a bit like, well, a garden party in Sloane Square, really. And yet now here we are only a few hours later and of a sudden, it's certainly no garden party, it's really rather real.'

'I'm afraid we really are going to have to go to war, alas and alack. And the country's not even halfway prepared. Not even a quarter prepared. We are just not ready.'

'Don't you think so? What—even with all these rehearsals? And drills?'

'My dear child, you can rehearse until kingdom come, but if you ain't got the ships, the planes and the guns—you ain't got a fighting chance.'

'Stop sounding so doomy and gloomy, David, or I shan't give you any more champagne,' Elinor scolded him, as she refilled their glasses. 'And can you really not make any more trips? What a wonderfully great big pity. I had a call only last night—'

'If I had a destroyer of my own, perhaps. Or a battleship, Madame Gran. Can you afford to buy me a dear little battleship of my own?'

'That bad, is it, Davey?'

As he failed to answer the three of them fell silent, Elinor wondering what at her advanced age she could possibly do this time round, now that her rescue service was being foreclosed, David wondering whether like his father before him he too was about to lose his life fighting for his country, and Meggie simply wondering what *it* was going to be like; wondering what was going to fall from the skies, what was going to cross their shores, what was going to happen to everyone if the Nazis decided to invade immediately. It suddenly seemed unimaginable that the scene outside Peter Jones would shortly become reality, real blood, real broken bones, no laughter as Dobsie did up pretend wounds; just sirens and terror.

'Enough of this,' David exclaimed, jumping up to his feet and clapping his hands together once. 'Let's all go out dancing. And drinking. Much more to the point.'

*   *   *

'What will happen to your nuns?' Meggie wondered some time later, as the three of them sat at their table in the Savoy, David Kinnersley just managing to keep his chin from touching the tablecloth with the aid of two clenched fists.

'Not my nuns. So how should I know?'

'It has been known for people to bundle 'em off without declaring their presence to the authorities—to some safe house in the countryside where they just *disappear*,' Elinor explained, quietly. 'They will have their use, believe me.'

Meggie stared past her grandmother into the ever darkening future. If the men were all called to arms, which they would be, then there was going to be much that needed to be done at home—not just keeping the home fires burning.

'Do you know something, Marguerita mine?'

David wondered, as he finally located his missing glass of whisky. 'The waltz you were playing—when us lot arrived this evening. You know when Ravel wrote that? On the eve of the last time Europe was at war, strange that, wouldn't you say?'

David eyed Meggie, and having drained the last drop of whisky from his glass, fell promptly asleep, his head on the table, his hands either side of his head. And so what he did not see, but Elinor did see, was the look in Meggie's eyes as she watched him, eyes closed, fast asleep.

'He has a right to be tired—and tight.' Madame Gran smiled and called for the bill. Nothing much had changed, alas.

CHAPTER FOUR

'Excellent turn-out,' Sir Arthur Melton observed to the Reverend Hodson, when the vicar eventually joined the rest of the party gathered on the lawns of the manor. 'You don't get that sort of a congregation 'cept at Easter and Christmas. Good show, I'd say.'

'One would rather have a full church in celebration than in dread, Sir Arthur,' the vicar replied with a shake of his bald head. 'I am afraid the fear of war drives us to God far quicker than the sense of our own iniquity.'

'Be that as it may,' Sir Arthur grunted, nodding in Hugh Tate's direction as he saw him arriving with his family. 'Good show all the same. Though pity about your sermon.'

'You didn't approve of what I had to say, Sir

Arthur?'

'Might have done if I could have understood it, Vicar. 'Scuse me, new guests to greet.'

Sir Arthur took himself off to welcome the Eastcotts who had just arrived hard on the heels of the Tates. While Lionel was engaged in conversation with his host Maude surveyed the crowd to see to whom she would most like to talk, rather than to whom she *ought* to talk.

Spying what looked like most of the Tates gathered on the opposite side of the still perfectly manicured lawns she made them her target, quite naturally encouraged by the fact that she had just seen Judy Melton join them. Maude hurried across, desperately hoping that she would be in time to learn what she could, as quickly as she could.

By the time she had joined the Tate family and engaged them in party chatter she had noted with increased interest that, far from John being the focus of Judy's attention, it was Walter, the middle son, who was obviously engaging her interest. Her discovery not only intrigued Maude, it also pleased her. She had always nursed a hope that her own Mathilda might catch the eye of the eldest Tate boy, a match that Maude considered would be quite definitely more suitable.

Nice though the Tates undoubtedly were, they were not as patrician as the Meltons. Hugh Tate might be both well educated and affluent, and be dividing his existence between his large flat in Wilbraham Place and his seaside house in Bexham, but he was still, none the less, New Bexham rather than Old Bexham.

The Meltons were the oldest family in Bexham. They were *le tout Bexham*, as Lady Melton's manner so often implied. Given all this, poor Walter Tate had precious little chance of winning the hand of Judy Melton, whereas either he or his elder brother would be more than welcome to take on young Mathilda.

'Are you feeling all right, Mrs Eastcott?' Hugh Tate wondered with a smile, taking another gin sling from a passing waiter. 'That was really rather a tragic sounding sigh.'

'Forgive me, Captain Tate. My mind was dwelling on the international situation. They say we shall be at war any time now.'

'I have no doubt about it, Mrs Eastcott. And if not, we bloomin' well should be, wouldn't you say?'

'You know, I'm glad to hear you say that, Captain Tate. So many people seem so bent on appeasement you wonder what we fought the last war *for*.'

Seeing his father drawn into conversation, Walter took the opportunity of taking Judy to one side in order to speak to her more privately.

'I need to talk to your father, Judy. When do you think would be a good time?' He cleared his throat and glanced across the lawn to Sir Arthur Melton, nerves setting in at just the sight of the upright figure.

'Oh, I don't know.' Judy hiccuped, laughed suddenly and then hiccuped again. 'Sorry. Nerves. No time like the present, I suppose.'

Judy gave another small hiccup, and laughed again as a Tiger Moth droned over, high above them. Walter looked up at the biplane and shrugged lightly.

'No. And I don't suppose there ever will be again.'

*   *   *

Summoned back to speak to Sir Arthur later that afternoon, Walter first walked Judy to the top of Point Hill, their favourite part of that particular stretch of downland. It was a very hot afternoon, but the heat was happily mitigated by the cool breeze that blew in from the sea, making the temperature at the top of the local beauty spot tolerable. Together they sat on the pile of large flat stones that marked the highest point, looking at the wonder of the Sussex landscape that spread out below them all the way to the estuary, until finally it met the sea.

Neither of them had any desire to speak their thoughts as their eyes finally strayed to, and stayed on, the stretch of water that separated England from the Continent.

Nor did they feel the need to talk about Walter's forthcoming interview with Judy's father. Instead they talked about things that hardly mattered, all the time trying to block the big things that did matter from their minds. Finally, when they could delay the moment no longer, they walked back down the hillside with Judy's long-haired sheepdog running happily in front of them, knowing that in less than an hour's time their joint fate might well have been decided.

*   *   *

Walter stood in the small hallway outside Sir Arthur's study door, waiting for the dreaded summons. He stared out into the courtyard garden that lay beyond the latticed windows, unable to focus on the roses, as he tried to prepare himself for the interview to come. He knew there was bound to be resistance to his proposal because the Meltons did not consider the Tates good enough. His family was not Old Bexham. Apart from anything else Walter's father worked for his living, and Walter's mother was an American which although perfectly acceptable was nevertheless not Old Bexham.

Hugh had told Walter just to 'be himself'. Advice that other people always seemed to give so readily, advice which might be quite easy to follow if you knew who the real you really was. Walter was quite certain that he did not know who he was, or anyone else for that matter, he just knew that he loved Judy. Realising yet again what a mountain he had to climb, even as the study door opened and the tall upright figure of Sir Arthur stood in front of him, Walter almost aborted his mission and fled.

* * *

As Walter's ordeal at the hands of his prospective father-in-law began, Judy was trying her best to make conversation with her mother. She had never found her mother easy to talk to at the best of times, but now, quite obviously suspecting the worst as far as Walter Tate was concerned, Lady Melton had clammed up to the point of turning herself into a Trappist monk. Sitting herself in an armchair by the window she stared out at the view, forcing Judy to sit on an inadequate footstool on the other side of the French windows.

To make matters even more difficult Lady

Melton had decided to read rather than listen, picking up her novel and pointedly opening it as soon as Judy tried to engage her in a discussion about Walter. Her only contribution to the conversation was to observe that she had no idea what Judy could possibly see in the young man. He simply was not their 'sort', regardless of how his family had improved themselves.

'Walter's father was in the Navy.'

'Walter Tate's father was a captain. Your father is an admiral.'

'Once upon a time he must have been a captain. When he married you he was a captain.'

'Your father retired as an admiral, while Captain Tate remained a captain.'

'He was decorated. He won a medal.'

'Your father was awarded the VC. That is not a medal, Judy, it is a piece of history.'

'Walter's father was awarded the George Medal for gallantry.'

'Do not be impertinent, Judy.'

'I don't mean to be, Mummy, really I don't. All right, the Tates may not be an old family—'

'I should say not.'

'But they happen to be one of the nicest sets of people I have ever met.'

'You are very young, Judy. And you have a lot to learn, particularly about people such as the Tates. Now if you don't mind I've just reached an interesting bit, at long last.'

Lady Melton returned to her reading, but Judy could not let the subject drop.

'What do you mean exactly, Mummy? People like the Tates. What do you mean by that, exactly?'

'Counter jumpers, Judy. The sort of people who

try continually to improve themselves through marriage. I won't have it. We can't have it. Really, we can't.'

For a second Judy almost lost her temper with her mother, who she knew was taking up a position which ill suited her. It was a little known fact in Bexham that Lady Melton was the daughter of parents who were solidly middle class, and although none the worse for that, they would have been considered a good deal farther down the social scale than Walter's own parents, her father having been a district bank manager and her mother from good solid yeoman stock. Indeed, Judy had heard it rumoured that her own father's parents had done everything in their power to stop their son from marrying *her*.

'Supposing Daddy agrees to my marrying Walter, what then?'

'You don't even know that's what your young man is seeing your father about. It could be naval matters. He could be seeking his advice for all you know.'

'But supposing Daddy does agree. Will you still object?'

'Your father is well aware of my feelings on the subject, Judy. So much so that there is absolutely no chance of his giving his consent. If that is indeed what is going on in the study, if that is what is being discussed, which I very much doubt.'

'Mummy—'

That is quite enough. I am trying to read. If you don't mind.'

Her mother glanced briefly at Judy over the top of her book, keeping her place with one long finger, before returning to the adventures of *The*

Heiress.

*　　*　　*

Eventually Walter found Judy anxiously pacing the garden, but before he even spoke Judy knew that what he had to say was not going to be good news.

'We have to wait, Judy. That's the long and the short of it, I'm afraid.'

'Wait for what, Walter?'

'To get married, of course.'

'You asked him, Walter?' she exclaimed, trying to ignore the more relevant part of Walter's statement. 'That's what you were doing? You were actually asking my father if you could *marry* me?'

'What did you think I was doing, muddlehead?' Walter smiled at her and took her hand. 'Discussing the weather?'

'You might have been discussing naval things for all I know. You might have been picking his brains about what to do to get on in the Navy.'

'I didn't join up to get *on*, Judy. I joined up because it's my duty to fight for my country. And for those I love. Which includes you.'

'And my father said we'd have to wait?'

'He seems to think it wouldn't be fair me marrying you just when war's about to break out. You might be a widow within minutes. You can see his point. So many war widows after the last dust-up. Well. You can see his point—although I must say I did not want to.'

'I had really rather be married to you than not. If you know what I mean.'

'Of course. Of course I know what you mean. Me too. But you're still only nineteen, Judy. I mean, you can see his point.'

'I shall be twenty in a few weeks.'

'You still haven't reached your majority. You're not yet twenty-one. Still a minor, in the eyes of the law, Judy.'

'I suppose I won't mind waiting,' Judy sighed, knowing that she would mind terribly. Because they were well out of sight of the house she leaned against Walter, allowing him to put his arms round her waist. 'At least the old man didn't forbid you. I mean at least he didn't refuse his permission, as Mummy hinted that he might be going to.'

'And what else was your mother busy hinting? No, don't tell me—that the Tates aren't out of a high enough drawer for the Meltons.'

'That's just her way. The Melton way, not that she was a Melton, but she has been one for so long now I don't think anyone can tell the difference.'

'What matters is what your father thinks, and he thinks we're to wait until the war—when it comes—which it will—we're to wait till the war is over.'

Judy turned and stared up at Walter. 'But suppose it went on as long as the last one? We could be a hundred and ninety by the time it's over.'

Walter shook his head and detached himself from her, taking her hand and leading her further away from the house.

'If you were twenty-one, sweetie, it would be different, but the fact is you are not.'

'We could—we could elope! Couldn't we? We could run away and get married, Walter. We could! We could elope!'

'We could—except I have to return to base

tomorrow, Judy. And I don't know when my next leave will be. So, much as I'd love to run away with you, I don't see it as all that practical. Not really.'

'So what are we going to do, Walter? If we're going to have to *wait—*'

Walter turned and took her back in his arms.

'I'll tell you what we're going to have to do, Judy,' he said. 'We're going to have to make darned sure the war, when it comes, lasts no longer than Christmas.'

* * *

That evening Walter ended up drinking with his brother John in the Three Tuns overlooking the harbour. The pub was not at all crowded, with just one knot of regulars grouped in one corner of the bar discussing the subject that was occupying everyone's minds, and another foursome forgetting their troubles with a darts match on the other side of the bar. John and Walter sat themselves in the bow window that looked out directly on the jetty and then beyond to the estuary itself.

'If I were you, old lad,' John said, tapping a Senior Service on his silver cigarette case, 'I'd do as she suggested, and run off with her right now.'

'Well, you're not me, and you don't have to report back on board tomorrow a.m.'

'That's a bit of a spanner in the works.'

'A spanner? It's a bloody sight more than a spanner, John, it's a bloomin' great pickaxe, that is what it is.'

'Judy's so pretty.'

Walter eyed his brother's dreamy expression, while quickly stealing one of his smokes. 'You keep off the grass, old man. Anyone straying on that grass will be prosecuted.'

'Don't worry, Walt. I'll be in uniform myself before too long. In fact I'm thinking of volunteering—like you. Thought I might join the Guards.'

'When last discussed you were talking about the Navy. So what's changed your mind?'

'Not putting all our eggs in one basket, that's what. As a family. Spreading it about a bit. You in the Navy, me in the Army, and young Dauncy—when he leaves school—he wants to go flying. Seems only sensible.'

'Sensible.' Walter stared into his drink. 'I don't know where sense as far as war is concerned comes into it, really, do you? Going out and killing other people's sons just because some twerp with his parting on the wrong side of his head is saying and doing things we don't agree with. Might have been a bit more to the point if someone had organised an assassination, I should have thought. Not that difficult, really. A great deal less difficult than full-scale war, but then that is the fault of the appeasers. Appeasers! Ditherers more like.'

'Come on, Walt, drink up. We've got a good bit of drinking to do—before we ship you and your opinions off back to sea.' John stood up and waited for his brother to empty his glass. 'And don't you worry about that old bag Lady Melton. There's not a lot she can do, you know. And even if you did have to wait for a year—so what?'

'So what?' Walter looked up at him, handing him his glass. 'A year is three hundred and sixty-five days, John—in case you've forgotten.'

'And in case you've forgotten, Walt—in the

last one the old man got through four and a half of them—at sea as well. Same again? No, as I say, don't worry about old Ma Melton. If you decide to wait, wait you will, and win you will. You will win through, and there's really very little she can do.'

'I don't suppose there is.'

* * *

'What are you doing, Mummy?' Judy protested, watching as her mother started packing her suitcase with her belongings.

'I'm taking you somewhere where you'll be a lot safer,' her mother replied, picking up another armful of Judy's clothes. 'You and I are going to Scotland to stay with my cousin, out of the way of the bombs.'

'But why? Why do we have to go to Scotland all of a sudden? We're perfectly safe here. Daddy says nothing's going to happen for weeks—if not months. If it does at all.'

'You don't know what you are talking about, Judy. Now just do as you are told and finish packing up what you will need. Whether you like it or not, you and I are going to Scotland.'

'For how long?'

'For as long as it is necessary. And please don't argue any further—this was your father's idea, not mine.'

'How long for? How long are we going for?'

'For as long as it takes to defeat Hitler.'

'But I don't want to go to Scotland! I want to stay here!'

'You are going to Scotland, and that is an end to

the matter.'

'I want to stay here and do something useful!'

'Like seeing that wretched Tate boy.'

'Like doing something to help if there's a war. And I can hardly see Walter if there's a war, can I? He'll be away at sea.'

'You are coming with me to Scotland, and that is all there is to it.'

'Please? *Please*, Mummy—'

'You would rather be made a ward of court?'

'A what?'

'You heard me.'

'A *ward of court*? What for? Because I want to marry Walter? You'd make me a ward of *court*?'

'You'd better hurry up, Judy. We are catching the early train in the morning to London, and then the sleeper to Edinburgh. So I expect you to be packed and ready to leave by half past seven. Goodnight.'

'Mummy? *Mummy*—'

But Lady Melton had gone.

* * *

While Judy was preparing to escape from her bedroom, once she was certain her mother was asleep, in the study directly below, her father was standing with a glass of brandy in hand in front of her mother's portrait. It was a charming oil painted of his wife when she was hardly older than Judy, seated on a stone bench under the old apple tree in what was now her favourite part of the garden. She had been such a beautiful young woman, slender, graceful and above all so good-humoured. He had fallen in love with her the moment he had met her on the tennis court at the local club. In fact so smitten by the young Elizabeth Watkins had he been that his distraction caused him and his older sister to lose an important match that they had been expected to win with ease, much to his sister's intense displeasure.

Sir Arthur shook his head and took another draught of his cognac, remembering the absurd despair into which his love for this tall, brown-haired, athletic young woman had plunged his family, and how he had invited her round one Sunday to meet his parents in the hope that they too might be won over by the character and originality of the girl he had fallen for so passionately. The day turned out to be a disaster. His mother had politely ignored his future wife, while his father had asked her the most embarrassingly direct questions about her family background, and his sister had directly snubbed her. Somehow they had weathered the storm, although for the life of him he could hardly remember how, since they had finally to wait two years before being able to marry and then another five years before his parents actually spoke to either of them again.

And now history was about to repeat itself, as it had a habit of doing. Elizabeth and he were trying to erect exactly the same obstacles his own parents had put in the way of Elizabeth, and with about as little reason. The more cognac he drank the more shame he felt, so that by the time he put the stopper back on the decanter he was determined to go and tell his wife that whatever opposition she might have to the prospective union of Melton and Tate, he himself could not go through with it. If they wanted to marry, marry they must.

With his inner self well fortified with his finest vintage cognac Admiral Sir Arthur Melton dropped his cigar in the fire, brushed the ash from his velvet smoking jacket and made his way slowly upstairs, determined on discussing the matter in order to clear the air. The last thing he wanted for his daughter was to have her prospective happiness jeopardised for no good reason, particularly at that moment, when they were on the brink of war.

He was just contemplating the idea of putting his head round Judy's door to wish her goodnight and chin up and all that when he noticed that there was no sign of light from under it, so, not wanting to wake her, he thought better of it and headed instead for his wife's bedroom. Much to his astonishment he found her door too to be locked and no sign of light shining from within her room either.

'Elizabeth. It's only me.'

'I'm a little under the weather.'

'But your door's locked. I wanted to speak to you.'

'Not tonight, Arthur. I'll explain in the morning.'

'Elizabeth—'

'Tomorrow, Arthur. When you're sober.'

Duly chastened, Admiral Sir Arthur Melton put aside his good intentions, considering that all told his wife was right and those matters of importance that he wished to discuss could wait quite happily until morning, when not only he but all three of them would be in a better state of mind.

Except by then it would prove more than a little too late.

* * *

Walter had just fallen into an alcohol-induced sleep when the first pebble rattled against his window. Due to the amount of whisky he and his brother had drunk that evening it was going to take more than a few small stones to rouse him. Getting no immediate response from her first cluster of pebbles, Judy chose a larger stone, aimed it carefully at her target and achieved a perfect bull's-eye. A moment later she saw a light go on.

'Who's there?' Walter called from his now open window. 'Is there someone there?'

'Ssshhh! It's only me! Judy!'

'Judy!'

'Ssshhhh! You'll wake everyone up!'

'Throwing stones at someone's window is not the quietest of occupations.'

'I need to talk to you!'

Grabbing his dressing gown Walter hurried quietly downstairs and out of the house.

Judy was waiting for him behind the large beech tree that stood on the corner of the front lawns. She was wearing a headscarf, a light raincoat, and a frightened expression. Walter took her hand and led her away from the house in the direction of the gazebo that was hidden from view to the right behind a shrubbery of azaleas and rhododendrons.

'I can't believe it,' Walter whispered after she had told him of her mother's threats. 'At least I can. After the warning off I got from your father.'

'I know. I—I really thought Daddy would take to you—you being in the Navy and all that.'

'It's your mother who is most against it, I think. Or rather, my mother thinks.'

'They used to be so much in love themselves—

my parents.'

'*My* parents think you're entirely splendid. If it was up to them we could get married tomorrow.'

'If only you weren't going back to Portsmouth tomorrow, Walter.'

'What? If only I wasn't going back to Portsmouth what, Judy?'

'I'd run away with you.'

'You really would run away with me?'

He took her in his arms and kissed her. Judy responded passionately, holding him as close to her as she could, her arms tight round his waist, her body pressed closely against his. They had never kissed in that way before, and the more they kissed the more it seemed to both of them that it really could be for the last time.

Walter put a hand to either side of Judy's head and studied her expression, trying desperately to remember every detail of that moment.

'I love you. More than my own life. Far more.'

'I love you too, Walter. If I could come with you.'

'I know. I know. But we must be patient. We must wait. It might not be as bad as everyone says. War might not be that imminent. There might be a respite—I might get home for another leave—there are all sorts and possibilities of might.'

'Too many, many mights. But not I *might* be going to Scotland, Walter, I *am* going to Scotland. No might about it.'

There was only one way to treat this immovable fact, and they both knew it.

CHAPTER FIVE

The following day Meggie found herself once more at sea, indecisive, on edge, unable to decide anything.

It was hardly surprising, such was the tension gripping London. Every newspaper hoarding, every news bulletin, was bringing the outbreak of war nearer and nearer to that particular second when it would be not about to be declared, but upon them. And in that second, as they all knew, their fates, everyone's fates, would be finally, and perhaps fatally, sealed.

Being alone she had spent most of the morning of the previous day, Sunday, in bed, as if afraid to face the outside world. Finally, summoned to lunch at short notice by a midday telephone call from her grandmother and unable to get a taxi, she had found she had awoken to a world teetering on the verge of chaos.

The pavements outside her flat had been thronged with both men and women in uniform: newly called up soldiers heading slowly but determinedly for railway stations and trains which could carry them to their barracks; auxiliary firemen, now no longer volunteers but full-time professionals, hurrying to hastily summoned drills; air raid wardens securing observation posts; sailors sea bound and young airmen looking no older than schoolboys making for craft that they had as yet no notion how to fly.

The roads had also been busy, jammed with traffic leaving the city, piled high with family possessions, luggage and pets, a sensible and for the time being orderly self-evacuation of people determined to be housed safely in the country when the bombs began to drop, as everyone sensed that all too soon they would.

Caught in a sea of dismay, Meggie had found herself being swept along in the opposite direction to that in which she was headed. Her sense of futile hopelessness was increased by her inadvertently interrupting the unloading of a couple of hundred wooden coffins. By the time she had finally reached her grandmother's house in Brook Street, on foot, war had become such a reality that, looking up at the skies above her while she waited for Richards to open the door, she had quite expected to see it already thronged with enemy aeroplanes.

After a predictably subdued lunch served by a still politely drunk Richards, Meggie had asked Elinor what she thought she should do now that the country was headed inevitably for war?

'What would you do? If you were me—my age now. What would you do? Because whatever *you* would have done, I shall do.'

'Something exciting, I expect. Can't just stand by.'

Elinor Gore-Stewart was always happier to generalise rather than give an opinion, refusing, as the old and the wise do, to give advice which they might later regret.

'Knowing you, you would have volunteered probably for the WRNS.'

'Possibly. They do have quite a smart uniform, darlin', except the officer's hat, which is hideous. Don't want to wear that, not for anything. Actually, if they'd teach me how to fly, as a matter of fact, I'd still quite like to join the RAF. Always did fancy flying. More and more women will be soon, you know. One of these days people will think nothing of it.' She paused, staring into some kind of future which only she could see.

'I have no sense of direction, which might make it a bit difficult. No, I think I shall join up, but not the RAF. Bit too much map reading, which is not my strong point to say the least. No, I think I shall volunteer and join the Wrens. Purely for the uniform, of course. But not, if what you say is true, the officer's *hat*.'

Elinor smiled at Meggie's lightheartedness, but only because it was better than weeping. It was all just as it had been before, and hardly twenty-one years later. Young people volunteering, dashing off to war, ready to do their bit, all courage and ignorance. For how else can the young face war if not in a state of ignorance?

During the silence that followed, Richards appeared with a dusty bottle of vintage cognac from which he generously filled three glasses.

'Good luck, and God speed to us all.' Elinor raised her glass to her butler and her granddaughter.

'And the very toughest of cheese to our enemies.'

'Hear, hear, Miss Meggie.'

Meggie laughed and raised her glass to the other two. Richards carefully replaced the cork in the bottle, which he had then proceeded to seal with a copious amount of sealing wax.

'May I enquire as to the purpose of this particular ceremony, Richards? We might have wanted another dram, myself and my granddaughter.'

'This bottle is now out of bounds, *réservé* for when we have beaten the beastly Nazi housepainter,' Richards told his mistress.

It was a sentiment with which Elinor Gore-Stewart must have concurred because she said nothing, but only continued to sip her cognac.

* * *

And now on the following morning, from the top of the bus taking her to Piccadilly where she was due to meet David Kinnersley for lunch at the Ritz, Meggie could see how inexorably fate was marching on. Bodies of men were busy sandbagging all the important buildings and digging trenches in the parks, while in the skies above the capital appeared not enemy aeroplanes but the first of the barrage balloons.

'You're very quiet,' Meggie said to David as they sat at the downstairs bar. 'For you, I mean. Very quiet. Mind you, given what's going on outside, I suppose that's hardly surprising.'

'I failed my medical,' David suddenly announced, nodding to the barman for two fresh drinks. 'Would you believe it? A great hulking brute like me? Volunteered for my father's old regiment—had my medical this morning. Blooming failed it. Hulking great brute like me.'

'Hulking no, great—possibly. Brute—certainly. Which bit of you doesn't work?'

'That would be telling. Suffice it to say it is a common complaint to do with the chest area resulting from a childhood disease, hence why I was sent down to Bexham to spend my childhood gulping in great hunks of Sussex sea air.'

'Sussex by the Seeeeeeee!' of a sudden they both finished, singing the proud Sussex song always played by the Bexham brass band on the village green as a finisher of a Sunday afternoon.

'Glad to hear there's *something* common about you, Davey. The way you go on, you'd think you were the noblest of them all.'

'Ha ha, very droll, Meggie Bore-Stewart.'

'So what are you going to do? A hulking great brute like you can't just sit around twiddling your hulking great thumbs when Your Country Needs You.'

'I shall find something, never fear. But *not* behind a desk.'

'I'm going to join up. In fact I am on my way to do so, once I've got tight with you.'

'So Elinor told me. She telephoned to me last night. Said, "Meggie's going to get tight with you, and then join up." You don't have to, you know.'

'What? Get tight with you? It's de rigueur, dear boy. How else does one prevent oneself falling asleep when one is with you?'

'You don't have to go so far as joining up.' David smiled, and then deliberately adopting a patronising tone to annoy her he went on, 'Lots of other things women can do.'

'I know, but I'm not really a knitter, Davey. Nanny used to have to undo all my plains and purls, let alone my moss stitch. No, I am afraid the only pearls I have ever been interested in are usually to be found on a string around one's neck. Nor am I cut out to work on the land. Besides, I think I'll look quite fetching in a uniform. The severity of the cut, you know—it will show off my perfect profile.'

'I think you'll look absolutely the ticket. But I'd rather you didn't stick your head over the parapet, soldiering, sailoring, and all that. Besides, it's not really ultra-feminine.'

'Oh, come on. You admire my grandmother for what she did in the last war.'

'Only because she was doing a feminine thing. Nursing. That's the sort of thing females do, not fighting with guns and so on.'

'Being a nurse in the Great War was most definitely dangerous.'

'It's not the danger, Megs. It's women in soldiers' uniforms. It don't fit together the way it should, not to my mind anyway.'

'I'm thinking of going into the Wrens, actually. They're very feminine, apparently, as long as you avoid the officer's hat.'

'Women in uniform. Full stop. Don't like the idea at all.'

'Nurses wear uniforms.'

'Ah, now. Now that is different. You'd look very nice in a nurse's uniform.'

'Better than you would behind a desk.'

'I am not going to sit behind a desk.'

'And I am not going to be a nurse.'

David contemplated their conversation while he ate some salmon.

'Won't be eating this delicacy for very much longer,' he said sadly, taking a draught of cold Chablis. 'Or drinking this kind of vino. Sardines and brown ale, more like.'

'You could try being an air raid warden,' Meggie told him, poker-faced. 'After all, you're very good at bossing people about.'

'You could try being a nice young lady,' David

replied, with a mock black look. 'And stay at home and learn to tat and knit better than you did with Nanny.'

'Why all the concern all of a sudden, Mr Kinnersley? And from Mr Devil May Care himself.'

'Call me old-fashioned, Miss Gore-Stewart, but I just happen to think a woman's place is not on the ramparts.'

'Where is it then? Home, hearth and kitchen? You're not going to dissuade me, you know. My mind is quite and utterly made up.'

'I know of a way to dissuade you,' David replied, looking her in the eye. 'I could marry you.'

'Only if I said yes, surely?'

'And will you? Will you marry me, Meggie?'

'No, absolutely not.'

'You won't? Why ever not? I'm one of the most eligible fellows around, for heaven's sake. We have everything in common, your grandmother is one of my greatest fans, and we have known each other in Bexham since—well, since we were knee high to the proverbial grasshopper.'

'I will not marry you, Davey, because I don't want you to be a war widower. Besides, I happen to know why you are asking me. You are asking me simply and only because you are determined to stop me joining the Navy and enjoying myself. You are a spoilsport. You don't wish to see anyone having as good a time as you are, or were, determined on, until the medical board found out you wheeze like a pair of old bellows.'

David stared back at her, trying not to laugh, but finally unable to contain himself.

'You are just too much, Miss Gore-Stewart, and

what is worse, I think you really mean it.'

'I do, David. Besides, I simply could not bear the thought of you sitting behind your desk, sad and miserable while I die a noble death in the field, or rather at sea. Leaving behind a war widower is not my idea of what I should do to you. You might never find another woman, and after the war, just think, you would be one of thousands.'

'If you'd say you'll marry me, Meggie darling, I should be so awfully happy, really I would.'

'If I thought you meant it—'

'Of course I mean it, Meggie! I always mean what I say.'

'But you hardly ever say what you mean. You—get married? And break practically every heart in town? I don't think you would find that particular marriage would last very long, Davey, do you?'

'And there was I thinking that you loved me.'

'That has nothing to do with my marrying you.'

'So you do love me, Meggie?'

'Of course I love you, Davey, I always have, and possibly I always will. But this is war, and the outbreak of war is no time to marry. We might wake up and find ourselves strangers once all the excitement died down, which is what kept happening after the last one. Besides, it's a bit ordinary, don't you think, to marry just because everyone else is. And you know me, I hate being ordinary, and like everyone else.'

They both looked at each other without saying anything for a moment. Meggie was wondering whether it was just the threat of war that was making her feel the way she did, as if she could see everything very clearly, not as she did normally, through a looking glass held over her shoulder. Everyone was getting married—daily, and almost hourly; it was a feature in most of the newspapers —and pretty soon everyone would be getting pregnant. It all seemed so wrong, as if they were all doing everything for the wrong reasons. The fact was that David would not be proposing to her if there was no war, and he knew it, and so did Meggie.

And David, probably because he was so used to getting his own way with women, was amazing himself by discovering what he really thought about Meggie Gore-Stewart of the impish, if crooked, smile.

He had always seen Meggie quite simply as one of his favourite flirtations, funny, attractive and original. Now, what with the barrage balloons and the sandbags, and her talk of joining up, he was finding out that he had other feelings for her. Of a sudden the thought of possibly never seeing her again, the thought that she might be killed in an air raid, was quite simply unbearable. He put his sea-bronzed hand over Meggie's pale-skinned one, and stared into her eyes.

'No,' Meggie said before he could say anything at all.

'Did I ask you something?'

'Didn't you just ask to marry me?'

'As a matter of fact the last thing I asked you was whether or not you loved me,' David said, offering her a Passing Cloud cigarette.

'Then the answer is *Pending*,' Meggie replied, taking the oval-shaped cigarette and lighting it from David's proffered match. 'After we've had coffee let's walk down to the river and along the

Embankment.'

'If we do that we could end up at Cheyne Walk. And have tea chez moi. And maybe some ultra-stiff whisky sours.'

'Perhaps we could. Yes. Let's go for a long and lovely walk, then end up having huge cocktails at Cheyne Walk.'

They walked through Burlington Arcade with Meggie daring her companion to whistle and David telling her in return that having been caught as a boy illegally doing so in the famous walkway it was a case of once bitten. In return Meggie called him yellow, made sure the Beadle was looking the other way, handed David her shoes, double-checked on the actions of the Watchdog, and then silently and successfully sprinted the length of the Arcade to the equally silent astonishment of the other pedestrians.

'You know what the punishment for that misdemeanour is, young lady,' David stated, once he had caught her up. 'The Tower.'

'I shouldn't mind. Once you're safely locked away, there's an end to harm.'

'Very Shakespearean.'

They walked arm in arm through the streets at the lower end of Mayfair, silent now as they watched the populace continuing their preparations for war. Blacking out the windows of a large showroom on the corner of Stratton Street, sandbagging a large anonymous-looking building in Curzon Street, digging deeper and deeper trenches in the parks.

Moving on they made their way down an equally preoccupied Sloane Street, past the site where what seemed like only a split second ago Meggie and Judy had pretended to be casualties in the mock air raid, and along the King's Road where for a while they stood and watched men on ladders painting out a department store's name emblazoned high on the side of a building. Finally, they found themselves on the Embankment leaning over the parapet and watching the river fast flowing out to sea.

'I think even the Thames is deserting London, Davey,' Meggie said, slipping her hand into his. 'Look—it's flowing out—never to come back in on the tide.'

'You and that imagination of yours. It'll be the death of you.'

'I don't think I want to die. Not yet anyway.'

'Don't worry, Meggie darling. I shan't let anything happen to you. Not anything terrible, that is.'

He kissed her just as a troop of soldiers marched by, earning them both a cacophony of wolf whistles and cheers.

'Cheerio, chaps!' David called after them. 'Good luck!'

Meggie waved, suddenly feeling strangely elated and desperately sad all at the same time.

'Can we go inside, David?' she wondered, clasping his hand tightly with both of hers. 'Before it all starts? Can we go inside?'

They went into David's house on Cheyne Walk, closing the door on the overcast August day.

CHAPTER SIX

When Rusty and her brothers returned home from the afternoon showing of *The Lady Vanishes* at the Odeon in Bognor at the beginning of September they found their father and mother sitting silently either side of the wireless. The young people's generally cheerful mood was immediately dispelled by the look on their parents' faces.

'What is it? Is it war then?'

'All but. Now quiet, the lot of you.' Their father waved at them all to be quiet, at which they sat round the table to listen to the end of the news bulletin, while Mrs Todd took up her knitting, her mouth set.

'The government are evacuating the cities? That can't be everybody, surely?'

'Children mainly, Rusty. Mothers where possible.'

Mrs Todd frowned at her four needles and re-applied herself to the thick wool sock, trying to hide the pain she felt from the arthritis in her hands.

'They said this doesn't mean war is inevitable—'

'Like heck.'

Mrs Todd clicked her tongue in time with her needles. '—but since they just announced the mobilisation of the Fleet and the RAF and the Navy have ordered their reservists to report for duty, I think we can take it all as good as read,' she finished, with quiet finality.

Mr Todd leaned forward to turn the wireless off but paused to listen to an extra announcement that the BBC would be broadcasting a special service of intercession later that night.

'Fat lot of good that'll do,' he said, finally switching off the set. 'As if all we have to do is pray. Fine thing.'

'There's a letter come for you, Tom,' Mrs Todd said, getting up from her chair and gritting her teeth as her arthritis caught her. 'On His Majesty's Service. It's there on the mantle. Dad?'

Mr Todd glanced at his wife as he fished his tobacco tin from his jacket pocket.

'Pass it down to him, Dad. It'll not answer itself.'

'It's all right, Ma,' Tom said gamely, taking the envelope down himself. 'I was expecting this. Seeing as how I'm the eldest.'

'Mine not arrived as well then?' asked Mickey, joking.

'Don't know why you don't just put a pistol to your head,' his father muttered. 'You're that keen to get yourself killed, putting in for bomb disposal, is it? I don't know where you get these ideas. You can't shoot a rabbit, let alone dispose of a bomb, our Tom.'

Rusty watched as her eldest brother carefully slit open the official brown envelope and took out his call-up papers. Even on the bus back from Bognor what talk there was had been about nothing but the war, so why did she feel so shocked at Tom's being called up?

'I'm not to start my training till the summer, it seems,' Tom looked up, 'being that I'm not quite nineteen. I put in early hoping they'd take me anyway. Can't wait to have a go at Jerry, really can't.'

Rusty followed her mother out to the kitchen to

help prepare the family's supper.

'There's no point in saying anything, Rusty,' her mother said, as she began to peel the potatoes. 'There's no point in saying anything, nor in worrying about it. It's just the way things are. The way things have to be. The way things have always been.'

'He's still a kid.'

'Your dad was seventeen when he joined up and went to war. In case you've not noticed, war's no respecter of age. And don't just stand there. You can do them carrots.'

'If there is a war—'

'Don't be daft. *If* indeed.'

'*I'd* like to do something.'

'Yes, well you can. Like I said, you can do the carrots.'

'I meant in the war. *When* it starts.'

'Any time now.'

'I'd like to *do* something.'

'There'll be plenty to do, don't you worry.'

'If the men are all going to get called up—'

'We're going to have to keep hearth and home. If men aren't here, we must be.'

'Not younger women. Not them that's not married—like me. Must be something useful I could do.'

'I'd like to know what. All you can do is mess about in boats. And I can't see them taking you into the Navy, girl. Even if they did, your father wouldn't have it.'

'Wouldn't be able to do anything about it, Mum. Not after my birthday. Not in another year when I'm twenty-one.'

'Talk sense, Rusty. I'm going to need you at

home. I can't manage too well with this—with the way I am, you know that.'

Rusty looked at her mother who was bent over the sink trying to peel the vegetables with a small knife. With a little sigh Rusty took the knife from her mother and her place at the sink.

'Dad's still hale and hearty. I mean, if I did find something useful to do—'

'Your dad's going to have his hands full in the boatyard, I imagine. He's also in the Local Defence Volunteers, remember.'

'Seems daft.' Rusty stared out of the window at the surrounding countryside. 'Millions of able young women with nothing useful to do. For the country, I mean. Except sit and wait to see if everyone will come home again. But that's governments.'

From behind Rusty her mother glanced up at her, before continuing with her preparations.

'As a matter of fact I'd like to help myself—but with this arthritis I dare say all I'm good for is socks and knitting. And even that's slow now.'

'It's only manual things, Mum. Fiddly things you're not too good at—like opening things, threading needles, scraping carrots.' Rusty dropped some perfectly scraped and portioned carrots into the saucepan her mother had put on the draining board. 'There's nothing wrong with your head. Nothing to say you can't use your grey matter.'

'What for, child? What sort of useful brainwork can someone like me do, eh?'

'You'd be surprised.' Rusty looked determined. 'You'd be surprised, Mum, really you would.'

Because they had been hoping so much for a boy it had often seemed to the Todds that their aspirations had somehow seeped through to their unborn daughter, who had finally emerged from her mother's womb determined to make up for the fact that she had disappointed them, by becoming even more of a boy than her brothers.

For as long as Mrs Todd could remember her daughter had been in a boat, first on the waters of the estuary and later the sea itself. She had learned to sail with her father, more by custom than tuition. Quickly picking up the rudiments of managing a small dinghy, she was sailing solo by the time most of her contemporaries were trying to learn how to ride their first bicycles.

By the age of ten she was managing the most sophisticated craft single handed. Ironically, although subsequently blessed with two sons, the Todds soon discovered that, besides Rusty, only Mickey showed a real interest in boats, and even that was a penchant that owed much to the fact that his older brother and his friends always left him out of their games.

Not that Rusty minded. Mickey, being the youngest, was her pet lamb, with the consequence that he followed her devotedly, even out to sea, where he was usually violently sick.

'Will Mickey get called up as well, do you think, Mum?' Rusty asked her mother, after a long silence. 'Soon, I mean?'

'Hardly. They're not calling them up at sixteen yet, I wouldn't say, Rusty.'

Mrs Todd sighed. Every time her children's ages were mentioned she always did sigh. Too many miscarriages and too little money had worn her to a thread paper. It was little wonder that she had ended up suffering with arthritis, what with the worry and the pain of it all; but, alas, her husband had shown little interest in Marie Stopes's contraception methods, or anything else, except boats and the boatyard.

'And if what they're saying's right—that it'll all be over by Christmas? Then there's not a lot of need to fret.'

'Familiar ring to it for your dad and me, that. It all being over by Christmas. Just what your grandfather said before he went off and got himself shot in the last war.'

Having completed her chores, Rusty excused herself and collected up her West Highland terrier, pretending to go for walk, but finishing by going up to the beautiful old Anglo-Saxon church. There were many others kneeling there where first the Saxons and then the Normans had built, or re-built, their church to the greater glory of God. For Rusty, as she imagined for her fellow worshippers, there was comfort in the peace beneath the early English stone arches, but desperation in her prayer, repeated over and over again. *Please, please, God, help there to be no war.*

* * *

David and Meggie learned about the invasion of Poland from the wireless on board the *Light Heart*, as with sails furled and engine idle she rode the swell three miles off Bexham Point.

'I shall remember this moment for the rest of my life,' Meggie murmured, as she sat in the bows staring at the invisible continent across the Channel to the south of them. 'To us. All of us. Most of all—' She stopped, staring across the water to the harbourside. 'Most of all, to Bexham.'

'That's the best toast yet,' David replied, handing her a tumbler of gin and French. 'To Bexham where we all grew up.'

'No, Davey,' Meggie said, and she shook her head, the look in her eyes suddenly quite old, 'where we all *thought* we *were* grown up. There's rather more of that ahead of us. Growing up. We won't know the meaning of it by the time all this is finished.'

* * *

At the garage on the top of the hill above Bexham village Peter learned the news from a succession of customers who drove in to fill their cars up, as if hostilities had already broken out and petrol rationing was already in place. As he manned the pump Peter tried to reassure all those who stopped at the garage that there was absolutely no danger of his supplies drying up in the immediate future, only to be greeted with general disbelief.

'There'll be tanks on the roads before you know it, young Peter my lad,' one of his regulars assured him. 'And let's just hope they're ours and not Jerry's.'

'He won't be setting foot here,' Peter replied. 'Not if I can help it.'

'Right—course, you're away to join up, eh, lad? When's the big day?'

'Day after tomorrow, sir. Can't wait.'

'Not like some,' his customer replied. 'And certainly not like before. Last time Jerry made trouble we were knocking each other over in the rush to teach him a lesson. This time—I don't know.' The man shrugged and shook his head sadly. 'You'd think it wasn't anything to do with us.'

This was certainly not the impression Peter got later on that day when he sat in the darkness of the cinema with Mattie Eastcott on one side of him and her friend Virginia on the other, listening to the sobs of some of the audience as they all watched an already meaningless newsreel about pre-invasion Poland.

The show over, the three of them drove home in Peter's Austin 10. Inside the car there was complete silence. No one could think of anything to say. There was nothing they could say, until, a few minutes out of Bognor, Peter rounded a corner and found himself being stopped by soldiers, and ordered to turn off all his driving lights.

'Haven't you heard about the blackout, son?' the sergeant scolded him. 'Come into force as from this a.m. and that means no lights. No lights. Got it?'

'I thought it was only headlights that were banned when driving?'

'Then you thought wrong, didn't you? Now on your way and make sure those lights of yours stay off! Now, and for the duration. Off, do you hear?'

Despite the fact that they all knew that Peter was right, the three of them bowed to the sergeant's demand and as a consequence endured an appallingly difficult journey back to Bexham, guided by nothing more than the light of an extremely pale and only occasionally visible moon.

Peter and Mattie sat in the car at the end of the lane that led to her parents' house. Virginia, sensing that she was about to feel even more of a gooseberry than she did already, had demanded to be dropped off first on their way through the now totally darkened village.

'Wonder what your parents would say if they knew you'd been to the films with me tonight? I dare say they'd faint from shock, wouldn't they?' Peter stared ahead of them, out on to the estuary.

'They'd say the same as if they knew I'd been out dancing with you,' Mattie replied, half turning to look at her tousle-haired companion.

'I shall miss dancing with you, Mattie.'

'Then hurry up and win the war, Peter, and then we can dance again.'

Mattie smiled at him, and as she did so she found herself hoping that she might get him to kiss her. But being completely inexperienced in such matters she had no idea if he would, only that she wanted him to. It just seemed so right, after all the weeks they had spent dancing together.

'Are you just doing this because I volunteered? Because I'm going off to fight?'

'Because you're going off to fight I'd rather I wasn't *doing this*. As a matter of fact. Really. Whatever *doing this* might mean.'

'Going out with me. Dancing with me. Being this nice.'

'In order of preference, then. I went out with you because I *like* you. I danced with you because I *like* you. I go to the cinema with you because I *like* you. I *like* you.'

'After the war's over—'

'When the war's over and when you come home again—well?'

'Well—will you? I mean will you still be here? I mean, will you?'

'Will I what, Peter? Will I what exactly?'

'I don't have the right to ask you. We've only

been dancing a few times—and I've only taken you out once, properly, tonight. To the cinema. With your friend. That's not very much, even if there is a war on, is it?'

Mattie took hold of one of Peter's hands and held it between her two far smoother ones.

'If what you're trying to ask is will I still be here, the answer is I jolly well hope so. And if what you're really trying to say is will I—well. Will I—will things be the same? Will I still go out with you—then of course I jolly well will. Just don't stay away too long, that's all. Just hurry up and knock the spots off Mr Hitler.'

Peter said nothing, silenced for once, only trying to make out her expression in the darkness, how serious she was, whether she meant what she said, was not still just teasing him, making light as she normally did.

'Right, I'd better let you go then, Mattie.'

'Not before—'

'Not before what?'

'Well, what do you think? Before we've kissed goodnight, silly.'

* * *

Judy learned the terrible fate of the world in the gloomy drawing room of her aunt's house on Mull. Left alone in the large grey-stoned house that sat at the head of a small seaweed-infested tidal loch on the western side of the island, she had been trying to keep herself amused with the latest variation of Patience which she had just taught herself from a book of card games when Mrs Craig, whose gloomy countenance matched the general mood of the house, appeared from nowhere to turn on the wireless.

'Ye'll be needin' to hear this, Miss. The Huns are in Poland.'

Despite knowing that war was, as it were, on the cards, Judy found herself standing up with the shock of it. She remained standing while she listened to the latest news bulletin in the company of the housekeeper, who regularly punctuated the silence with a sharp clicking of her tongue.

When the bulletin was over Mrs Craig switched the wireless off as briskly as she had turned it on.

'Now then, if ye have any washing that needs doing, Miss, I should take it off you.'

Judy frowned at her. 'Washing? You want my washing now?'

'If ye'd rather be caught with your linen dirty.' Mrs Craig sighed with a shake of her head. ''Tis all the same to me.'

So while the housekeeper washed the household linen clean rather than be caught napping by any invading force, Judy took herself out for a long walk in the woodlands by the side of the loch until she reached a point with a full view of the Atlantic ocean.

Below her the tide was racing in and a strong wind was up, swishing her rich dark hair away from her face, and high as she was she could still feel the tang of salt on her skin and taste it on her lips. The ocean was green-grey and angry-looking, breaking vast white-capped waves against the granite rocks before scuttering away in lethal whirlpools. Judy stared at the sea, unable to take her eyes from it, knowing that somewhere below its fury soon, if not right at this moment, Walter would be hidden from sight, submerged in a dark steel tube loaded with deadly weapons, in search of those who were now their mortal enemies.

Please God, she whispered into the wind. *Please God keep him safe and bring him home. Please, please God.*

Wheeling high above her some big dark bird called a loud cry before folding its wings backwards to dive swiftly down into the seething seas and disappear from sight, leaving Judy with the feeling that God was not listening.

* * *

Afterwards, not only Judy but everyone would always remember where they were and what they were doing at 11.15 a.m. on Sunday 3 September, 1939, when the prematurely old and seemingly already war-weary voice of Neville Chamberlain announced on the wireless that, since Germany had failed to respond to the British government's ultimatum to withdraw her troops from Poland, a state of war now existed between the two countries.

The congregation gathered in St Mary's Parish Church, Bexham, received confirmation of what they had all been dreading when the vicar's eleven-year-old daughter walked solemnly up the aisle and broke the news to her father as he was about to climb into the pulpit to deliver his sermon. He at once abandoned his prepared text to convey the message to his parishioners, before cutting short the service so that everyone could hurry back to their now threatened homes.

'Bad news,' Loopy Tate said to Sir Arthur as she and Hugh hurried past him on their way back to

Shelborne. 'Terrible news.'

'Yes, terrible,' Sir Arthur agreed, 'but at least it means we got let off the vicar's sermon. I wish the clergy wouldn't talk about themselves so much. I, I, I. That's all they seem to ever say. *I.* Aye, aye, and that's naval, everyone knows that, not church.'

Ahead of them the main street of the village was thronged with people, not all of whom had been attending Matins. Windows had been flung open and neighbours who had barely exchanged a word with each other during all their years of residence in Bexham were now talking animatedly to each other about the news.

Cups of tea and glasses of sherry were being handed out to anyone gathered round the bay window of the Lupins, a large and rambling house at the end of the high street which was the home of two spinster ladies, Miss Penrose and Miss Henshaw, known to all as Penny and Henny, while PC Ambrose was to be seen cycling slowly and carefully around the village announcing the outbreak of hostilities through a megaphone he had strapped to his head.

To Hugh and Loopy's astonishment they saw the landlord of the Three Tuns sitting at a table outside his pub being comforted by one of his barmaids, his great round red face suffused with tears, while not ten feet away from him on the quayside a group of children were happily spinning round in a circle as they celebrated the indefinite closure of schools for the duration.

'War brings nothing good in its wake.' Hugh turned from the sight of the children making themselves dizzy going round and round, and round and round, as they sang *No more Latin, no more French, no more sitting on a hard school bench.*

Loopy walked on with him, thoughtful and preoccupied, until at last, hurrying towards them from the estuary where they had been fishing, they saw Rusty and her two brothers, with their still assembled rods slung over their shoulders.

'Heard the news, have you, you three?' Loopy called to them, as they ran past.

'Colin the Lobster told us!' Tom called back. 'Heard it from the coastguard!'

'By the by, I think you're wrong, Hugo,' Loopy said once the youngsters had passed by. 'About wars not doing anyone good. Some people gain from war.'

'I'm leaving aside the arms boys, Loopy, you know that. They who make arms always support war.'

'I'm thinking nearer home. When I was in the stores yesterday, a couple of the local farmers were in. They sounded pretty darned pleased at what was about to happen. Reckoned it would stop the present agricultural slide to ruin.'

'We're certainly going to need all the food we can grow, of that there is no doubt.'

'Only thing is, Hughie—if they call up all the able-bodied men, who's going to see to the land?'

Hugh stopped by the gate, looked quizzically at his wife, and then squeezed the bicep of her right arm.

'Not you, my dear, and that's for sure. I don't want you to break your fingernails,' he teased. 'Now come on—I could kill a whisky sour.'

* * *

As the Todds ran past the Eastcotts' house they saw Lionel Eastcott hauling a Union Jack up to fly on the staff in front of his house. They stopped to watch him stand and salute the flag now unfurling in the stiffening breeze, an action that prompted Mickey to try to imitate him, before picking up again and running on towards their cottage where they found their father and mother busy with black adhesive tape at the windows.

'What's that for, Dad?' Mickey wanted to know. 'They won't be bombing Bexham, will they?'

'Seeing we're right on the coast, boy, there's no telling what they'll do. Now go and give your mum a hand with the blackout stuff. Half them screens need blacking.'

Rusty led the way, stopping as the three of them hurried upstairs to stare through the window at something in the glass-clad lean-to outside.

'Mickey?' she called, continuing up the stairs. 'I want to ask you a favour!'

Once they had finished helping their mother to paint some extra blinds she had made the day before with a mixture of lampblack and size and left them to dry out on the grass, Rusty took Mickey back to the lean-to shed and pointed out the young sapling that her brother had been growing in the little patch of ground their father allowed them to garden for themselves.

'Can I have it?'

'I won that, I did, when it was a conker. I won that.'

'I know that, Mickey, but I have a place for it, a special place.'

'But I'm growing it till it gets as tall as Brighton Pier.'

'I'm not going to stop it growing, silly. Come on, and I'll show you.'

Taking her doubtful brother by one hand Rusty hurried him off to the green at the other end of the village.

'Here,' Rusty said, choosing a bare, uncultivated spot near the cricket pavilion. 'This is where we'll plant him.'

'Can't see as to why,' Mickey said, scratching at his thick head of hair, and looking about him. He pointed across the grass. 'They've got trees here.'

'Yes, but no chestnuts. A village green should always have a chestnut.'

'Don't see why.'

'Because it's lucky, see? The horse chestnut is a lucky tree. Not like yew, which is for graveyards, and that. Now, come on. We'll go back and dig him up. For luck. See?'

'I still don't see the point.'

'The point is, Mickey, there's a war on now. If you remember. So I thought we should plant something to last out. Something maybe to outlast us all.'

But Mickey looked obdurate, and Rusty, knowing that look all too well, decided to leave her plan to another day.

* * *

'With Norway, Hitler's bitten off more than he can chew.'

Meggie looked across at her grandmother with a sudden frown. 'Do you think?' she asked, absently. She had just received a letter from Judy Melton, marooned, poor soul, in Scotland with her mother

and a gorgon of a housekeeper. 'Madame Gran?'
'Yes, darlin'?'
'You know Lady Melton, don't you?'
'For my sins, on occasions, yes, darlin', I do. Richards! Stop playing that dreadfully morbid piece, and play something a little more lively.'
'Madame.'
The butler looked across at his mistress, a hurt expression in his eyes, and started to play a Strauss waltz instead, always popular with Madame Gran.
'That's better. So.' She turned to Meggie. 'So, what is it you want me to do, or say, or write? Is it one—or all three?'
'Write would be best. Could you write and ask the Meltons to come and stay at Cucklington with us?'
'Cucklington? But we haven't any intention of going to Cuckers. We are staying in London. No one, not even Hitler, moves us out of London, darlin', certainly not. Brook Street is Brook Street, and here we stay, Richards and I. For the duration.'
'But supposing it becomes Brook Strasse?'
'Not while I am in it, it won't. No, here we stay, for the duration, Richards and I. The royal family are in Buckingham Palace, and Mrs Gore-Stewart is in Brook Street, and has been since war was declared seven months ago.'
'But Madame Gran, I really would, please, please, like you—really—to go to Cucklington, and then we could ask Judy to come and stay with us and be organised into something useful. That way her mother would bring her back to Bexham, and, eventually, Judy could live happily ever after with Walter, when he gets back from Somewhere Terribly Secret. You see, the stuffy old things,

the Meltons, are terribly against Walter—you remember Walter Tate? Lovely, lively family, and if you were on their side, well, it would all be different, wouldn't it? I mean, quite eventually, it might bring them round.'

There was a pause while Mrs Gore-Stewart considered this plan. Meggie knew that Madame Gran was deeply romantic, and against the older generation's interfering in the matters of the young.

'She's a terrible old snob nowadays, old Elizabeth Melton, and nothing much to be upsy dupsy about either, I mean ancestrally speaking, that is the silly thing. Really. But there you are, admirables' wives do get a bit hoity toity on occasions—all that gold in the yacht clubs, and people saluting so hard they fall over.'

'So you will write to Lady Em and ask her, darling Madame Gran?'

'Oh, very well. Doubtless she's sick to death of Scotland now, anyway—nothing but mountains, lochs and sea, not to mention heather. I dare say she can't wait to bring Judy back to Bexham, if only to get her hair permed.'

'What will you say?'

'Say? I shall say she is needed for my classes. I shall say that I need Judy.'

Meggie's mouth dropped open, but only for a second before she burst into laughter. 'Your what?'

'I know, I know. Don't laugh, naughty Meggie. It's Richards. He's heard on the grapevine that what will be needed is groups of people, in sort of classes, making things. Not socks so much, although those too, but perhaps much more ghastly things—nets for hiding under and all sorts and stuffs of things. Much better than just knitting socks, which let's face it they usually only used, in the last war anyway, to clean out their guns. Yes, Richards came to me with the idea, and we were going to start it up here, part of the WVS initiative and all that, but I do see, we should go to Cuckers, because there is yards more room there, and we could have teams and teams of people all making and doing like mad. But we are not leaving London because of bombs, is that understood? We are leaving London because of jobs. Jobs is what women are good at. Jobs, and managing men.'

Just at that moment Richards stopped playing the piano, finishing on a nice round of gaiety from Vienna, of all places. Still, Meggie realised, it was awfully difficult to play something classical without straying into the German composers, and that was the truth.

'Yes, managing men and jobs, that is what we women are best at.'

Remembering the long conversations that she and Richards had enjoyed over the past days, and catching him raising his eyes to heaven behind his mistress's back, it occurred to Meggie that managing *women* might be Richards's forte. So, as darkness fell, plunging London once more into blackout, Richards took Madame Gran's letter to Lady Melton, demanding Judy's presence at Cuckers to help the war effort, to the post.

Naturally, it being wartime, it was some considerable time before Lady Melton received it, due to one thing and another—mostly the fact that the postman's bicycle had received a hit, not from enemy aircraft but from a wall he crashed it into after a visit to the local hostelry. But whatever the reason, the bicycle had taken ages to mend, because most of the spare parts had to be made at the local garage, the owner of which was also recovering from a similar sort of accident.

On the last night before the letter finally reached its destination, Judy tossed and turned in her narrow, uncomfortable, iron-framed bed. Outside, rain driven in hard from the Atlantic swept up the glen and lashed the windows of the granite-walled house, and the image of Walter hundreds of feet down in the sea would not be moved from Judy's sleepless head. Finally, ashamed of her self-pity and yet at the same time more determined than ever that she and Walter should not be kept apart, Judy made her mind up once and for all. She would take whatever money she could find, even if it wasn't enough to get her as far as London, let alone Bexham, and then she would hitchhike the rest of the way. She had to get back to Bexham, to where those she loved lived. To Bexham, while it was still there, and while they were all still there.

* * *

'Where on earth have you been, Maude?' Lionel demanded, peeling off his khaki tunic top and carefully placing his broomstick-cum-bayonet in the umbrella stand. 'You keep disappearing.'

'Since your lot are none too keen on letting ladies join in your fun and games—'

'Fun and games?' Lionel thundered, hanging his military headgear on the peg he normally reserved for his motoring cap. 'I'll have you know, Maude, the British Local Defence Volunteers are not being assembled for the purposes of fun and games.

There is a war on, may I remind you?'

'Which is precisely why I am learning to drive, Lionel. So that I may also play a part in the defence of our country.'

'This is not women's work, Maude. War is men's work, not women's work.'

'Broomsticks are usually women's work, Lionel.' Maude threw a disparaging look towards the dummy rifle in the hall.

'It is not a broomstick. We have been issued with new wooden rifles. And if you shake it, it makes a sound like a machine gun. Little bits of metal inside, d'you see?' Lionel fetched his new weapon and demonstrated its capabilities.

'Oh, goodness, Lionel, I should think my driving will frighten the Nazis more than that thing.'

'You and your driving. Anyone would think that no one had ever been in a motor car before. And I trust to it that you're not encouraging young Mattie to take to the wheel. We can do without too many women drivers, thank you. Where is she, anyway? I haven't seen her for days.'

'Mattie is also learning how to drive, Lionel. And before you go working yourself into a blue fit, it was her own idea. She and her friend Virginia thought of it altogether separately. They want to drive ambulances. Virginia is even talking about joining the army so she could be a staff driver.'

'So she could gad about with men in uniform more likely,' Lionel grumbled. 'Man mad, that girl. Not a good influence on our Mattie at all.'

'Lionel, there's a war on, remember? Things are going to get a lot different all over the place, round here included, if it goes on for some time—which they say it will. I mean, it has certainly not been all over by Christmas, has it? And we are now in April, if you hadn't noticed. So if I were you I'd get used to the idea of some of us doing things you lot wouldn't approve of us doing in peacetime.'

'Us lot being?'

'Men, dear,' Maude replied tartly. 'As if you didn't know. Now don't you think you had better go out and shake your fake gun at someone? If there's an invasion we are going to need every fake marksman around.'

She stared at Lionel. He suddenly seemed much older. Not capable of frightening her, let alone a Nazi. Oh well, they could only hope that it would not come to that.

*   *   *

'I told you it'd be fun,' Virginia said to Mattie as they walked in the pitch darkness back towards the village. 'And I told you he was a good kisser.'

'I thought he was meant to be teaching us to drive, not to kiss.' Mattie raised her eyes to heaven, thinking of Peter.

'Think how useful it will be to be able to kiss *and* drive.'

'He was quite forward though. Wouldn't you say?'

'Because he kissed me?'

'Because he seems to try to kiss everyone.'

'Whoops—' Virginia stopped as she bumped into something—or somebody—in the darkness. 'Sorry.'

'Do you always apologise to pillar boxes?'

'Was that what I just bumped into?' Virginia peered at the shape of the object now behind her.

'I could swear it was moving.'

'Are you really thinking of joining the WRACs, Virginia? I mean really?'

'I've got this thing about being in uniform. I see myself driving this super staff car, with a general or someone like that in the back. Blast! Oh, blast and dammit!'

'Whatever is the matter now?'

'I only walked straight into a blinking lamp post, that's all. I think I've broken my nose.'

Having located her troubled friend, Mattie fumbled in her pocket for her Swan Vestas. 'We should have brought a torch with us.'

'Underwoods have run out of number eight batteries,' Virginia replied, through the hankie she now held to her nose. 'God, this hurts. Anyway, we're not meant to use torches.'

'Yes we are. Long as you point it downwards, and put tissue paper in front of the bulb—'

'As if enemy aeroplanes are going to spot some feeble little pocket torch.'

'Crikey!' Mattie examined Virginia's nose by the light of the match. 'You look as if you've been in a boxing match.'

'I feel as if I have.'

'Is it broken?'

'No, course not. Come on.'

'What's the big rush?' Mattie's match had long gone out as she trailed behind Virginia, who had hurried ahead in the darkness.

'I'd rather not hang about, Mattie! I think someone's following us! Listen!'

Mattie tried to listen without stopping. 'I can't hear anything!'

'*Listen!*'

The two young women both stopped together, colliding with each other as they did so.

'Can't you hear it? Listen?'

Now Mattie could hear their pursuer all right. It seemed they were being followed by someone who preferred to make up his ground in a series of quick rushing steps rather than a steady, heavy tread. Which somehow only served to make their pursuit even more frightening.

'Quickly!' Virginia urged, grabbing Mattie by her coat sleeve. 'We'll have to make a run for it!'

The two of them began to run, stumbling along in the darkness, somehow miraculously staying on their feet for the next fifty yards or so until Mattie fell off the verge into the small ditch that ran alongside, pulling her friend with her.

'Help!' Virginia screamed as she tripped on top of Mattie. 'Please, someone help us—please!'

Both of them screamed as the noise of their pursuer increased, if anything sounding even louder.

'It's all right, Virginia!' Mattie yelled over her still screaming companion. 'It's only an old box!'

* * *

'What a sight,' Maude sighed as she shut the front door behind her daughter. 'What have you been up to, Mattie? You'd better not let your father see you like this. And you're very late.'

'It's a wonder I'm home at all, Ma. We couldn't see a thing—not a thing. And then we thought we were being followed—I mean this blackout thing is *spooky*.'

'Not as spooky as it will be if the Germans invade. Better safe than sorry. Now come on into the library and we'll steal some of your father's gin. And compare notes on our driving skills.'

Mother and daughter found their way across the hall and along the corridor with the help of a couple of lit candle stubs, the only post-curfew lights allowed in the house by the ever-vigilant Lionel, settling themselves around the remains of a fire to sip gins and orange while recounting their progress.

'You know your father still doesn't approve. Of either of us driving, I mean. And more so than ever if you ask me.'

'Makes me even more determined. We must be doing the right thing, Ma.'

'Oh, I know exactly what you mean, dear. If he did approve of something it would have to be something safe—like knitting. Or sending food parcels. Not that there's anything wrong in knitting or making up food parcels, Mathilda—'

'It's all right, I know what you mean, Ma. But safety hasn't anything to do with anything now, has it? Not now.'

'No, and just because we're meant to be the weaker sex doesn't mean we have to sit at home twiddling our thumbs. Besides, your grandmother used to say that if men had to have babies the human race would have stopped long before Adam.'

Mathilda looked at her mother across the table in the candlelight, and seeing the look in her eyes and the smile on her lips all at once realised how little she knew the woman who had given birth to her.

'You know how dangerous it is, what we all want to do, Ma? I mean really, it is dangerous, joining up, learning to drive—it is dangerous, and no quarter given.'

'I have learned that there is something far, far worse than danger, Mattie.'

'And that is?'

'Boredom,' said her mother crisply. 'To be bored with yourself worst of all—it means you can't even taste your food—'

Maude stopped mid-sentence as overhead the sky was suddenly filled with the droning noise of heavy-engined aircraft.

'No siren,' Mathilda said. 'At least not yet. Must be ours.'

'I love the sound of aircraft. Or rather I used to,' Maude said, reaching for her comforting and much appreciated packet of John Players. 'Now they give me the shivers.'

Mathilda unscrewed the top of the green gin bottle and poured another two drinks.

'God save the King,' she proposed, getting to her feet.

'Absolutely,' her mother agreed, also rising. 'And death to his enemies.'

They held their glasses aloft, as if toasting the skies, then downed their drinks in one. Mattie stared over her glass for a second at her mother. She did not know why, but since war was declared—what, seven months ago, something like that—not only had their lives changed, but they had all changed, most of all her mother. There was a new light in her eye, a new spring in her step. She looked younger. It was almost shocking.

CHAPTER SEVEN

Six weeks later the small and normally quiet harbour of Bexham was alive with activity. Everywhere it seemed people were readying boats, crafts of all shapes and sizes. Press-ganged into service by their elders and betters, village boys ran full pelt along the waterfront with empty jerry cans to be filled to spilling at the fuel pump that stood at the head of the quay, while a stream of flat-footed girls with sacks of provisions slung over their shoulders stumbled along in the opposite direction towards the boats bobbing on the water, some with their engines already running, others with last-minute adjustments being made to their mechanics by their crews.

'What's happening?' Mickey asked Rusty, catching up with her as she ran towards the grocer's shop next to the pub. 'Mum said something about some of our soldiers bein' stranded like—'

'That's what the rumour is, Mickey!' Rusty replied over her shoulder. 'Now if you want to make yourself useful—'

'I do! What can I do?'

'They could use some more help up at the store!'

'Provisionin'! Which was where I was headin'! Unless you'd rather do the fuellin'!'

'What a madhouse,' old Dan said, from his permanent seat on the capstan. 'Madder even than Regatta Day.'

'They want every possible boat,' Rusty gasped, pausing to draw breath, having despatched her brother to help pack up provisions. 'We been told to get every boat possible on the water.'

' 'A t's what I 'eard on the wireless, din't I?' Dan replied, filling his old briar pipe with dark shag. 'Anyone and everyone what can sail a boat must go, they says. Our army is stranded, we must get our boys home, and that. God bless 'em.'

Rusty stopped paying attention, having just caught sight of David Kinnersley jumping down off the quay on to the deck of his blue and white yacht. At once she ducked out of his sight, hoping he had not seen her, for if the rumours were true and things were as bad as they said they were the other side of the Channel, then Rusty had no intention of remaining at home twiddling the knobs on the wireless and scraping carrots for her mother—although at this particular moment she had only the vaguest idea of how she could be useful.

Since the majority of the young men in the village had either been called up or volunteered, Rusty knew there was going to be a shortage of able sea hands, as surely as she knew that no one would entertain the thought of a girl's helping to man a boat cross-Channel. Women were only being required to help victual and fuel up the boats. Experienced though she might be at sea, and as good a sailor as any she could think of, she knew that, being a girl, no one would want her on board his vessel.

'Rusty!' Mickey yelled to her down the quay. 'Come and give us a hand with these boxes, will you?'

She hurried to where Mickey was struggling with a couple of cardboard boxes, one under each arm. Rescuing some of the small packets and tins of groceries that were already spilling on to the quay,

Rusty took one box from him and asked which boat they were intended for.

'One's for Mr Marcus, and one for Mr Kinnersley. This one.'

'I'll take him his. Then I have to run an errand for someone, so if anyone's looking for me, I'll be back later!'

Inevitably, in the hubbub, Mickey failed to catch much of what Rusty was saying, most particularly the last bit, thanks to a hooter blast from a departing fishing smack, bound for France, and cheered off by those on the quay.

Hardly giving it a glance, Rusty hurried as fast as she could to the smart blue and white motor yacht bobbing on its mooring at the end of the quay. Seeing David Kinnersley in conversation with another outward-bound sailor, Rusty held up the box of groceries in indication, before shouting over the noise that she was taking them below. Happily David Kinnersley paid her about as much attention as Rusty had given the departing smack.

'Depends what actual beach they're on, I suppose,' she heard him saying as she clambered on board. 'If there's too much shallow water then the Navy won't be able to get in close. It'll be up to craft like ours to ferry them out, or home. Vital that we do.'

'They say over half our army is stuck there, sitting ducks for their bombs. It doesn't bear thinking about.'

David looked up at the sky. After being given the thumbs down over his army medical, he could not wait to get going, do something, for God's sake. These last months, up in front of this army board and up in front of that army board, he had become convinced that he was only half a man, as the bureaucrats tried to decide what to do with a man with only half a lung.

'If this weather holds, should be an easy enough trip. Going out, anyway.'

'Sailing single handed, what happens if you get taken out?'

'Every inch will count on the way back. Space below, space on top. Space is what I need to fill the boat up with our boys.'

Rusty listened from below. She could curl up small, and then, she reasoned, reappear when most needed. Guide the boat through the water for Mr Kinnersley as they neared France, leave him to pull the boys on board. Through the porthole she could just see him and his companion disappearing into the pub at the top of the quays, for all the world as if it were an ordinary day and they were two friends intent on a drink without a care in the world, rather than two men about to risk life and limb in a harebrained plan to try to snatch the members of the British Expeditionary Force from under the noses of the advancing German army.

She knew no one at home would miss her, at least not immediately. The quays were thronged with people whose only thoughts were on the rescue mission ahead of them, so if anyone came looking for her and was unable to find her it would be all too understandable. By the time either her brothers or her father realised she was actually missing, it would be too late, and with a bit of luck, should their mission prove successful, she would sail home alongside her hero, for, as Mickey was forever teasing her, David Kinnersley was very much Rusty's hero. Watching him as she had, month after month, sailing *Light Heart* into Bexham with his mysterious human cargo, human cargo that her father with his boatyard was only too willing and able to help conceal, she could not, after all, regard him as anything else.

'You keep your mouth shut, our Rusty. Remember, if it weren't for men like Mr Kinnersley, these poor creatures would be dead meat.'

That's what her dad had said, when Rusty had first confessed to witnessing some of the mysterious goings-on. And that was all he had said, before sticking his pipe back into his mouth and walking out of the house to the Three Tuns for much needed refreshment.

Rusty looked around her appreciatively. The boat was entirely shipshape, and everything that was necessary for the voyage was stacked and folded neatly: life belts, extra ropes, lanterns, flares, blankets and towels, leaving little or no room in the cabin proper. Beyond the sitting area in the next compartment were two bunk beds. Realising quickly that every space would be needed for a soldier, Rusty was beginning to despair of finding a bolthole, until she spied a hatch on the foredeck.

Hurrying back to the cabin, Rusty grabbed a thick wool blanket and one of several torches before returning on deck and dropping herself down into her hidey-hole. Pulling the hatch carefully shut over her head, she settled herself down in one corner, a place that to her great dismay she found to be under a couple of inches of water. Pulling an old empty flare box out from the other corner, she perched herself on it, making herself as comfortable as she could against the curved side of the boat, but unable to keep her feet out of the cold water lapping all around her.

After half an hour she heard someone jumping back down into the boat, then the sound of feet hurrying about the deck as the skipper made ready to cast off and set sail. Moments later the engine throbbed into life and the next thing Rusty knew they were at sea.

Light Heart sailed as smooth as glass down the estuary, chugging steadily at moderate speed until finally—to judge from the sudden pitching—they reached the open sea. Rusty had no idea of what sort of seas they might encounter, and although it hadn't concerned her earlier when she had begun to hatch her plan, since she had been born a good sailor, now that she was shut in a tiny dark space which was beginning to fill with diesel fumes, she began to have serious doubts as to the strength of her stomach.

But no sooner had they endured the rough waters that generally occur where estuaries become the open sea, the pitching stopped as the boat obviously ran into millpond conditions. The calming of the seas brought no respite from the continuing engine fumes, and after enduring it as best she might for another half an hour Rusty finally gave in and did the only thing possible in the circumstances. Damp or no damp, swell or no swell, she fell into a diesel-induced sleep, waking from it what seemed like hours later.

This time she could stand it no longer and burst through the hatch only to collapse on the wooden seating around the cockpit, her head still spinning from the fumes. For one awful moment she thought she was going to let herself down completely by being sick, which would have seriously dented her reputation as an experienced sailor, but happily the moment quickly passed.

'I wouldn't make a habit of doing that too much, old thing, really I wouldn't.' David Kinnersley eyed her, one hand on the wheel and the other skilfully lighting a fresh cigarette as he put his pistol away.

'I heard that some of our lads were beached in France, Mr Kinnersley.'

'So you thought you'd come along for the ride.'

'Reckoned you'll need someone to take charge of the boat, while you help them get on board, and that.'

David nodded. He knew Rusty Todd, old Todd's only daughter, only vaguely, but enough to know that she was as good as a boy in a boat.

'All right, Rusty. Soon as you've recovered your sea legs—'

'It's not my sea legs. It was the fumes below. Enough to make a horse sick.'

'Well, if you're recovered then, why don't you rustle us up some refreshments?' He nodded across at the flotilla around and behind them. 'Glad to see we are not alone, eh? Half Bexham seems to have come with us!'

Five minutes later David was eating a plateful of thick-cut cheese sandwiches washed down with a bottle of Spellings Best Light Ale while Rusty took a turn at the wheel, keeping the craft steady as she went across the millpond waters.

'We were told it was a planned withdrawal,' David said in answer to Rusty's questions. 'Don't think they wanted us to know what's really going on—that our boys have been cut off and if we don't get 'em off the beaches somehow, they can't get themselves off.'

'What about the RAF? Dad said they were giving the Germans a right pasting.'

At that very moment they both looked up to see three fighters heading back for England, one of them streaming smoke from its tail.

'Good luck, young feller,' David murmured, watching them go. 'Pray to God he makes it.'

Moments later they caught their first sight of the French coastline, flatlands that seemed to be almost wholly hidden under a heavy pall of black smoke.

'Lot of oil installations around the port, one gathers. Looks as though our bombers were on target. Good show.'

To Rusty, setting out, stowing away in the hold, it had, at first, seemed just like an adventure story, but now, staring ahead of her, it was so no longer.

Perhaps it was the sight of the ships that brought the reality of it all home to her so forcibly. Naval vessels, like great helpless whales, but lying, not basking, well off the coast, too far out for the marooned soldiers to reach by wading or swimming, but quite near enough to attract the attentions of the enemy fighters and bombers, so that even as David swung his boat to, it was apparent they were mounting another raid on their sitting targets. The noise of their bombs exploding and the crackle of returning gunfire began to reach their ears, so faint at first that the actual noise of war sounded almost harmless.

'You'd better get below for a bit.'

'I didn't come all this way just to go below, Mr Kinnersley.'

'Captain's orders,' David replied, looking round at the flotilla of small ships that was beginning to assemble over a couple of square miles.

'You got a mutiny on your hands. I take it we got to get as many of our lads home as we can?'

'The original idea was to ferry as many of our boys as possible on to the Navy's boats. But—' David looked ahead now, spotting more enemy planes heading out from the coast, 'but, given the current activity, I'd say we're going to have to play it by ear!'

Most of this sentence was lost in the din of sudden gunfire as an enemy fighter swung hard right over the fleet of little boats and opened both machine guns. Bullets burnt the sky right over their heads as David flattened them both on the deck just in time.

'Bet you wished you'd stayed at home with your mum like a good girl now,' David said in Rusty's ear, as they remained resolutely face down.

Rusty said nothing. Going to someone's rescue, their boys in France, had certainly spelt a kind of pleasant danger to her, but death, her death in particular, had never really entered the equation. Now she found herself shaking like a leaf while the air around *Light Heart* screamed from the hail of bullets.

'Well, now Jerry's got that little lot off his chest'—David raised himself slowly and carefully to look over the rail—'time to go a-rescuing, I'd say.'

Slowly increasing the speed of the boat, David steered towards the first group of soldiers he could see in the water about half a mile forward. Rusty eased herself up on to her knees to look where they were going and saw some of the men holding their rifles above their heads as they tried to wade towards them.

'Must be dead shallow here. I mean they're some way out.'

'Poor buggers. Couldn't have chosen a worse spot to be stranded.'

'How many can we take aboard?'

'Hadn't thought really. Twenty—no—more, I'd say.'

'We goin' to take 'em to the Navy?'

'Let's just try to get some of these poor chaps on board first, shall we?'

They were nearer now, and the nearer they got the more clearly Rusty could hear the shouts and the cries of the men. Some of them, hurrying now they saw rescue so close at hand, stumbled and fell forward into the sea, while those more fortunate stayed upright long enough to grab hold of the side of the boat.

'Here!' Rusty shouted, extending her hand. 'Here! Come on! I'll pull you up!'

'They'll pull you in more like!' David shouted at her, killing the engine. 'Don't pull anyone till they're over the side or you'll be in the briny! And lads! Not all one side or you'll have her over!'

Leaving the boat in Rusty's charge, David reached out wherever he could to help the soldiers aboard. Some threw their rifles in ahead of them, others clung to them as if their lives depended on them rather than the rescue craft, while others, exhausted by their ordeal, fell back into the water, losing their places to their fitter companions. Appalled, David stretched out to try to help a young lad who had obviously been shot in the shoulder to judge from his bloodstained tunic, but his grip was not strong enough to haul him on board. Just about to lose him again to the sea David felt someone else come to the rescue from behind, a stubble-chinned Tommy with a soaking wet butt of a cigarette still clenched between his teeth. He shoved away a soldier who had been trying to take the wounded boy's place at the side and one-handed hauled the boy on board, where the poor lad at once collapsed on the deck.

Still in charge of the boat, Rusty tried to keep her mind on her duties. It helped to take her gaze away from the sea which seemed to be turning from blue to red.

'All right, chaps!' she heard David yelling. 'That's enough of you! That's enough for the moment, I said! Or none of us will get home! I mean it!'

'You 'eard!'

It was the unshaven soldier again, the self-promoted leader of the pack. With the end of his rifle he started to push men back into the water, bringing the butt of his gun down on one pair of hands determined not to let go of the boat.

'Hey!' Rusty yelled at him. 'You can't do that! You could break someone's hands like that!'

'Leave him alone, Rusty!' David shouted. 'We can't take any more on or we'll all be drowned!'

Seeing the logic of this, Rusty stared helplessly and hopelessly at the crowds in the water, some of them reaching out pathetically to try to grab hold of a boat that was already turning away to leave them, while others more intent on survival were already heading as fast as their wading would let them for the next craft in the flotilla. Every boat she could see was swarming with soldiers, and it seemed the same scene was being played out everywhere. Men were clambering up the sides of motor launches and dinghies, yachts, smacks and even the odd long rowing boat, the sort used just off Bexham and other small harbours for near-shore fishing. And everywhere men were either being forced back into the sea or dropping off boats already too full to take any more. Some of the craft now headed back for England were sailing with men still holding the sides of the stern, where possible.

'We'll be back!' David was calling out to them, once more in control. 'We'll be back again soon as we can! Promise you!'

Rusty could hardly bear to look any longer. Instead she started to attend to the men sitting along the benches that lined the cockpit who were obviously injured, offering drinks and food first before darting down below to fetch the first aid kit stored there. The boy with the badly wounded shoulder was being supported by his burly rescuer, who had managed to light himself a fresh dry cigarette. Rusty crouched down on the deck and opened her first aid box.

'Not a lot in there'll do him good, girl,' the soldier told her with a weary shake of his head. 'Needs blood, that's what he needs.'

'Is he going to be all right?' Rusty asked helplessly, as the young soldier slouched even more heavily on his companion's shoulder. 'Shouldn't we try—I don't know—try to clean his wound or something?'

'Leave him be, sweetheart. You're a good girl, but best thing all told is just leave 'im be, OK?'

Rusty closed the lid of her first aid tin, watching the young soldier's face grow paler while the deep red stain on the left side of his chest grew ever darker. She suddenly felt faint. Swallowing hard and taking a deep breath she nodded at the burly soldier and moved on to see if anyone else needed her attention.

As if sensing that his second in command might be losing consciousness David called, 'Brandy in the locker, First Mate. Take a good shot then bring it out here. Couple of these chaps look as though they're in need of it as well.'

Rusty did as she was told, gulping a shot of the brandy straight from the bottle and finding to her astonishment that it pulled her together in no time. By now they were well out of the firing range and heading back to England as fast as David could run his boat. The sea was still flat calm and the visibility so good they could see dozens of other small craft to either side of them, some making their way back home fully laden, others hurrying full pelt across the Channel bent on further rescue. The next hours passed in near silence, punctuated every now and then by desultory remarks.

'Where the bloody 'ell were they?' one man kept asking, time and time again. 'They was shootin' us to ribbons, throwin' everythin' they 'ad at us—and where was the bloody RAF? Sittin' at 'ome on their bleedin' backsides playing cards, most like.'

Rusty was just about to point out that the RAF had been overhead the whole journey, when her eye was caught by the sight of yet another flotilla. A familiar boat passed some distance away. Rusty found herself automatically ducking, a habit of years when she was somewhere she should not be and suddenly caught sight of her dad.

'That was my dad and my brother Tom,' she told

the old corporal next to her.

'Good on him. God knows what will happen if those poor sods are not reached in time. Sitting bloody ducks, if you'll forgive my language, miss.'

'Oh, swear away,' Rusty told him. 'I mean, if you can't swear during a war, when can you?'

Miraculously, when they reached Bexham harbour the badly injured young soldier was still alive, and Rusty was relieved to help him, and others who were wounded, into one of the waiting ambulances.

As the final soldiers were disembarking and Rusty was, for the first time in her life, considering not only visiting the Three Tuns but taking up cigarette smoking too, seemingly from nowhere Mickey pounced on her.

'Where the heck you been? I been looking all over for you! Dad was looking too. He wanted you to go with him and Tom. They're gone—'

'Mr Kinnersley and me've been already, Mickey. Over to France. That's where we've been. To Dunkirk.'

'You were on board *Light Heart*?' Mickey asked admiringly, then he frowned. 'You went over to help in the rescue? You could have taken me.'

'Not enough room for three, stupid. Not with all the soldiers we got to bring back, ask Mr Kinnersley. Besides there's blood over there, lots of it, and you don't like blood, Mickey.'

'Mr Kinnersley, sir, you'll take me next time, won't you?' Mickey caught at the arm of the disembarking David Kinnersley. David smiled, but shook his head.

'No.'

'Aren't you going back there, then, Mr

Kinnersley?'

'I most certainly am, but not before I've had a pint at the Three Tuns.'

David walked off in the direction of the pub, lighting a cigarette and whistling at the same time, something which Rusty suddenly knew she wanted to emulate.

'Here, you going back too?'

Rusty nodded absently, still watching David.

'Can I come and all?'

Rusty shook her head. 'Can you imagine what Mum would say?'

'She knows you've gone.'

Rusty stared into her youngest brother's bright blue eyes. 'She does?'

'Yes, she sat down sudden when I was having my dinner, and said "Rusty's gone with the rest, hasn't she, Mickey?" '

Rusty nodded. That would be Mum all right. She always knew when things were happening to her family, even when she could not see them. It was just the way she was. Dad always said that she was half mermaid half woman, and that he had only married her because she sat combing her long hair on a rock and playing music that dimmed his senses.

'But you haven't seen me, you understand? I don't want Mum coming down here, see?' Rusty eased her way round the blind side of the boxes, completely out of sight. 'Now go home, Mickey, there's a good lad, and help Mum, or something. Go on.'

Mickey looked at her, his heart in his eyes, longing to stay, but knowing that Rusty would never take him back with her and Mr Kinnersley on

Light Heart. Not in a million years. She just never would.

He ran home as fast as he could. He could not wait to tell his mum about what had happened, about all the soldiers coming off of the boats, and the blood, and Mr Kinnersley, and everything. But when he got in his mum was gone, and he sat and ate his milk and biscuits quite alone while all the time making a plan for an adventure of his own—some way that he could prove he was as brave as the rest of his family, something he could do that would make him a hero in everyone's eyes.

CHAPTER EIGHT

In the event Meggie did not join the Wrens as she had promised herself she was going to do, once Madame Gran and Richards, not to mention a newly arrived Judy, had settled into Cucklington House, on the outskirts of Bexham. Instead she joined the WVS, and persuaded Judy to do the same.

'WVS—it stands for widows, virgins and spinsters, Judy. Which one are you?'

Seeing the colour that Judy turned at her question, a colour that exactly matched her brand new WVS pullover, Meggie turned away, laughing.

'Oh, touché, Miss Melton! Life catches up with all of us.'

'Walter is home on leave soon, and I am so hoping against hope that we—you know.'

'I know, you and Walter are going to marry, in fact I am sure of it, and up the aisle you will go in Madame Gran's old white dress, and I will wear a Parma violet toque on my shining head of hair, and cry and cry and cry, which is just how it should be.'

'Oh, bother the white dress!' Judy stared out of the window towards the harbour. 'What do dresses matter when we all have so much to do?'

Meggie lit a cigarette and smoked it in silence, before pulling on her red felt hat and staring at herself in the mirror to study the effect of the grey-green uniform and matching red jumper, all so carefully designed by Digby Morton for the WVS to look beautifully chic.

'How is your mother taking your still being in love with Walter and all that, Judy?'

'My mother?'

'Yes, duckie, Lady Melton, remember? Your mother?'

'I wouldn't know, actually. As you know, I have hardly seen her since we got back from Scotland, but I had the impression that being so isolated up there for so long, I think that pulled her up a bit. I think during that long and dreary winter she came to realise that there were things in life, in war in particular, which were really rather more important than whether or not Walter and I choose to get engaged. And since my father has decided it matters less whom I marry than that we win the war, the whole subject seems to have been put to bed.'

'In the event, rather an appropriate expression, that . . .'

They both started to laugh.

'Actually, at this moment, my mother is in Weymouth helping to organise the evacuees from the Channel Islands. My father will be lucky to see her for the duration. The old boy is having a rare old time in the Local Defence Volunteers with all the other fuddy duddies, or fuddy daddies. Fire watching, digging trenches, putting up booby traps in the woods, and keeping his eyes peeled for parachuting Nazis dressed as nunny wunnies arriving from the skies. Not bad considering his age. Actually, I think the LDV has really given all the older men a new lease of life. You should see them marching—soon you won't be able to tell them from crack infantry. Marvellous really. Mind you, meeting my father and his friends on a dark night would be enough to scare most Nazis to death. And I mean it. Talk about no quarter given. Firearms, the lot—he's becoming a crack shot, too. Given up drinking spirits, in case they affect his aim, and since his eyesight is still perfect the Nazi housepainter had better watch out.'

Having satisfied herself that her felt hat was now moulded into the perfect shape for her face, Meggie turned to Judy.

'Right, Miss Melton, off we go, to do our duty for God and the king.'

The two young women about-turned in mock imitation of a march and left the bedroom.

Downstairs Elinor Gore-Stewart and Richards were sorting clothes for the village evacuees. Jumpers in one pile, skirts in another, trousers in yet another, all now returned immaculately darned from the various knitting and sewing circles around Bexham, and ready to go off to the collecting points being organised by the WVS.

'We're having a knitting circle in the dining room, a sewing circle in the drawing room, and making cocktails in the cellar,' Richards told Meggie with more than a hint of pride in his voice.

'I know your mixes tend to be lethal, Richards, but not so lethal you have to mix them in the cellar, surely?'

'Madame Gran's mix, not mine, Miss Meggie—Molotov cocktails, for throwing at German tanks.'

For a second both young women turned back and stared at Richards, lost in admiration for Mrs Gore-Stewart and her butler, before making off towards the garage and their next destination—the coast, and the new arrivals from France.

'Chummy's not going to be much use soon, once the petrol rationing worsens, so let's enjoy her while we can.' Judy patted her little car on its bonnet before getting into the driving seat.

Nothing could prepare them not just for the sight of the troops returning from Dunkirk, but for the look of them; not the blood and bandages, but their air of utter disbelief, the mortal wound of defeat seeming not to have left even the heartiest of them unscarred. Since they had elected not just to feed and comfort the young men, but to accompany the worst of the wounded back to London on the train, Judy and Meggie found it difficult not to be affected by the sight of schoolchildren, parents and teachers running up the grass embankments to the small country stations, to the halts, to everywhere they knew the trains might or would stop, however temporarily, to bring food and refreshments to the dirty, dispirited, and wounded troops.

'I lost my brother somewhere back there,' a pathetically young, horribly wounded corporal suddenly told Judy, bursting into tears.

'You can't think about that now, son,' one of the older occupants of the carriage remarked, 'not any more. None of us can. All of us is going to lose someone. That don't matter, same as Churchill keeps telling us, not compared to what we got to do. Victory, that's what matters. We're the only ones left waiting to punch Hitler in his Nazi face. Only us and the Empire, but punch him we will. Just you see.'

* * *

Light Heart was outward bound once again, and near to completing the less than thirty miles to France. In the distance bombs were exploding along the beach and among the lines of soldiers wading out to sea. It flashed through Rusty's mind that being brave once was one thing, but being brave twice was quite another. Looking ahead, she no longer felt even faintly courageous, in fact she felt appalled at her own cowardice.

'How far in are you going to try and get this time?' she called out to David Kinnersley.

'As far as I dare!'

The lines of wading soldiers formed slowly advancing semicircles in the shallow waters, almost perfectly formed where they began, but disintegrating into ragged disorder the further the troops got out to sea. From where *Light Heart* was now positioned it seemed to Rusty that everything was moving in slow motion. Even the shell and bomb bursts seemed to have no real appearance of reality, happening as they did before the sound of their explosion was carried out to the flotilla of rescue ships waiting bravely, patiently, at last holding out hope to the waders.

But as David eased *Light Heart* in across the shallow waters the conflict became hideous. Rusty could hear the shouts for help from the men they were all bent on trying to rescue, and, far worse than that, the screams and cries of their wounded companions seemed to have welded into one hideous, long drawn out wail that appeared to come from the bowels of human despair. All around, now, she saw that this time there were not just patches of red, but the whole sea had turned to a dull brownish scarlet as the dead, some limbless, some whole, floated past the boat. On the beach and in the shallows men were being shattered by shells, bombs and gunfire from the German fighter planes, ending their lives in the very sea in which, perhaps only a few months earlier, they might have been enjoying themselves on holiday with their families. Caps and berets, long parted from their owners, floated past the boat, as did waterlogged wallets, letters from home, postcards from sweethearts, mementoes of young lives now nothing but macabre confetti on the sea of blood.

It was too real for Rusty to be able to summon up the strength either to scream or to be sick, but she found herself momentarily closing her eyes before turning to hurry to the opposite side of the boat where the sea had erupted around a line of panic-stricken soldiers who had suddenly turned their joint attentions to climbing on board. This time too there was no burly unshaven soldier to come to Rusty's rescue, just herself and her skipper trying to control the gang of men pulling themselves up from the sea and on to the deck. They tried to shout warnings, aware the boat could only carry so many, but their admonitions were either lost in the noise or simply ignored. Already overloaded by a good third more than the number they could safely carry, David yelled at Rusty to turn about and go full steam ahead for one of the waiting naval frigates that lay out well beyond the shallows, but before Rusty could swing the yacht round another ten men had clambered and fought their way aboard.

'There's too many of you! We'll sink!' David bellowed at them. 'Just wait, we'll come back for you.'

So overladen was *Light Heart* that the sea was already lapping over her sides. To add to their plight Rusty could now see that an enemy fighter had swung about just beyond them and was heading back, already beginning what promised to be a lethal dive.

'Get down, everybody!' she yelled, pushing those nearest her as hard as she could. 'Get down! Get down!'

But so tightly packed were the troops that there was no room to get down. The most they could do was duck and cover their heads as the fighter levelled out and opened fire from its twin machine guns. Wedged upright amidst a bunch of sea-soaked soldiers Rusty tried to make herself as small as possible as a line of strafing bullets cut through the sea and ripped into the side of *Light Heart*. Someone in the pack of men screamed in agony as he was hit, at the same time as another trooper not more than two away from Rusty yelled that he'd been hit in the legs. Another held his face in his hands, through which blood was seeping as his mate began to cradle his stricken companion in his arms. Turning her head as far as she could Rusty searched the skies to see if the fighter plane was returning to take care of its sitting duck of a target, but to her infinite relief she saw the plane swinging hard left to the shoreline, finally to disappear in the pall of black smoke from the still smouldering oil installations.

They were now well in reach of the frigate, and men were starting to climb all sorts and sizes of ropes and ladders on its side when two more fighter planes appeared from the clouds above them to swoop down as if to strafe them once again. But as they levelled out and roared overhead a cheer went up as everyone saw the round red, white and blue emblem of the RAF on the underside of their wings. Another great cheer arose from the soldiers as they saw the Spitfires rushing to engage the enemy.

Once they had seen their passengers safely on board the frigate, David paused to examine *Light Heart* for damage. There were several gaping holes in the starboard side of the boat, but whereas when she had been fully laden the damage had been well below the water line, now it was clear.

'Come aboard with us,' one of the officers yelled down to David.

'Captain and First Mate never abandon ship, however many holes,' David yelled back. 'We never abandon. Never!'

Rusty's heart sang on hearing these proud words. She had always worshipped Davey Kinnersley—'Mr Kinnersley' as she had always thought of him—and now she knew she would die for him.

The fact that he did not even bother to turn for

confirmation to Rusty, but restarted the boat's engine before heading back to the mayhem behind them, would always be one of the great moments of her life.

For a few seconds she found herself smiling proudly at his back.

'As I see it you will have to regulate the numbers a bit better this time, Mr Kinnersley,' she called to him, as they turned about.

'Regulate, no less.' David stared back briefly at Rusty, poker-faced. 'Suppose we could always try issuing tickets.'

'All aboard the *Skylark*, trips around the bay—' Rusty sang out suddenly, for no reason that she could think feeling braver than ever.

'I thought we might not go in quite so far this time. Can't risk that much more damage to *Light Heart*!' David called back to her, over the noise that was increasing the nearer they drew to the scene of battle. 'Just try and pick up a few stragglers.'

Rusty hardly heard him, already searching the waters in front of them for any soldiers detached from the main body of men.

'There!' She pointed. 'To port, Mr Kinnersley! Hard to port!'

Within the next ten or so minutes they picked up a few lone soldiers who were all trying to make it on their own.

'Got room for another couple, chum?' the last trooper aboard asked, as he flopped down exhausted on the seat in the cockpit. 'Poor sod over there's just had his boat blown out of the water.'

The soldier pointed to a couple of men making heavy weather of it about a hundred yards away, while in the distance Rusty caught sight of a couple of enemy fighters appearing on the scene.

'Came in for us and then got blown out of the water,' the soldier shouted to David.

At that moment Rusty also called to David, pointing upwards as yet more enemy aircraft circled ominously overhead. 'I don't think we can go back now, Mr Kinnersley.'

But as she protested the soldier grabbed *Light Heart*'s wheel from her and directed the boat towards the two men. David reached out as one of them, obviously the more seriously wounded of the two, slipped from his mate's grasp and began to float away from the boat.

'Boat-hook!' David cried. 'Where's the damn' boat-hook? Rusty?'

Rusty started to look as David leaned over ever further until finally, and inevitably, he was in the water.

'Mr Kinnersley!' she yelled, hurrying to the rail and sticking the boat-hook out as far as she could. 'Mr Kinnersley—here! Grab this!'

But it was too late. David was swimming away from the boat.

'Mr Kinnersley!' Rusty screamed, realising the futility of her skipper's heroics as he closed the distance between himself and the two sinking bodies ahead.

But even if he heard her, David was not for turning, although one of the enemy aircraft was completing the half circle it was making over the beach to head back out to sea and the ragged flotilla of rescue boats.

For a moment it seemed the plane was heading hard to the right towards a group of four or five craft, but at the last minute it appeared to switch direction and the next thing Rusty knew it was heading straight for them, guns blazing.

'Bloody hell!' one of the soldiers nearest to Rusty yelled. 'Bloody hell, he's coming straight at us!'

The Messerschmitt was over and past in a second, somehow miraculously missing its target altogether, its torrent of bullets screaming overhead to tear into the sea beyond *Light Heart*. Seeing the plane fast disappearing, Rusty turned her attention back to David and his rescue mission. Still swimming strongly, by now he had reached his target and turned himself on his back half underneath him to begin the slow and laborious task of returning to the boat with the first of his burdens. It was not until Rusty helped haul the man aboard that she realised exactly why David had already started back for the other.

CHAPTER NINE

Loopy stared around the small cottage that backed on to fields behind, and was fronted by a narrow country road that led past its neat iron railings. One way and another she had been keeping an eye on Owl Cottage ever since the last of the two Misses Harding had been *gathered*, as the Reverend Hodson always called it—and now, with a dip into her precious savings, she had gone one better and bought it from their estate, with one person and one person alone in mind—her second son Walter, at sea somewhere.

Walter had been gone for what seemed to his

mother like years not months now, but being of a golden nature he never forgot to write to his parents, his usual amusing and cheerful letters, whenever it was perfectly possible.

'We're not going to live at Owl Cottage, are we, Mother, because of the war?' Dauncy asked her, his expression anxious as he bounced a tennis ball endlessly against one of the cottage walls.

'No, darling, we're staying at Shelborne for the duration, I keep telling you that. What we're doing is—we're doing it up for Walter, in case, you know, he should need it when he's on leave. You know, Walter's quite an old boy now.'

'What about John? John's an old boy too.'

'Oh, John's different, he's not thinking of settling down with anyone, at the moment, darling.'

'John loves Judy.'

Loopy turned quickly. 'Stuff and nonsense, Dauncy Tate, John does nothing of the sort.'

'He does. He loves Judy.'

'No, darling, you've got that *wrong*. *Walter* loves Judy, and Judy loves *Walter*. That is why I—that is why *we* bought the cottage.'

Loopy snatched at Dauncy's ball, caught it, and, fearing that he might break a now all too precious light fitting with it, put it into her picnic holdall.

'Now, come along, enough of that, and you must help me get the old paint tins from the garage out of the car. We're going to try to get this place as fresh as new-churned butter by the time Walter comes back on leave.'

They changed their clothes in the spider-infested bathroom, putting on old paint-bespattered togs for the task ahead of them, and, Loopy having once more plugged in her old wireless and placed a battered kettle for tea and coffee making on the old-fashioned wood-fired stove, they started to rub down the walls of the old cottage.

'Does Father know we have bought this, Mother?'

'Not yet, darling, he's in London all week now, you know—at the War Office, so I didn't want to bother him about it, not really. I told you yesterday, this is our secret, yes? Owl Cottage is our secret, just the two of us.'

Dauncy smoothed his hands down his old painting shirt, a look of sudden pride on his face as he realised just how responsible sharing a secret with his mother made him feel.

'Do you know this is the first secret I have had with you, Mother?'

'Is it, darling?'

Loopy put down her paintbrush, resting it against the side of the tin, and lit a cigarette. Paint, cigarettes, buying cottages, they were all part of peacetime; so much so that she actually felt guilty. She should not be smoking, or painting. She should be joining the WVS and escorting children on trains, or making meals for pilots when they returned from their sorties, that was what she should be doing. Or helping out with the new netting circle that Elinor Gore-Stewart had organised in place of what she now called the 'utterly boring knitting circle' at Cucklington House. All in all, she should be doing the things that the rest of the women in the village were busy doing. But while Walter was away at the war it seemed to Loopy that her heart was away with him; that somehow, by buying the cottage and doing it up, she was willing Walter to come home to

Bexham. Willing him to come home safe to her and Hugh, John and Dauncy—but, most of all, to Judy.

*   *   *

Meggie poured herself yet another stiff gin and It, lit a Black and White and took a further turn around her bedroom at Cucklington. She had heard nothing from David since the morning she had woken up in his bedroom in his house in Cheyne Walk and found him gone with just a note left for her on the pillow. *Left you a kiss on your nose to be had at your leisure*, the note read. *Got to go off to sea for a little while—nothing serious. Dinner at the Ritz on my return. On me. Love, your Bad Man.*

The result of Davey's note was that Meggie was in no hurry to see him again. She felt that since he had let things slide, so must she, and because of this, and for no other reason, she had decided that not only was it a bad idea for her to marry in wartime, it was a bad idea for Judy too.

'But if you love someone, surely it's only logical—to want to marry them?'

Judy paused, staring into her own eyes in the mirror in which she was making up her face, as she remembered her night with Walter in the summerhouse.

'Well, of course it's logical, but not in wartime, Judy, surely? And marrying a submariner? A submariner who joins up at the start of the war? Not exactly long odds for a marriage. I mean, girls of our generation, don't you think we should do *something*; I mean other than just wait around to make brief wartime marriages? And have babies.

Or not. Our first concern should be for what's going to happen to this country, I mean isn't it? Shouldn't it be? I mean, think about it—we could be having babies who are going to have as brief lives as we ourselves.'

'Don't say that!'

'It's true,' Meggie stated. 'War is not a time to fill one's head with silly romantic notions.'

'But I thought you were all for Walter and me—'

'Well, I was, but since then I've thought about it, and I'm not so sure. Love is fine, but marriage, well, I just don't know, Judy. I mean really, if you think about it, we must all be mad to even contemplate it at this moment in our lives.'

'Are you saying it's unpatriotic?'

'Yes, I suppose I am. I think we should all wait until the end of the war, you know, see which of us is left, and, if any of us are, count heads not hearts. Rather than rushing off in a flurry of romantic feelings because any minute now we might all die.'

Judy turned from the mirror. 'You're just repeating what Madame Gran always says, aren't you?'

'Yes. And no. She only says what I believe to be right, that we must learn from what happened to the previous generation, not to marry in haste just because there is a war. More important by far that we put our shoulders to the wheel and forget about the rest, until it's all over. You saw those poor men we escorted up to London on the train, Judy. They were shattered.' She paused, stubbing out her cigarette before announcing, 'Davey proposed to me, twice, in London,' and as Judy turned but said nothing, she added, 'but I refused him, twice. That is how strongly I feel.'

Meggie looked over to Judy and smiled her crooked, impish smile, trying not to remember the vulnerable look on Davey's face when he proposed to her the second time, after they had made love in his house in Cheyne Walk. Davey was the most wonderful lover, so passionate and yet so considerate. She would never regret making love with him, and yet at the same time the idea of taking some sort of advantage of him, taking him up on his marriage offer, somehow seemed awfully wrong.

'Why won't you marry me, Meggie mine? Don't you love your Bad Man?'

'You know I love my Bad Man, I've told you I love you with all my heart, but—be fair to yourself, Davey. You wouldn't be proposing if there wasn't a war on, and you know it, and I know it.'

There had been a long silence after that, as there was a long silence now as both girls resumed brushing their hair.

'Will we *never* hear?' Judy finally broke the agonising silence. 'I mean, not ever? Could it be that we will be like this for years and years and years, Meggie?'

'Like what?' Meggie asked, knowing perfectly well.

'Like this, waiting and wondering, over and over, where they are, the men we love. I mean, I know I will never love anyone the way I love Walter, and you will never love anyone the way you love David, however much you try to pretend otherwise.'

Meggie stared at Judy knowing she was right, and hating her for it.

What seemed like hours later, hours during which they talked and pretended to read books, and then talked some more, there was a discreet knock at their bedroom door.

'Who is it?'

'It's me, Richards. Madame Gran sent me to tell you, Miss Meggie. *Light Heart*'s come back—'

Meggie ran to the door and wrenched it open. 'Is Mr Davey back? It's Mr Davey's—he's back, isn't he?'

But one look at Richards's face told Meggie that *Light Heart* might be back, but Davey was not.

* * *

Mrs Todd seemed to be staring not past the vicar but right through him, to something that she could see but the Reverend Hodson could not. Although her husband was still unconscious she had insisted on bringing him home. If he, like Tom, was to die, then she was determined that he would do so in his own bed, as he would have wished. He was suffering from a terrible blow to the head from which, but for Mr Kinnersley, he should have died. The wrong man had come back, and both she and the vicar knew it. Tom and Mr Kinnersley were both lying at the bottom of the sea somewhere near the coast of France, but nothing, not even that tragedy, could turn her into the kind of churchgoing type the reverend so clearly wished her to be.

'If it is of any interest to you, Reverend, I always thought my Tom would be taken from us early, and as for poor young Mr Kinnersley, well, he was always such a daredevil, it's amazing he lived as long as he did really.' The expression in Mrs Todd's eyes was resolute. 'And kind though it is of you to stop by here, I am sure, with your words of comfort and that, there's no need, I do assure you, no need at all. My Tom was about to start his training. See, he was the clever one. About to train to join them young men that dismantle bombs. That's right,' as the vicar dropped his eyes, and looked away. 'His death, well, it's come sooner rather than later, that's all.' She paused. 'It's funny really, because I knew from the time he was born that God only meant my Tom to be with us for a little while.'

'So you do believe in God, if not in church, Mrs Todd?' The vicar's expression brightened.

'Oh, I believe in God all right, Reverend.' Mrs Todd glanced towards her unconscious husband as if looking for some kind of affirmation from him too. 'I believe in God in the garden, in God in the fields, in God in the sea, but not in a church. My husband always said, my husband always *says*, folk like you sending off young men to fight in the Great War is what stopped the rest of us going to church. It was the vicars and the priests who blessed the guns and sent them to their death and where's Jesus in that may I ask? Sending off young men to kill other women's sons, that's not what Jesus taught us to do, is it, vicar? So thank you for your kind words, but I'm best left to just be at this moment. After all, no amount of prayers will bring my Tom back, and we both know it.'

The vicar stood up. He was a good man not unused to being sorted out by women such as Mrs Todd, and as far as he was concerned he had done his duty, offered his sympathy, and there was really no more that he could do.

He closed the door quietly behind him and let himself out of the Todds' brightly painted cottage.

Happily the wind was blowing strongly in towards the village, making him bend his head to hold his hat, and the seagulls were crying loud and constantly overhead, so, luckily for him, he was unable to hear Mrs Todd's sobs as he made his way along the towpath and back to the village and his church. For this reason perhaps he was able to comfort himself with the thought that Mrs Todd might come to church, eventually, perhaps to a Sunday service, or perhaps just to seek refuge there, together with the rest of the village, if there was an invasion. As it was he could do no more than he had.

Inside the cottage Tom's father lay where Rusty and Mickey had laid him so carefully, still breathing, but also still unconscious, shielded from the world, and—happily for him—the grief that awaited him if and when he awoke.

His wife was in no such state, as seated by his side she stared at the only photograph she had of her little Tom, aged ten, wearing his Scouts uniform. Every now and then she held it to her as she rocked to and fro with grief, her unconscious husband beside her.

* * *

At the cottage hospital Meggie and Judy passed down the men's ward, Meggie's eyes desperately searching for some sight of someone they knew who might be able to tell them if David was alive.

But all the time they were stopping, and staring at the bandaged faces of sometimes younger and sometimes older men, all Judy could think of was Walter. No one ever got to bury a dead submariner, unless they were washed up, and even then it was unlikely that anyone would find them. Even as she stared at these other wounded men, men she did not love and only a few of whom she vaguely knew, Judy felt desperately lonely and depressed in the realisation of what she might soon have to face.

Now that they were coming to the end of the ward, and there was no Davey, no one from *Light Heart*'s second rescue mission, Judy and Meggie, for no reason, both sat down suddenly and stared back down the ward, as if they could not quite believe that they had not found David, as if should they wait just a little longer they would suddenly realise that they had missed him. That he was sitting up in bed, probably with a broken arm, cuts and bruises, but very much alive and calling for a dry martini, making light of everything, raring to go back across the Channel to rescue more of the benighted British Expeditionary Force stranded on those beaches in France.

'Meggie.' Judy glanced down to where Meggie was seated, still staring vacantly down the ward, and touched her lightly on the shoulder. 'Meggie. Why don't we try the women's ward? There might be someone there who saw him, or saw what happened? Why don't we try there?'

'I suppose we could,' Meggie agreed, the despair never leaving her eyes.

'Time for visitors to leave!' Matron called down the ward. 'All visitors to leave. Oh, hallo, Miss Melton,' she went on in a gentler tone, recognising Judy. 'I am afraid I have to ask you to leave. We're a bit over-crowded and under-staffed, as you can see, so we will have to ask you to go now, I'm afraid.'

Judy drew Matron aside. Edith Hargreaves was one of the old sort, strict but kind. She knew the Meltons well since Sir Arthur was one of the hospital directors.

'We *are* leaving, Matron, it's just that we were looking for someone. David Kinnersley. He's been back and forwards to Dunkirk in his boat *Light Heart*. I expect you know him—always in the wars is David.'

'Yes, of course. A bit of a regular here, especially when he was younger, was young David Kinnersley.' Of a sudden Judy found her body turning to ice as she noticed Matron's eyes leaving her face as, placing her hand on Judy's arm, she walked her even further down the ward. 'His boat did come back, Miss Melton, I know because we have one of the crew in the women's ward, just called in for a bit of treatment for a burn—Rusty Todd. *Light Heart* came back, but without her skipper. I'm afraid David Kinnersley died, my dear, trying to save poor Tom Todd, Rusty's brother. They were both killed.' Then noticing Judy's pallor, her expression tightened. 'I am so sorry to have to break this news to you. Were you engaged to him, my dear? I am so awfully sorry.'

'Not me, no.' Judy looked quickly over to Meggie who, pale-faced and tense, was still seated just staring in front of her. 'No, I was not engaged to David Kinnersley—no, Miss Gore-Stewart, just there, sitting down, she was.'

'Would you like me to tell her for you? It's sometimes easier if it is done by someone less close.'

Judy said nothing for a few seconds, her throat

tightening so hard she could not find her voice. Finally she whispered, looking across at Meggie sitting upright and white-faced on a visitor's chair, staring in front of her, 'I don't think there's any need, Matron, I think she already knows.'

* * *

Loopy and Dauncy had found it impossible to keep their secret for very long, so, at weekends, Hugh had now joined them at the cottage, helping with the decorating and generally making himself handy, making up drinks for the workers, singing Gilbert and Sullivan at the top of his voice. Somehow the decorating, the smallness of the cottage, its cosiness, was comforting to all three of them, and Hugh, away from his desk at the War Office in London, was more than grateful for the distraction that Owl Cottage brought him.

Like everyone else's in Bexham, the Tates' wireless was always turned on, waiting, forever waiting for more news of the war.

'Do you think we will win?' Dauncy gave his father his most serious look.

'Of course. Just as soon as we can get your mother's people on the other side of the Atlantic to join in, just as soon as America comes to help us, we'll thrash the Nazis, no trouble. We must. We have to. Everyone knows that.'

'We saw so much fighting in the skies yesterday I think we must be winning, don't you, Father?'

'You bet.' Hugh nodded at his son, determined to look casual. 'Of course we're winning, Dauncy.'

'The machine gun fire was fantastic. And my friend Donald, he picked up a German parachute in the next door field, lucky devil.'

Hugh paused in his painting to stare across at Dauncy for a second. At first it was almost shocking to hear his youngest son referring to what might be the end of their country in such cheerfully sporting tones, but then, remembering that the newsvendors in London were chalking up the results of the dog fights overhead like cricket scores on their billboards, he turned back to his painting. Then too, he realised that at Dauncy's age he would have been exactly the same. Fascinated by war, not frightened by it, only frightened by such things as his parents selling their house, or not seeing his school chums again, that kind of thing; but the actual reality of it—death, the death of friends, or lovers, husbands, or brothers—that would have meant little to him, until or unless it happened.

'Good man,' Hugh told Dauncy admiringly. 'Good man. I hope the pilot was not in the parachute when Donald dragged it off?'

'No, he wasn't, worse luck. Mr Gurney from the post office had already arrested him, with his pretend gun.'

Loopy frowned over the top of Dauncy's head, and Hugh turned off the wireless before the next news announcement. God alone knew why everyone in Bexham was so keen on listening to the news, since so little of it was good. However determinedly they all switched it on with jolly expressions, pretending to each other that they thought it was going to be cheering, it never was, it was just more of the same. The Nazis were winning, we were losing, and everyone knew it, which was why their conversations were so consciously bright, so delightfully ordinary, as if everyday tasks must be made to matter, when really everyone knew that they did not matter, as Loopy would say, 'a hill of beans'.

Loopy seemed to understand and approve of Hugh's switching off the radio, because she put down her paint brush and lit a cigarette, preparatory to starting a conversation.

'Judy's friend Meggie's coming over to help us, later this evening, if she can, but you know she's running about for the WVS while also helping with the netting circle at Cucklington, and goodness knows what else.'

'How *is* the netting circle at Cucklington?'

'Anything with Elinor Gore-Stewart at the centre of it is bound to be invigorating.'

'And Judy's mother, how is she?' Hugh's face assumed a mock serious expression, as it always did when Walter's perhaps-may-be-could-be in-laws were mentioned.

'Well, you know Lady Melton, she is never *not* Lady Melton, except when Mrs Gore-Stewart is around, when she becomes a little less Lady Melton, but not *much* less.'

Hugh laughed. He always loved Loopy's line on things. God, she was so refreshing. He looked across at her trying not to imagine the unimaginable. Life without Loopy. He loved her, with all his heart and with all his soul. She was the opposite of him. Together they made one whole, because they were so different. Loopy so New World, so stylish, such fun, so zesty, while he was so Old World, so Gilbert and Sullivan, so Bexham, so British.

'I don't know how you put up with me,' he told

his wife suddenly.

Loopy smiled. It was her *pas devant* smile, because of Dauncy's being there. But it was also the smile that a woman gives a man she loves with all her heart.

* * *

Although the Tates could not know it, even Lady Melton had been forced to forget all about the niceties of life when faced with her new task, namely the urgent setting up of net-making frames in her house, for the sole purpose of producing camouflage nets to *protect our army*.

Elinor Gore-Stewart too had set up a netting circle, and, as she soon discovered, it was the filthiest job imaginable. Even after long hours spent darning socks, most of the women volunteers would have willingly run back to darn the worst holes in the least attractive socks rather than continue with netting, but net they must, and they all knew it. Netting was more important than darned socks, or salvaged saucepans, or clothing of any kind. It was the most important job you could help with, on top of whatever else you had taken on, and it could only be done by hand.

'I say, I suddenly realised, Richards, that no good will come of our netting groups unless we can also get hold of some tea urns,' Elinor told her devoted butler. 'It's the dust and the fluff from the scrim—it chokes you fit to bust. I suppose all those old school teapots and so on have gone to make aeroplanes?'

Somehow Richards managed to scrounge, if not tea urns, then some of the largest teapots around—

the kind that are normally only found in institutions—and since the weather was so fine, and despite the dog fights going on overhead, the sound of the machine gun fire, and rumours of an impending invasion, despite the comparative success of the Battle of Britain, despite the young men lost who would never come back, despite the fact that some households were already in mourning for some young life lost—and in between everything else they had to do—the women of Bexham lined up to volunteer to start knotting the scrim on to the nets.

Crawling about with bruised knees and aching backs, there was not a woman in Bexham who did not volunteer at some point of their week to help out with this dire but urgent task. When they were not darning socks or knitting, helping out at the cottage hospital, or making armbands for the LDV, not to mention clearing glass from the bombed streets of neighbouring towns, or in Judy's case ferrying WVS members and officials to and from Bexham in Chummy, they dropped in to help out with the netting. Mrs Todd, with her arthritic fingers, was no exception, arriving with an appropriately knotted headscarf covering her hair, and sidling quietly into the room.

'How is your husband, Mrs Todd? How is Mr Todd?'

Elinor Gore-Stewart broke the awkward silence that Mrs Todd's entrance had engendered, no one quite knowing how to broach the subject of the bereavement that the black armband on her coat proclaimed.

'Mr Todd has now quite recovered consciousness, thank you, Mrs Gore-Stewart.' Mrs

Todd nodded.

'We were very sorry to hear about your son, Mrs Todd.'

'Thank you, but, as his dad and I see it, our Tom's only been taken a little earlier than we expected, since he was due to be trained in bomb disposal. To our eyes he would not have been with us that much longer, if you understand me. He was just taken early.'

The group fell silent once again, none of them quite knowing how to take this practical, courageous but somehow almost shocking statement.

'And I'm very sorry, we all are, all the village, about Mr Kinnersley, Mrs Gore-Stewart,' Mrs Todd continued. 'He was a brave man. Mr Todd always said, if David Kinnersley could have taken out his heart and put it on a plate for you, he would have done.'

'That is very true, Mrs Todd.' Elinor turned away. Whatever happened there would never, surely, be a better or more fitting tribute to poor young David. Even now she could hardly believe that he had gone, despite the fact that he had seemed to be risking his life so many, many times over the past years. Always so funny, and rueful, self-deprecating, delightful, warm-hearted—the fitting adjectives for beautiful young David seemed to gallop through Elinor's mind in the small hours of the morning, the few small hours when Richards insisted that she pretend to sleep.

'Very well, now, I am going to make tea for the netters—outside.'

Elinor cleared her throat, breaking yet another awkward silence, at the same time nodding to Richards who had just abandoned his darning circle to bring in a fresh supply of sandwiches to the netters. As she watched him with gratitude—always so practical—Elinor thanked God, yet again, for her butler. He had been the mainstay of the house since Meggie's heart had been broken by David's not coming back, right down to galvanising Meggie into realising that she had to get up and get going, get on with her life.

Richards's motto was, 'It's always better to do something rather than nothing.' In his book anything else was unthinkable.

Although she was ostensibly only going to make tea for her outside group, Elinor still changed out of her netting clothes, pulling out her white hair from under its scarf, and climbing out of her faded dungarees. For, old as she was, she still insisted on joining in the netting. Still determined to choke on the dust and the fluff with the best of them, seeing this, as she did, as almost the most urgent part of their war effort. For, as they all now appreciated, one extra hour spent netting meant that many more feet of precious cover for their army. When they were netting it was as if they were making a shield not just for their own, but for everyone's loved ones. Besides, it was one of the few things they could actually do that they knew might really make all the difference to their boys, the difference between life and death. Between their boys coming home to them, or their boys not returning to them.

Masks were another necessity for this filthy work, but neither masks nor headscarves nor dungarees—nothing could stop the netting staining the skin and hands dark with its rich dye. Yet the netting at Cucklington regularly continued until just before midnight, when many of the regulars would crawl off to take over a fire watch, or to make hot meals for incoming pilots at the local aerodrome, or to relieve some other volunteer at one or other of the rest rooms in nearby towns, leaving Cuckers, finally, to Madame Gran and Richards, and to an exhausted Meggie, if she was home. Then daylight struck once more, and the whole routine started again. It was the same night in night out, day after day, Judy, fresh from ferrying some of the wounded from the cottage hospital to a larger hospital near Churchester, also made a practice of dropping in on Mrs Gore-Stewart's group at around midnight before retiring to bed for a few hours.

On this particular evening, she saw at once that Mrs Gore-Stewart was overdoing it. Watching her excessive zeal, Judy knew that she was exaggerating her devotion to the task in hand, because of her feelings of loss over David Kinnersley and Tom Todd, the first of the Bexham young to be sacrificed to the Nazis, but only, they all realised, the first. Soon there would be many, many more.

Her arrival fresh on the scene meant that Judy was perhaps more observant than many of the others, exhausted as they were by their own discomfort from both the work and the long hours. Judy could hear that Madame Gran's breathing was becoming affected by the dust and the fluff, not to mention the agonising struggle her poor old arthritic hands were being subjected to by the work itself.

Within a few minutes of her arrival Judy made sure to kneel down to talk to her.

'Tea. Please have some tea, Mrs Gore-Stewart. Please, stop and take some tea, won't you? You've been at it night and day now, and for far too long. Please? For my sake, please?'

Richards, himself now masked and choking from the dust, looked up at that, and nodded smartly at Judy as if to say, *Yes, for goodness' sake get some tea down her.*

Elinor drank her tea, quickly, and in the event most ungratefully, since her eyes were quite evidently still fixed on the work yet to be done. Judy, feeling guilty at such a display of energy from someone so much older than herself, immediately set to herself to help with the work, and tired though she was, as she knotted, and choked, knotted and choked some more, she could not help thinking of all the young men who might be going to be saved by the work they were doing—young men like Walter.

The previous day she had taken a few hours off to visit Walter's family, but not at Shelborne. The invitation had come out of the blue.

Meet us all at this address, if you possibly can, at one o'clock.

Loopy thought she would always remember the expression on Judy's face when she handed her the key to the cottage and said, 'Happy birthday, Judy. Hugh and I want you to have Owl Cottage—it is for you and Walter.'

'But we're not even properly engaged—'

'*Yet*—not even properly engaged *yet*. Of course you will be married, but until then this is yours—both of yours—until the great day dawns.'

Loopy looked evenly at Judy, who immediately blushed, suddenly realising that the Tates must know about—well, about *everything* that had happened between Walter and herself. Not that

Walter would have told them; she knew that Walter would never be indiscreet, but mothers knew these things about their sons, so perhaps they knew all about girls who were in love with their sons too?

'This is everything that we would have chosen.' Judy stared around the low-ceilinged rooms, their white walls now immaculate. 'It's as if you had done it up for us, but exactly—it is as if we had done it up *ourselves*! How did you manage to guess—'

Loopy shook her head, interrupting her before she could go on.

'I must stop you there, Judy.' She smiled. 'I mean, really, dear. You don't think Walter would go to sea without telling us everything about you, including that you had told him that when you were able to have your first home together you would like cornflower blue covers and pink cushions, and that you wanted a pale yellow bathroom? I mean to say, Judy, what kind of a family do you Meltons think the Tates really *are*? We would hardly have taken it on had we not known exactly what you both liked.'

Loopy laughed delightedly, ignoring Judy's look of embarrassment at her light-hearted reference to the Meltons' intransigent attitude to the Tates. They had all worked their legs off, in between everything else that was required of them, to get Owl Cottage ready for Walter and Judy, and selfish though she knew it was, and not even remotely patriotic, seeing Judy's delighted face as she wandered about touching everything, unable to believe that this was really going to be her first home, that Owl Cottage was a gift to Walter and herself, Loopy could not find it in herself to feel sorry for what they had done.

Owl Cottage was all about willing Walter home, about Lady Melton's allowing Judy and Walter to get married, about everything they were meant to be fighting for, which was why it was so terribly important.

'Your mother still on the outs with you about Walter, is she, Judy dear?' Loopy asked later, at a discreet moment, when Hugh and Dauncy were busy in the back garden trying to fix the bucket in the top of the little well.

'I am afraid so, Mrs Tate.' Judy looked away, embarrassed to be the child of such a mother.

'It's because you're an only child, isn't it? You are her ewe lamb, and that makes it very difficult. I mean let's face it, Judy, as far as your mother is concerned, the only person who is suitable for you is someone who has not yet been invented!'

Loopy laughed to take the sting out of her remark, and, happily, so did Judy.

'Don't worry, she'll come round. Parents usually do. I say *usually*. Some *never* do. My English mother-in-law always thought my American cooking would kill Hugh, never mind what it would do to her grandsons, and she was probably right, so just as well I've never cooked for him much, until now, but look—by God's grace, Hugh is still alive. At least, I think he is!'

Loopy stopped, suddenly remembering that even if Hugh was alive, Walter might not be, but Judy was hardly listening, only looking round, realising, more and more, the love and care that had gone into Owl Cottage.

'You did all this for me and Walter to bring Walter back, didn't you, Mrs Tate? It's like lighting a candle and leaving it in the window, isn't it? This is Walter's candle, lit for him.'

Loopy nodded, and immediately lit another cigarette.

'Of course. If you love your children you would do anything to bring them back to you, safe and happy.'

* * *

Lionel stared at Mattie. 'What the devil do you think you look like?'

'A bit better than you in your uniform, if we can call it such,' Maude chimed in.

'You've joined up?'

'No, Daddy, actually.' Mattie gave a hearty sigh. 'No, actually, I am going off to a fancy dress party! Of course I've joined up. Goodness gracious, what do you think the driving lessons were all about?'

'He thought they were all about your driving instructor,' Maude put in, and Mattie laughed.

'Oh, old hot hands Blundell. Mmm, well, he *did* help me to concentrate. And believe me, if you can learn to drive while all around you are trying to grab your knees, you can drive anyone through anything.'

'So, this is it. It has really come to this. You, my only daughter, have joined up, joined the army of all things.' Lionel sat down suddenly in his armchair, before turning on Maude. 'This is all your fault, all your fault. You and your driving lessons, encouraging her to be a man. I don't know what you are all about, really I don't. Except I do. Bungling, that is what you are all about, as usual. Bungling, Maude.'

Mattie went and stood in front of her father's chair, her uniform giving her a sudden authority. She was determined to defend Maude.

'No, Daddy, it is not Mummy's fault, believe me, it is not Mummy's fault, and it is not my fault, it is the fault of Hitler. I have to join up, simply because I *am* your only daughter. Don't you see? I have to prove myself the same as if I was—well—either sex. Just because I am a girl doesn't mean to say I don't have the same feelings as a boy. Not that I want to be your son, nothing like that. I like being a girl; I like being your daughter, but just because I am doesn't mean that I don't have the same call to do my duty as everyone else. I had to join up, I simply could not sit at home darning socks, or making tea, or joining the WVS and minding the rest room, I'm too young for all that, really I am. Besides, I am a very good driver. I have just passed all my army tests, first class, A1. And I can pack a mean punch, believe me, just ask my dear driving instructor.'

'You could have told me,' Lionel said, still staring at Maude. 'You might have told me.'

Maude turned away, her husband's eyes telling her, *if anything happens to Mattie it will be your fault, all your fault and no one else's, and I will never forgive you.*

* * *

What Maude was not telling Lionel was that, at Mattie's instigation, she herself had just bought Peter Sykes's car from him—since, having joined up, he was going to have no use for it for the duration—and she had bought it with the sole intention of joining the WVS car pool. Maude was quite determined that Mattie was not going to be the only one of the family in uniform.

Frankly Maude could not wait to put on the grey-green uniform with its ruby red jumper and felt hat, which was deliberately designed so that it could be shaped in any way the wearer desired. Up off the face, more flattering for the older woman, was how Maude was going to wear hers, she told herself.

Presenting herself for recruitment was a different matter, though. After all—she could not help wondering with sudden awareness—after all her long, tedious years of marriage, seeing only to Lionel and Mattie's needs, what had she to offer the Women's Voluntary Service, except a mild ability to play bridge, and a new ability to drive a motor car?

She confessed as much at her interview.

'I am pretty useless, I'm afraid.'

'Nonsense,' the woman behind the desk told her, and since she was probably about the same age as Maude, Maude was prepared to believe her. 'That is the whole point of the Women's Voluntary Service. We turn *no one* away, because we know that there is always something that a woman is good at. Always something useful she can *do*. To give you an example, there's an old lady near here, near Bexham, who walks six miles three times a week—in her seventies she is too—just to come here and clean the offices. She makes them look like a new pin, and do you know something? She's twice the person since she started doing her bit, and why? Because she knows she *is* doing her bit, pulling her weight. That's what it's all about, the women doing their bit, pulling their weight, not sitting at home just knitting and listening to the wireless.' She paused before leaning forward and confiding to Maude, 'Do you know that I admire her cleaning as much as I admire Churchill's speeches? And why? Because both of them are doing what they're *good* at. That's what it's all about, believe me,' she repeated.

'Can you find *me* something, then?'

The woman nodded, her eyes already searching for the necessary paperwork.

'Find you something, Mrs Eastcott, and you the owner of a motor car? If the WVS has anything to do with it, your feet will not touch the ground, that I can promise you!'

* * *

Gwen, the Tates' housemaid, had been a member of not the WVS but the WI for over five years before war was finally declared. It had seemed a nice, busy thing to do, and, since she was a Quaker, perfectly in line with her beliefs. The WI had actually been started to help food production during the Great War. It was not, as rumour always suggested, absolutely not an organisation just to do with jam making and singing *Jerusalem*. It was a practical institute, as practical as anything that had ever been organised by some stupid government, as Gwen was always telling her husband whenever he took time out to mock it.

Now it had been brought home to Gwen most forcibly, most especially by the non-Quaker members, that the WI might be going to be once again about vital food production, and more than ever before, more even perhaps than during the

Great War. Jam making would of course be *part* of it, for if there was no butter to be had, at least if there was jam to put on their bread the children of the nation would obtain some vital vitamins from the home-grown fruit.

Perhaps because she was what Hugh Tate always called 'a bright little thing' Gwen, among others, was sent up to London to learn how to organise a 'Jobs Mending School', for not only did every housewife now have to learn how to mend a fuse and many another job they would have normally looked to their men to do, but they had also to learn how to grow vegetables from seed, plant currant bushes, and make more and more jam to a new and firmer consistency, so that it could be transported all over the country to WI centres without any chance of spillage. The last part of the short training was in what Gwen called 'the silly games half hour'. Central to the work that members of the WI contributed to the war effort was the recognition that with all that had to be borne, with all the strains under which the women fighting on the home front were being put, letting down their hair for half an hour was not just a good idea, it was vital. Matchboxes on the nose, musical chairs, charades, going round the room without touching the floor—whatever *could* be done to make the women laugh and forget their troubles *must* be done.

* * *

Yet some troubles could not be alleviated by lighthearted treatment, and Elizabeth Melton's netting circle was one of them. While quite as vital to the war work as her neighbour and acquaintance Elinor Gore-Stewart's, it seemed that Lady Melton's was not the netting circle in Bexham that anyone wished to join.

No matter what the hour, or how tired they were from their other occupations, everyone in Bexham flocked to help with the netting at Cucklington House. Such was definitely not the case at the Melton house. In fact only two ladies regularly attended Lady Melton's netting circle. One was an old lady who lived in the former groom's cottage, and the other was Mrs Molly Woodhouse, a woman remarkable only for her bridge-playing prowess and her narrow view of life, but whose bad-tempered ways had to be borne because, after all, when all was said and done, there was a war on.

Even Judy Melton never called in to net with her mother at the family home in Old Bexham, a fact which was actually so hurtful that Elizabeth Melton could hardly bring herself to think about it. Very well, Judy did lodge now with the Gore-Stewarts, on account of Meggie and Judy's both having joined the WVS, but even so, a visit once or twice a week from a daughter to her mother would not go amiss.

Tonight, however, not only was Judy not present, which was hardly unusual, but neither was old Mrs Crescent, nor even the ill-tempered Mrs Woodhouse, so that, unsurprisingly, as Elizabeth Melton surveyed how little work the three of them had accomplished, her heart sank to the bottom of her prim, dark brown, side-buttoned shoes.

Even so, she pulled on her mask and with a look of resignation and a sinking heart approached the ghastly task of knotting quite alone, which it had to be said was a first, even for her.

'It seems to me, old girl, that at this rate the biggest net you're going to produce for our army is a hair net!'

Sir Arthur would keep making that joke. And he was making it again now, as he put his head round the door and stared into the ground floor room set aside for this vital work, before going off fire watching.

Tonight Lady Melton sensed she was not just alone, she was alone and quite ridiculous. Yet to give in and not continue to work on the netting for the army would be unpatriotic, and worse than that it would give more than a little ammunition to *that lot,* as she thought of the rival Bexham netting circle at Cucklington House.

She had been hard at work for some few, and considering there was a war on, strangely peaceful, hours, and it was now after midnight, so Elizabeth was expecting no one when she thought she heard someone knocking at the front door. Grabbing her husband's ridiculous old family musket from beside the fireplace, she went into the hall and tiptoed quietly towards the sound. The blackout made it impossible to make anyone out, and at the other side of the heavy front door she could hear only heavy breathing.

'Who's there?' she called out, trying, pathetically, to deepen her voice in such a way that anyone on the other side might perhaps become doubtful of her actual sex.

'It's me, Lady Melton, Gardiner.'

Elizabeth Melton unbolted the door, and held it open a few inches, shining a torch in her visitor's face.

'Gardiner!' Lady Melton stared at her former maid, long ago married and gone to live in the village. It was years since she had seen her, but naturally she pretended it was not, for some reason that she herself could not have said. 'Gracious, you're very late, Gardiner. But better late than never, I do agree. I myself, as it happens, am working through the night.'

'Thank you, Lady Melton.'

Gardiner slid through the narrow gap allowed to her, and followed Elizabeth into what had been the old sewing room.

'Good, now we have a chance of going a bit faster, Gardiner. With your hands at the ready we will do better.'

Lady Melton handed Gardiner a mask to cover her nose and mouth, and looked on approvingly as she did so, as if Gardiner was trying on an Ascot hat which had once belonged to her ladyship, and they were both now finding that it suited her really rather well.

'Anything the matter, Gardiner?' she asked as Gardiner took the mask off again, almost at once, as if of a sudden she could not breathe.

Gardiner looked away and then back again, concentrating her gaze entirely on the pearl buttons on her former employer's blouse, before she could at last bring herself to speak.

'Just a little bit, Lady Melton, yes. That's why I came along up to the house really. Got to do something to take my mind off everything, because—my son—you know, fire fighting in London? Well, I just heard, he's been killed, and I gotta, I just gotta do something to take my mind off it.'

Elizabeth Melton stared at Gardiner. It had been a year since they had all first expected the bombing of London, but now it had started in earnest, and the very worst thing that can happen to a mother had just happened to her former maid. Forgetting that she was Lady Melton, wife of Admiral Sir Arthur Melton, a woman who had grown stern with the years, for no reason that she could now quite remember, Elizabeth held out her arms to this woman called 'Gardiner' whose Christian name, incomprehensibly as it now seemed, she had never even asked of her, and drew her into a warm embrace.

* * *

'You're looking pale as a coming-out frock, Madame Gran.'

Richards stared into the face of his employer with some concern.

'Stop being such an old woman, Richards. That's my role in life, to be an old woman, and not yours; yours is to be perfect, which of course you are.'

'I am your ladyship's devoted man of all seasons.'

'Well, think of yourself as you will, Richards, but I prefer to think of you as my guardian angel, come down to earth and made flesh, the wings upon which I fly, you are really, Richards,' Elinor told him, suddenly. 'Now I am going to bed. For as usual you are right. I am very tired. Feeling my age. Better in the morning.'

Richards stared after her. He had never known Madame Gran admit to tiredness, not even when she crawled in from the Dorchester at five o'clock of a summer morning singing 'The Nightingales Sang in Berkeley Square'. Even then she always had time for a nightcap, usually even demanding of Richards that he put a record on the gramophone for a bit of a dance.

He glanced at the old grandfather clock in the hall and saw that by the light of his torch the old man in the moon on the gold face of the clock was telling that it was only one in the morning. The netting circle was still as busy as ever, and consequently Richards was as busy as ever, torn between the netting and the tea making, knowing all the time that the chances of victory were as slender as a single hair.

Of course Miss Meggie being Miss Meggie, now she had joined the WVS, would be in the centre of it, busy taking someone's children back to the East End where their mothers were eagerly waiting for them. For some reason that no one could understand, least of all the WVS, the insane idea that it was safer and better for them to be in London with their mums rather than in the Sussex countryside with some caring family had, of a sudden, become popular once again.

'Where's Miss Meggie tonight, Richards, by the way?'

Elinor shone her torch up her staircase, illuminating the straight-nosed, delicate-eyed faces of a few of her ancestors as she did so.

'Miss Meggie is due to come back here by—er—two or so,' Richards lied, quickly and adroitly. 'I believe she's meant to be busy at one of the WVS rest centres, that is what I believe, Madame Gran.'

'You were never very good at lying, you know, Richards. Where is she—struggling through

London in the Blitz, rescuing people from burning buildings? Anything as long as it is dangerous, knowing Miss Meggie.'

'Whatever she's doing, she's very busy, Madame Gran,' Richards went on, ignoring her. 'These days sleep is just not something she is in touch with. And when she is she tells me she goes out like a light, which is strange because as a little girl, if you remember, Madame Gran, she never really slept, did she? Miss Meggie never really slept.'

'No, I think you're right, now I recall, Richards. She never was one for sleeping, was Miss Meggie. Very well. When she joins you,' Elinor turned towards her bedroom, 'tell her—tell her I send her my dearest love, won't you, Richards? And keep an eye on her? Well, I know you will, you always do.'

Richards was too busy forging ahead to Madame Gran's bedroom to make everything ready for her to pay much attention to this last remark.

Madame Gran missed her personal maid these days, as you would when there was a war on, but most of all she missed the order in which everything had once been kept for her. Never had been used to doing everything for herself at home. Neatening up, straightening up, clearing up, pulling and twitching, was not Madame Gran's style. It was Richards's style, but not that of Madame Gran.

Richards stopped. He stared around him as he heard his mistress walking slowly off towards the bathroom for her late night ablutions. Madame Gran's bedroom was like a new pin. Everything was in its place, but to such a degree that it had probably never looked so neat in all its life. He opened one of the cupboards. The line of Madame Gran's frocks had never been so straight; indeed so straight were they, they might have been Guardsmen on parade. The coats, too, were all hung in perfect lengths, and their protective covers pulled over them. Madame Gran's fur tippets and fur muffs were all neat and tidy, the hats normally in total disorder were now in total order, her shoes in perfect lines, her handbags and reticules all the same.

Richards knew that he should feel pleased, but as he made a mental note to check that she was safely asleep before he himself finally called it a day as dawn was about to break, he did not know why, but his heart turned over a little. It was as if someone else was now occupying the lovely bedroom on the first floor with its pale and tasteful furnishings, not his Madame Gran; as if—but he turned away from the thought. He had always told Madame Gran she would outlive them all, but only a little later, when he knocked on her door on some lame pretext, Richards found that he was wrong. The unthinkable had happened. His *Madame Gran*, as so many of the gravestones in the churchyard at Bexham read had, *fallen asleep in God*, leaving Richards not just bereft, but, it seemed to him, for the first time in his life, utterly alone.

EARLY 1942

CHAPTER TEN

Walter was singing at the top of his voice as he drove at top speed towards Bexham. He was on forty-eight hour leave, enough time to get married to Judy *and* have a twelve-hour honeymoon. After all that he had been through it seemed to him that he was in heaven already. Against all the odds, he was going home to be married. Of a sudden his steering wheel started to play up, and he stopped singing as the three passengers to whom he was giving a lift, yelled, 'Flat tyre!'

Turning into the nearest farm entrance he drew to a stop outside a cow shed, the owner of which, a red-faced farmer more used to counting sheep on the Sussex Downs than searching for pilots shot down over England, volunteered to help him.

'I found a machine gun pellet in my milking pail yesterday,' he told Walter cheerfully, peering at him from under his steel protective helmet, 'and two enemy parachutists landed in the middle of my ewes last week. But my son and I held them hostage with our pitch forks until the Home Guard arrived, not that they were much better armed than myself—broomsticks and fire pokers is what they arrived with!'

He chuckled as he handed Walter the necessary trappings for his now mended tyre, and then, nodding affably from Walter to his two companions—hitchhikers in army uniform Walter had picked up on the road—he sighed with envy.

'Darned shame, I told my wife, but I was passed unfit this time around, otherwise I would be fighting alongside you young fellows, believe you me.'

Walter smiled, and handed him a tip, which he refused at first, reddening as he did so, before finally pocketing it quite gratefully.

'I should think he got blind drunk with gratitude when he was passed unfit,' Walter observed to his passengers, and they laughed, knowing that the idea that everyone who lived in Britain was simply dying to join up and fight for their country was ludicrous. 'Where can I drop you fellows off?'

Seeing the time, Walter put his foot down. He had forty-eight hours' leave. Forty-eight hours in which to get married to his darling Judy. He had hardly been able to believe the news when he was told that Lady Melton had, of a sudden, given in to the idea of Judy's becoming Mrs Walter Tate. He started to sing 'A Maiden Fair to See' in a creditable baritone. For two whole days he was going to put the war behind him, no matter what went on elsewhere.

* * *

Some weeks before Walter was given his forty-eight hours' leave to get married, Lady Melton had gone to see Loopy and Hugh, or rather she had gone to see Hugh and Loopy, because Elizabeth Melton, Loopy realised, was one of those women who, when faced with a man and a woman, completely ignored the woman. It was as if Loopy was not even in the room.

'Mr Tate, as we are all now quite aware, my daughter has fallen in love with your son, Walter, and they wish to get married. The admiral has never been against it, as you may or may not be aware, but I, as Judy's mother, have always been against it. Now, however, I am *not* against it. Let the marriage take place, with all our blessings. Let them be married as soon as the young man can obtain some leave, although forty-eight hours is the most they can expect at the moment, I am afraid, and even that is difficult. We will hold the reception at our house. Not too much fuss, since there is a war on, you will agree.'

'Of course, not too much fuss.'

Loopy had put in her pennyworth, in a vain effort, she realised afterwards, to attract Elizabeth Melton's attention. But it was truly vain, for Lady Melton continued to stare at Hugh, her expression not unlike that of a bedraggled bird which has arrived at her destination after a long and stormy flight.

'I wonder what made her change her mind so suddenly?' said Hugh a few minutes after she had gone, leaving Hugh and Loopy to discuss the incredible volte face with which she had presented them, not to mention the prospect of arranging a wedding in a very short space of time.

'The war, Hugh darling. Even women like Lady Melton are not impervious to what is happening outside their front doors.'

'But, Loopy, don't you realise, this is such wonderful news. We must get in touch with Walter, somehow, we just must.' Hugh gave a sudden and brilliant smile, thinking of Walter. 'Like Tom Kitten, he will burst his buttons—'

'Oh, but you are so right, Hugh, he will burst his buttons.'

'He will be so happy,' his father agreed, and then

turned to his piano and played a rousing rendition of yet another Gilbert and Sullivan song, one that both he and Loopy knew young Walter had always loved since he was a little boy in short trousers. 'We sail the ocean blue . . .' Hugh and Walter had always sung it together at the piano before the little fellow hopped up to bed of a summer evening at Shelborne.

*   *   *

Following her mother's almost historic visit to the Tates at Shelborne, Judy veered between treading emotional water, because it looked as if everything was going to be all right after all, and becoming dizzy with the sheer dread of how much she had to accomplish before her wedding day. To begin with, it was still winter, so the all important question of what she should wear posed itself.

'My old wedding dress, Judy dear!'

Judy could hardly bring herself to look into her mother's excited face, or down at the simply beautiful silk dress she was cradling in her arms.

'Mother—'

'I can't tell you how many yards of silk this took.'

'Mother—'

'You may remember from the photographs—and thanks to your grandmother's extravagance, bless her—I was attended by twelve flower girls and boys. What a splash we made in all the newspapers. It was too wonderful.'

Judy had never seen her mother like it. Now that the wedding was a reality the normally cool Elizabeth Melton with her frosty demeanour had become as excited as a *vendeuse* in some

Knightsbridge salon.

'I love this dress so much, Judy, and to think that you will be wearing it to get married in Bexham church—well, darling, it is really the most cheerful thing I can remember since the outbreak of war. And Daddy will be so pleased, too. Really he will, proud and pleased to take you down the aisle wearing my dress, the dress I married him in.'

'Mother.' Judy sat down, and her mother, seeing the expression in her daughter's eyes, sat down too, still holding the dress in her arms as if it was a baby in a shawl. 'I cannot marry Walter in a long white dress, Mother. I cannot look every inch the happy bride, not during a war. I am just not that sort of person. What about all the other brides who haven't a chance of getting hold of a dress? I should feel terrible.'

Her mother stared at her. 'Whatever do you mean, Judy? Whatever do you mean?'

'I mean, there is a war on. People have lost their sons, and husbands, their loved ones, and here am I about to gallop up the aisle of Bexham church sporting thirty yards of silk. I can't. I really can't. I want to, believe me. There is nothing I would like better than to marry Walter wearing your dress, Mummy, but in war, with so much that is so sad, I don't believe that I can, not in all honesty.'

'So what do you propose to marry in?' Elizabeth asked Judy in a suddenly flat, hard voice. 'A mourning dress? Because if you do, I have some of those too!'

'I am going to get married in my WVS uniform.' There was a stunned silence as Lady Melton stared at her daughter. 'But with a small bouquet,' Judy went on, a little too quickly, because her mother's expression was one of such bewildered hurt that she could hardly look at her. 'And we're allowed to pull the hat, you know, into any shape we wish, so I can make it look quite pretty. Off the face, I thought. And the bouquet to be of dark leaves and flowers, to match the pullover, and the hat.'

'The one thing that I have always wanted to do,' her mother said, after a long silence following this information, '*always* wanted to do, was to see you married in my beautiful, beautiful wedding dress, and now all *you* want to do is to scramble through the ceremony wearing the uniform of the WVS. Well, all I can say, Judy, is that you are certainly not taking our dear Queen as your example, are you? Do you see the Queen picking her way through the rubble and the horror looking like a common soldier? No you do not.'

'No, Mummy, but then she is the Queen. I am only Judy Melton, and I am thinking of people in the village who are grieving, people whom Walter and I want to invite, people whom we have known all our lives. How will they feel if I am not dressed in some appropriately sober way? As if I am ignoring their grief, as if I am some sort of callous young thing out for people only to admire me.'

Elizabeth turned away. It was difficult to explain to someone like Judy, always so wrapped up in herself, so wilful, so difficult, just how much she hurt other people, most especially her mother, by her insistence on doing things *her* way.

'I suppose this is all Walter's idea,' she said, before leaving the room, still carrying her dress.

She was sure of it. All Walter Tate's idea, all this sort of false nicety about other people's feelings had to have come from him, she was sure of it, she repeated to herself. She went upstairs to her bedroom and started to fold the dress back into its protective wrapping, and as she did so tears fell on the old black tissue papers in which it was always stored. Just one thing, that was all she had asked of Judy, just one thing, that she marry in her mother's dress. But no, she could not, could she? She had to get married in a Digby Morton grey-green suit with a cherry red jumper and matching hat, had to get married looking as if she was just off to ferry someone to hospital, or escort them to London on the train, or any of the other things that she was always doing.

Elizabeth sniffed, and then, remembering that the bride's mother could not be expected to be in uniform, she turned her attentions to her own choice of outfit.

*   *   *

Private Mathilda Eastcott sat at the wheel of her Humber staff car waiting for General Michael Rafferty to reappear after his meeting with the Heads of Staff. She had been the tall, laconic North American's personal driver for some months now, taking him from pillar to post whenever he was in London. One of several high-ranking officers sent to Britain by the US government, he was engaged, Mattie imagined, on work that was both top secret and highly influential. But that was all she could do—imagine.

At first he had barely addressed a remark to her. In fact so involved had the general been with military matters that on their first few journeys he had addressed Mattie, on several occasions, as *son*.

It was either that or *driver*, and finally rather more correctly *Private*—until that evening, the Friday evening when after a long and exhausting meeting in Whitehall General Rafferty flopped into the back seat of his staff car and instructed Private Eastcott to recommend a movie.

'I've had a bad day on top of a hard week, Private,' he'd told her. 'So let's go see something good and light and entertaining. None of this big Russian stuff they keep showing, and none of that Mrs Miniver type of nonsense either. Let's go see a cartoon—or a musical, you hear me?'

Mattie had deliberately ignored the implicit invitation to accompany her distinguished charge to the cinema, preferring to imagine that General Rafferty liked to think of and refer to himself in the plural in the same way as royalty. She had recommended *Holiday Inn* starring Bing Crosby, which she knew was showing at the Odeon Leicester Square. General Rafferty readily agreed with her choice, saying that sounded *just fine*.

'I'll need to go home and change first,' he'd said. 'You want to do the same?'

'I have to get the car back, General,' Mattie had replied, buying time. 'I'm still on duty, sir.'

'Long as you're with me you are, Private. And I'm certainly not in the mood to go to the movies alone.'

'If you would like to arrange for someone to accompany you, sir, I can certainly drive you to the cinema. And wait for you, if needed.'

'You're too pretty to be left outside sitting in the car—Private.'

At this Mattie had glanced at him in her rear view mirror and seeing him smiling, cajoling, she had relented and taken him back to his rented flat in Marble Arch, waiting in the car while he changed, having politely refused the invitation to go upstairs. However, at the general's behest the staff car was finally locked up and left in the street while they took a cab to the cinema.

Almost before they were settled into their seats in the smoke-filled fug of the picture palace, the red lights went on by the screen to indicate that the sirens were sounding to warn of an impending air raid.

'You want to go to the shelter?' The general carefully and calmly placed his folded mackintosh under his seat. 'Personally I hate to miss even the news.'

'Me too. Public service films, trailers, the lot.'

'That's my girl.' The general offered Mattie a Lucky Strike, making it seem as if it was some sort of reward for their mutuality of tastes. 'You smoke American?'

'I smoke anything, sir. But particularly American.'

'You like candy, too?'

'Yes. Sir.'

'You sure you don't want to go to the shelter?'

'One hundred per cent. Sir.'

'My thoughts entirely. Private.'

That seemed to be the general mood of the very mixed audience that night, since only a handful of people got up and left when the warning lights went on.

Everyone else settled down to lose themselves in the film, to watch, smoke, hug and kiss their joint way out of the misery that lay beyond the solid concrete walls of the picture house. Incendiaries might land on the building's flat roof, the next-door building might go up in flames, Leicester Square might not even be there when they finally emerged, but, of a sudden, no one seemed to care. All anyone inside the cinema that night seemed to be concerned about was that at that moment they were still alive. They were with friends or lovers, and they were being entertained by one of the great singing stars of the age via one of the great inventions of the twentieth century. So, for three hours, while they were in the two and sixes, or the one and sixes, the war, according to that strangely enraptured gang of people, could go hang.

This particular evening, as the cinema, of a sudden, shook with the impact of something particularly fearful, the general put a comforting arm round Mattie as they, and the rest of the audience, automatically ducked forward, waiting for a further blast.

'You all right, Private?' the general asked in a low voice.

'Perfectly, General.'

Mattie did not dare to turn to look at the tall, dark-haired man with his arm round her. For God's sake, he was a general! The most senior member of the American army, and he had his arm round her. Meanwhile, she stared up at the screen, immobile, feeling frozen with horror. Privates did not slap the faces of generals, nor did the driver of a general remove his arm from about her waist. The driver of a general waited until he did that of his own accord.

A minute later, the general did remove his arm, as if once reassured that Mattie was in fact all right he felt it was safe to resume his normal polite if courtly pattern.

Such was not the case with Mattie. For once he had removed it, she found to her astonishment that General Rafferty's arm round her had not just been comforting, it had been electrifying. Never mind what was happening outside, it was what was happening inside Mattie that surprised her. Moreover, it was something for which she had never, ever bargained. Perhaps it was because the general was not like Peter Sykes; he was not gentle, shy and diffident. He was powerful, strong, hypnotic, dynamic—any word you could name that brought about the singular sound *wow*! So much so that Mattie knew, without any doubt, that if that arm ever returned, she would not have a chance.

* * *

In the event even Elizabeth Melton enjoyed her only daughter's wedding to Walter Tate. Perhaps it was because she herself was looking really rather lovely, so lovely that as soon as he saw his wife the admiral was induced to cross the floor of their chintz-decorated drawing room and congratulate her.

'Might just as well be *your* wedding day, dearest, might just as well be. You look so beautiful, darling, really you do.'

Elizabeth was wearing a Watteau-style suit in blue velvet with a long, waist-cinching jacket and a flurry of lace at the cuffs and neck. On her head was a matching blue velvet hat, very fetching, pulled down slightly over one eye.

'It is actually pre-war, but I never got a chance to wear it. Bought it for the Cosgroves' do, remember? But then Claudia Cosgrove broke off the engagement and ran off with one of the Howards, I think it was.' She paused, trying to remember. 'At all events, I never did have an occasion after that to which I could go in it. So here we are, and at rather a big event too, as it happens.'

As her mother was preparing to leave for the church with Gardiner, who was supervising the flowers that they had all arranged together, Judy had come down the stairs in her WVS uniform, holding a large bunch of matching red roses, and wearing a very dainty pair of pre-war shoes, and matching gloves.

Perhaps it was the radiant expression on her face that made it a little difficult for the admiral, who so prided himself on his ability to conceal his emotions, to look at her. Or perhaps it was just that it was such an affecting sight, so much a wartime sight—a young bride on her wedding day in her smart Digby Morton uniform—that so filled him with paternal pride, both for the way she looked and for her patriotic statement. Whatever it was, the admiral found himself blowing his nose on his special handkerchief normally only used for snuff, and quite by mistake throwing it into the drawing room waste-paper basket before offering Judy his arm.

They could walk to Bexham church through the village, and since it was a sunny day, with winter just beginning to give way to spring, that is what they did, although the village seemed oddly empty until they reached the church, when it rapidly became apparent that absolutely everyone had turned out to see Judy Melton marrying Walter Tate.

'It's a Bexham wedding all right,' Gardiner, who

had helped Judy make up her bouquet, kept saying to anyone who would listen. 'A Bexham wedding, between Bexham families, and all the better for it.'

*   *   *

As Judy and her father made their way on foot to the church, chatting and waving to the occasional passer-by, all of whom smiled back in the way everyone seemed so anxious to do in wartime, Loopy and Hugh were trying to hurry Walter, John and Dauncy towards the church. They had to be there first, not only because Walter was the bridegroom, and John the best man, but also because Hugh was playing the organ and Dauncy was singing a solo.

Loopy was in that semi-hysterical state with which every mother of three sons, let alone the mother of the groom, can readily identify, in that she was dressed and ready, but quite, quite alone in her readiness.

She had often observed that, for some reason best known to men, when it came to dressing themselves for a special occasion, nothing was ever completely arranged or ready. If their shirts were ready and clean and they had actually managed to put them on, then they would inevitably decide that they really must clean their shoes, because, after all, by vigorously cleaning their shoes they would greatly increase the chances of getting polish on their freshly laundered white cuffs. If they had remembered to have their suits cleaned—which was a miracle in itself—then a tie would go missing, or a cuff link, or a belt. Most women only had to cope with one or two of these dramas on a day of solemn celebration, but having three sons and a husband Loopy found that she always had to cope with it four times over, and yet it never occurred to her to lose her temper.

'What a business, Gwen.' She sat down suddenly on the staircase, as the distant sounds of four men looking for something they had suddenly realised they needed echoed round the house.

'I know.' Gwen gave her employer a sympathetic look. 'I don't know what it is about men, Mrs Tate, but I always think it's nature's last laugh, to make them so strong physically, and yet so weak in their brains that they can hardly dress theirselves.'

Loopy lit a cigarette and drew on it hard. Boy, did that taste good! For a second she laid her head against the wall bordering the staircase. She almost felt like offering Gwen one; only the fear that Hugh would come down and become dreadfully upset at the sight of both his wife and their housemaid smoking prevented her. Hugh was stuffier than Loopy, which was unusual, because, as Loopy had had cause to observe over the years, in England it was usually the wives who were stuffier than the husbands.

'Well, as long as Mr *Walter* makes it to the church, we can wait for the other three.'

The two women looked at each other, knowing that neither words of encouragement nor sympathetic offers to find whatever it was that was missing would make any difference at all. The male Tates would appear, fully clothed, only when they, and the Almighty, decided it was both good and appropriate.

'The flowers is looking something lovely, Mrs

Tate. The reverend says he hasn't seen them done better in a long while, not since his wife did them for the last wedding.'

This compliment, as it happened, proved to be neither a comfort nor a distraction to Loopy. Flower arranging had never been her forte, and hardly had she herself entered the church, ready to do what she could to brighten the place up, when her efforts had come under fire, not least from Lady Melton.

'Gracious, Mrs Tate, how—well, *original* your arrangement is! But, if you don't mind my saying, taller flowers should be at the back, and smaller to the front, and bulking out your arrangement by keeping the leaves on will not, I fear, do. Leaves are never left on the lower part of the stems. Not ever. It is the number one rule, Mrs Tate.'

Quickly finishing her vase as best she might, Loopy had promptly abandoned all pretence at further effort and leaving the other ladies hard at work on their arrangements she had slunk out to have a cigarette in the graveyard at the side of the church.

Inevitably it was a lowering experience, because, although Bexham had not yet received a hit, there were quite a few freshly dug graves, decorated by small bunches of wild flowers and leaves in jars—jars that she knew it was increasingly the habit of amateur jam makers from all over the village to steal, so precious had glass become.

She turned away from the sight, remembering poor old Mrs Gore-Stewart's funeral, and the grief of Richards and Meggie, losing not only Madame Gran, but dashing Davey Kinnersley too, the losses coming so close that it would have knocked anyone for six.

To take her mind off that sad afternoon Loopy stared instead towards the small country road, the well-worn path, which led back to the village. Any one of her boys, John, Walter or Dauncy, could be lying beneath that same earth, and who knew when they might not, and herself and Hugh too? Since the beginning of the war, in common with many other women, Loopy had taken to keeping certain pills in a secret drawer in her household desk. Hugh had brought them back from London for her. In case of invasion he did not want her raped and tortured: she must have the means by which she could take her own life, as must anyone else in the household. It was something they had both agreed. The pills were codenamed by Loopy *my bare bodkin*, an expression used by many smart ladies who had taken the same precaution, with the agreement of their husbands.

Loopy had crushed her cigarette beneath the heel of her shoe, and went back inside. Although voices were being kept appropriately low, nevertheless life rather than death was most definitely in evidence all over the church. Lady Melton and Gardiner with their arrangements, the ladies polishing various brass vases—everything was to do with life and the living.

Not only that but the church was still standing, which in itself was a miracle, seeing that Bexham was on the south coast and only a relatively few sea miles from France, and Hitler's army. With this realisation Loopy had pulled herself together, and throwing off any sense of a cold hand being placed on her shoulder had gladly plunged back into the hectic preparations for Walter and Judy's wedding with a sense of gratitude that was almost tangible. They were about to celebrate two young people falling in love, for heaven's sake. What could be more life enhancing than that?

*   *   *

'I love everything about the way you love. Your kisses particularly. You kiss just like no one else.'

'I'll bet.' Mattie turned on her side to look at him better. 'Want to know what I love about you? Your mouth.' She traced the line of her lover's lips with one finger. 'You have such a good-humoured, sweet mouth. Not the mouth of a soldier at all, I'd have said. In fact sometimes you don't seem one bit like a soldier. Like a terribly important general. Someone with the power of life and death over others.'

'That's what I am, Mattie.'

'That what you always wanted to be?'

'Since you ask, no.' Michael turned on his back, an arm round Mattie, holding her to him while he stared up at the ceiling in the dark. 'What I wanted to be was an actor. A movie actor.' Mattie turned her head towards him in surprise. 'Sure—I even bunked off to Hollywood with a couple of pals and got myself a screen test. From a guy I was at high school with who was directing movies. Ed Childs. Nothing sensational, but he was making movies just the same, and he got me a test.'

'And?'

'I got offered a contract.'

'So why aren't we looking at you up there with the stars, Michael? Instead of down here on earth?'

'Lots of reasons. My mother fell ill at that exact

time, and I had to go home. She got to be seriously ill—and I got to stay at home to look after her. Dad was a soldier as well—a general, just like *his* father. So I guess it was kind of inevitable I'd end up in the military, rather than on the screen. Take it from me, if my father had even dreamed I'd been to Hollywood, let alone had a screen test, let alone been offered a contract . . .'

'I imagine you wouldn't be here.'

'He'd have court-martialled me, personally.'

'I sort of thought you weren't just an ordinary soldier,' Mattie said, resting her head back on his chest. 'I thought there was something distinctive about you.'

'There's something distinctive about everyone on this earth, Mattie,' Michael replied, reaching for his pack of Lucky Strikes. 'That's one thing being in the military teaches you. The unaccountability of folk.'

'But what do you really think about killing people, Michael? Does it bother you?'

'Well, of course it bothers me, Mattie. Except I don't see it as killing people. I see what I have to do—the way I see it my job is to stop people killing people. We didn't start this damned war. So what the likes of people like me have to do is do their utmost to bring it to its swiftest possible conclusion. And that's something else I have to talk to you about, sweetheart. So why don't we get dressed, OK? And I'll take you dancing.'

* * *

Since Michael had never taken her out anywhere where they could dance, once in his arms Mattie was bowled over. She'd only really been used to dancing with young boys at the local hops in Bexham to which she and Virginia Morrison had sneaked off, and exciting though those adventures had been Mattie had never really known what it was like to dance with a really good partner. Now she did. As the quintet played 'The Nearness of You', muted trumpet, clarinet, piano, bass and brushed drums, Mattie felt as though she were floating on air, so perfectly did Michael hold and guide her. He took just enough of her weight with his left arm to make her feel her feet merely brushed the floor as she followed the steps Michael was taking. His left arm was crooked so that they could dance cheek to cheek, and now and then his lips brushed either her hand or her face, while his legs and hips moved with hers almost exactly as they had only an hour or so ago when they had been making love. Yet somehow to Mattie dancing like this seemed more intimate, seemed to say even more about how they felt at that moment—the music, the words of the song now being sung in a soft husky voice by the trumpeter, the presence of other people around them all dancing in like fashion, while outside and barely two blocks away they could hear the bombs dropping, the air raid they had again chosen to ignore rather than break the spell they were in.

'You know I love you, Michael. I shouldn't—but I do.'

'You know I love you too, Mattie. And I guess I can't help it either.'

'So what are we going to do?'

'Go on loving each other for as long as we may. For just as long as we can.'

'How long is that going to be, Michael?'

'I wish I knew, sweetheart. You see, in one way I want this damned war over like tomorrow if it were possible. To spare any more lives. To stop all this suffering. And the other part of me wants it to go on for ever.'

Michael looked at her now as they danced. This was the one topic that was never broached, the other life of General Michael Rafferty: his home life, the life of someone completely different from the man holding Mattie in his arms. He had joked earlier in the night, as they had sat at their table drinking shots of whisky, that the only similarity between actors and soldiers was that anything was permissible on tour or at war, but although Mattie had sensed an opportunity to open that particular can of beans, as Michael referred to such matters, she had resisted the temptation and continued with their game of pretence—that there were no responsibilities other than the ones they had to each other, temporary ones, transient ones, unspoken ones: a duty not to hurt each other or deceive each other any more than was inevitable in such circumstances, a need not to intrude too much into each other's lives, not to let the very real and deep emotion that existed between them jeopardise any previously existing associations.

Mattie had known that Michael must be married from the moment she first saw him, yet she had chosen to pretend that he might not be since self-deceit was the only way she could allow herself to become his mistress. As long as she pretended Michael was single and free, they could be lovers. The moment that the question was asked and answered fully and truthfully she knew their affair would be over. So she did not ask the question. She had not even hinted at it—not, that is, until that evening.

She had regretted her question even before she had asked it.

How long is that going to be, Michael? she had heard herself saying, as if she was somewhere miles away, down the end of a long, dark and echoing tunnel. *How long is that going to be?*

And when he had answered her, inevitably, all she could hear was an echo in return.

As they danced on her thoughts continued.

Perhaps he wants to tell me. Perhaps he's terribly unhappy—wants a divorce, wants to be with me for ever, because that's what he means, surely? Maybe all I have to do is ask him—and the whole thing will become clear. The burden will be lifted, he'll be free to do and say as he wants.

She so nearly asked him. The question was ready there, waiting to be asked. All she had to do was put it to him. And she so nearly did—so very nearly, before something pulled her back. At first she thought it was her conscience, until she became aware of the voices, mostly a man's voice, scolding.

I cannot imagine what you think you're playing at. A married man indeed. What sort of person are you? Is this the way you were brought up? To behave like this? To have an affair with someone else's husband? You must have taken complete leave of your senses—I cannot for the life of me imagine what you thought you were doing.

Mattie looked round the dance floor and there they were—there were her father and mother dancing alongside, her father holding her mother rigidly with his left arm outstretched and his right hand held high on her back. Her mother was looking away, as if too ashamed to set eyes on her adulterous daughter, while her father glared at her from under his oddly twisted and waxed eyebrows.

'I didn't know he was married!'

'What was that, Mattie?' Michael had stopped dancing and was holding her slightly away from him, staring at her. 'What was that you just said?'

'I don't remember,' Mattie replied, alarmed, looking round the tiny dance floor for the spectre of her parents. 'Someone said something to me—but I didn't see—I mean I didn't see who it was.'

'What did they say?' Michael persisted. 'I thought I heard you say something?'

'Only that I love this tune.'

'No, I definitely heard you say something about marriage.'

'Why should I say anything like that?'

'I don't know, perhaps because it's on your mind?'

To escape from the intensity of the moment, Mattie said quickly, 'I'm sorry, Michael, I feel a little dizzy, could we sit down?'

He led her by the arm back to their table, stopping on the way to ask a waiter to bring them some iced water. Mattie sat down gratefully, putting her head in her hands, trying to pull herself together. Perhaps she was tired or something, but she could have sworn that her parents had passed them on the dance floor, so close that she could smell the French scent her mother always used; that was how close they had seemed to be to her.

* * *

While Michael fussed over her, pouring her glasses of water to sip, and anxiously patting her on the hand, Mattie stared at the floor, slowly regaining her sense of reality. Of course she had not passed her father and mother on the dance floor, so if she had not, it must be that her conscience had. If her mother and father had actually been in the ballroom they would have been right to upbraid her so publicly, for the truth was that she had not been brought up to do what she was doing. Having an affair with a married man was against everything in which she had been brought up to believe. And there was Peter—her Peter—back there in that place called Bexham, a place that, ever since she had left it, she thought of every day, and every night before she fell asleep, even when she was with Michael. If her parents would be shocked, what would Peter think? She turned away from the thought. Ever since she had come to London, Peter and Bexham—her whole former life—had seemed less than real; it had seemed imaginary in its honesty and simplicity. The person she had been at Bexham would be shocked at the person she was now. More than that, she thought the old Mattie would not even like the present Mattie now.

Yet, at that moment, it seemed to her that she loved Michael so deeply, she simply could not imagine her life without him. In fact the more she was with him, the less she found herself able to survive without him. It was unfair on Michael, and it was wrong in the eyes of everyone righteous. But, at that moment, it seemed to her that she couldn't live without him. More than that, she *wouldn't* live without him.

Not that she would ever dare ask him *the* question. She would just let things be. Let them remain precisely how they were. While the war still raged and Michael was still with her in Britain, they had each other, and that, Mattie knew, had to be good enough. She would never ask him about his wife or family, if he did indeed have one, which she shrewdly imagined that he must. She would only ever talk about such matters if, and only if, Michael brought the subject up himself. Otherwise she would just take each and every moment as it came, treasuring them as if they were the last, and if she was killed in a bombing raid and found herself in hell, it would surely have been worth it?

'You sure you're OK now, sweetheart?' he was asking her, taking both her hands in his. 'You look awful pale.'

'I think it's just because this place is so smoky—and so crowded. I just had a funny turn. Stupid. I am sorry.'

He took her outside, leaving the warm, thickly smoky nightclub to hurry back across a darkened and almost deserted city. Their cab had just reached the wrong end of Oxford Street when the air raid siren sounded.

'If it's all the same to you, guv,' the cabbie shouted over his shoulder, 'I'd rather not chance it!'

'Very well!' Michael shouted back. 'Head for the nearest subway.'

The cabbie decanted them outside Goodge Street tube station, whose entrance was already crowded with people seeking refuge from the imminent attack. Without even bothering about his fare, the driver disappeared as fast as he could below ground, leaving Mattie and Michael standing in the darkened street jostled by the local residents pushing and shoving their way into the station.

'Don't let's,' Mattie said to Michael, gripping his arm tightly and trying to turn him away from the stream of people, many of whom were in nightclothes under their topcoats. 'Please?'

'You'll be a lot safer down there, Mattie.'

'I know, but I get terrible claustrophobia in crowds, really I do.' She paused for a second as hundreds of people, panicked, and oblivious of anything except their own safety, pushed by them. 'I'm sorry, I just can't. I'll pass out completely if I go down there. I am sorry, Michael. You go.'

'No, Mattie. Without you? Absolutely not.'

Michael took her arm and started to push against the tide of people streaming past them, and back towards the emptying streets.

'You don't have to do this,' Mattie said, turning. 'You can take shelter if you'd rather.'

'Now you're being funny. Think I'd leave you wandering the streets alone in an air raid? While I sat all safe and sound down there? You're an even bigger nut than I realised.'

Once the sirens had finished wailing and silence had fallen back over the city there was no one else to be seen. In this way they found themselves wandering into Oxford Street. Behind them somewhere a dog howled, abandoned by its owners while they sought refuge from the raid, and just as they started to hurry towards some other form of shelter a cat fight broke out, sounding painfully loud in the eerie silence before gradually, so gradually, inexorably the heavy drone of bombers approached. Now they could hear the clatter of the ack-ack guns, but nothing stopped the persistent advance of the enemy. Michael pulled Mattie into a doorway, putting both his arms round her, sheltering her as closely and tightly as he could at the very back of the entrance.

'I don't know why I let you talk me into this—I am meant to be a sane person,' he murmured against Mattie's hair.

'You didn't have to come with me.'

'Oh sure. I could have just turned tail and gone underground cosy as can be, leaving you to roam the streets in the middle of an air raid. I always knew you were nutty. But now I know how totally nutty you really are.'

'Sorry. But I just couldn't have stood it. Being bunkered up with hundreds of strangers.'

'Like I said, nutcase. We could be killed, you know, as in d for dead.'

'I don't mind. At least we'd die together.'

'So that is what this is all about!'

Michael was joking, but he could not make out the expression on Mattie's face. Instead he tried in vain to stare at the skies above them, as if to search for what could be the harbingers of their fate, but from where they stood sheltering it was impossible to see the night sky. Still he stared because he did not know what else to do or to say. He knew what Mattie meant because that was exactly the way he felt as well. He knew—they both knew really—that one way or the other, what they were feeling for each other at that moment had a hell of an end date stamped right across it.

Logically, either Michael would be killed in the war, or else when it was over and victory won he would have to leave Mattie to return to America and his wife and three young children, who were all waiting, hoping against hope, for his safe return. He could never leave his wife, could never hurt her in that way, any more than he could bear the thought of not seeing his son and daughters again.

He was just about to suggest moving from the doorway and making a run for it back to the tube station when the first bombs of that night began to fall. The next thing they both knew was darkness as they were picked up and hurled into the air, blasted out of their shelter by the explosions. Miraculously they were thrown clear of the falling masonry, the nearest bomb having dropped on a building the other side of the alleyway that ran behind the shop in whose doorway they had been sheltering. But the blasts were sufficient to knock half the roof off the building above them, as well as blow out several of its windows and loosen much of its brickwork. Michael was so stunned by the impact that he had no idea what was happening or indeed even where he was. Deafened by the explosions and all but blinded by the dust and debris, he found himself staggering into the middle of the street while the world seemed to be quite literally falling around him. Water was gushing up from somewhere in the ground nearby and there was an overpowering smell of gas from a fractured main. Fully conscious now, Michael realised Mattie was nowhere near him. He yelled her name above the now distant noise of yet another stick of bombs exploding and the rumble and thunder of tumbling masonry.

'Mattie!' he yelled. 'Mattie, where are you? Mattie! Mattie, answer me! I'm right here! Mattie!'

With a sudden ominous *thump* the fractured gas

main exploded into fire, pitching Michael forward on to his knees but at the same time lighting up the vicinity in a dull red glow.

At first all he could see was rubble, brickwork and concrete blown from nearby buildings, display goods and debris from broken shop windows, and rubbish and litter already lifting in the winds caused by the explosions. Then he saw a pile of bodies lying in the street, their clothes torn from their backs, their broken limbs twisted at all angles and sticking up in the air.

CHAPTER ELEVEN

As Judy walked down the aisle on her father's arm to the sound of the old church organ, with all the flowers set about the transept in perfect order, Loopy could hardly believe that they had actually made it. It simply did not seem possible that she had her three sons, and Hugh, all present and correct, and that everything needed for the reception was ready and waiting for them back at the Meltons' house in Old Bexham.

And what was more and what was better, no bombs had dropped either on the church or in the harbour. No bad news affecting the village had yet filtered through from London or elsewhere, but what *was* affecting was that Walter was there, and alive and well, and not dead at the bottom of the sea. Indeed at that moment, as Walter turned at the altar to see his lovely young bride with her bouquet of red flowers, his face was so filled with joy, it seemed to Loopy, that there was not a person in the church who, if they observed it, could remain unaffected.

We are gathered here today . . .

The words of the wedding service never failed to affect Loopy. Perhaps the longer she was married, the more years Hugh and she knew each other, the more she realised just how fortunate she was to have met and married someone with whom she had remained so very much in love. The fact of loving someone, no matter what, was just such a miracle, and for the marriage to last was an even grander miracle than the miracle of meeting and falling in love in the first place. Loopy bowed her head in prayer, for, to her mind, if God was a mystery, so too was love, but if God was love, then there was no mystery at all.

*   *   *

'I thought the flowers were beautiful, simply lovely, didn't you?'

Not only the woman who had just voiced her appreciation of the floral displays, but all the guests at the reception back at the Melton house were agreed upon this point. They must be, because they had all said so to Loopy, over and over again, as if weddings were all about flowers, not people.

To Loopy the flowers, although very pretty, were completely outshone by the radiance on the young people's faces. That was what she would remember for the rest of her life when she stared at the photographs of Walter and Judy on their wedding day—their radiant happiness at finding each other and sharing their mutual love—not the flowers.

Meggie, who had acted as lone bridesmaid to

Judy, had found the wedding almost more difficult than Madame Gran's funeral. Both she and Judy knew that neither Madame Gran nor Meggie herself approved of wartime marriages, and yet a part of both of them, a large part, could not help wondering whether, if Meggie had married Davey when he had asked her, that afternoon in London when they shut out the war and life, when they had loved each other so passionately, if she had done as Davey had asked and married him, he would not be dead. They might have been on honeymoon, they might have set up house together, he might have abstained from joining the flotilla that went out so quickly, so bravely, to Dunkirk to rescue the stranded British army.

'You're practically bilingual in French and German, aren't you, Meggie?' Hugh was suddenly at Meggie's shoulder, refilling her glass with gin, and wearing his most innocent expression, which if Loopy had been by his side she could have warned Meggie meant that whatever was coming next would be, to say the least, unexpected. But since she was not, Hugh merely went on, 'I think I remember Mrs Gore-Stewart telling me that, shortly before she died. Yes—I think I do remember that's what she said, that you were brought up to be not bilingual, I mean, but trilingual.'

Meggie nodded. She still found it impossible to believe that Madame Gran had gone, let alone Davey, and yet at the mention of either of their names it was as if she had been stabbed through the heart. It was ridiculous, but she still went in and out of Cuckers expecting to see the busy figure of Madame Gran, hear her distinctive tones, listen to her mischievous conversation, watch Richards following her about, his usual adoring expression in his eyes, but his eyebrows always about to be raised in potential disapproval at whatever new scheme she was proposing. And then again, looking out, daily, towards the harbour, or walking by the Three Tuns, she still expected to come upon Davey, his sailing togs rolled up to the knees, canvas shoes on slim, brown feet, his eyes on seeing Meggie lighting up as if he had just won a yachting race in the *Light Heart*.

Hugh Tate must have been about halfway through his little pep talk about how useful Meggie could be—if she really wanted—when Meggie looked up at him and said the single word he really wanted to hear.

'Yes, Hugh. Of course. Just tell me where to be and I will be there.'

Hugh stopped talking, suddenly aware that his personal recruitment drive had worked. 'Really, are you sure?'

'Quite, quite sure. I've finally realised I have to leave Bexham. Too many memories, Hugh. You must understand that.'

Meggie gave him one of her piercingly honest looks, and Hugh dropped his eyes. He had to confess that the thought had occurred to him that Meggie might well want to put a great many miles between Bexham and herself.

'Yes, I must say, I thought you might.'

If Hugh had been anything less than honest at that moment, then Meggie might have changed her mind, but since he was not, the die was cast.

* * *

There was an old shoe, but no rice could be wasted, and although the wedding cake had tasted a trifle strange, and there was more gin and sherry than champagne—and those bottles that there were had been donated by Richards and Meggie as a present from Madame Gran's cellar—nothing much mattered to Judy. For, as Walter carried her over the threshold of Owl Cottage, all she could think of was the wonder of the fact that she was alone with Walter, and he was home for another twelve hours. A whole twelve hours to make love and more love. A whole twelve hours to kiss and talk, and kiss again, and talk some more. It was perfection, although not the honeymoon of which Judy had dreamed when in exile in Scotland with her mother.

* * *

That honeymoon was to be spent abroad, in a Europe at peace. She would have worn a beautiful coat and skirt by Molyneux. Walter would have hired a private carriage on the luxury train to Paris, where they would have started their honeymoon in a palatial suite in an old grand hotel on the Île St Louis. From there a chauffeured car would have taken them to the South of France, where, once more followed by little page boys carrying her endless luggage, Judy would have made herself at home in yet another luxurious hotel. Their suite would have a double set of French windows which opened on to a brilliant view of the sea, and there would be a yacht to take them out for picnics to remote beaches where they would swim and laze until it was time to return for dinner. Every night she would change into gowns so stunning that Walter would hardly be able to look at the menu, let alone the wine list. After dinner they would dance until the early hours to a ten-piece orchestra before retiring to make love in a vast, gold embossed bed made up with silk sheets.

* * *

Of course they had both seen Owl Cottage before, individually, but now they were actually married obviously it looked more beautiful than ever. Because it, like them, was now a fact, a big, beautiful fact. The blue covers, the pink cushions, the kitchen like a new pin, cupboards painted pale blue, walls white, every spoon and fork that could be spared, and saucepans too, were admired by Walter and Judy.

But admiration is a dull word when it comes to the wonder of a first home, where the gleam of the first tin opener or corkscrew, the shine of a saucepan lid, or the colour of a plant by the back door, assumes an importance that is remembered by the owners for the rest of their lives. How much more so, therefore, if war has put a time limit on those moments. How much more for a young man to take in, knowing that in such a short time he would be gone, perhaps for ever. To have found each other in peacetime would have been joy enough, but to do so in war brought an intensity of beauty and colour into each second. So much so that it seemed to Judy, for the heartbreakingly short time they spent together, that such was the passion of the love that consumed them, their hearts might stop, and they might be extinguished, long before Walter was once more in uniform, his officer's cap under his arm, his eyes bright with a courage that he could not have been feeling.

After he had left her, Judy, refusing to risk bad luck by waving goodbye—while at the same time instructing him not to turn to look back at her—shut the front door, and went upstairs to lie on the bed they had left only an hour before.

There were tears now that Walter had gone; but although there was no one else there to comfort Judy, she was comforted.

She would have a baby. She would have Walter's baby. Whatever else happened she was going to have Walter's baby, something of Walter for her to love, some child that would remind her of him, for ever. And that being so, nothing that might be going to happen to them now would matter quite so much. She placed her hands on her stomach. She *would* have Walter's baby.

* * *

Yelling Mattie's name again in anguish, Michael stumbled over to where the bodies lay, only to discover that they were not human beings, but dummies from a nearby department store window.

Turning round in helpless circles where he stood, he looked in vain for any other sign of life, but could see none.

'Mattie!' he yelled once more. 'Mattie—can you hear me! Mattie!'

'Michael?'

He could see her now, beginning to try to scramble to her feet from where she had been thrown to the ground. Hurrying to her side, he steadied her, urging her to stay where she was until they could find out whether or not she was hurt. There was blood on her face, running from her nose, and there was blood in her hair, matted with debris and dirt.

'It's all right.' Mattie took hold of Michael's arm with both her hands. 'I think I can move everything. Yes, I can—I think everything's still working.' She pulled herself slowly to her feet. 'Are you all right?' She pushed back a tangled knot of hair from her face. 'I thought you had to be dead.'

'I thought *you* had to be.'

Michael put his arm round her back, at the same time looking round to see if there was anywhere safe to shelter, but hardly had he done so when there was another crash as another lump of masonry fell to the ground. Quickly deciding against the idea he turned Mattie away from the target area and led her into the semi-darkness behind the flaring gas main and the smaller fires that were breaking out around it.

'I've got a feeling, Private Eastcott, that suffering claustrophobia down the subways might have been a great deal less uncomfortable, but let it pass.'

'Sorry, General. I must have been mad.'

'Mad-*der*. Any idea where the nearest hospital is?'

Mattie shook her head, wincing with the sudden pain.

'I don't need a hospital. Honestly. I just have a few scratches and bruises, that's all. What about you?'

'I just need a new pair of pants. Lost my hat as well into the bargain.'

'I'm so sorry. You shouldn't have listened to me, really you shouldn't.'

'And miss all the fun? Listen, kid—it's not everyone who gets blitzed and lives to tell the tale.'

'You shouldn't have had anything to do with me.'

'I knew that the moment I met you, sweetheart.'

They picked their slow way across the rubble lying in the street. As soon as they seemed to be well clear of all apparent danger, Michael stopped and looked back west along the line where the bombs had been dropping. The all-clear was sounding now, and rather than the sound of droning aircraft and the thud of exploding bombs the night was filled with the sound of rescue vehicles, the fire engines and ambulances already rushing towards the scenes of carnage. Raised voices were carried on the wind, shouting instructions and directions, and now there were screams as well, faint cries for help from beneath the rubble, louder shouts from those lucky enough not to be buried but unlucky enough still to be injured. Hand in hand Mattie and Michael threaded their way back through the chaos of the bomb sites, avoiding the side streets that were still plunged in darkness, preferring to stick to the long, wide route that was Oxford Street. As they crossed the Circus a member of the WVS, catching sight of the blood on Mattie's face by the light of her torch, offered her first aid. From somewhere appeared two mugs of steaming tea, borne by a diminutive grey-haired woman in carpet slippers and a thick tartan dressing gown, tea which they gratefully consumed.

Continuing on their way to Michael's flat they passed the emergency services busy removing a line of bodies from a smouldering building nearby, taking them to await identification in a makeshift morgue just around the corner in the church hall.

To Michael's surprise Mattie stopped to watch, before hurrying on. When they eventually reached the flat, she said, 'I feel oddly selfish. The way I've been thinking, carrying on. Does it take bombs to make me realise that you and I don't really matter any more?'

'Oh, we matter, we matter very much, but not the way we perhaps think we do.' Michael paused. 'Actually I've been putting off telling you—I have to go, Mattie. I am being moved on.'

Mattie nodded as if she already knew this to be the case. 'Yes, but when? When do you have to go?'

Of course Mattie had always known this must happen some time, but, rather like her determination to walk home in the middle of an air raid, she had put the reality of their situation aside, preferring to carry on living in the belief that things were going to continue indefinitely in a strange sort of wartime status quo, with Michael based in London and her continuing to act as his driver.

'Can't say when, or where, just soon, but I do have one idea. You still have two days' leave left, isn't that so?' As Mattie said nothing, he went on, 'Happily enough I actually have a couple of days' leave due as well. Thought we might take a little trip together. I thought you might drive me to this famous Bexham of yours that I'm always hearing so much about. I'd really like to see where you come from. Where you live. I want to see you there, for real, before I go, so I can picture you back there when I'm gone.'

'You do?'

Mattie tried to look enthusiastic, but the prospect of trying to hide how she felt about Michael from her parents, her mother especially, was not one to which she could look forward.

'Sure.' Michael, perhaps sensing a certain

reluctance, went on enthusiastically. 'It would mean a lot to me to see the part of England where you were raised. We could stay somewhere. A little inn maybe. That's something else I've always wanted to do, stay in an old-fashioned English inn, with an old-fashioned English girl.'

'You want a guided tour?'

'You bet. And I get to sleep with the guide.'

* * *

Mattie knew she couldn't take Michael home. There was simply no possibility of her arriving back at her parents' house with a four star United States general in tow, the man whom they knew Mattie was driving. Even if the subject of his marital status was not brought up, Mattie knew that in Bexham, anyway, assumptions would be made, instantly.

Besides, Mattie had no wish to share the precious few hours she and Michael had left to spend together with her father and mother. Nor could they stay in the Three Tuns. It was much too local and Mattie was far too familiar a face with the regulars. Instead she recommended to Michael that they stay some way from Bexham, and perhaps only visit it if it could be arranged to be part of his official itinerary. Naturally this would mean staying in uniform, but if Michael really wanted to see Bexham, it was the best way.

'I just love this place,' Michael exclaimed after he had started to explore Mattie's choice, which providentially was not just a safe forty minutes' driving time from Bexham, but also happened to be one of the oldest inns in Sussex. A place so famous for the famous having stayed there that perhaps only the arrival of William Shakespeare ordering a pint of mead in the bar would cause a mild stir. 'Quite apart from anything else, it creaks everywhere. And everything is crooked, and just breathes history. How old is it anyway?'

'I'm not sure. Old enough. Judging from all the old panelling and what have you, I don't know—Tudor certainly, probably much earlier.'

'Steeped in history, I bet. Feels as if you're tumbling backwards in time, somersaulting, even.'

Mattie smiled, thinking that whatever might have gone before in the ancient coaching inn, nothing that she had planned for that night would surprise any ghosts or spirits that might still be lingering in its rooms.

* * *

Everything about her new training felt unreal to Meggie. Despite being determined on it, completely committed to it, even at her final briefing she kept thinking that any minute now Hugh Tate would turn round from the map of France to which he was pointing and laughingly say, 'Ha, ha, just a tease, Meggie. You don't have to go. It was just a joke really.'

It was then that it came to Meggie that becoming an agent, volunteering to be dropped into France, turning up at Baker Street and various other places, being kitted up with everything that would be needed—and some things, like her own personal cyanide pill, that she hoped would not be needed—must be very like having a baby. The idea was fine, volunteering for the experience not that difficult, and the conception even quite enjoyable, but actually having to face up to the reality—blooming terrifying.

Although she did not know it, in her grief for her loved ones Meggie looked more beautiful than she had ever done. If mourning had any reward it was in the luminous quality it had given to her large, sad eyes, and in the pallor that showed up the dark lines under her eyes since her childhood inability to sleep had returned. Of course she was not aware of this as she stared at herself in the mirror; she was only aware of the change in how she looked as it affected her chances of being passed off as a Frenchwoman. It was not only because she had already adopted a French style of dressing—very smart—or that her blond hair was drawn back underneath her navy blue hat in a new, slick, Gallic kind of style. It was not that her make-up was more evident than it would be normally; it was because she herself, as she stared into the mirror, saw how afraid she was. She would have to be a fool not to be afraid, she told herself, even as she heard David's voice in her head begging her to marry him, as the sirens sang and people pounded past his Chelsea house, their feet pitter-pattering on the pavement, the sound somehow seeming to echo their heartbeats.

He would have known it was as useless to say to Meggie as it had always been to say to him, *You mustn't do this, because it's very, very, dangerous*.

Of course it was dangerous, and of course she was fearful. It was because it was dangerous and because she was fearful that, of course, she must go.

'Have you thought what you will do if you make a splodge?' Hugh looked at her, the look in his eyes purposefully casual.

'Of course.'

Meggie paused by the door and her eyes drifted towards everything and nothing; the future, the past, maps with little pegs that told where agents were, pinholes that showed where agents were no longer. Drawers full of cyanide pills, desks with piles of papers on them, most of which seemed to say 'Top Secret'.

'Anything I can get you while I'm over there? I hear roast rat's a speciality in Paris *en ce moment*.'

Hugh turned away. 'Off you go, Meggie Gore-Stewart, and don't forget what I said.'

She closed the door behind her, and Hugh went back to his desk and sat down. Hardly had he seated himself when every swear word he had ever known started to run like some ghastly repetitious song through his head.

He tried to block them out but they went on and on, in the same way that such words sometimes occurred to him suddenly and incongruously in church, shocking the life out of him, and increasing his already profound belief in the devil.

He stood up, knowing that a change of scene was the only way to stop himself from being overtaken by the guilt he felt each time he sent an agent off to France. Going quickly into the corridor outside he called through a colleague's door, 'Coming for a drink, old man?'

They wandered off together, not really thinking about anything much, because when all was said and done, there was really too much to think about.

* * *

Meggie lay safely hidden in a hay barn in deep

Normandy countryside some thirty miles from her destination. Given the amount of time that she knew she would have to stay out of sight, she found she could no longer put off having to face reality for the first time. Even if she accomplished her first mission successfully, or rather *once* she had accomplished her first mission successfully, her reward would be quite simple: she would be sent back. Only now did she realise that being an agent was not a job, nor was it a vocation, it was a marriage. Once you knew enough you already knew too much, and that was something the Service appreciated to the full. She had been told that some agents had been dropped so many times into France, the rumour was that they ended up staying there rather than return to be dropped again. Not funny really, but not unfunny either.

Happily, however, she was not alone in the barn. Equally well hidden in the hay bales were two Englishmen, commandos who on an otherwise successful raid on Le Havre had got cut off from their party and perforce been left to find their own way home. The Resistance had come to their rescue, just as the commandos had been promised in advance, and now the two battle-weary soldiers and their glamorous saviour were sitting it out until word came that it was safe to undertake the next part of their journey north to the coast.

* * *

The floorboards of the inn had creaked all the way from Michael's bedroom to Mattie's, so badly that by the time Michael arrived at his destination it was as much as he could do to stop laughing.

'There's no law to say you can't walk down a hotel corridor,' Mattie had remarked as she sat brushing out her hair at the dressing table. 'Who's to know where you're going?'

'At this time of night? With a look like this on my face?'

Mattie had started to laugh too when she saw the deliberately exaggerated expression on Michael's handsome countenance. There was something indefinably appealing about his looks that made Mattie inwardly sigh with hopeless adoration every time she looked at him. Dressed as a general he looked handsome, strong and full of the right sort of authority. Lying naked in her arms he looked every inch what he had originally thought he might be, a heart-throb, a sort of grown-up version of every girl's dream.

'Do you think you'll always be a soldier, Michael?' Mattie had asked him as they both lay on their backs peacefully smoking a couple of Lucky Strikes. 'Maybe when the war's over—'

'Maybe *what* when the war is over?'

'You could still take up acting.'

'Oh sure. Like I could always become President of the United States.'

'I don't see what's so preposterous, General. After all, what's the difference between playing soldiers and playing other people?'

'Quite a lot, Mattie—I mean in the army the bullets are real and kill you, whereas, although you in Britain probably don't know this, in films the bullets are not real, and—'

'No, don't joke. I understand—you'd rather not think about the future. I understand.'

'Would you?'

'Yes and no.'

'I'm strictly a *no* on this issue. Hell, Mattie—the war's not even halfway won yet. Suppose it doesn't go according to plan. And we lose?'

'Shouldn't we be prepared for that sort of thing to happen? We can't just get through every day thinking we're bound to win. I'm sure you don't believe that. You wouldn't be a four star general if that was the way you thought.'

'What would you do if we did lose, Mattie? And this lovely country of yours became occupied by the Germans?'

'I think I'd probably kill myself. Actually. But then as long as your lot's still fighting the good fight, I suppose it's going to take some sort of miracle for Hitler to win.'

'I guess. Just as I guess that my job is to try to ensure that that particular miracle never happens. Now is that enough about the future, honey?'

'No . . .'

Michael had glanced at her, before turning away to stub out his cigarette. 'Stay right where you are while I get us a whisky.'

Mattie had watched him as he got out of bed to fetch a half bottle of Scotch. There were no lights burning, but the curtains were pulled back and a full moon bathed the room. She knew she should shut up. It would be neither right nor fair to go on trying to ask Michael for some kind of commitment. Besides, little did he know, but he had already made it.

* * *

'Mademoiselle?' a voice called quietly from below

the hayloft. 'Your friend is here.'

Having dropped off into a catnap, Meggie started, before easing her way to the edge of the trapdoor and looking down. Below her stood two figures, one the ample but comforting shape of the farmer's wife. Dressed in a shapeless dark grey dress with a once white pinafore over it, her grey hair in a tight bun under a triangular black scarf, she smiled up at Meggie. Beside her was the figure of a stranger, a tall loose-limbed man with a large beaked nose and flat black hair, dressed in a pair of cord trousers still bicycle-clipped at the ankles. Apart from his corduroys he wore what looked like a home-knitted bright red polo-neck sweater and a loose dark blue canvas jacket. Even though Meggie had become quite accustomed to the thought of having to trust her life and those of her compatriots to complete strangers, there was something about the cut of this man, the way he was shifting uncomfortably from foot to foot while he waited, or perhaps his habit of what appeared to be incessant sniffing, that put Meggie on her guard. She knew she was right to be wary, although her caution was necessarily academic, for by the time her latest contact discovered her whereabouts her cover was already as good as blown.

The man introduced himself as Pierre Roux, sent as part of a line that stretched as far as Argentan. He was courteous, apologising for the delay in his arrival and explaining it was due to the present intensity of German patrols in the area, and efficient in the way he explained the details of their proposed route and the concomitant timetable.

'I would have preferred to have made the entire journey by night, m'selle,' he said. 'But alas, thanks to these wretched patrols we shall have to make some of the journey by day, otherwise we shall not make your rendezvous. As it is, we shall have to hurry.'

Meggie—known as Martine on French soil—said she quite understood and that her party was prepared to take whatever trouble was needed to ensure a safe and speedy journey. Not only were the lives of her two commandos precious, but the men also had vital information about the harbour installations at Le Havre. Of course Meggie said nothing about this to her escort, other than to stress that it was their mutual top priority to see the two commandos on board their rescue craft and safely on their way back to England.

So, after a supper of cold goose, homemade cheese and freshly baked bread washed down with rough cider, the four set off into what was left of the night.

The sky was clear so the journey was not too arduous, nor were there any undue alarms, so that by the time dawn broke they had covered nearly half of their eighteen-mile journey. They stopped for a rest to catch their breath in a vast barn on the outskirts of a tiny village well off the beaten track, where Meggie and her two soldiers hid themselves behind a collection of old farm machinery and abandoned vehicles, while Pierre took himself off into the village to meet up with the contact who was due to escort them for the second leg of their journey.

He was gone well over an hour, rather more time than had been estimated. Meggie started to become anxious, realising that she was left with absolutely no option other than to wait for the promised new guide, since none of them had any chance of finding the pickup point on a stretch of totally unknown coastline. She wished she had experienced times like this before, moments which caused her heart to beat faster and her mouth to dry up entirely. She felt that if she had she might know better how to deal with them. However, as the first hour started to stretch towards two, she and her companions came to understand that they were in trouble. Realising that they were on a hiding to nothing by remaining where they were, Meggie started to make a new plan. By now either Monsieur Roux had been captured and was telling all under interrogation or else—something she herself considered more than likely—he had already betrayed their identities and whereabouts to the Gestapo.

'So,' she announced with one last look along the road that led away from the barn to the village. 'We're just going to have to chance it, chaps. Even if we can't find the beach and pickup point, we can probably lie low somewhere, under cover. Whatever happens we can't stay here.'

She led them out single file through the back of the old barn, using the hedge as cover along the side of the road until they reached the small wood at the end of the field. Meggie was armed with a Lüger, a weapon proudly presented to her by the farmer in whose barn they had been hiding, and claimed by him to have once belonged to a German officer whose throat he had cut swiftly and silently one night in a daring raid on Gestapo headquarters in Rouen. After their encounter in Le Havre her comrades in arms had been left with only their service issue knives.

Being no match for any handpicked squad of German officers, they all three knew their only chance of survival was to keep hidden. Yet once they had found their way through the coppice and saw nothing but open countryside ahead of them for the next four or five miles such a task seemed to be a complete impossibility.

'We can hide out in these woods until nightfall,' Meggie suggested in a whisper. 'Hope that Pierre hasn't either turned traitor or broken down under interrogation, and then try and find our way across these farms until we get to more cover.'

'These woods are too close to the village, surely?' one of the commandos asked. 'We might be better—since they're not on our tail as yet—to make a dash for it over in that direction, to those hills.'

But just as he was pointing to a mound of undulations on the far western horizon his companion shut him up, indicating with a backward nod of his head to listen behind them.

All three did, and all three heard the same thing: the quiet but definite tread of others in the same woodland, of people tracing their steps; the heavy fall of soldiers' boots as they advanced across beds of dry twigs and small fallen branches.

* * *

Mattie and Michael had parted at the inn, as they had both known they had to do. Mattie left Michael to meet some War Office contacts at a nearby hotel, and she herself, being allowed some time off, made her way happily to Bexham.

As always when approaching the village where

she had been brought up, Mattie felt her usual surge of joyous expectation. It was as if she was young again and cantering along on Virginia's old pony, the light Sussex breeze making her hair stream out behind her, and any minute now they were going to jump a stream or a ditch; that was how excited she suddenly felt as she neared Bexham.

And then, there it was, slumbering in the early spring sunshine almost complacently, as it seemed to Mattie, like a contented cat on the back step of a cottage. Dear heavenly Bexham with its bobbing boats and its flint-packed walls, its pub and its village green, its residents of old and new, how she loved it. Of a sudden she felt as if she had sloughed off the person she had been in London. She was herself again, not confused and terrified and trying to pretend that she was more grown up than she really was, and ending up being all too grown up. Now she was back, she knew that the old Mattie was back too, and might even be back to stay.

It was not until she walked up to the front door of her parents' house that it came to her that not all of Bexham was unchanged. There was something about Magnolias that was different. It was not the fact that her mother's little motor car was not there, or the lack of flowers in the pots set about the door. It was not just that the blackout blinds in the bedroom overlooking the front were drawn, despite its being day.

When the front door slowly opened to her long insistent ring and eventually her father stood before her, one look at his forlorn, colourless face, the expression in his eyes, told Mattie that something quite terrible had happened.

CHAPTER TWELVE

Richards looked across the room at Judy Tate. She had just removed her mask, and was coughing fit to bust at the dust and the scrim that had been choking all the regular netters at Cucklington House for over a year now, but that was not what was worrying Richards. What was worrying him was that Judy was as white as a sheet, or as pallid as tapioca, as Mrs Gore-Stewart would have had it.

'Time for a well-deserved cup that cheers, Miss Judy.'

He took her by the arm and led her to the room next door, a room that he had, in the now permanent absence of his beloved Madame Gran, given over to the making and preparing of tea and small morsels to eat. It was after all, he reckoned, the least he could do for the regular netters. The irregular netters, however, were never allowed in the new tea room. Those who just popped in for a bit of a show, and then did not come back for weeks, Richards comforted only with a glass of water and a patronising smile. Tea, not to mention milk, was by now far too precious to waste on the flotsam and jetsam of this world, of that Richards was quite sure.

'You look a little pale, Miss Judy.'

Judy had been staring ahead of her, but now her eyes, still watery from the netting next door, looked up at Richards.

'As a matter of fact, I feel a bit pale, Richards.' She smiled a little wanly. 'I don't know why, but this last week everything has started to get me down. It is just not *me*, to be got down, at least I hope it isn't. I suppose it's only natural, but it's so—so self-indulgent, and yet I can't shake it off.'

Richards, who had his own worries, not least about the whereabouts of Miss Meggie, nodded sympathetically.

'You need something to take your mind off the war, Miss Judy. Perhaps Mr Walter will be home again on leave soon?'

'I don't think so, somehow. Anyway we've heard nothing more.'

'You just need something to take your mind off everything,' Richards repeated, still staring down into Judy's over-white face.

'I suppose that is it, Richards. I must admit that I had so *hoped* that I would be left with something to take my mind off everything, as you say, but—well, I know that, alas, I probably won't have now for a very long time.'

It was a very discreet way of putting something that Richards knew must have been uppermost in Miss Judy's mind. He understood intuitively how envious she must feel, seeing that half of Bexham seemed to be pushing prams out nowadays, and so he patted her on the shoulder, but, being the soul of tact, he forbore to comment.

'Tea is good for everything.'

Judy smiled wanly, and he took her cup.

'Have another one, Miss Judy, and let me tell you a joke. Know the one about the Yorkshire man who ordered a pint of beer and as it was being served to him the barmaid said "Looks like rain"? "Well, it certainly doesn't look like beer," came the reply.'

Judy laughed. Richards loved to collect jokes

from the wireless, or from the regulars down at the Three Tuns. There was no joke anywhere that he did not write down in his little black book and memorise especially for cheering the netters, or others engaged in war work in Bexham.

As the atmosphere was lifting and Judy was beginning to tell Richards about all the little field animals that came up for scraps to her kitchen window at Owl Cottage, Rusty Todd put her head round the corner of the door.

'Come in, come in, Miss Rusty, tea is at hand,' Richards called to her.

'Very good of you, Mr Richards, but I won't, if you don't mind. I must be on my way. Father, you know—he gets restless now that Mother is away so much doing night work.'

Richards nodded, his face wearing only a most impassive expression. The whole of Bexham knew that Mr Todd had recovered consciousness only to become all but bedridden on hearing of the death of his son Tom; that he blamed himself for taking the boy with him across to Dunkirk; that his physical recovery from his own injuries, miraculous though it was, was as nothing compared to his subsequent mental decline.

'Oh, come on, have just half a cup, Miss Rusty, warm you up in this weather with no heating in the house.'

Richards went to the tea urn and poured Rusty a cup, despite her half-hearted protestations. As he did so, Rusty turned her large eyes on Judy.

'You heard about Mrs Eastcott, didn't you?'

'Yes, I was so sorry.'

'Tried to rescue two young children and their mother from a burning building. What a brave woman. Dad says she will be posthumously awarded with the George Medal, or something.'

There was a small silence as both Richards and Judy tried to envisage what the *or something* might encompass. They began again together, '*Do you think*—Mattie will be staying with her father now?' Judy finished, as Richards added, 'I was about to ask the same thing, Miss Judy.'

Rusty shook her head. She had no idea. After a few days' compassionate leave Mattie had returned to London. Apparently she had been determined to go back, although for how long Rusty was uncertain.

As to Mr Eastcott, he was still insisting on going on fire watching duties, despite the fact that his wife had just died in one.

Rusty shook her head again as she once more prepared to leave. 'I must rush. I've been behind all day, I don't know why.' As Judy followed her into the hall, she picked up a small potted tree. 'I have to be with Dad at night, you know. He never sleeps since his accident. I read to him. Very good for me really, not being bookish, but I shan't be able to do it for much longer. I'm off to work in the munitions factory at Plimpton. With Mum going netting and all sorts, there's not much for me now at home and I can't spend the rest of the war reading to him, and running round after him, and nor can Mum. I meant to plant our Mickey's tree today, and look, I haven't even done that.'

She sighed, staring at the tree that she still had a mind to plant by the village green. Mickey had been against it, but now he was gone, well, it seemed as if as long as she could plant it somewhere it would bring him back, because their Mickey, he was such a little daredevil, he would do anything provided it took courage, Mickey would.

'We'll plant it for you,' Judy told her, taking the small tree from her. 'Won't we, Richards? We'll take care of it, Rusty. After all, as you know, no one in the village dares counter anything that Richards wants to do, do they, Richards?'

Richards took the tree from Judy, stroking its leaves as if it was a monkey tree from Kew, or some other rarity, which at that moment, it seemed to him that it might be.

'Oh, I don't know about that, Miss Judy . . .'

'Yes, you do, Richards. With all the men gone, nowadays you run Bexham, and we all know it, even if you don't.' Judy loved to tease Richards.

'Well, I must be off. See you when I get back.'

'Take care, Miss Rusty, won't you?'

Once he had heard the front door shutting quietly behind her Richards said in a worried voice, 'I don't think Miss Rusty realises what she is in for, I mean, after Bexham. I really don't think she understands what she is in for joining a munitions factory. Dunkirk will be a roller coaster ride compared to life in a factory. Some of the women in there, well, Miss Judy, I hear they'd scare the moustache off a Nazi.'

But of course, concerned though he might be for Miss Rusty, with Madame Gran gone all Richards really dreamed of was seeing Miss Meggie, alive and well, and safely returned to Bexham. Every night before he indulged in a few hours' sleep he imagined allowing himself to be hugged by Miss Meggie, before hurrying off down to the cellars and bringing up a bottle of champagne to celebrate. It was all he could really think about, which is why, the following morning, he took Mickey Todd's tree, now grown to really quite a good height, and went out and planted it on the edge of the village green.

Perhaps because there was a war on, or because he took care to have one of his friends from the Three Tuns build a protective fence of netting around it, no one thought to question the tree's sudden appearance. Everyone assumed that someone else knew why it was there, so it stayed where it was, growing slowly, blossoming in good time for spring, and bearing conkers once autumn came.

* * *

Rusty peered round the door at Father seated in front of the fire. He was still awake, if you could call sitting staring in front of him 'awake'.

'What, still not in bed, Dad?'

'Waiting up for your mother.'

'No, don't do that, Dad. She could be anywhere at this time of night. Might have gone netting, might have gone fire watching . . . and old Mrs Gardner, she has the measles caught from one of her evacuees, so I know that Mum had a mind to step in for her at the hospital. All sorts and tykes of occupations she could be doing this time of night, and you know it.'

'I'm waiting up for her, until she gets back. God, your face and hands aren't half a funny colour. You'll never get a man looking like that.'

'Just going for a wash, Dad, don't have to tell me. Netting's filthy work, you know.' When Rusty came back she picked up a book. 'If you're set on staying up I might as well read to you. Now where were we?'

Her father tried to look vague, as if he did not quite remember where they were, because he never liked to admit to Rusty how much her reading to her old dad meant to him. It settled something inside him, for a few moments anyway. The great black sadness that had come on him after Tom's not coming back from Dunkirk, it all seemed to seep away once Dad got interested in the adventures of Tom Sawyer, and the descriptions of the great river by which Tom lived. And then there were the marvels of the characters that surrounded Tom. Well, *they* reminded him of his boyhood in Bexham, and all the old characters who would drink at the Three Tuns, when he was a little lad.

'Chapter Five . . .'

Before she began Rusty looked across at her father. His legs uncrossed themselves, and his hands came to rest on the sides of his armchair as he heard her voice start to read to him once more. She had noticed that this was the only time he did not twist and turn in his chair, moving restlessly this way and that, as if he was suffering from some sort of ache which would not leave him, which of course he was.

'You don't have to go and leave us for that munitions place or whatever it is, Rusty, really you don't.'

'Don't start, Dad, please. You know we've been over all this, time and again. I have to. You know single women can get sent to prison if they're found without a job nowadays.'

'But you've got a job, here in Bexham—'

'A desk job, Dad, that's something a married

woman, anyone, could do. I want to make something to well and truly get back at Jerry for taking all those gallant soldiers of ours, for taking Tom, and Mr Kinnersley.' She paused, knowing that she should not have mentioned Tom and Mr Kinnersley, but it seemed to her that it was the only way to get her father to understand what she was about now. How she could no longer cope with a desk job that kept her dulled and anxious. She had to *do* something. 'Anyway, it's not munitions or explosives I will be making, I'm not that daft. No, this is balloons. I'm joining the balloon girls. Cheer up, Dad, it'll bring in money and that, and the factory manager said I had nice neat small hands, perfect for that type of work.'

'Women making bombs and guns and barrage balloons, don't see it myself.'

'I hate to disappoint you, Dad, but women are better and faster at that kind of thing than you lot.'

'You should have been a boy.'

'I know, I know, now do you want me to get on with the story, or don't you?'

'Oh, very well. But just you mind out for soldiers at that camp near Plimpton. Don't want to sell yourself for a pair of nylons, as I hear some are doing.'

Rusty stared at the book in front of her and sighed the deepest sigh she had sighed yet that day. Just because it was inward, and could not be heard by her father, did not mean that it was not heartfelt. Father was so full of the nonsense he heard at the Three Tuns, girls selling themselves for a pair of nylons, jitterbugging through the night and turning up for factory work as hung over as ten sailors. She sometimes felt that the men in the village were more horrified by the fact that it was now compulsory for women to register for war work than they were by the war itself and all the casualties. As far as the men were concerned the worst had happened: women were working and that meant that women were independent, and what was even worse was that the government was behind them. It was a filthy plot, the men both behind and in front of the bar had told Mr Todd, nothing more and nothing less than a filthy plot to free women.

She started to read to her father, seated beside him in their usual way, while all the time they both knew that they were listening out for her mother. When Rusty at last heard her, her father had long ago fallen asleep to the sound of his daughter's voice detailing the adventures of Tom Sawyer.

'Where you *been*? I was so worried, it's nearly two o'clock, no, nearly half past two, new time.'

'The blackout, Rusty dear. I went up to Cucklington House for a go at the netting, and then on the way back I stopped off.'

'You stopped off, Mum? Don't tell me at the Three Tuns?'

Mrs Todd coloured slightly. 'No—no—I dunno why, no, I dunno why, but I just had a mind suddenly to go to the church and say a prayer for our Mickey, and course when I came out my torch went and had it, didn't it. Found myself clinging to one gravestone, and then another—well, I thought I'd never see home again, and that was all before I walked into a lamp post and apologised to it!'

Mickey had run away from home three months before. They had not dared to tell Rusty's dad. Mrs Todd had thought it would kill her husband, so they had just told him that he had gone off to stay with relatives in Yorkshire. Rusty had even forged a letter from him, which was not that difficult since Mickey's writing was so bad that her father never bothered to even ask to read the letter, but seemed quite happy for it to be read to him.

Now her mother's voice was barely above a whisper, but Rusty was so pleased to see her back safe that she answered her in a normal voice, 'Well, thank God, you're home anyway.'

This woke her father who called out, 'Who's there? Rusty? Who's there?'

'It's all right, Dad, it's just Mum home.'

'At this hour!'

Both women waited, resigned expressions on their faces, knowing only too well what was going to come next.

'You been out jitterbugging with some GI?'

Every night it was always the same. Rusty turned away. 'You would honestly have thought he would have got bored with saying that by now, wouldn't you?'

Her mother smiled a little hopelessly, knowing that her father's obsessional behaviour, his inability to rouse himself just a little from his physical collapse, was one of the many reasons that Rusty was leaving home and taking a job in the factory at Plimpton, and she could not really blame her.

* * *

Meanwhile Mattie was saying goodbye to Michael.

They had parted temporarily in Sussex, but now they both knew in all likelihood they were parting for good, since Michael had been called back to

America.

It was strange, after so much intimacy, after sharing so much love, Mattie's sudden and terrible grief over her mother's death, everything—it was strange to find that it was so difficult now to know what to say to each other. The fact was there was nothing *to* say except 'goodbye', but even that was both too small and too big a word for how they were both feeling.

As she kissed Michael for the last time Mattie knew, without any doubt, that she should tell him that she had, finally, obtained a commitment from him, albeit without his knowledge.

'Can I get in touch with you?'

'Of course, at Bexham, my father's address.' It was ridiculous, but she realised suddenly that she had not given him directions, and yet perhaps that was not so ridiculous. 'I'll send it to you, soon.'

'No, give it to me now.'

'I haven't time,' Mattie lied, turning away from Michael towards the staff car. 'Just haven't. And—and Major General Allington is waiting for me, sir, you know how it is . . .'

'Gerry's always fried, he won't notice what time you pick him up.'

'No, really, General. So long. We'll keep in touch. I promise. Somehow.'

The hurt in Michael's eyes at her dismissal of him was not reflected in Mattie's, because she knew what Michael did not, that she would probably always be in touch with a part of him, and in a far more tangible way than via a letter or a card. And anyway, what good were letters and such like when everyone knew that war, and heaven only knew what else, was just about to come between them? Besides, it would be very possible, men being so careless, that his wife might find a letter, and Mattie was the last person to want to hurt his wife, because that would mean she would hurt Michael too, and just at that moment if she was sure of one thing, and one thing alone, it was that there was too much hurt in the world, without adding to it.

'Don't you know there's a war on, General?' she joked, at the same time saluting him smartly, only for him to catch her hand.

'Mattie, please.'

But it was too late. She shook his hand free of hers, and flung herself behind the driver's seat. She had lost her mother, she had lost Michael, she just hoped that she could hang on to his baby.

*   *   *

For a moment Meggie had lain in utter silence, the only noise being the constant swish of the spring crop around her, blown softly by the breeze, a slight wind on which she suddenly heard voices being carried her way, German voices shouting commands and directions as a small army of them poured out of the woods.

Half standing to try to gain sight of them, Meggie parted the tall stalks and got a good view of the grey-uniformed and helmeted soldiers as they stood in a broken line surveying the crop fields and the landscape beyond. There were about twenty or so men, Meggie reckoned, having made a quick head count, led by one officer who had just emerged from the copse on the eastern end of the line. One of his men suddenly shouted, pointing at the same time to something west of them, movement it seemed in the grain, so Meggie gathered from what they were shouting. The next thing she knew shots rang out. Then more shots and more shouts as some of the soldiers were despatched after what could be their quarry.

Meggie dropped at once back to the ground, not daring to crawl either forwards or backwards lest the soldiers caught sight of her as well. Looking over her shoulder she knew she had left a telltale path of entry into the field, and she also knew there was nothing she could do about it, other than hope none of the soldiers decided to come this way. For a long, precious moment it seemed that her wish had come true as all she could hear were the voices of her enemies growing ever more distant as the chase went westwards. There were several more shots fired, then silence—more or less. Silence apart from what Meggie now realised was the sound of footfalls behind her.

She lay with her face pressed as hard as she could against the cold earth, her whole body flattened into the ground in fact, as if she was trying to bury herself. She knew there was someone there, but she could not look round. She really did not want to look into whoever's eyes it was, as they shot her.

More silence followed. No more footfalls, just utter silence—until a slow click, the sound of a revolver being cocked, or the safety catch coming off a pistol. Unable to bear the suspense any more, Meggie all at once rolled over, deciding that perhaps it might be best to brazen it out with her captor, to look him in the eye.

He was standing not a yard from her, smart as

paint in his captain's uniform, and almost absurdly good-looking. Not the traditional Teutonic blond, Meggie had time to notice as she lay on her back staring up into his face, but a tall dark-eyed, dark-haired man, looking at her.

'Hello,' Meggie said in her perfect French. 'Lovely day for a picnic.'

His gun was pointed not at her heart but at her head, which Meggie did not consider very gentlemanly.

'If you're about to shoot me,' she continued, 'I'd rather it was in the chest rather than mess up these features of mine, which I have often been assured are really rather fine.'

Her captor said nothing. His face showed absolutely no expression as he blinked slowly, before obeying her orders and lowering his gun in line with her heart.

'Don't you speak French? Would you rather I spoke German?'

'I speak French, thank you,' the German replied in equally impeccable French.

'Fine,' Meggie replied. 'Then why are you hesitating? Or don't you have the nerve to shoot a woman in cold blood?'

The officer held his gun rock steady, pointing at Meggie's thumping, racing heart. 'Why aren't you frightened?'

'Probably because I've never died before. If I had, perhaps I would be.'

'I haven't seen you,' the captain told her, finally, lowering his voice and replacing his revolver in his holster.

Meggie stared back at him, suspecting a trick. 'So what am I meant to do now?' she wondered, still not daring to move.

The German officer pursed his mouth while he thought, before looking across the fields in the direction of his troops.

'At the north end of the village,' he said, 'there is a large, red-bricked house with a broken white front gate. The house is empty. You'll be perfectly safe there.'

'For how long?'

'That depends on you, Fräulein.'

'On me?'

'Entirely. You will be perfectly safe in this house, Fräulein. You have my word. Just wait fifteen minutes, and then go. But if you try to go anywhere else, you will not succeed. The area is crawling with our soldiers. You would not get another hundred yards.'

'Thank you.'

'My pleasure.'

The captain suddenly smiled. Their eyes met and held for a brief moment, then the officer inclined his head to her once more in a half bow, before straightening himself up in answer to a distant call from one of his men.

'No!' he shouted in his native tongue. 'Nothing at all! There is no one here! They must have all gone the same way!'

Then he was gone, quickly and as quietly as he had arrived, leaving Meggie, her heart still pounding with the impact of having faced death and somehow, heaven only knew how, having got off.

'That's one life down, eight to go, Bad Man,' she said, sending David a message up to the heavens, and God a silent thanks, because interesting as being shot might have been, it would mean that she would not be able to meet up with 'les chaps' as she called her two commandos.

Later she sat in the corner of a downstairs room in her supposedly safe house, which she had found with surprising ease. There seemed to be no one about in the tiny village, other than one very old man asleep at a table outside what Meggie supposed to be the only café-bar in the place and an equally old woman tending her vegetable garden to the side of a small paintwashed cottage. The old man had remained fast asleep as Meggie had sidled her way towards the red brick house with the white picket gate, and the old woman had had her back turned to her, and since the entrance to the house was at the back of the building and out of sight of the old woman Meggie had every reason to believe they were ignorant of her presence as she explored the deserted house.

Now as she waited, seated on a pile of old newspapers in a dark corner of a bare room, she realised that she had to decide on her next move. Getting up, she crossed to the window to consult the small but well detailed map of the region that she carried in the lining of her mackintosh overcoat, and outlined what she could only guess to be the best route to the pickup point, having been robbed of her promised guide. But her study of the map also made her realise what a difficult if not impossible journey it would be to make in daylight, particularly if what the German officer had told her was true, and the area was crawling with enemy patrols. There seemed to be plenty of cover in the way of woods and farms on the way to the coast, but there were too many roads that had to be crossed and no apparent way of avoiding them, not if she was to take the quickest route. Meggie knew the ropes too well by now; five minutes the wrong side of the right time at the appointed rendezvous and the rowing boat coming in to pick up her party off the beach would be gone—that is, if the two soldiers in her charge were still alive.

None the less she felt it her duty to try to make the rendezvous in case the commandos had indeed survived, either injured or uninjured. Since she was alive and in one piece, Meggie felt that she should not write her responsibilities off until she knew the exact state of play, which meant she had to make it to the appointed beach.

But risking her life unnecessarily could prove to be counter-productive. Even if the commandos had escaped unscathed from the German hunting party, since Meggie had become detached from them, they would have to find their own way to the beach. If they did manage to do so, then their instructions were to hide until the rowing boat arrived to pick them up and carry them back to the waiting rescue craft.

Searching for a cigarette, she found she had one half-smoked stub left. Carefully turning away from the window, she lit the stub and sat herself down once more with her back to the brown-painted wall. As she relished the last of her smokes Meggie allowed her thoughts to drift back to her pre-war life in London. She saw herself dancing at the Savoy with David, dressed in her favourite green silk evening dress. So immersed did Meggie become in this gorgeous memory that she did not observe the two men creeping up to the window behind her.

*   *   *

Rusty found that she had to report for duty at the balloon-making factory at six forty-five p.m., prompt. Once she had been kitted out with her uniform and scarf and all that, the factory forewoman told her that in future she need only report at ten past seven, which since it was quite a walk from her digs in the town to the factory was a bit of a relief. What was not a relief was the realisation that she, and everyone else of course, was expected to put in a twelve hour shift. It seemed it was the only way if they were to keep up production.

The first thing that struck her amidships as she started to cross the factory floor, following the young woman in whose charge she had been put, was the noise. For a girl brought up in Bexham, used to sailing for hours on end all alone, the racket was almost unbearable.

Noise, noise, noise, and noise of such intensity that it seemed to Rusty that she would not be able to bear it for one hour, let alone twelve. Indeed, despite passing her medical the previous week with flying colours, she even thought she might be going to pass out, and that was before she settled to the work, the so-vital work. Stitching, stitching, stitching. Rusty of all people stitching, Rusty who had always made fun of women who liked to knit and sew and such like, wanting only to run out of the house and sail her boat, run about on the beach, fish and swim, wanting nothing to do with womanly crafts.

'Rusty! I say, Rusty Todd! Here, stop! No, stop.

Rusty Todd!'

Rusty had just begun her break and was sipping the precious, permitted hot drink from her Thermos flask when she heard the voice calling her name. She stared around her, her head already throbbing to such a degree that she thought that had she been in her boat, she would have been able to use it as an outboard motor.

The lavatories nearby were filled with women going in and out, but the young woman who had shouted her name was still discernible, coming towards her at a rate of knots. The scarf knotted on top of her head in the accepted wartime manner at first made her unrecognisable, but as Rusty stared at the face, bit by little bit, it became quite clear who it was.

'Virginia Morrison!'

'Yes. You remember me then, Mattie Eastcott's friend?'

'Course I remember you.'

'Well then. God, I can't tell you how glad I am to see someone else from Bexham. Really I am. I never thought I'd be blasted homesick living twenty miles from the village. God, it is so good to see you. But, Rusty, I mean to say.' She gave Rusty a curious look. 'What made you come here? I thought someone like you, you'd have joined the Wrens.'

'Partly money, partly Dad, partly Mickey, our youngest who we think's gone for a soldier and lied about his age, though we don't dare tell Father. And—you know—if I joined the Wrens, I'd hardly ever get home, so that was out. But I needed to get away from my desk job. Anyone can sit behind a desk, but here,' she nodded back towards the still terrible noise, 'well, we're really needed here, making barrage balloons, and that. It's like Mother says, it's women's work, this sort of stuff. We've got the hands for it, we've got the patience, we can do the job better than the men, and quicker.'

'Rusty. Look. Tell you what, why not come back to my lodgings with me when we finish here? Mrs Grady won't mind, she's Irish and kind, and you can stay with her, I'm sure. That will make it so nice when we go dancing, coming back together in the blackout, not on our own being chased by something that turns out to be an old box, which is what happened once to Mattie and me.'

'But I'm putting up at Mrs Blacker's—'

'Not any more you're not. We'll call by and explain. She won't mind. For every bed that's let at Mrs Blacker's there's another five hundred from the factory queuing up to take your place. No, you've got to come to Mrs Grady, be with me. You'll like Mrs Grady, she makes Irish stew that would curl your hair, and I don't mean in a good way, and has beds with lumps in them, and when you taste her tea and dried cake with cocoa filling and listen to her singing you'll wish you were back on your twelve-hour shift. See you later, eh?'

Virginia laughed, and was gone, back to the unbearable noise, the endless work, the sweat of it all. Virginia of all people who before the war, as Rusty well knew, seemed only to be interested in men and going to the films.

* * *

'Why do you stay there then, if it's that bad?' Rusty wanted to know, following Virginia out of the factory door into the grim darkness of the blackout when they finally finished their shift.

'Take my arm.' Virginia took hold of Rusty's hand and tucked it into her elbow as they walked uncertainly away from the factory towards the town. 'I stay there because when we have our two days off Mrs Grady, like the good Catholic woman that she is, turns a blind eye, and a blind ear, to what time we get in. That is why I stay there. How's your jitterbugging? No, don't tell me. Knowing you, you can't?'

Rusty remained silent, feeling absurdly dull and old-fashioned.

'Well, that's something we'll have to get down to the moment we get to old Ma Grady's house. The jitterbug is not just the only dance to dance, it is the only dance that anyone under thirty is dancing. You have to learn or quite simply you will end up as a blooming old wallflower, and we can't have that.'

Rusty clung to Virginia's arm, following her along the very narrow path that led past the railway, past waste ground, to the town.

'Watch out you don't stamp on anyone's head, or trip on their underwear. This stretch is usually more crowded than the London Underground at night. But still, a girl's got to earn her nylon stockings somehow, hasn't she?'

Listening to Virginia's chatter, for a second Rusty found herself wishing against wish that she was back reading *Tom Sawyer* to her father. She had been frightened that she might be going to be out of her depth the moment she entered the factory. To a girl brought up as she had been to independence and quiet, to sailing with only the sound of the wind, to the cheerful hum of village life that eventually dropped to silence as night came, it had become immediately apparent that, however much she had boasted to her father that she could put up with any kind of war work, she was not going to fit in at the factory. But now that Virginia was going on about nylon stockings and such like—well, she really did know that she was out of her depth, and well and truly so. Just because she lived in Bexham did not mean that she was entirely innocent, but on the other hand going out with men who gave you nylon stockings in return for favours was not something she had planned to do with her life. She thought of David Kinnersley and Dunkirk, of Mickey, wherever he was, and felt desperately homesick. Why had there to be a war? Without a war Tom would be alive, and she would be sailing with him, going out to deep sea fish together, and Mickey would be going into the village bakery which was owned by a family friend and bicycling back with hot loaves from the last baking of the day; and her father would still be all right in his mind, not seated in front of the fire staring ahead of him, useless to everyone.

'Fer chrissakes! Do you mind!' A male American voice seemed, of a sudden, to detonate in front of Virginia in the darkness.

'So sorry, so sorry, so sorry, madam—oh—I mean, yes, so awfully sorry.'

Despite the fracas, and the fact that there might be other bodies hiding in the shadows, Virginia carried on, pulling Rusty behind her, until at long last they reached the main road that led to the town, upon which she burst into fits of laughter.

'I told you, I told you!' She caught Rusty by the

hand and continued to laugh as they ran. 'Oh dear, that is so funny! What did I tell you? That was only Mrs Grady earning her nylons with a GI!'

* * *

'Martine!'

Meggie had hardly been able to believe her eyes; as well she might not. There, alive and well, and looking as relaxed as anyone who had just spent several hours evading German soldiers in Normandy could look, were her two commandos. And shortly after, there was their rescue boat, coming silently into thankfully still waters. And after that, England, and debriefing, and all that, but not, for some reason she simply could not understand, peace, as in peace of mind. For Meggie, after only one drop, was now hooked on an immensely heady drug, and, although she did not yet realise it, one that once it had you in its power was, as with so many drugs, almost impossible to shake.

Once she returned to Bexham, and Richards's relieved welcome, she took care not to let him know that she was intent on returning to France, to do it all over again.

'Champagne, Miss Meggie. Been saving this for you, for your safe return. Vintage too, thought you would like that.'

'Thanks, Richards. Happy landings, eh?'

'So. Back home for good, now?'

Meggie stared past Richards, neither willing nor able to answer his question. How could she tell him about the thrill she felt at actually doing something dangerous and brave, how when your blood was up you found that being so-called courageous was nothing of the sort, it was exciting, dashing, daring, spine-chillingly fascinating; it heightened everything and lowered nothing? She was determined to go to France, again and again and again, and each time she went, each time she inflicted damage on the Nazis, she was doing her bit to avenge Davey, and everyone else for that matter. Victory at any price was what was wanted; anything else was unthinkable. Line after line of agents had already been tortured and shot, and if she was to be one of them, well, that was how it had to be, but until then she could not wait to get back.

Meggie looked across at Richards, the expression in her brilliant blue eyes opaque, unfathomable to anyone who did not know her.

As it was, Richards did know her, had known her since she was a tiny waif-like figure who had been deposited on Madame Gran at a moment's notice. Knowing not just her, but her grandmother, the butler felt a chill run through him as he saw the expression in Meggie's eyes. He knew that look. It was exactly the same look as Madame Gran used to have, and it always and inevitably signalled dangerous times ahead.

CHAPTER THIRTEEN

Within a few days of his wife's heroic death Lionel Eastcott was insisting on going out on fire watching duties again, and carrying on as normal. As an active member of the Home Guard, he was determined to carry on his life as it had been before Maude had been so tragically killed. And to his friends' and comrades' astonishment, and even admiration, he had managed to do just that. If when he appeared for his duties as usual he looked a little dishevelled, where before he had presented, courtesy of Maude, an entirely neat appearance, if his shirts were grubbier and his suits not pressed as they used to be, that was, they all quietly reasoned, only to be expected.

What his friends could not witness, however, what Lionel was at pains to keep from them, was the depth of the guilt he felt now that Maude was no longer there.

He found that not only had he come, far too late, to appreciate everything she had done for him, he had come to appreciate everything he had not done for *her*. When had he ever thanked her for fetching his suits from the cleaners? When had he ever appreciated her kitchen battles with Cook and the maids before the war, battles that had resulted in the good plain cooking that Lionel enjoyed? When had he ever brought her home a bunch of flowers unexpectedly, or offered to drop her at the hairdresser's? When he was not fire watching, or helping out as a volunteer at the hospital, when he was not doing his Home Guard duties, the answer came to Lionel over and over again—never. He had never ever, not once, appreciated what Maude had meant to him.

Worse than that he had scorned her. He had made fun of her to Mattie and her friend Virginia. He had made jokes about women like Maude at the golf club, he had even rolled his eyes behind her back at the maids to make them laugh at her, conveying the impression that instead of being worthy of their respect, their mistress was in fact, in his eyes, a stupid woman. He had made fun of her driving lessons, and then, too, he had mocked her joining the WVS, pointing out, over and over, that the WVS would take just about anyone.

All this had run through his mind, time and time again, but never more so than now as he waited for Mattie to arrive for a rare visit to Bexham. Now that Maude was gone he knew that every time Mattie looked at him it would be with Maude's eyes, that if she laughed he would remember her mother laughing. The evening when Maude had begged him to dance with her came back to him now, as he dusted the records near Maude's favourite little gramophone, a gramophone that he always used to turn off whenever he came back into the room, preferring to listen to the sound of his own voice rather than one of Maude's records.

He stared round the sitting room. Try as he would he had not been able to make it look as it had when Maude was alive. He had attempted to arrange a few wild flowers in a vase on the table that always stood ready and waiting by the couch, but he realised now that they looked stupid—silly even. He had pulled the curtains about, trying to arrange them in their usual confines, tied neatly with silken ties, but his bows looked crooked and untidy, and the curtains the same. The cushions too on the sofa, he tried to remember how Maude had always put them. He thought she always put them not straight as he had done, but crooked, or was it straight not crooked? Now he could not even remember that. A lump came into his throat as he pulled the sitting room door shut behind him.

Mattie would be sure to laugh at his

housekeeping the way he used to laugh at Maude, and with good reason. He was useless, as useless as he used to think that Maude was, his beloved Maude, who had died so bravely, in a way that he would never have believed possible of her. Maude, who had seemed only to love to dance, to drink martinis, to listen to the wireless, had run into a burning building to rescue someone else's family, and then against all advice she had gone back, even after she had rescued them, to search for more possible survivors, whereupon the building had collapsed on her.

Sometimes, in the middle of the night, Lionel imagined that he could hear Maude laughing at him. Perhaps saying, *Finding the going tough on your own, Lionel?* Or again, *Didn't think I was capable of anything much, did you, Lionel, but finally I have proved you wrong*.

Again, this morning, as he hovered about the kitchen checking his list of what to do and ticking off the various items, Lionel tried not to imagine, if Maude was watching him, how she would laugh at his attempts to put together a good and welcoming wartime Sunday lunch for Mattie. Since it was Mattie's birthday, he had even tried to make a birthday cake.

He had been able to do this because Mabel Constanduros, the famous wireless cook, had, only the week before, dictated a make-do wartime cake recipe out of flour, syrup and powdered ginger. Not content with this sortie into higher cuisine, Lionel was also proud to be able to serve chocolate buns for pudding; buns made by one of his Home Guard friends from wartime ingredients. Lionel had already tasted one. It was delicious, although he had no idea whether it had really tasted so delicious because it was so long since he had eaten a chocolate bun, or because the recipe, apparently culled from a magazine, had been so clever in its use of its ingredients.

'Mattie!'

Mattie stood at the door. The house still smelled of a mixture of lavender polish, floor polish, and other cleaning materials, as it had done in her mother's time. This surprised her since she knew that her father had no help, for the very good reason that there was no help available now that everyone was being urged to take up war work. Indeed everything was as clean as clean could be, and not a thing out of place.

'How have you managed it, Daddy? It's just like—well, it's just like it's always been.' Mattie's eyes took in everything from two precious oranges arranged in a bowl to wild flowers in a vase and some women's magazines, *Woman's Weekly* and so on, laid out carefully, as they had always been. 'You are clever, really you are.'

Lionel coloured. He had hardly had more than a few hours' sleep for many nights now, but he had been determined, in between everything else, to make the very best of everything, make things look as near as possible as when Maude had been alive. To him, of course, the whole place was a shambles, nothing quite as it should be, but he saw now that to Mattie it was far from being so, and that thrilled him.

'I wanted it to be nice for your birthday, Mattie.'

'Nice? It's wonderful, Daddy. You are such a poppet, doing all this for me.'

'It is . . .' Lionel paused again, 'it is,' he could not

think of a better word, 'it is nice that you could get back, on leave, be here with me, Mattie. We haven't had a Sunday together for so long, have we?' Lionel looked away, clearing his throat. 'How's London been?'

'Well, you know London, always something on!'

Mattie smiled, and Lionel laughed. It was something that Maude had always said when she got off the train after one of her trips to the West End, shopping and lunching with a girlfriend.

'Now sit down, don't move, this is your birthday, and I wanted it to be special for you. Kept my cheese ration for you, all two ounces, so we'll be sitting down to up to five courses, if I have anything to do with it. But first—a gin.'

'Er, Daddy—no gin, thank you.'

'Come on, only a small one.'

'Very small, Daddy. Don't want to use up all your gin, really I don't.'

'Don't you worry. Us old chaps in the Home Guard, we have an indefinite supply, thanks to the Three Tuns . . . oh, yes indeedy.'

Her father hurried off to the drinks cabinet. The familiar tune of 'When Irish Eyes are Smiling' started to play as he opened the cabinet doors to bring out the gin bottle, and the two dancing figures twirled endlessly in the reflecting mirror.

Mattie looked round the room, inspecting it more closely. Everything was, as she had been anxious to reassure her father, just the same as it had always been. The long blue silk curtains, the material that her mother and herself had chosen at Peter Jones, what now seemed years ago. The cream covers, the flowered chintz cushions, the Chinese prints, the mock Chinese Chippendale cabinet, the spare piano stool covered with a tapestry that her mother had sewn in a rare fit of domesticity. It did not seem more than a matter of weeks since she had returned to Bexham by chance and received the news, and yet it was only now that she was viewing each object by turn that Mattie realised just how long it really must be, because, looking round the sitting room, of one thing Mattie was now completely sure. Maude was well and truly gone.

At this realisation an overwhelming sadness filled her daughter, a sadness that she had never felt before, even when Maude had just been killed. She had never truly appreciated her mother until now. More than that, she had never really needed her. Now she felt the need of a mother more than ever before, but Maude had vanished, for ever.

'Cheers, darling.'

'Cheers, Daddy.'

They clinked glasses and Lionel smiled happily at his daughter. She was looking very well, as well as he had ever seen her look.

'Bottoms up!'

'Up the Nazis!'

Michael and Mattie had used to say that. Mattie turned away from the memory of her love affair, because at that moment it seemed as dim and distant as the memory of her mother did not.

* * *

The roast beef that Lionel cooked was surprisingly excellent, the potatoes the same, and if the Yorkshire pudding made with dried egg came out exactly the same size as it had gone into the oven, that was not his fault. No one in Bexham had yet been able to make their batter puddings rise by using dried egg.

'I am afraid I ate my egg, last week. If I'd known you were coming . . .' he turned back and nodded at the pudding lying on the sideboard, 'it might have turned out a bit better.'

'You've turned into a splendid cook, Daddy, better than Mummy. That would make her laugh, wouldn't it?'

'I hope so.'

Lionel got to his feet and began to tidy away the plates, but as Mattie started to follow suit, he pushed her back into her chair.

'No, no, you stay there, darling. I've got you a present, and I have to go and get it.'

He hurried off, leaving Mattie to stare round the dining room this time. This too was the same as when her mother had been alive, but less touched by her absence, perhaps because the dining room is always something of a male preserve. The sepia tints of India before the Great War, the furniture, heavy and oaken, the decanters, cut glass, Waterford. A very pretty claret jug decorated with a delicate silver top, its lid engraved with some unknown cipher belonging to its original owner. The room in which she sat was very much more Lionel than Maude, and that in a strange way was comforting.

'There.'

Lionel placed a brown paper parcel in front of Mattie. He had hand-painted flowers in bright watercolours on the paper, and Mattie recognised the ribbon doing up the parcel, giving it an air of both gaiety and decorum—it was from one of her mother's summer nightdresses.

Unwrapping it, Mattie naturally wondered at the contents, all the more so since it had always been her mother who had chosen Mattie's birthday presents, while her father had contented himself with looking on and frowning at her extravagance. Furthermore, it was wartime, and there were no luxuries—no, as it were, *presents*—in the shops, no frivolities, no lace, no ribbons, no sugar, no clothes, no hats—especially not hats. Everything was rationed, rationed, rationed, and not just her father's beloved cheese, and weekly egg. Everything was in short supply; even orangeade came marked simply orangeade with no maker's name on it.

Of course as soon as she saw what he had bought for her Mattie tried to smile, but she failed. It was a beautiful dress. Where her father had managed to find it she had no idea, but as soon as she saw the look of pride in his eyes, and heard him saying, 'Go on, try it on, try it on—do, you will look wonderful in it,' she could not help herself.

Far from plucking the dress from the box and rushing off to try it on, to Lionel's consternation his daughter burst into tears.

* * *

Virginia was busy cutting the top off a stocking, and at the same time staring at Rusty's head as if it was some part of their factory work, instead of just Rusty's hair, long, thick, red and curly.

'You're a very pretty girl, Rusty, but you haven't made the best of yourself. I mean, a fabulous film star like Veronica Lake you will never be, ducky, but we can make you look a bit better than you are now.'

This was Virginia all over, and if Rusty had not previously made her acquaintance in Bexham, if they had not, for the last few years anyway, stopped to greet each other as they shopped in the High Street or queued for cinema seats or—nowadays—ration books, she did not suppose she would have accepted such condescension from Virginia. But after five days of a twelve-hour shift in the factory, quite frankly Rusty could not have cared if Virginia had decided to shave her head, so willing did she feel to trust her new friend's taste. Now she lay staring up at the ceiling wondering what their two days off together in Plimpton would bring, for in her heart of hearts she really rather dreaded going dancing and such like with Virginia. Virginia was obviously nothing if not fast. What worried Rusty more than anything was that Virginia thought nothing of *earning her nylons*, as she euphemistically called it.

'What we do now, Rusty Todd, is put this on your head. Sit up, come here, that's right. We put this stocking top on your head, and we curl the hair upwards, and don't ask where I got all the hairpins and Kirby grips, and I won't tell you a lie!'

Rusty sat on Mrs Grady's shabby dressing table stool and stared straight ahead of her. She did not care what Virginia made her look like; she just adored someone paying attention to her. It was probably because she had never had it before. Her mother and father had always treated her as either just another boy, or a spare pair of hands. For Rusty, to be treated as a potential woman was something quite new.

'You doing me a Victory Roll?'

'That's the ticket.' Virginia nodded at both their reflections in the three-sided maple dressing table mirror. 'I pin this up all round the roll made by the stocking, which is very flattering. Leave you a bit of a fringe, or *bangs* as the GI Joes always call them. The good thing about the Victory Roll is it saves putting your hair in curlers at night, see?'

Rusty nodded. She did not like to tell Virginia that she had never, not once, put her hair in curlers at night. That she had never done more than just wash her thick Titian locks, dry them, and shake them out like a dog after a dip.

'I've never slept in curlers,' was all she said.

'No one ever *sleeps* in curlers, Rusty Todd,' Virginia laughed. 'The only thing you can do in curlers at night is stay awake. Why do you think so many of the girls at the factory come to work with the blessed things under their headscarves? Because it's better than sleeping in them, and not only that, it's a great deal easier to brush 'em out when you do get home.'

'I hate my curly hair. I wish I had straight hair like yours.' Rusty glanced up at Virginia's classic pageboy hairstyle. It looked as though it had grown on her head unaided, so natural did it appear.

'You wish you had straight hair like mine like you wish yourself a head of lice, Miss Todd,' Virginia told her, handing her a powder compact and lipstick to try out without any reference to the fact that Rusty never wore make-up. 'Thanks to your natural curls you will never have to have a Marcel perm or a Eugene wave, think of that. Besides,' she looked at Rusty in the mirror, and her eyes glinted with the thought, 'besides, just wait until you've been out on the town with me, Miss Rusty Todd. Now come on—time to go to work and turn back what Mrs Grady thinks passes as carpet and jitterbug, jitterbug, jitterbug.'

Having finished powdering her nose and putting on lipstick Rusty looked at herself in the mirror. It would seem that Virginia had indeed performed miracles on her. She leaned forward and stared intently at her own image. She looked, well, she looked really rather girlish, not at all like Rusty Todd, more like—well, more like Virginia, a red-haired Virginia. For a second she wondered what her father and mother would say, but then, remembering how sad everything was back home in Bexham, she winked at herself. Nothing could be worse than how she had been, half boy, not wholly girl. Not even David Kinnersley had treated her as a girl. She turned back to the room and Virginia's chatter.

'Come on, ducky, time to dance!' Virginia caught her hand, and of a sudden it seemed that Rusty really was dancing, just like people on newsreels in London. War it seemed was not all patriotic duty.

* * *

For Judy, that night, though, it was. Driving for the WVS she had clocked up many, many miles around Sussex, sometimes not returning to Owl Cottage for several days at a time, as she found herself in demand for everything from hospital services to transporting much needed forage for livestock. The call for help had come to her late this particular evening, just as she had sat down for the first time for what seemed like weeks and, turning on the wireless, had started to eat a small pie that a grateful passenger had given her earlier in the day.

'Raid on the dance hall at Churchester, many hurt.'

Arriving there a scant half hour later Judy had never seen so much carnage in one small location, and yet like other more experienced members of the rescue teams she realised that it was the sort of civilian disaster that they had all been told to expect, but had not yet experienced. Dozens of young girls and servicemen of all nationalities dancing and enjoying themselves in one small area meant that they did not have a chance against a direct hit. The task of identifying the bodies of the victims was made virtually impossible by the thick cake of burnt dust that had been seared on the skin of their faces by the sheer force of the explosion. In the company of both fire and ambulance services Judy and her team worked ceaselessly, comforting the bereaved and helping the uncertain, feeding and sustaining.

But as she said later to John Tate when they met by previous arrangement at the Three Tuns in Bexham, 'What do you say to a woman who has just lost all her children in such an appalling way? And there are so many who are unidentified at this moment, so very, very many. People at home, quite unknowing, thinking their children are all right, not knowing, because they can't identify the bodies. What do we tell them, and how?'

John was home on leave from a desk job in Yorkshire, and although he was sympathetic, because he had so little time to spend with Judy he really did not want to talk about her work. Besides, she was looking so pretty, her dark hair loose for once, not bundled in a workaday wartime scarf, just caught up in slides on either side of a middle parting. Quite simple, but also feminine and appealing because her hair was long and shining. It was particularly appealing to John, after the really very married, very, very permed ladies who shared his military office in Yorkshire. So appealing that he found himself wanting to lean forward and stroke Judy's hair, but he lit a cigarette instead.

'For some reason it is always me whom they choose to break the bad news to the bereaved,' Judy went on, staring out of the window towards the water outside. The rain had come too late to put out the terrible fire she had witnessed; the mist had come too late to put off the German bomber. It had all come too late—perhaps, she wondered, just like her and Walter. 'The powers that be seem to think that I have a sympathetic face. Little do they know! Walter used to say that large brown eyes always make a person seem as if they are a good listener.'

She smiled and turned her own large, brown eyes once more towards the darkness outside the window, towards the water that lapped the steps of the Three Tuns when the tide was in, towards the places where they had all kept boats as children, sailing off into the wide blue yonder with picnics tucked into the hold, or under seats, towards little coves where they could swim and run about without a thought for anything.

'Mother told me that you heard from Walter, a few weeks ago?'

'Yes. But you know. No leave, all leave cancelled. I suppose he's too valuable, isn't he?'

'He'll be home soon, Judy, I'm sure.'

Judy stared at John suddenly. *Are you sure*, she wanted to ask him, *are you quite sure, because I'm not. I have a definite feeling that I may never see Walter again.*

'It's almost as if I was actually married into the Tate family without having a husband,' she had said some days earlier to Mattie Eastcott, now back living with her father in Bexham, for reasons that the village thought they all knew, but still only guessed at. 'And I can't divorce myself from them, because I am so terribly fond of them all, but, you know, none of them are Walter. I married Walter.'

'But John?' Mattie had wondered. 'He's nice, isn't he? You like John.'

'John is not Walter, Mattie. Although he *is* very kind; and I know that I haven't been very fair on him. As a matter of fact John is so utterly nice, it is almost embarrassing. He's utterly, utterly nice, completely and utterly decent.'

'And?'

Judy had looked quizzical. 'John is just not Walter, Mattie.'

Now Judy thought fleetingly of her conversation with Mattie as she sat opposite John in the crowded pub. Due to the noise of the other drinkers, most of whom seemed to be naval officers and sailors on leave, it was difficult to have a sustained conversation, but that was a relief in a way, because she could see that John really was not that interested in her WVS work, any more than she was fascinated by his desk job in the north, which was just as well, since it was top secret.

'You'll find my mother's changed a bit, Judy,' John said to her as they walked the mile back to

Shelborne from the pub. 'She says there's nothing the matter with her, but actually we're all a bit concerned.'

'What is it?' Judy asked anxiously. 'Has she seen Dr Adams?'

'You know my mother.' John smiled. 'Doesn't think a lot of doctors.'

'She likes Dr Adams.'

'She likes to play bridge with Dr Adams. As a physician she thinks he's a complete quack.'

'What exactly seems to be the matter?'

'You'll see for yourself. She seems to have lost her famous zest. If only she could get involved in the WI or the WVS or the cottage hospital again, but—and we none of us know why—about a fortnight ago, she suddenly stopped all her usual activities and took to her bed; only comes down now in the evenings. Dad is not allowed to play his piano, nothing like that. The house has to remain quite silent. She says it's in case of bombs, that we must listen out for bombs, but it's not that at all. I've watched her; she seems to flinch if someone so much as shuts a door. It's as if everything hurts her, or as if she thinks everything is going to hurt her.'

'Or as if someone turned off a switch in her somewhere,' Hugh said to Judy later, after Loopy had retired to bed having hardly uttered to Judy, or anyone else.

'Perhaps she needs iron. Quite a lot of people do at the moment. I have a good contact, I can get her iron tablets, if you think that would help?'

'Could you, would you?'

Hugh looked almost pathetically grateful as Judy got up to take her leave. Judy was not sure whether his gratitude was based on the idea that iron tablets might give Loopy back not just her zest for life but her personality, or whether it was because, despite Judy's being a member of his family now, he really rather preferred to be alone with John and Dauncy, the all male household, able to talk about male things, not having to be distracted by a woman.

She herself felt relieved, despite the blackout, to be able to walk home to Owl Cottage quite alone. As usual she went the back way, via the church, and then up to the right, following the ancient pathway that led to the row of cottages whose very aspect somehow, no matter what had happened during the previous days and nights, always gave her hope. The ancient thatched roofs, the crazy paving paths that ran round the front gardens that grew both vegetables and flowers, the sound of the old brook that ran on the other side of the tiny country road—it was all so reassuring. She pushed open her front gate, and taking out her key and flashing her small torch she went quickly and expectantly up to the front door. Sometimes when she put her key in the latch she imagined that she heard Walter's voice from inside calling to her, which was ridiculous, because he had never called to her from indoors, not once. Why should he, since they had only ever had twelve hours at Owl Cottage together? At other times she thought she could hear him laughing and talking, and she hurried through, hoping, always hoping that as she closed the door behind her she would see Walter in front of her, perhaps reading a book, or just 'slouching' as he loved to call sitting and thinking. Tonight, before pulling down the blackout blinds, she shone her torch on the table in front of the blue-covered sofa. There was a note on the table. She picked it up.

Mrs Tate, you were out, but a telegram come, so I took it for you. Next door when you want it. Dora Niven.

No one in the war was ignorant of what a telegram meant, most especially not a young newly married woman. It meant that in all probability she was now a widow.

* * *

Of a sudden the tables were turned and Judy knew what it was to be given bad news, rather than to give it. And the following morning, having slept not at all, as she went next door to Mrs Niven, and long before she opened the telegram with its carefully phrased message *Regret to inform you Walter Hugh Edward Tate RNVR missing believed killed*, she also knew that Walter's mother must have known, long before the War Office, long before the Navy, just what that telegram would say.

Loopy had taken to her bed in premature grief, because, as happens with mothers, she had already known. She had realised that Walter was 'missing believed killed' long before anyone else, even before Judy, who now found that she almost felt resentful of Loopy's precognition, believing passionately as she did that she had loved Walter enough to have known the same, to have had the same feelings.

Walking up to Shelborne later that morning, her uniform carefully straightened, her face properly prepared, telegram in her gloved hand, Judy tried to imagine that she was just any member of the

WVS preparing to tell a member of the public that their son might not be returning from the war.

But as the ever faithful Gwen, now also in the grey-green uniform and plum-coloured jumper of the WVS uniform, opened the door to Judy and dropped her eyes to the buff envelope, and Judy's large, brown eyes gazed steadfastly ahead, not all her WVS training, nothing, could stand her in the sort of stead for which she might have wished. The fact was that she did not have to say anything, and in some ways, as she walked past the silenced Gwen, Judy knew that it would be the same when she walked into the drawing room, the room in which they had all been so happy that weekend just before the war, when the piano had been played so joyfully, and Hugh and Walter had sung a duet of Walter's boyhood favourite from *HMS Pinafore*: 'We sail the ocean blue, and our saucy ship's a beauty . . .' The room where she had danced with John, and Walter had teased his elder brother that he had a crush on her. That had all happened, and, like Walter, all of it was now missing—believed dead.

Now the piano would remain silent, perhaps for ever. Now Walter would no longer be seen, so dashing and handsome in his naval uniform, waving to Judy from the garden. Nor would there be enough gaiety to fill a thimble, let alone the room in which she now stood listening to Hugh sobbing, as upstairs Loopy lay silent, inert, a graven image unmoving in her awful grief.

* * *

No telegram had arrived for Virginia's mother, the

former fast Gloria Bishop, scourge of the tennis club in nineteen twenties Bexham, nor indeed for Rusty's mother and father. While other parents and relatives who lived much nearer to the dance hall had searched in vain for their children and loved ones, while boyfriends who had turned away for what had seemed to them only a minute or so to go outside for a cigarette, or a breath of fresh air, now faced the horrors of the morgue, and the sometimes worse horror of everlasting guilt, neither the Todds nor the Bishops knew anything of Rusty and Virginia's escape.

Nor would they ever know, Rusty thought to herself as, together with Virginia, she returned to the site to try to help the ambulance and fire services. The Todds, churchgoing and God-fearing as they were, would never understand Rusty's leaving her digs to go dancing *dressed up like a fancy woman*, as her father would have said. And, if anything, the Bishops would understand even less, although for a completely different reason.

If Virginia admitted going to a dance hall and thereby narrowly escaping being bombed, her mother would have said in her husky voice, 'Well, dear, if you do something as common as working in a factory you really must not expect to live!'

So while Rusty and Virginia, together with the two American soldiers in whose company they had left the dance hall only fifteen minutes before, worked alongside everyone else to try to clear the rubble, they both knew, without saying anything to each other, that they would never ever mention how close they had come to death that night, not to anyone, least of all their families.

Once back at the factory, and despite the noise

and the din and the seemingly endless days that they worked, Rusty would run the whole catastrophe through her mind and wonder, over and over, what it was, who it was, that had ordained that she should be spared when so many others had died. It did not seem fair, to say the least, that she and Virginia had left the dance hall to go to the common with their jitterbugging partners and thereby ended up alive, when so many, perhaps far more virtuous, less forward girls, more innocent girls, and their partners, were now dead.

Of course Virginia liked to make a joke of it, saying many times to Rusty afterwards, 'You have to face it, Rusty ducks, our escape from death was the reward for sin!' but it simply did not do for Rusty.

Rusty knew in her heart of hearts that, fortified by too much drink and excitement, she had been quite prepared to 'earn her nylons' on the common that night, and that knowledge frightened her almost more than the idea that she had only just escaped being laid out in the morgue by the seemingly stoic rescue teams.

Let me not to the marriage of true minds admit impediment.

For some reason that she could not name—she could not have even said which play it came from—that famous line from Shakespeare, which she had heard only recently on the radio, kept running through Rusty's mind as she worked her twelve-hour shift.

Soon she would have another two days off, after her five days on, and she knew exactly how she would spend it. She would not be going dancing with Virginia, or anyone else; she would be going home to Bexham. She would be going to see young Mickey's chestnut tree that he had grown in a pot, and so lovingly tended, before he ran away to join up at too young an age, before he broke what was left of their mother's heart. The tree that Richards had written to tell her he had planted on behalf of them all by the green.

'The tree of life we call it now.'

That was what Richards had named it. The tree of life, a symbol for all of them that no matter what, come what may, things still grew, and what was more and what was indisputable was that, despite everything, things were still worth growing.

WINTER 1942

CHAPTER FOURTEEN

Of course the beautiful dress that Lionel had obtained, with such difficulty, for Mattie for her birthday had not fitted her, any more than the idea that his beloved only daughter was pregnant and unmarried had fitted into what he might, before the war, have considered to be his scheme of things for her.

But war changes everything, and Lionel, to his own amazement, as Mattie grew more and more obviously pregnant, instead of being embarrassed by her condition, had become fascinated by the idea of this new life about to burst upon the scene, this new person who would, he imagined, take up all their time, all their interest, and had already done much to take his own mind off his guilt about Maude.

'There, there, never mind, eh?' was all he had been able to say to Mattie as she had tearfully confided the news of her pregnancy. 'There, there, worse things have happened at sea, I am sure.'

What Mattie would never, could never, tell her poor father was that she had become pregnant quite deliberately. For Mattie to have made a mistake would be, in time of war especially, understandable. After all, the whole of Bexham was rife with rumours of how so-and-so had succumbed to what was known, euphemistically, as 'the prevailing disease' by being given a 'fright' in an Anderson shelter. Or of how such-and-such had been led, quite falsely, to believe that some GI would marry her, but had, to her amazement, instead been left holding the baby with no wedding ring in sight. No one but no one, it seemed to Mattie, had of late become pregnant on purpose—except Mattie.

Mattie had not just wanted Michael's baby, she had longed to have his baby, and that night at the old inn she had prayed that she would become pregnant by him. But now—it was so different. Now that she was actually having it, now that she was nine months into her pregnancy, she was, she had to admit, dreading the birth. The idea of having a baby was one thing, the actuality of it was quite another.

However, vast though she might now be, she still felt the need to what her father always called 'titivate'. She picked up her bath towel, and letting herself out of the house she proceeded to walk, albeit slowly, towards the main part of Bexham, passing the harbour and the inlet. The familiar sights of the village were still much the same, the flint-encrusted buildings, the sign of the Three Tuns swinging in the wind, and in her present state of dread they were pleasantly reassuring. Even the new sights, the barricades and the coils of barbed wire, were not without comfort, compared to the anticipated ordeal of the birth.

Since she was going to the hairdresser's, she was taking some knitting with her as well as her own towel and some liquid soap, soap that she had managed to obtain through a friend of her father's, someone in the Home Guard who had some kind of private access to the precious commodity.

As she walked along in her pregnancy coat, made from an old blanket once belonging to her mother cut out into an A shape complete with a fur collar and fur trimmed cuffs, Mattie noticed Rusty Todd, also carrying a towel, and walking smartly towards Virginia Morrison's new hairdressing salon. Ever since the bombing of the dance hall, not only Rusty but Mattie's old friend Virginia had shown a marked reluctance to return to the all important manufacturing of barrage balloons. And although no one else knew how close they had both come to death, it was not just the Todds and Virginia's mother who were glad to see them return to Bexham—the girls themselves were more than relieved to go back to other wartime occupations. Virginia, having returned with more nylon stockings than anyone in Bexham had ever seen gathered in one place, had needed no urging when several friends had begged her to open a much needed hair salon, because no one could now be certain of driving to Churchester and back without the kind of undue incident which might make a perm or a Marcel wave seem just a little too costly.

'Go on then, if you want new for old, send your wife to Churchester to have a perm!' was the joke that passed as being only fairly humorous in the Three Tuns, particularly since one of the buses to and from the town had been hit, with a resulting complete loss of life.

So now, meeting up with Rusty, Mattie paused before going on her stately way.

'Going the same way as me? We can shout our gossip over the sound of the hairdriers, and shock the village,' she joked. They both turned as they saw Judy Tate approaching Virginia's from the other side of the green.

Judy smiled, her eyes avoiding Mattie's very

pregnant state and concentrating on her face, for many reasons, the main one being that each time she saw Mattie looking both beautiful and blooming in her present condition, she felt a terrible stab of jealousy.

'It must be something in the air. We all want our hair done today, and it's not even Friday,' Mattie went on gaily, because of a sudden it seemed to her that there was no war on, and she was not going to have a baby any minute. It was just a fine winter day in Bexham, and they were all going to the hairdresser's. With only a little bit of effort she could imagine, with no sirens going, and a wintry sun above them, everything was just normal. Only the fact that they were all taking their own towels to the hairdressers, and their own soap if they could find any, made it seem any different from a day in peacetime. That and the fact that Rusty Todd had abandoned the boyish look and was now wearing a hairstyle that was bang up to the minute for wartime, nylon roll and all.

Whatever their private opinions, they all knew that there were currently two prevailing attitudes to women beautifying themselves despite all the shortages. The first was that it was vain and insensitive to think of such things as your hair or make-up during a war, and the second was that it was cheerful and necessary for the war effort for all girls and women to look as glamorous as was perfectly possible.

As far as Mattie was aware not only Judy and herself, and obviously now Rusty, but most Bexham women had decided to opt for the Our Women Must Look Glorious argument being urged by the majority of the newspapers and women's magazines, all of which were anxious to point out that to look dreary meant that the war was getting you down, and therefore Hitler and Goering were winning the propaganda campaign.

Look Marvellous For Our Boys was the message that seemed to be winning.

Rusty was aware of all these mixed feelings, but, much as she admired Virginia, and grateful to her as she was for helping her to discover that she was actually a young woman, and not a tomboy, she was quite sure that she could no longer aspire to be the kind of girl that Virginia, before the incident at the dance hall, had thought she might be quite happy to be. Rusty was not willing, or even able, to set about earning herself nylons by 'going out' with American servicemen. It was just not her way. Not that she intended to slide back into being the old boyish Rusty again; that particular Rusty had, thank God, gone for ever.

And just as Mother had now started to go out to work on the buses as a clippie, Rusty started to make secret plans to save every scrap of money that she had earned at the factory, with the intention of building up her father's boatyard again. With Tom gone, and Mickey no one knew where, Rusty set her heart on making new plans for the boatyard, plans that might bring Todd Senior back to life. Her mother might have given up on her husband, and no one could blame her for that, but Rusty now dreamed of bringing her father back to how he had been before the war and guilt over Tom's untimely death had set in. His emotions, felt but not expressed, seemed to have eaten away at him, numbing his ability to do anything constructive except visit the Three Tuns, or fall asleep in front of the fire, waiting for Mother to come back and cook him something hot.

Rusty, freed from her new job in the Food Office for a precious lunch hour, now pushed open the door of Virginia's small, cramped hairdressing salon, and held it open for Mattie. While Judy felt a stab of jealousy every time she saw her burgeoning shape, Rusty only pitied her. To be pregnant in war was just so awful. However, it had its compensations. It was not unusual to see the queue to the shops crammed with pregnant women, all happily clutching the green ration books that allowed them privileged access to certain foods during their nine months. Mattie could not count the times that she had been hauled to the front of the food queues on account of her green ration book. It had become a joke at home, with Lionel quite able to tease her that she had become pregnant simply to get her hands on the precious green ration book.

Virginia, looking more glamorous than anyone could have thought possible and wearing, of all things, a boiler suit, greeted her three customers with pecks on the cheek, and open delight when she saw that they had all brought not just towels and soap, but also hairpins, and even that most precious commodity, Kirby grips.

'You are my favourite customers,' she declared.

Rusty looked at her new friend, and found herself feeling vaguely amazed at the way in which Virginia could look so immaculate. There were no real beauty aids to be had anywhere in Sussex, and yet Virginia's make-up and hair could have done justice to any movie star.

Unfortunately, they had hardly pushed through

the door into the little salon when the siren sounded.

'Oh, thing and blast.' Virginia pursed immaculately red and enviably shiny lips, and glanced at her watch. 'I say, what if we just carry on?'

Rusty knew that it might be all right for the rest of them to take the risk of carrying on, but it could not be so for Mattie. As soon as she heard the siren she pushed her pregnant friend ahead of her and out the back towards the Anderson shelter. Shortly afterwards everyone else duly followed, including the lady whom Virginia had been brushing out the perm. A village woman, she sat down calmly beside Judy, looking as resigned as any housewife waiting for a bus, her hair still in Virginia's home-made curlers.

As the siren continued its long drawn out threnody it occurred to Judy that women would do anything to make themselves feel better, no matter what. Come bombs, come battle, women would improve on their natural assets, which was probably why they were such survivors. They would not go under. They would endure. She had heard that women in prison wiped whitewash off the walls to powder their noses and keep them from shining.

In the event, Virginia, with her usual panache, made sure that none of her customers wasted their time in her Anderson shelter. As she finished brushing out her first customer's perm, she passed on her own beauty tips to her fascinated audience.

'See my lips? They look good, don't they? Well, that's not lipstick, it's beetroot, finished off with Vaseline, which gives a nice shiny effect, don't you think? Eyelashes?' They all leaned forward, deeply impressed, as she lowered her face to them, and shut her eyes and opened them again to demonstrate their immaculate appearance. 'That's burnt cork; eyebrow pencil—same. You *can* use boot polish, but if you're involved in what we will call a close-up with a member of the armed forces, or your Mr Regular, it can prove a bit smelly, at least that's what I've found.'

She gave her usual devil-may-care laugh, and proceeded over the next half hour not just to wash and style Judy's long, shining hair, but to advise on the best way to make face cream out of the most unlikely ingredients, and put perfume into melted down soap to add more glamour to a shampoo.

'There you are, my dear,' she finally told her seemingly expertly permed first customer. 'You're finished; and what's more the all-clear has just sounded. And no thanks to the Nazis I'm only three hours behind in my day, which is a bit of a miracle.'

Back again in the salon, Virginia watched the woman walking happily out of the door with a mixed expression on her face.

'Poor soul, she does so love a perm, she had to have one, nothing else would do,' she said, as she stared after the lady in question who was now sashaying proudly down the street. 'I only hope she makes it home because the poor dear's been here since early dawn and just won't admit she's popping.'

She turned on the wireless and started humming along to 'Some Sunny Day', while Judy waited patiently for Mattie to be washed and set.

'Come back to my house this evening. Come and have Green Ration Book supper, on me.' Mattie was looking and feeling better than she had been for days, and as the other three looked doubtfully at each other she clinched it by saying, 'Daddy's out, so please, all come, will you? We can be quite private, if Daddy's out.'

'We'd love to, Mattie ducky,' Virginia told her briskly. 'Course we'll come.'

Returning to her dull but vital job in the Food Office after having her hair washed and set, Rusty, like the other three, not only felt glamorous, but found herself looking forward to a girls' evening in. It would be most enjoyable to spend an evening somewhere other than her parents' house, or the Three Tuns. At the end of a long day dealing with nothing but filing cards, which were about to be moved to Bexham Library for safety, she duly returned home and changed into the lovely dress that Mattie Eastcott had given her.

Turning round again and again in front of the mirror, she realised that a beautiful dress really did turn you into a beauty, by its cut, by its allure. Mattie's dress made Rusty look slim and glamorous, and set off her Titian hair. It was pale blue with pretty sleeves; the design a little old-fashioned because it was from before the war. Apparently Mattie's father had given it to her for her birthday, but Mattie had not been able to get near it, due to her pregnancy. Rusty shook out her hair proudly. She loved the new look that Virginia had given her, managing somehow by dint of her strange potions to straighten Rusty's curls into a shining bob.

At Mattie's house, Virginia opened the door to her, wearing slacks.

'I say, Mattie, do look—the war's turned Rusty

into a girl, and Judy and me into boys!' Virginia looked thoughtful for a second. 'Just think,' she said to Rusty, 'before the war if any of us had walked down the street in slacks there would have been cat calls and goodness knows what else. Shocking stuff, a woman in *slacks* of all things. And now look, no one turns a hair.'

'The vicar is *still* shocked by slacks,' Judy said, lighting a cigarette. 'Won't have them in *his* church.'

They all laughed. Mattie too, but unlike the others she also gasped. Naturally, because they were all too busy pouring drinks and lighting cigarettes, no one heard Mattie gasp. She hardly heard herself, although a minute later, when she laughed again at something outrageous that Virginia had just said, she found that she had cause to gasp once more. This time everyone in the room heard, even Mattie. They turned first to her, and then to each other.

'My God, Mattie, you're starting, don't tell me you're starting. My God, you are, you're starting. You can't start yet,' Virginia told her. 'We haven't even mixed the second gin and It.'

'Where does the midwife live, Mattie?' Judy asked, gently, as she saw what was happening, and Virginia ran for towels.

'The other side of Bexham, you know, you go up Badger Lane on up towards Peak Farm, past there, and on—oh, you know—' Mattie gasped again. 'You know! Mrs Ripley—Chick Mill—that's her house, except it's not a mill any more.'

At that moment the awful wail of the siren started, its very tone seeming to be conveying only doom.

'Mattie, you can't have a baby here, not without the midwife.'

'I must be early! I can't be. I must be. Blimey, I wasn't due for another fortnight.'

Mattie stared up at them all, calmly. She was the only person who *was* calm, although not the only person staring. Judy, Rusty and Virginia all now stared at each other.

'We'll have to go down to the basement, duck,' Virginia told Mattie, suddenly practical. 'We will, really. And then one of us will have to go for Mrs Chick at Ripley Mill.'

'No, Virginia—Mrs Ripley at Chick Mill, except it's not a mill any more—'

'Oh, do shut up about the mill, Mattie,' Judy exploded suddenly, 'and let's get some more towels, because you really are in need of some!'

Virginia, knowing the house from before the war, quickly organised towels and bedding in the basement, and then volunteered to go for Mrs Ripley.

'See you,' she called cheerfully from the top of the steps, turning round and smiling as she did so.

Rusty looked up at her new friend for a second and smiled. Virginia looked so chic, changed from her boiler suit to slacks and a zip-up jacket, homemade, but elegant. She was now twisting up her hair underneath a scarf and knotting the scarf on top of her head. She kissed the tips of her fingers to Judy and Rusty, and seconds later she was gone.

'I don't know why you didn't book yourself into the nursing home in Churchester like everyone else in the village is doing. It's only cheap, you know—everyone else has had their babies there, and it's everything you could want, apparently,' Judy said suddenly to Mattie. 'The nursing for mums during the war is meant to be better than it has ever been.'

'I didn't want to go to Churchester.'

Mattie could not say why, but having Michael's baby in Churchester was just not something she wanted to do. It was as if, having his baby at home, she could make believe that somehow she and he had been in touch all the time, and any moment now he would come through the door, tall, handsome, American, in his impeccably cut uniform, his smile as wide as the marriage bonds that would always separate them from each other.

Because a part of her, although only a very small part of her, hoped against hope that, knowing she lived in Bexham, one day Michael would come and search her out there, and by-mistake-on-purpose find the baby too.

* * *

Later, once the all clear had sounded, they managed to shift Mattie from the basement to her own bedroom where they made more proper preparations for the arrival, all the time hoping that the baby would make his or her entrance into the world in a nice slow fashion, giving the midwife time to arrive.

'I hear there are no anaesthetics to spare now, not for civilians, so there would be nothing to give her to relieve the pain, anyway, even if she was in a nursing home.'

Rusty tried to look philosophical. She and Judy had left Mattie to try to have some sleep in between the pains, which were still only coming every twenty minutes, and were now attempting to make themselves a hot drink in Lionel's over-tidy kitchen.

'Oh, look, orange juice, how jolly. Let's boil some water and make hot orange.'

As they did so, Rusty asked after the Tates, knowing that in doing so she was really asking after Judy too.

*   *   *

It seemed that Loopy had done her very best to keep some sort of spark burning, initially in the hope that everyone was wrong and one sunny spring day she would look up and see Walter strolling up the garden with dog at heel, cigarette as always in one corner of his mouth, perhaps a bunch of wild daffodils for her in one hand.

But when she could no longer fool herself that 'missing believed killed' did not actually mean lost for ever, she tried to keep the spark alive with other things, at first with prayer. Then, when she thought that God had failed her, she stopped bothering with God, which was understandable, because no one could know what the loss of a son felt like to a mother. This savage tearing of the heart, this seeming irreparable damage to mind and soul. Not God, not Judy, not Hugh—perhaps least of all Hugh who had high-tailed it back to London and the War Office as soon as he could.

She knew it was wrong to love Walter and miss him as much as she did, because, unlike so many other women, she had two other sons. So she thought she wouldn't leave yet. She would wait for Walter's birthday. And she would wait to see Judy again, brave little Judy who was holding the fort at Owl Cottage, still not really able to believe that Walter would not be coming home to her.

As they had embraced, under Loopy's silks and fine wools Judy had felt her frailty, the inner thinness of this valiant, elegant woman. And when she stepped back to look at her better it seemed to Judy that her mother-in-law might have already left for another world, that while her thin, taut body might be present at Shelborne, Loopy herself had, in fact, gone, caught the train.

* * *

But now, facing Rusty across the table, Judy merely said, 'Oh, you know, she's going along as best she might. She has her bad days and she has her good days, but all in all, well, that's the best *I* can say, that she's doing *her* best. John comes home, Hugh's in London, Dauncy's home quite a lot actually because the east wing of his school received a direct hit. Sometimes when I have a little time off Loopy comes to visit me at Owl Cottage. I think that's a comfort, because of Walter's things being there. But it's difficult. And, you know . . . anyway, how is everything at your place?'

There was no time to find out from Rusty just how things were at her place, how they never heard from Mickey, how Tom's memory seemed to fill the house all the more because he remained unburied at the bottom of the sea, how her father's mind now seemed to be actually wandering, and sometimes when she went in to see him of an evening he appeared to think that she was her mother, and at other times that it was before the war. How he spoke to her in different voices—sometimes in the deep seafarer's tones of the former strong, confident man with his own boatyard, sometimes in the pathetic voice of an old man, and how confusing it all was, and how she longed to make it all different. There was no time for all this because from upstairs there was a sudden loud cry. Mattie was, it seemed, not only awake but this time bearing down, her baby about to make its appearance, and not a sign of Mrs Ripley of Chick Mill, or any other place.

Before leaving, Virginia had carefully laid out scissors and cotton, and written instructions, but faced with the reality of a birth both Judy and Rusty wished that Virginia herself, who always seemed so unflappable, so redoubtable, was there, rather than just her instructions on a piece of paper.

'It says here we must boil the scissors—I'll go and do that.'

Rusty rushed out of the door, not just because she realised, as Mattie gasped and swore, that cutting the umbilical cord might be imminent, but because she could not wait to get out of the room anyway. Childbirth did not frighten her, it terrified her.

'And bring some more towels!'

Rusty flew down the stairs as fast as she could. God, having babies was almost as bad as Dunkirk, perhaps worse, since there was no Mr Kinnersley there to reassure her in his deep voice, no man there as it were to conduct proceedings from the helm.

However, no sooner had Mattie yelled out once again to her Maker for a new and terrible strength to cope with the pain she was enduring than Lionel, coming off his fire watching, sea watching, all seeing duties with the Home Guard, fitted his key into the door of the house, only to be greeted as he opened the door by the worst scream that Mattie had yet let loose.

Lionel knew nothing of childbirth except that there always seemed to be a great need for boiling water, so on hearing his daughter's quite terrifying scream he thought he knew at once not only what was happening, but what was wanted, and went straight to the kitchen and started to boil water. He knew from the lack of ordered sound upstairs, the constant drumming of female feet as they rushed to and fro, that there was no midwife, as yet, present, and that being so there would be nothing to relieve poor Mattie of the awful pain. Even though all the major anaesthetics had to go to relieve the war wounded—and whatever pregnant women were, or were not, they were not that—most Sussex midwives, although not equipped with anything sophisticated, travelled about with their own pills and potions.

As he watched the kettle coming to the boil, more slowly than it seemed it had ever done, he realised that he was in a state of mind that was somehow frozen. It was exactly as if it was not really him standing watching the kettle, and as if the kettle was not really going to boil. While this sense of unreality floated through his body, a much darker sense of reality marched through his head, and it seemed to him that all he could hear was his own voice, when he returned from the Three Tuns, just after Mathilda was born, saying complacently to the nurse, 'Well, that wasn't too bad, was it, Nurse Miller?' and wondering why, in return, Nurse Miller had given him such a very cold, very pitying, and very old-fashioned look.

Ever tried having a baby, Mr Eastcott?

But now it was not Nurse Miller speaking, but a really very lovely-looking Rusty Todd standing in front of Lionel waiting for him to hand her the kettle, before she shot back upstairs with it.

'No, Rusty, as a matter of fact I haven't. I believe it's too painful for men to have babies. Besides, as I now know, men are far too cowardly. As my wife used to say, if it were up to us to have the babies, the world would have stopped years ago. Left to us males the whole human race would stop, just couldn't take it, that's what I think anyway, since you ask.'

Rusty Todd seemed somehow mollified by the humble tone of this anti-male speech, but nevertheless her whole demeanour, like that of Judy Tate, seemed very close to despite when it came to poor Lionel. It was as if, by standing in the kitchen helplessly boiling water, he represented the very worst in the whole male species. Or as if he had made Mattie have this unwanted child, his grandchild, as if he had made her come home and have a baby, when it was truly the last thing that he would have wanted—until he saw him.

* * *

It was not something that Lionel was prepared for, not something to which he had ever even given a thought, the idea that he would have a grandson, that someone would hand him a bundle of laundry which contained a small, perfectly formed face crowned by a halo of dark hair. The overwhelming feeling that came to Lionel as he gazed down at the little chap was that his life had, after all, somehow been worthwhile, that for all the bitterness and boredom that had lain between himself and Maude, for all the constraints and strain, he was now being given a second chance.

He put his finger out and felt the power of life in the small grasp. He kissed the top of the baby's forehead, and after all the horrors of the war, after all the dead bodies, after Maude's heroic death, despite everything that was happening, and even what was to come, he felt able and whole once more. He felt a purpose coming back into his being. Here was someone he could take sailing on the calm summer waters, here was someone he could teach to hold a cricket bat, someone he could guide and understand. His grandson.

* * *

It was a cold, cold early morning into which Judy and Rusty finally found themselves, leaving Mattie and the baby with Lionel.

'No midwife, no Virginia. Strange, that. They must have been stranded up there in them there hills, cowboy,' Judy joked to Rusty as she shivered in the cold of the day that was creeping towards them, the feeble light of her silly little torch hardly making an impression on the ground more than a yard ahead of them.

They groped their way along the narrow path that led back to the main part of the village in silence. Of a sudden Rusty found that she was really looking forward to telling her mother that she had helped to deliver a baby. Judy was looking forward to telling John Tate the same thing, when he next came home on leave. She thought it might interest him in a way that nothing else she said did. She was also, as always, looking forward to going back to Owl Cottage, hoping, praying that she would somehow, against all the odds, find Walter there waiting for her. It was a ridiculous fantasy of hers, and one that she re-enacted every day. Perhaps because there were no funerals for those who were missing believed dead, Judy could not get over the idea that Walter would come back to them, that he would prove the authorities wrong, that he was not missing and dead, but missing and alive.

Only Loopy Tate's despair in the middle of this awful war defeated Judy's optimism. Seeing her mother-in-law nowadays was not something to which Judy could look forward. It was not something to which anyone could look forward, and when she parted from Rusty, finally and thankfully arriving outside the front door of Owl Cottage, she was so tired, so fagged out, that she could have sunk down and fallen asleep on the doorstep. Instead she found a note from Dauncy tucked into the old brass letterbox.

* * *

'I think she's taken the pills that Father gave her, Judy!' Dauncy looked both much older and much younger as he stared at Judy, white-faced. 'I went in to take her a cup of tea, and I just can't wake her.'

'Why the hell didn't you call an ambulance?'

Judy heard herself demanding, despite knowing at once that the look of anger on her face was frightening the younger boy.

'I can't, Judy, I couldn't, because, you know, Gwen—she told me . . .'

He looked over towards his mother's maid, who nodded encouragingly for him to continue.

'Gwen told me, if Mother has tried to do something, she'll—you know—she'll be put in prison, that's what she said. You know that is the law, Judy. Even though she's still alive, they will put her in prison if she's tried to take her own life.'

Judy stared at Gwen, embarrassed and grateful at the same time. My God, she had quite forgotten. Or perhaps she had never known. To make an attempt on your own life was a serious offence, a crime. She closed her eyes momentarily, putting out her hand to Dauncy's shoulder.

'Oh, Dauncy, I am sorry. Of course, of course, you did quite right.'

'She's still breathing all right, that's why I sent Gwen with the note, she won't tell anyone. And anyway, she knew already. She knew what Mother has been like, not herself at all, just lying about upstairs, hardly eating, never coming down. I've been glad to go back to school, I tell you, I have.' Dauncy's tone was almost bitter.

Judy followed Dauncy upstairs as he continued to relate the facts. Loopy was still breathing. Her pulse was slow. He just could not wake her, that was all.

Judy went into the room. The curtains were drawn. The place smelt unaired, not at all like a room which the elegant and fastidious Loopy would inhabit. Not only that, but with Hugh's bed still primly made, and Hugh spending more and more time in London, not coming home even at the weekends—perhaps wanted for his duties at the War Office but perhaps also trying to escape the utterly wretched sight of his wife falling to pieces with grief—it was as if Loopy was already widowed, which knowing the exigencies of war she might well yet be.

'What shall we do, Judy? I tried to move her but I was afraid I might drop her,' Dauncy told her, digging his nails into his hand with anxiety.

Judy leaned over the bed. Loopy looked dreadful, her face un-made up, her hair dishevelled, all glamour gone, and there was a strange scent pervading the pillows upon which she lay. Judy leaned down, lower and lower, until she could smell the older woman's shallow breath.

'It's all right, Dauncy. Your mother's going to be all right. She's not dead—just dead drunk.'

* * *

It took many visits to the bathroom, much black coffee and continual dragging up and down the bedroom, forcing her to walk, but finally Loopy came to, and seemed able to understand where she was, and who they were, and so Judy and Dauncy, convinced that she was fully conscious at last, put her in a chair, and sat down themselves.

Silence reigned. It was as if everything they had ever thought or said had escaped them, and they could think of nothing. All ways of expressing their emotions seemed to have finally flown from both of them. Besides, Judy thought miserably as she stared ahead of her, what was there *to* say?

'Are you all right, Judy?'

Dauncy was staring at her, a worried expression on his face, as Judy lurched forward suddenly, putting her head between her knees.

'If you wouldn't mind fetching me a glass of water, please, Dauncy?'

She wanted to shout, *No, I am not all right! There is positively no reason for me to be all right. It's almost a day since I have had time to eat, not that that would matter if I had not had to deliver a baby, and resuscitate my mother-in-law, so, no—I am far from all right*, but instead she took the glass of water from Dauncy when he returned, sipping at it, still keeping her head between her knees, before finally straightening up and glancing towards Loopy.

'Where am I?' Loopy asked suddenly of both of them. 'I'm not drunk, am I?' Judy and Dauncy looked at each other.

'*No.*' They both told her at once, unable for some reason to bear to tell her the truth.

'No, you're not drunk, Loopy, you're just lonely,' Judy heard herself saying. 'So. You and Dauncy, you're coming to Owl Cottage to stay with me for a while. Gwen can keep the house dusted and looked after for you, but you both must come to me.'

'I don't want to come to you. I want to stay here, and wait for Walter.'

Judy went across to her, and taking her hand she said, 'Walter's missing, Loopy, but if he should ever not be missing he won't come back here, he won't come to Shelborne, he'll come back to Owl Cottage. That is his home now.'

Loopy looked up at her daughter-in-law and tears fell from her large eyes.

'Yes, yes, of course, Walter's married now, of course that's where he'll go,' she agreed, sounding relieved and worried at the same time.

'Which is why you are going to go there with me, you and Dauncy, and we'll play the wireless, and make jokes, and try to do recipes with dried egg and that awful fish that everyone says no one, but no one, can eat, and all sorts, see if we don't. And you and I, and Dauncy, just for a while, we'll be a little family together, just until you're better.'

Judy turned away, but hardly had she finished speaking when she realised with a jolt that what she was suggesting was really *all she needed*. She actually dreaded the idea of Loopy and Dauncy's living with her at the cottage, but she could not risk any more alarms and excursions. Besides, what she had just said was true. If Walter ever came back to them, he *would* go to Owl Cottage.

* * *

Morning, although always welcome because it brought light, was less than usually welcome that day to Rusty. She had thought it strange that Virginia had not returned to Magnolias, blackout or no blackout, in her usual cheerful flamboyant manner, bringing the midwife in tow, but in war the disappearance of people—and indeed the reappearance of people—without explanation was completely normal. Communications being what they were, after the first months, after the so-called Phoney War, few people attempted to get in touch with loved ones who were gone longer than usual, any more than they expected to hear bad news via anything except the dreaded telegram.

This morning there was no telegram, only the stoical expression of Judy calling in her WVS capacity to tell Rusty that Chick Mill had received a direct hit and that Virginia and all the Ripley family had been killed.

'The pilot crashed. He was killed too, if that is any comfort.'

Judy stared out of the window. Perhaps the pilot, like Walter, even if he was a German, had a mother, and a young wife. Perhaps, poor young man, he had gone to do his duty for his country, unable to do anything else, because that was war.

Rusty knew not to cry publicly over Virginia. None of them did nowadays; it was just not on. Instead she turned away and she too stared out of the window to the inlet, and in her imagination from there to the sea. Her father was still in his bedroom, still in his pyjamas, despite the fact that it was mid-morning. She felt like running through to him and slapping his face, telling him to get up, that if *they* were all coping, so should he.

'We hadn't been friends very long, not like Mattie and Virginia, they've known each other so, well, for so long, but nevertheless we had a grand time, for the bit that we were friends. She was a one hundred per cent person, Virginia was.'

Judy nodded. She had been to see Mattie already, and perhaps because she had just had a baby Mattie had given way immediately, crying into Judy's clasped hand as if her heart would break. 'Life will have a great deal less gaiety now that Virginia's not here,' she had said, remembering Virginia in the Anderson shelter making them all laugh, demonstrating how to put beetroot juice on their lips and then cover it with Vaseline.

'I just wish there was some good news from somewhere, and then perhaps we could all perk up a bit,' Judy said now. 'Still, Mattie's baby is fine this morning, you will be glad to know. So perhaps that is our fair share of good news after all. He's feeding well, and looking far less crumpled. Despite everything that we could do to him, he appears to have survived. She's calling him Max, by the way,' she added inconsequentially.

'Is war always this difficult, do you know, Judy? I mean Virginia; I'd only *just* got to know her.'

'Yes, yes, I know. And yes, I think it *is* always this difficult, and the effects—well, they go on for centuries, at least that is what my mother thinks. Such muddles, and such bitterness, you know. But we just do know one thing, Rusty, we do.' Judy clasped her gloved hands tightly in front of her and her words too seemed to be squeezed hard. 'We—do—know—that—we—have—to—win this war, or all those lives, all the people we have known, everyone, all those pilots, they will all, all of them, have died for nothing. And we just can't let that happen. We can't let anyone, not one person we have known, die for nothing. We have to win for Virginia, for your brother Tom, for Mickey, if he's still alive, for Meggie. We have to win for Walter, who may yet be alive, for little Max who is hardly a day old, for all of them. We just have to win, and if we give in, give way, to tears, to tiredness, to grief, or to sadness, if we get drunk or kill ourselves because we can't stand the pain of it all, we will have lost. So, don't give way. Be like you are now, struggling, but winning. Or . . . or . . . be like Virginia always was—laughing and pretending to be gay even though she knew there was nothing to be happy about. That is the only way.'

Rusty nodded, and turned away. Judy was right, of course she was right.

'Thanks for coming to tell me, Judy. Really, thank you very much.'

Judy left, and Rusty watched her walking down to the path that led back to the main part of the village. From inside the house, from his bedroom, she could hear her father calling out in a feeble voice for a cup of tea. She sighed. Despite Judy's fine speech, despite the fact that what she said was completely true, she still felt like slapping her father's face. Worse than that, because of Judy's speech she felt like slapping his face more than ever.

* * *

What pulled Rusty through the rest of that awful day, walking belatedly to work past the now darkened hair salon, trying not to remember how Virginia had turned her from being what she called 'a blasted tomboy' to someone who could go dancing and be admired, was a telephone call to the Food Office.

'Guess who?'

'I can't.'

'Peter Sykes, remember me—in the garage?'

'Oh, yes, of course.' Rusty tried to sound normal, and interested, and failed.

'The thing is, I—er, I called on—er, Mattie Eastcott, I called on her, and, well, I never realised . . .' He paused, obviously searching for some way of putting his shock at finding Mattie with a baby.

'No, well, you wouldn't—none of us did, not until lately.'

Rusty waved goodbye to someone as she gripped the heavy black telephone receiver under her chin and continued filing at the same time. She was in a hurry to get home and make her father some tea.

'She gave me your number at the Food Office because she said although she was otherwise occupied, you might not be. I mean would *you* fancy going out this evening, just for a drink at the Three Tuns?'

'Thank you, yes, Peter, I would. I'll—er, I'll see you there.'

Rusty replaced the telephone. Anything to get out of spending yet another evening listening to the wireless and reading to her father. She paused, frowning, before she started to lock up, last as always to leave the office, everyone else hurrying home to their tea and the news. She had known Peter Sykes all her life; she just could not remember exactly what he was like. She had never owned a car, but she had often walked past the garage, stroked his dog, passed the time of day. She remembered now that he had gone out with Mattie once or twice, because Virginia had told her, and she knew that his father had died in the bus that was hit on its way to Churchester. But other than that, really, Peter Sykes might just as well be a stranger. In fact she realised that having a drink with Peter could prove most embarrassing. She sighed. It could be more than embarrassing; it could be really awkward.

Perhaps because of this, once she was home and had given her dad his tea, Rusty changed quickly into the blue dress that she had worn the night before. It would, she reasoned, give her confidence in herself the way that wearing slacks and a headscarf would not. However, leaving nothing to chance, as she was now becoming determined never to do, before leaving for the Three Tuns she sat down at her mother's kitchen table and made a list.

The restoration of Light Heart.

That was a good subject for conversation, well away from the war.

The birth of Max Eastcott.

She sucked the end of her pen. She really could not think of anything else that might be cheerful about which they could talk. And then it occurred to her to suggest that instead of spending the evening drinking watery beer in the Three Tuns, they might go to the cinema. There were always queues a mile long for the cinema, far greater than before the war, not just because everyone in Bexham wanted to watch a film to take their minds off their troubles—even the Food Flashes and the Board of Trade fashion films being more interesting than staying at home knitting or talking—but also because of the news, which was always from *somewhere in England*. The film itself was much less important. And although ice cream was now banned, on Rusty's last visit she had volunteered to try the jelly sweets of which the very new and very young projectionist was so proud. Of course they proved to be quite disgusting, and not even better than nothing.

One last look in at her father, sleeping once again in front of two small pieces of dully smoking coke, one last look at herself in the hall mirror, and Rusty stepped out into the night, putting behind her the evening before when Mattie had still been a pregnant woman, and not yet a mother, when Rusty had set out wearing this same dress with her homemade coat over the top, when Virginia had still been alive, and they had all begun the evening laughing and talking at Magnolias.

Judy was right, she told herself as she walked along, winning the war was about not giving in, about enjoying any snatched moment you could, about putting anything tragic that had happened behind you, before it swamped you, as Judy's mother-in-law had been swamped, overcome by the loss of her beloved Walter. She walked into the Three Tuns thinking of all this, and not really thinking of Peter Sykes. After all, Peter had been out with Mattie, and if he had fallen even halfway for her, he could never be interested in Rusty. Rusty was from a different background from Mattie's, and although war had made all that kind of thing a bit unrealistic, old-fashioned, stuffy, yet it was still a consideration, because, as Rusty well knew—which was why she had written out her list of suitable conversational topics in her mother's kitchen—she was still not yet very socially adroit with the opposite sex. She had realised this during her ill-fated evening with Virginia and the American GIs, when, whereas Virginia had been the centre of attention, full of gaiety and fun, Rusty had been really rather the opposite. That was why she had always liked sailing so much. Once out on the briny there was no need for talk, just the sound of the water, the call of the birds, the boat tacking and tacking about. Words were superfluous.

But now as she entered the Three Tuns it was not Rusty whose conversational flow failed her, but Peter Sykes, who, despite seeming a great deal better-looking than she remembered him, on seeing Rusty walking towards him, hand outstretched, had apparently become completely tongue-tied.

'I—er—I—er . . .'

He shook Rusty's hand, the look in his eyes openly admiring of the change in her, but whatever his eyes said he still seemed lost for words as Rusty sat down beside him at the pub table.

Rusty smiled.

'The beer's awful,' he finally finished.

'I don't mind.'

Following his fetching her half a pint of what he called 'best watery', Rusty realised that something had to be done or the silence between them might threaten to become eternal.

'Shall we go to the cinema? I don't know what's on, but it has to be better than the beer.'

'Good idea. Let's do that, let's go to the cinema,' Peter agreed.

As they queued and finally passed the cinema manager—the 85-year-old one with the shock of white hair and white moustache—Peter turned to look at Rusty.

'What happened to Dennis the Menace who used to run this?'

'Called up. Nowadays you'll find it's either the youngest Browning boy in charge—and don't for goodness' sake try his jelly sweets—or it's Grandpa Appleby back there. Only the projectionist is exempt from war service, it seems.'

They had barely settled into their hard won seats when the siren sounded. The rest of the audience, also barely settled, booed and hissed as despite the darkened auditorium the curtains failed to part.

When Grandpa Appleby attempted to clamber on to the stage and warn that there was a bombing raid and they should take shelter, the audience in the now acknowledged tradition shouted, 'We know, we know! Get on with the picture!'

They did not know, of course, where the bombs were dropping, but the truth was the audience had all decided that they preferred to stay and watch the picture rather than be bothered to move. Cinemas had actually been found to be much safer than houses, with the result that some audiences had to be almost forcibly evicted, having shown a marked reluctance to leave at the end of the completed programme.

As soon as the first of the Board of Trade films came up, Rusty became well aware that Peter's eyes were more often on her than on the screen. After the first few minutes it was difficult to even see the screen, such was the smoke now rising from the audience, so she leaned forward in her seat and tried to pretend that she had not noticed that Peter, having lit a cigarette, had put his arm across the back of her seat, which meant that should she lean back it would be round her.

As it happened Rusty did not lean back when the news came up on the screen and item after item went merrily by, stirring stories being made of everything and anything, good cheer pouring out of both the commentary and the images from *somewhere in England*, because she knew that to do so would be to make some kind of commitment to the evening. Finally, as yet another item came up, showing jolly British troops enjoying themselves in a camp, peeling potatoes, waving to the camera, as certain of victory as the audience were not, Rusty found herself leaning forward even further. More than that, she found herself clutching the seat in front of her, half standing in her excitement.

‘Peter, look! Look! See that boy,’ she did not turn to look at Peter, afraid of missing a moment, staring up all the time at the screen, ‘see, look, that’s—that’s my brother Mickey.’

DECEMBER 1943

CHAPTER FIFTEEN

The result of the great battle being fought at that moment near Cassino, in Italy, was not in the forefront of Lionel's mind as he went upstairs to see his young grandson tucked up in bed. He was looking forward to listening to the story that Mattie would be going to read to Max. And whereas formerly when Maude was alive, or when Lionel became a widower, he would have moved his chair close to the wireless to hear the voice of Alvar Lidell, or Bruce Belfrage, read the latest news, now he was much more interested in the adventures of Little Grey Rabbit, and Hare joining the Home Guard, which both Lionel and Mattie joked they probably enjoyed more than Max, who was still a little young for the lively duo.

And yet when Hare fired his sandwiches at the enemy, and Little Grey Rabbit put on her spotless white apron, there was no doubt at all that the Eastcotts felt more secure, and as the sound of bombers passed overhead their world seemed more than doubly precious.

So it was that the importance of the stirring news from abroad did not hit him until much later, when he and Mattie eventually sat down to eat their two sardines with boiled potatoes, and sip their much appreciated tots of whisky, as they both listened intently to the news on the wireless. It seemed that the battle for Italy was under way.

*   *   *

Somewhere in Europe Meggie was listening to the same news as the Eastcotts, but not read by Alvar Lidell or Bruce Belfrage. She was listening to it in German, and as usual wondering how to translate the more ambiguous details.

She had been dropped into France upwards of half a dozen times now, and, as she and Hugh knew but never mentioned, each drop increased the risk of exposure. The more she made contact with the French underground, and strolled about the streets of provincial France, albeit causing valuable disturbances, the more likely it was that she would, finally, be betrayed.

Yet, for some reason that she did not fully understand, of late she had lost all sense of anything but exhilaration. She knew that Madame Gran would murmur, *Your blood's up, darlin', nothing to be done*. And possibly that was more true than she cared to think. Her blood *was* up. She hated the Nazis more than she could ever say. Their reprisals—shooting whole villages in return for the ambush of one of their cars, torturing a local priest, the officer in charge bringing his floozies to watch as the man was slowly put to death—made Meggie more than ever determined to carry on with her work, which was, as Hugh Tate had reminded her many times, *disruption at all costs*.

Some events had proved not just exhilarating, but almost hilarious. Hearing two ambushed Nazis begging tearfully for mercy to be shown towards their beautiful new Mercedes motor car, before driving it, and them, into the sea. Surprising a local Nazi officer in bed with not one but three local prostitutes, and making quite sure to send a photograph of the event back to his wife in Germany. Which, as Meggie remarked, 'might just help to lessen her grief *un tout petit peu, n'est-ce pas?*'

When she looked back Meggie realised that everything would have been all right that particular day, now six months ago—she was posing at the time as a provincial French girl working for a doctor in a local practice—had she not strolled out of the surgery and gone to seat herself in the sunshine in the little square. Of course there were German officers lunching in the restaurant there, but then there were German officers lunching there every day; it was just that this particular day, as she glanced up at one or two who were passing her to go inside, she found herself looking straight into the eyes of the man who, what now seemed a lifetime ago, had refused to shoot her in the Normandy field.

All at once they both knew.

He knew.

She knew.

And do what she could, there was nothing to *be* done.

'Ah, mademoiselle,' he said, pleasantly. 'We meet again?'

'Yes indeed,' Meggie agreed, hoping that the sweat was not apparent on her upper lip, or her hand as she shook his much larger one.

'Why don't you join us for luncheon, mademoiselle?' he went on. 'Yes, please, do, join us for luncheon.'

'That will be difficult . . .'

'For my sake, for *Heinrich*'s sake.'

'That will be difficult, *Heinrich*.' Meggie smiled

into his pale blue eyes. 'You know I have to get back to my job at the doctor's surgery.'

'Ah yes, how *is* the good Dr Ebel?'

'He is very well, a little overwhelmed with all the work—as you can imagine. The children in the village are much in need of vitamins, and they are difficult to get hold of.'

'Come and have luncheon, and I will personally see to it that whatever he needs is facilitated.' He put his hand under her elbow and guided her firmly into the restaurant.

To try to eat while seated between two Nazis was about as easy as trying to eat in front of a starving man. And to make matters worse, the proprietor could not look Meggie, or Martine as she was known there, in the face. Why would he be able to? These were men who would have helped to hand over men and women from surrounding villages to the Gestapo. These men with whom Meggie now shared a table would not just have blood on their hands, they would have torture.

After what seemed to be the longest three courses of her life, watching the older man, his gold teeth flashing in the light of the café, telling a story of catching some of the Maquis and handing them over to the so-called proper authorities, Meggie found herself longing for the friendly little cyanide pill with which Hugh Tate always made sure that all his agents were issued. And Heinrich, who had once saved her life, now also made sure to guide Meggie back across the square, in the full view of what felt like half the town.

From that moment on, both he and she knew, Meggie would be put down as a collaborator at best, a double agent at worst, and her greatest danger would come now not from the Nazis, not from this handsome German officer who had already spared her life once, but from the Underground.

The Maquis would never forgive, could not afford to forgive, a double agent. She would be lucky if she stayed alive until morning. She might as well take her own gun and shoot herself, or swallow her pill.

And yet of course Meggie could not help thinking, as the officer followed her into the worthy Ebel's house, how her Bad Man would laugh at her situation. She imagined him saying to her, *Well, Meggie, you really are in hot water this time, old darling, aren't you? There's going to have to be some pretty quick thinking to get you out of this hole*.

'I can't spare you twice, you know that, don't you?'

The handsome officer in his enemy uniform looked down at her politely, not sorrowfully. They both knew he was right. This was war, and sparing people was not what war was about.

'Of course not. Anyway, I've enjoyed my last meal, so why should you spare my life? And, I mean, you paid for it, which was jolly kind of you.'

Meggie took her hat off and shook out her long, blond hair. This time she knew that she had really had it at last, but reasonably she realised that she had at least had a good long run for her money.

And what was more, and what was better, she had given those bastard Nazis the same—a good long run for their *argent*!

'Why are you shaking out your hair like that?'

'Because, Heinrich, if I am going to die, which I realise I surely am now, I want to look my best, don't I?' She took out a comb and flicked it casually through her tresses. 'Besides, you've really buggered everything up for me anyway this time, haven't you?' she said, jokingly using the colloquial German word, which she knew would shock a man from his obviously patrician background. 'I really must thank you from the bottom of my heart for making sure that you were seen drawing my hand through your arm as you crossed the square. So, really, you might as well shoot me here and now, if you don't mind, before the Maquis do it for you. Anyway, being a crack officer you're more likely to be accurate. I'd rather be shot by a professional, thank you.'

Heinrich did not seem to have taken the point because he said, 'What time does the doctor get back from lunch?'

Meggie stared at him.

'About three o'clock—you know us French,' she said, carefully keeping to her disguise. 'Why? Do you want an appointment?' she added facetiously, determined to remain flippant to the end.

'Very well. You wait out the back, and I will collect you. Your only chance is for me to continue to pass you off as a double agent. Your one and only chance. I am due to be moved to Cologne today. You can come with me, and the Maquis will not find you there.'

'I can't just walk out of my job. Anyway, if you don't mind my saying so, I really don't want to *go* with you, as you call it.'

Heinrich, tall, handsome, blue-eyed and extremely fit, gave Meggie what is called in French '*le regard rouge*', that look that passes between men and women who within seconds of meeting each other know that they could and will please each other.

'You have two choices, Mademoiselle Cool Eyes,' he told her quietly. 'Either you come with me, or, as you say, you are shot by the Maquis and laid out by the good doctor, in the morgue.'

Meggie shrugged, her mind already formulating a plan. If she went off with Heinrich she might at least gain access to more information than either Hugh or herself had ever dreamed of, and that, when it came down to it, might be more positive than being shot, either by him or by the Maquis. The truth was the German officer was right; she did have no real option. Meggie smiled, and putting her hat back on followed him out of Dr Ebel's back door, and so to a whole new history.

* * *

All that *was* now history, and as she sat listening to the same news as Lionel and Mattie, albeit not in Magnolias in Bexham, but in an elegant drawing room in Cologne where Heinrich had found her not only lodgings, but work as a receptionist in a well-known local restaurant, Meggie found herself praying not only for the Allied forces in Italy, but also, perversely, for Heinrich.

He had already been wounded once on manoeuvres, seriously enough to be sent back to Cologne to recover, becoming in the process a more than willing patient to Meggie's ministrations. But on finding Meggie's apartment too bleak to be romantic he had promptly moved her to his own family's apartment, housed in one of the most lovely and elegant squares in the city.

To Meggie this had, at first, seemed ill advised, although now that she was actually living there with Heinrich, his sister Anna, and a large but generally silent household staff, she had to admit that the cleanliness and order of the place, if appealing as both immoral and illicit in time of war, was also comforting; and since Heinrich's father was permanently absent in Berlin, she did not seem to be in any immediate danger.

She hardly spoke to Anna, leaving, whenever possible, too early for Heinrich's sister to have finished breakfasting, and coming back too late for her to be still up. Naturally, once he had moved her to the family apartment, Heinrich could not understand why it was that Meggie wanted to go on working in the restaurant. Meggie sensed that he considered it more than a little unsuitable for someone associating with him, but she nevertheless insisted on doing so.

She had good reason.

First, if the war turned against Germany, as it well might, judging from what they were not being told, she would need some civilian occupation to pass herself off as part of the local scenery. And secondly there was Anna, Heinrich's sister, Anna in whom her brother could see no wrong.

'Anna is a lovely girl,' Heinrich would say.

'A laugh a century,' was Meggie's laconic reply.

Heinrich was different. Despite the war, despite his kidnapping of Meggie—which it undoubtedly was—despite his falling in love with her and her finally falling in love with him, thereby placing them both in the gravest danger, Heinrich loved to laugh. Perhaps that more than anything had finally made falling in love with him so easy—that and war.

Heinrich had never even bothered to protest to Meggie that he was not a Nazi. The moment he let her escape from the field in Normandy, Meggie had known that he was no supporter of Hitler. And, again, the moment he looked down at her and his cool blue eyes met her cool blue eyes in that square in France, she had known that the same thing applied. Just as, the moment she removed her hat and shook out her long blond hair, and the expression on his face turned from one of concern to momentary amusement as he appreciated that like the good agent she was she was using her hair to make him take his eye off the ball, Meggie had known that she would end up in bed with him, and not, if she was honest, just for espionage purposes either.

Worse than that, she suspected that her courage and belief in Allied victory might yet fail her, when it came to having to kill him.

For the moment, thankfully, he was alive and she was alive, and they were both, as people in war can be, in love with each other. Yet despite his assertions that Anna and his valet Klaus were not Nazis, Meggie continued to avoid them as much as she could, particularly when Heinrich was away. She clung to her job, working in the restaurant, and maintained her separate lodgings in the old cheap quarter of the city.

* * *

Rusty had never really liked Dr Adams, not since she was a small child, but now she thought she might truly dislike him, as he leaned forward and putting his head in his hands said, 'Tell me, can none of you think of getting married first?'

Rusty's hazel eyes focused on Dr Adams's bald spot, which she found particularly uninteresting.

'It is just a little difficult, Dr Adams, in case you haven't noticed, to get married when your—fiancé-person—only has forty-eight hours to be with you. Only just time to get pregnant, and *not* enough time to buy a marriage licence,' she ended sarcastically, still hating the doctor as much as she ever had; perhaps even more.

Of course the reason that Rusty felt so particularly unhappy with Dr Adams was that she herself had been horrified to find out that she was pregnant.

She had already seen one birth, and now, having seen it and been terrified by its reality, and having been unable to forbear congratulating herself on not being in any danger herself, she had fallen in love with Peter Sykes, and not just in love. She had truly fallen, for his baby.

'Does your father know about this, Miss Todd?'

There seemed to be a veiled threat in the question. As if Dr Adams was saying, *Because if he doesn't know already, just wait until I tell him*.

'I don't think my father knows about much these past years, Dr Adams, but of course my mother and I will tell him. He might even sit up and take notice a bit more if there is a squalling baby in the house, who knows?'

Rusty sighed. She knew that Dr Adams abused his position as a medical man, taking gifts from under the counter, queue jumping at any opportunity, and making sure that everyone in Bexham was in his thrall, and therefore quite likely to be putting him in their wills too. And goodness, were wills important in wartime!

So, with a bit of luck, Dr Adams might even make more money than some of the counterfeiters, thieves and arms makers who would end the war far richer than they had ever dreamed possible. Because, it had to be faced—and having seen life from behind a desk in the Food Office, Rusty was well aware of this—there was still a double tier of people in Bexham, the haves and the have-nots. It was just that they had all changed positions since war was declared. The people who plundered buildings and shops after a bombing were the most despicable, of course, but there were others nearly as bad, and Dr Adams was one of many. He would not be found giving up his rations for some poor child, he would not be seen collecting week in week out for the Penny a Week fund, he would not even busy himself all day and all night at the hospital as other doctors in the village were doing. No, Dr Adams was always 'called out', and the name of the lady who was always 'calling him out' was all too well known in Bexham. It was obvious that he was in such a filthy mood this morning because, for once in his life, he had actually been found in.

'Been a bit sick, have you?'

'Could say. Bit of a waste of my egg ration this morning, let's put it that way.'

'Putting on weight?'

'What do you think? I'm certainly not taking it off.'

Such stupid questions. Dr Adams always asked such stupid questions. It was as if by asking stupid questions, which you could only answer stupidly, he could prove to himself just how stupid his patients really were, and therefore justify his neglect of them.

To take her mind off the questions, and his form filling and chit chat about orange juice and green cards, Rusty remembered the night she had walked back to Peter's house with him after seeing Mickey on the newsreel. It had been one of the high points of the war, seeing Mickey, after that awful twenty-four hours, with Mattie's baby being born, and Virginia being killed. It seemed to her that there was a God after all, and that He really had looked down on her and smiled, because like it or lump it, Mickey had always been her special brother, and not just because he liked sailing.

Peter seemed to feel the same sense of euphoria and they both ran through the darkness, laughing and talking, so that by the time Rusty pushed in after him into his house, and they were floundering about in the darkness trying to find some candles and matches because he had no light bulbs left, and anyway they were in terribly short supply, she could not believe that before setting out that evening she had sat down in all solemnity and made out a list of subjects for her and Peter to talk about.

He was the easiest person in the world to talk to, and, it had suddenly seemed to her, after a shot or two from his treasured whisky bottle, the most sympathetic. She told him all about Mickey disappearing and Mother and her having to pretend to Father that they were hearing from him every now and then, but actually faking the letters to read to Father. It was strange to think that all the time both of them had been resigned to the fact that not only was Tom lost to them, but Mickey was too.

And yet Mickey had been alive—and not just alive but up there on the screen, *somewhere in England*, laughing and waving to the camera. It did not matter now that he had never got back in touch with them; it did not matter that he might never have given a thought to the worry that he had put Mother and herself through. All that mattered was that, like his chestnut tree, Mickey was alive, and perhaps even, like the tree, blooming.

Of course in telling Peter all this, in confiding in him, inevitably Rusty realised that not only was he now a friend, but he was very probably, before the night was out, going to be her lover too.

It was not difficult to make love during a war. Why would it be? With guns and sirens breaking the normal silences of everyday living, with a heightened awareness of life's being all too sweet because it was all too short, with everything and everyone being taken away, and only sometimes being sent back, with the news either getting worse, or getting better, what—against all that—was a little lovemaking?

And besides, Rusty wanted to make love with Peter because she could tell that he was bowled over by her, that, as he said, her transformation from tomboy to film star was so complete that when she walked into the Three Tuns, if it had not been for her red hair he would not have known her as the girl who had stopped to talk to him now and then when she passed his garage with her dog before the war.

What surprised Rusty was not that they made love, but that it was so easy to make love, that making love was not nearly so complicated and difficult as she had always imagined it when she had a crush on Mr Kinnersley. What surprised her even more was that she became pregnant just as easily as she had made love, and having made the discovery, had found that she had no idea at all how to find Peter to tell him. It could not of course be kept a secret from everyone in Bexham, but it seemed that, as far as Peter was concerned, it was going to prove to be just that—a secret, until such time as he came back, which she prayed every night that he jolly well would. Peter must come back. He had to come back, to her, and to whoever she was now expecting.

* * *

Meggie's secret was different. The reason she was insisting on working in the restaurant was so that she could continue to pay the rent on her original lodgings. There she had constructed a small but effective radio transmitter which Heinrich had given her, just before he moved her into the family apartment.

'You may need this in the days to come, and I might not be here, in fact I will most probably not be here,' he told her, casually. 'I don't want to think of you alone, not knowing. You might be cut off from everything and everyone, but this way you will be able to get messages out to whoever you need to.'

Of course he knew that Meggie would be using it for all sorts of purposes long before he was called back to his regiment, and that she would, at some point, have to disappear.

But since he was no Nazi, it seemed that he did

not care. Meggie was not on his side, but that did not matter to him, as he kept telling her whenever they were alone. The only thing that mattered to him was that she should try to get out of Germany as quickly as possible once the end came.

'It is no bad thing to sleep with the enemy, is it, Martine?' he would joke, and then they would make love again.

It was also no bad thing to work in the vicinity of German officers, who like their male counterparts the world over enjoyed not just their food, but their drink too, and drink, Meggie was not the first person to discover, was a grand lubricator of tongues. Once drunk the Germans became as indiscreet as any other officers, if not more so. Once drunk they discussed their regiments' movements, their lack of belief in their superiors; all manner of things that they should not discuss were often aired over restaurant tables in that café in Cologne.

Besides all this, Meggie's regular attendance serving at tables in the restaurant ensured that she, being easy on the eye, and a natural blonde, captured the interest of the wining and dining German hierarchy, who were always most anxious to tell this young beauty endless stories about the Third Reich and their own courage. How they loved to shoot wild boar, the wilder the better; how they revelled in skiing down dangerous runs in the Alps, adored to jump the most formidable obstacles on their thoroughbred horses. On the way, gratifyingly, she also learned about the deployment of their regiments, the still grandiose military ambitions of the Führer, and Berlin's certainty of final victory over the Allied forces.

Whenever this last boast was made Meggie was

sure that the truth was quite the reverse, that they were all becoming less and less certain of any final victory. Innocently feigning ignorance about the actual state of combat she would find herself happily bombarded with information about proposed future strategies by officers who were clearly more intent on trying to climb into Meggie's bed than on repulsing the Allied forces in Italy.

Of course she was aware that she was playing a highly dangerous game, but then she had known that when she first volunteered to work for SOE and be dropped into Occupied France. She had also known that she was raising the stakes to a very high degree when she agreed to accompany Heinrich to Cologne as his mistress. But none of that mattered, really, compared to the information that she was able to transmit from the laundry cupboard of her lodgings. She understood the stakes all too well, because she was Elinor Gore-Stewart's granddaughter. Yet none of this stopped a cordon of fear tightening around her heart when she discovered one morning that Heinrich had mysteriously vanished from the family apartment, without either saying goodbye to her, or leaving her a note.

No good thinking now that she, a Gore-Stewart, should not feel fear, because not even the strongest genes can overcome human feelings. She had come in much later than usual, and because of that had decided not to disturb him, creeping to the spare room that she used as her dressing room, and falling thankfully asleep at last, only to wake up and find that he was no longer around. Not just him, but everything to do with him. His uniforms, packed and gone, his shaving brush, shoes, boots;

everything had gone, including a photograph of his mother that he always kept by his bed.

'If you're looking for Heinrich, you will not find him.' The voice came from a large, winged armchair. 'He left early this morning, didn't he, Klaus?'

Anna glanced over towards Heinrich's manservant, Klaus, who was busy laying an immaculate tray of coffee on one of the tables. He nodded, before straightening up and glancing back at Anna. It was as if they too had a secret. The look between them seemed to confirm it.

'Any idea where he might have gone?' Meggie asked idly, as she helped herself to coffee, or what now passed as coffee. 'I was asleep when he left. He usually leaves me a note.'

'How odd that this time he did not.' Anna looked almost complacent. She looked across at Klaus again.

'He is usually so good in that way.' Meggie looked pointedly at Anna, making sure that not just her mouth was smiling, but her eyes too, because although Anna might be humourless, she was not a fool. Meggie knew that she would look into Meggie's eyes and would sense the smallest tension, the least tiny pipsqueak of fear, and Meggie would be finished.

'It is very strange, Martine. Apparently, Klaus tells me, Captain Von Hantzen took a large suitcase with him. So what do we make of that?'

Meggie shrugged her shoulders and managed to look vaguely puzzled, while sipping at her coffee. 'Perhaps he has some important papers in his suitcase, papers that no one else must see.'

'Yes, yes, of course.'

Meggie liked the sound of this less and less, and

she liked the look of Anna and Klaus even less, but there was little she could do at that moment that would not arouse suspicion. She tried, unsuccessfully, not to dwell on all the possible explanations for Heinrich's strange behaviour. What she feared most of all was that he had, somehow, been trapped. Or was going to be trapped, and that part of that trap would involve turning Meggie over to the authorities.

Except it did not somehow seem likely that if that were the case he would have packed an overnight suitcase. That was not the kind of action a man being taken in for questioning by the Gestapo would take. So where had he gone? Back to his regiment? Or sent on some kind of mission perhaps by his high-ranking father? The unaccustomed fear of an hour before had been replaced by the more familiar relish of danger, and so, with cold resolution, she merely left Anna and Klaus to their thoughts, and continued with her day as usual. Hugh and she had always agreed, and everyone at SOE knew, that whatever happened, whatever you suspected might be going to happen, you did not rush, you did not change your habits. You just kept on doing what you normally did.

She picked up her coat, an expensive coat that had once belonged to Heinrich's mother, and let herself out of the elegant apartment, making her way, as always at that time, first to the restaurant. As was her habit, and in case she was being followed by either Anna or Klaus, she changed into her waitress's uniform in the basement, and then, because she always took care to arrive too early to be needed, promptly left again, going the back way to her old lodgings, her coat concealing her uniform.

She ran up the sixty-eight steps to her old apartment, let herself in, and went quickly to her transmitter, out of breath, but determined never to neglect what she saw as her absolute duty to the cause of Victory: the daily transmission of even the smallest detail. Heinrich's leaving Cologne and not returning as always, his simply disappearing, was not a detail she would leave out. Every little aspect of life behind enemy lines at that moment would go to help London to build up a picture of the Nazis' state of mind. Even the fact that Captain Heinrich Von Hantzen might have been called back to Berlin under special orders, or might have been taken for questioning by the Gestapo, was vital.

Living with Meggie who was, with his help, posing as a Frenchwoman born in Strasbourg, and therefore understandably speaking perfect German, was not on the face of it particularly suspicious, and Heinrich, being a high-ranking officer, would not necessarily be under observation, and yet—war being war—he might be, not least since it was he who had supplied her, piece by tiny piece, with all the parts for her radio transmitter.

Double, double toil and trouble was her code warning to London to tell them that she thought she was under suspicion, and that in his turn Heinrich, because he had, of a sudden, disappeared, might also now be under suspicion.

When it came to espionage the most successful device that any nation could use against another was the double agent. Double agents trod a minefield, the risk so high that it was almost incalculable. They were the least likely to be successful, and the most likely to be discovered. Heinrich might be just such.

Having completed her task, Meggie wrapped her coat around her once more and started the downward descent to the street. It was not until she stepped out on to the pavement that she saw the black Mercedes parked at the top of the narrow thoroughfare. Slowly and carefully she stepped back into the protection of the building, realising at once that only the Gestapo could occupy such an expensive motor car. She remembered with a sinking heart that somehow or another, in her flight from France, she had lost not only many precious belongings, but also, most precious of all, her cyanide pill.

She started to re-mount the steps back to her apartment, intent only on destroying her transmitter and any other evidence there might be, when a voice behind her called, 'Fräulein!'

* * *

The Grannies' Charter, as it was called in Bexham, had roused a storm of opposition. The idea that every able man and woman in the country up to the age of eighty must do war work, must put their shoulders to the wheel and work for Victory, was greeted with something close to horror by everyone except the grannies themselves.

Mrs Todd was already hard at work as a bus conductress, so this new government edict affected the Todd household even less than Rusty's pregnancy, during which, happily, her quite evident change of shape appeared to affect her father's state of mind for the better.

Lady Melton was different. She was not just determined to go to work in a real wartime occupation, she actually could not wait—not only that, but she found it most agreeable to be able to tell Sir Arthur that if she did not engage in some activity outside the home, she could be put in prison.

Like any other husband in Bexham, Sir Arthur took the news that his wife would not be in to make his breakfast, lunch, tea or dinner—which with the lack of staff in the village was now expected of her—very badly indeed.

'What are you going to join up *for*?'

His wife's eyes glinted behind her new spectacles. 'I am signing on for the same job as Gardiner. She has found a new and most enjoyable occupation. Not netting—something much more congenial to a lady and her maid.'

By now, Sir Arthur was not listening, too intent on switching on the wireless for the news. Really, he did not know what the war was coming to, his wife going out to work, his wife's former maid going out to work, soon all the women in Bexham would be working, doubtless looking like those propaganda films that the Communists liked to show, with Russian women wielding great sheaves of wheat, wearing dungarees and laughing and smiling, pretending to enjoy their work, of all things. As if that was any kind of reality.

* * *

Naturally Meggie had stopped on hearing someone calling *Fräulein*, because since there was no one else to be seen it would seem more than a little suspicious if she had carried on. Instead she turned, smiling.

'Goodness, you startled me!' she told the speaker in her impeccable German, to which she had added a light French accent.

The large man smiled up at her, his surprisingly small shoe resting on the first of the steps.

'You startled me too, Fräulein. I heard your pretty little feet on the steps outside my flat. Going out much earlier than normal, I see?' He looked strangely important at this, and putting his hand in his pocket he took out an envelope. 'You paid me too much money last month, so I am returning it to you. You are not a rich woman, although very well connected, I must say. Not many of the girls are as well connected as you.'

He looked up at Meggie, a fleeting appreciation of her feminine attributes coming into his eyes.

Meggie took the envelope he had offered her, and continued up to her apartment, calling down her thanks as she went, and adding, 'Forgot my hat, silly me!'

Once back in the flat she set about destroying or hiding every piece of evidence that might incriminate her. It was only when this task was completed and she took out the envelope with her landlord's rent rebate in it that she realised it contained more than money.

Gone to rejoin my regiment, you must fly tonight. Heinrich.

Meggie burned this note too, and tucked the money into the front of the same brassiere about which she had complained to Judy on the day of the 'war rehearsal' outside Peter Jones. The blasted garment was *still* uncomfortable, damn it! Realising that she would in all likelihood not see Heinrich again, and that she might still be going to have to run the risk of passing the parked Mercedes outside, she nevertheless went back down to the street, secure in the knowledge that she had done her duty as far as her orders were concerned. *Destroy all evidence, if at all possible.* It had been, and she had.

'Good day, Fräulein! I wish all the girls were as pretty as you. You fill the eye, do you know that!' a voice called out in a country German accent.

Meggie just had time to think *dirty old man* before she saw the Mercedes backing down towards her, and it had to be her because there was no one else in the street at that moment.

'Ah, good day, Fräulein!' another voice with a different accent called. It seemed everyone today was intent on wishing Meggie good day. 'A little late for our job at the restaurant, are we?'

'No, no, I am not on the first shift,' Meggie answered gaily, smiling, at the same time taking in the black clothes of the men inside the Mercedes, their matching black eyes, their fixed expressions, the way they were eyeing her up. She had no gun, she had nothing. To have a weapon while in Cologne, she and Heinrich had agreed, would be too incriminating.

'In that case you have time for us.' The driver's door swung open, and all at once he stood in his leather coat in front of Meggie, smiling. Well, he was smiling if you could call showing your teeth smiling. 'May we come up?'

Meggie thought quickly of her apartment. There might still be a lingering smell of burning. She would pass it off as burning love letters. She thought of where she had hidden all the pieces of the transmitter, having first taken it to pieces—a bit here, a bit there.

'Come up to see *me*, you mean?'

'But of course.' He was still showing his teeth. 'We have been waiting for you many times here, in the past week, whenever we could. Such a very pretty girl does not often come our way—in the course of our duties, naturally. We spotted you first in the restaurant, and we have followed you here several times, but missed you. You have always left by the time we called.'

'Oh, naturally, just in the course of your duties. Heil Hitler!'

'Heil Hitler!'

'How very flattering you are, gentlemen, but you must understand, I am at the moment . . .' Meggie leaned forward and whispered.

The Gestapo officer looked startled.

'Fräulein! Forgive me! I am so sorry! Of course, we had no idea. We were just so taken with your looks, and seeing that you live in this red light district . . .'

'Perfectly understandable, but you know how it is. If you are reserved for the Top Command, you are reserved. The Führer is insistent that all near to him are clean and healthy at all times. Hence—I am reserved, I am afraid. Nothing to be done.'

'Fräulein! Of course!'

The Gestapo officer was now so distracted that he forgot he was the driver of the car, and stepped into the back of the Mercedes. Meggie turned smartly away, not wishing to add insult to injury by noticing, and hurried off to the restaurant.

She had to leave Cologne tonight.

She just hoped that it would be in time, that Heinrich had told her the truth, that the handsome, kind, sensitive man with whom she had been having an affair was not going to be found to have betrayed her. Ten hours was a very long time. By the time it was finally up Meggie knew, from painful experience, that it would seem to have been a thousand.

INTERLUDE
LONDON, MARCH 1944

In the war room the men were grouped around a large rectangular table lit only by a low-hanging overhead lamp. They sat in silence as they read the papers in front of them. When they were all done, the siren-suited figure at the head of the table nodded towards one of the higher ranking officers at the other end of the same table, who took this as his cue to stand up to address them all.

'As you know, thanks to Operation Fortitude and the information coming from sources behind German lines, we have successfully created the illusion that we wanted, which is that of a super-strong American force preparing itself in readiness in the south-east of England, directly opposite where the 15th Army is positioned. Furthermore, it would appear from one agent's report that there could well be dissension in the enemy ranks as to the final control over Hitler's crucial reserve of armoured divisions in France, sir. The Panzergruppe West.'

'I should imagine that Rommel would want them as close to the beaches as possible, would you not say?'

'I agree, sir. While it seems Rommel's field marshal might prefer to hold them back to counterattack us should we successfully make it inland.'

Someone else in the room now spoke and all eyes turned to him.

'I have to say that in my opinion this information is invaluable as it confirms the apparent success of Operation Fortitude. This being so, the plan is to invade further west.' The uniformed speaker got up and switched a light on above a wall-hung map of France. Taking a long ruler he pointed at given destinations along the coast, moving the ruler to each place as he spoke.

'The plan is to land here—from as far west as Barfleur to approximately Villers, on the five beaches which have been unofficially code-named Utah, Omaha, Gold, Juno and Sword. I think this is a correct procedure. From what we know from information coming out of Germany, this is what Rommel has in mind.'

He continued in the fashion of generals everywhere to make what the Allied forces had in mind sound, as near as possible, like a bit of a tea party, while the figure at the top of the table seemed happy to remain silent until the end, whereupon he remarked, 'However it goes, gentlemen, it is going to be a hell of a long day.'

1944

CHAPTER SIXTEEN

Long before Rusty's baby had started to make its presence evident, Rusty herself was contemplating moving to the next door village, if only for a little more privacy. She had a deep-seated desire to be alone, away from her parents—despite the fact that her mother's arthritis had improved beyond recognition and she seemed happier than Rusty had ever known her.

Rusty would have liked to put her mother's happiness down to knowing she was to have a grandchild, but Rusty was not sentimental like that. She would have liked to put it down to knowing that, against all the odds, Mickey had succeeded in joining the army, and had looked well and happy in the newsreel. She would have liked to put it down to the fact that her father seemed much more cheerful nowadays, and was up and doing of a morning, making tea for Rusty and himself before she went off to her job, but Rusty knew all too well that to sentimentalise in that way would be ridiculous.

The plain fact of the matter was that her mother's arthritis had improved in leaps and bounds from being on the buses. She liked the life of a clippie, the odd hours, the companionship, the sense of freedom, the realisation that she was wanted and appreciated, far more than she had ever been as a mother. There was just no comparison to being at home peeling vegetables, sitting for hours knitting on her own, or waiting for Father to come back from the Three Tuns.

The knowledge that independence had given her mother back her health did nothing for Rusty. She knew she should be happy that Mother was now much more relaxed, that she seemed well able to cope with her arthritis, not to mention her husband, but knowing that in three months' time she herself would become the kind of person she had always pitied her mother for being—the kind of human being that everyone else felt quite free to despise, pity and love in seemingly the same measure—was not making Rusty at all happy.

Of course part of her loved the idea of a baby, because she had always liked small things, but the much larger part of her hated the idea that she would become permanently tied to this tiny person who would, as is the way of things, become bigger and bigger, until finally he or she would look back on childhood as part paradise, part hell, and might even blame Rusty for both states.

Motherhood, Rusty now realised, was all about becoming a prisoner, all about not being able to escape. Besides which, she also had the ordeal of childbirth to look forward to. It might have been easier if she had not already seen Mattie go through it, in graphic detail. If she had not seen how hard it was for a mother, alone, to cope with a fatherless baby. No one to hold your hand when you were anxious, no one to share a drink with you of an evening and listen to the day's mishaps, no one to comfort you with love at night, when you had just been woken for what seemed like the hundredth time. Mr Eastcott might be doing his best for Mattie and Max, but the plain truth was that no grandfather, and no grandmother, could replace the strong shoulder to cry on that a young woman bringing up a child really needed. Someone of her own generation to whom she could turn for support and understanding, for love.

For all these reasons, Rusty moved out of Bexham and into a small cottage in a neighbouring village, which was where she received a letter from Peter.

Rusty dear, when I come back to Bexham, I hope you don't mind but I would like to marry you. If this comes as a terrible shock, I hope it won't. Please forgive this letter, we are on the move SOMEWHERE IN ENGLAND!!! I love you, don't forget. Peter.

The letter was not date stamped, nor was it marked, but it was extremely grubby, although blessedly free of the censor's blue pencil. Her father, who had brought it over on one of his all too regular Friday afternoon visits, looked across at Rusty after she had finished reading Peter's few lines for the sixth or seventh time.

'Bit old, that letter, isn't it, Rusty?' he wanted to know, trying not to appear curious. 'But that's letters in wartime,' he went on comfortably. 'It was the same in the Great War, believe you me. Some of them arrived two or three years late. You're lucky if that's only six months out of date, mark my words. Letters. Some of them blow up, some of them get chucked in hedges, some of them get intercepted, and that's letters. And of course, the trouble is,' he took his pipe out of his mouth and waved it at the fire in front of which he sat as if the fire itself was another human being, not just a feeble little blaze made up of a few pieces of wood and coke, 'the trouble is, letters is all about human beings and their lives. So that is another victim of war—letters.'

* * *

Seated beside Mickey Todd's chestnut tree by the village green Mattie rocked Max's perambulator up and down, down and up. Her father was agog with excitement, all the regulars down at the Thee Tuns were agog with the same, and there were rumours flying about everywhere, but none of it meant very much to Mattie compared with the fact that Max had fallen fast asleep, at long, long last.

That morning, she had received a parcel from the WVS—a parcel from America. It was ridiculous, but just seeing that American stamp on the precious brown paper had made Mattie's heart turn stupid somersaults, which in turn had made her realise that Michael, wherever he was, still had a rather more firm grip on her emotions than she had known, or wanted. She could have kicked herself for feeling so happy and excited as she undid the already partially unwrapped parcel. But of course it was not from Michael, it was just one of many distributed by the WVS to women with young babies. It seemed that Mattie had been allocated two sets of rompers made by a lady in Connecticut.

Instead of indulging in any more sentimental thoughts, she had pushed Max out in his pram to the village green. Above her was a clear blue sky, and beyond the mouth of the estuary lay a millpond of a sea. Sea gulls swooped and screamed around her, ducks shepherded their newborn along in perfect order. Further on, wading birds prodded the wet sand with their long curved bills, in search of tasty morsels of shrimp or grub, while where the water was deep enough a boy in a rowing boat sat patiently fishing for whatever might take his bait. The only difference between this day in wartime and any day in peacetime was the huge coils and runs of barbed wire along the shores of the estuary, the distant signs warning of mines on the beaches, and the concrete pill boxes and gun post towers dotted regularly along the lovely coastline. Yet so calm and peaceful was the day that Mattie found it almost impossible to believe the rumours that any moment now one hundred and fifty thousand men were about to land in France to begin an invasion that was meant to herald the end of the war.

Not only were there rumours about an imminent invasion of France, however, there was also an excitement of a more personal nature that was involving the whole of Bexham. Something to distract everyone from whatever they needed to be distracted from, be it the pain of past or immediate loss, a relationship fracturing under the strain of constant deprivation, or just the news.

Peter Sykes was about to return home a war hero, having won the VC in Italy in the second battle for Monte Cassino. It appeared that he had saved the lives of three of his comrades while under heavy enemy fire. It was also rumoured that he had been severely injured in the battle, and subsequently invalided out of the army. Mattie had seen Peter only once since he had joined up at the outbreak of war, despite knowing that he had in fact returned home on leave several times. Mattie had been in London. She had been with Michael. She had been behaving scandalously, having an affair with a married man. Remembering how much her parents had disapproved of young men like Peter simply because they ran such things as garages now seemed, in retrospect, both ludicrous and hilarious, particularly since she was now staring down at Max, the living image of his American father. She sighed inwardly. *If only* was ridiculous, but, in some ways, *if only* she had not gone to London, her life might have been a great deal simpler, but also, perhaps, a great deal poorer.

By the time she had pushed Max's pram back into the heart of the village what remained of the local brass band was making itself ready to play a selection of popular tunes in preparation for Peter's arrival at the head of Bexham Quay—conveniently near to the Three Tuns. A table had been placed ready for the local dignitaries to welcome Bexham's first VC. The church clock struck twelve and on cue a black Humber pulled up in front of the pub. Like everyone else Mattie strained forward to catch sight of the hero. At first all she could see was the army driver's back bending into the Humber. A moment later a pair of arms was clasped firmly around the driver's neck and the younger man was helped out of the car. His appearance was greeted at first in total silence, as both band and crowd watched in dismay while he was assisted on to a set of crutches and it became clear that Peter Sykes VC had lost most of his right leg.

Finally the silence was broken by the sound of the fanfare, cued in too late by the bandleader with the result that what had been near perfect in rehearsal now sounded at first as if it was being improvised. The bandleader tapped his baton on his music stand to cut short the cacophony and allowed his players a second bite at the apple, a chance that mercifully they fully embraced, so now the quayside echoed with familiar airs, like the National Anthem, of a type that everyone would know at least the opening verse. As soon as the fanfare was over, the crowd broke into spontaneous applause, applause that swelled as the onlookers were rewarded with the very broadest of smiles from the homecoming hero.

With his weight on his left leg, supported by the sturdy crutch under his left armpit, and with some difficulty, Peter took off his military cap and held it in the air by way of both a salute to his birthplace and thanks to all those present. Standing by her pram, Mattie found herself amazed at how well he looked, in spite of his incapacity, suntanned, strong and even more good-looking than the day he had left Bexham to join up as an ordinary foot soldier. Miraculously he had survived campaigns in France and Africa as a member of perhaps the most vulnerable of all fighting regiments, the infantry—*gun fodder* as Mattie's father always called them, having served as a rifleman himself in the Great War. Not only had Peter survived, he had proved to be a brilliant and courageous soldier, as shown by his promotion from private to first lieutenant, by the coloured stripes of service decorations sewn on to his uniform above the breast pocket, and by his winning of the greatest accolade of all, the Victoria Cross.

Not that he needed to win a medal to prove to Bexham that he was the epitome of a true hero. He was one of them, a young man in his prime, a man who without any thought for himself had saved the lives of three of his fellow soldiers. Returning again and again, constantly under heavy enemy fire, he had dragged each wounded rifleman back to the safety of a dugout, where other members of the same regiment lay sheltering themselves.

Home had come the hero, perfect and untarnished in every way, save the loss of one of his limbs. In the eyes of his proud village, long before he joined the army Peter had been a great sportsman, the captain of the village football team and the very devil of a fast bowler for the Bexham XI. Now they saw with cruel reality that he would never kick a ball or bowl one for fun ever again. Never go on long, joyful walks with his dog, or—perhaps worst of all, Mattie thought, staring across to where he stood—captivate and charm the young women he took in his arms to lead elegantly around the village hall dance floor.

Pretending to check that her baby was still sleeping soundly, Mattie bent over the pram and wiped the tears from her eyes with the edge of his pram sheet. When she looked up she found Peter was looking directly at her. As she caught his look she smiled, and after only the slightest hesitation Peter returned the smile, and made his slow and doubtless painful way over to where she was standing by the pram.

Rusty too was watching the ceremony, half hidden by the crowd on the other side of the quayside. Seeing Peter crossing over to kiss Mattie on the cheek, she slipped away, back to her cottage.

'You got to tell him, love,' her mother had said, not once but about twenty times. 'You've got to. No good hiding out in the next village hoping that something will happen, because being war, most likely nothing will. You have to tell him. It's only fair.'

'No "got to" about it. I've thought about it a lot,

Mother. I know I have changed, for better or for worse, it's just a fact, so why should I think that he hasn't changed too? It's the war, one minute people are one thing, and the next quite different. If I have changed, why not Peter? Specially now he's coming home a hero. Besides, I don't want him to think *he's* "got to" marry me. That would be worse than anything. No, I'll tell him, if I think it's right, and not otherwise, Mother.' And then as always by way of distraction Rusty asked, 'Heard anything from our Mickey?'

INTERLUDE

ST AUBIN, NORMANDY, JUNE 1944

Mickey was certainly in no frame of mind for heroics. Having endured a beach landing in a craft half full of water from seas that on first sight every fighting man considered were far too rough to suit the intended invasion, and having seen three-quarters of his companions cut down by machine gun fire the moment the landing craft's flap fell with a mighty crash into waves well over head height, all he could think of was self-preservation. Sheltering up against a breakwater while all hell broke loose around him, Mickey who was normally as brave as the soldier next to him found himself shivering with terror as men with whom he had been sharing cigarettes and tea only a matter of an hour earlier were literally blown to bits around him.

He had now seen plenty of action but nothing quite as hellish as this. He had never seen or heard fire like it. It was as if God had become sickened with this terrible war and determined to exact His revenge on His creation by unleashing every thunderbolt in heaven.

Somehow he had to survive this holocaust. He held on to his sub-machine gun for dear life. Somehow he had to do his duty as a soldier too, but first he had to survive. He had not come this far to die at the eleventh hour, which he most certainly was going to do if he stayed where he was, fighting for self-control in the shadow of a large hulk of timber that was slowly being shot to bits around him.

But how? Orders that moments ago had seemed crystal clear now in the light of this sheer mayhem seemed quite nonsensical. This was obviously the moment that every fighting man dreaded—the moment when strategy and tactics went out of the window and it was every man for himself.

Taking a quick peek round what he hoped was the safe side of the breakwater Mickey caught a brief glimpse of someone he thought was his sergeant signalling for his men to take position around him, only to see him blown to pieces the very next moment, as were most of the soldiers kneeling and lying close to him.

One second later and something took the top off the breakwater, blowing the prop behind Mickey into a thousand pieces. A huge jagged splinter of wood embedded itself in the sand beside him, missing his leg by inches. Now he had to move, so searching desperately for cover further up the beach—since there was no going back, only up the beach and on—Mickey saw the burning wreck of an amphibious tank lying on its side. Keeping as low as he could he pelted forward, in full military gear, jumping the bodies of the fallen, the dead, the dying and the terribly injured, until he was ten feet or so from the burning tank. Hurling himself at it, as if doing the long jump, he just made it to the lee side of the smouldering vehicle as the very ground upon which he had been running a second earlier erupted in a huge explosion, filling the air with sand, stones and the remains of soldiers. Minutes later Mickey was another thirty feet up the beach, taking cover this time behind a huge length of severed drainage pipe that had been hurled down the slope by the force of some other enormous explosion. Two other soldiers joined him, both British, one of them with a face almost totally covered with blood.

'You OK?' Mickey screamed at him. 'You got hit?'

The soldier shook his head and wiped the blood from his face with the sleeve of his torn uniform.

'Some other poor sod's!' he yelled back. 'Where to now?'

Mickey, who was lying on his back against the pipe, turned to his left and pointed towards a headland some two hundred yards to the east.

'Machine gun nest at the top of that! Got everything covered from here to the same distance the other side! If we could get there—'

He was cut off by a series of huge explosions, seemingly no further away than the other side of the huge pipe which was affording them shelter. The shock of the blasts was so great it threw the three men bodily ten feet or more from the pipe. At once they turned on to their bellies and snake-crawled their way back to its shelter.

'I'm going to try and make it to those rocks there!' Mickey pointed to his intended destination, an outcrop of scaleable rocks that lay behind the German machine gun. 'If any of us can get there and up those rocks, we could surprise the gunners and take the bastards out! You with me?'

Both the soldiers nodded, checking on where they were to go.

'Right! I'm with you!' one of them shouted. 'Said to my mate here—this ain't no place for no bloody picnic!'

After what seemed like half a day but was in fact only a matter of ten minutes Mickey found himself still unscathed and in one piece behind a huge rock. Another minute or so later one of his companions threw himself down in the sand beside him.

'Where's your chum?' Mickey yelled.

'Copped it! Cut down by the machine gun! Nearly bloody made it!'

'All the more reason to get the bastards!'

Mickey looked upwards. Most of the climb would be protected by the pile of rocks that had formed against the finger of land pointing out to sea. As long as no one was on lookout above, their climb would be slow but a simple one, a matter of keeping round the back of each rock and working their way carefully ever higher. Twenty minutes later they were at the very top of the rock pile, leaving only a stretch of ten to twelve feet of unguarded land to cross to another handily placed lump of rock positioned in the middle of the path that led to the end of the cliff and the enemy machine gun nest.

'Take a breather, mate,' Mickey whispered in his companion's ear, pointing to the rock. 'Then on a count of five, leg it to that rock! I'll cover you!'

They both made it, finding on arrival that the rock was not one lump but three, with a cleft in the middle large enough to house them both in perfect and invisible safety, which was just as well, since unbeknown to them not a hundred yards away in a well-prepared dugout ten feet below the level at which they were sheltering was one of the many rabbit-hole tactical sub-headquarters of the defending German regiment.

'I could do with a smoke,' his companion whispered in Mickey's ear.

'I could do with several,' Mickey replied with a grin. 'How many in a nest usually? Three, isn't it?'

One to load, one to fire, one to take over if one of

you's hit.

They had two grenades between them, and enough rounds to take out half a dozen nests, were they to have the chance. But no amount of ammunition would be sufficient for their survival if there was a look-out posted. Between the rocks and the nest there was nothing but low-lying scrub.

'Bellies,' Mickey whispered. 'Snakes right up to near as we can get. Then the grenades. Then open fire if still necessary. Got it?'

'Roger.'

* * *

A hundred yards away a land periscope was trained on the three rocks.

'There is no sign of anyone, sir,' the watcher reported, eyes still fixed on the target.

'I swore I saw someone,' his officer replied. 'As the smoke was clearing I swear I saw someone disappearing into those rocks.'

'Still no sign of movement, sir.'

The officer picked up his field telephone and cranked it one last time, but it was as dead as before, as dead as the two soldiers lying at his feet and the three who had failed to return from an earlier sortie.

'Looks like it's going to be you and me, Corporal,' the officer said, taking a cigarette out of his inside pocket and lighting it with a gold lighter. 'How much ammunition do you have?'

'About a dozen rounds, sir.'

The officer, cigarette clenched between his teeth, checked his Lüger.

'I have precisely four. Now.' He took a deep

draw on his smoke, leaving the cigarette where it was in his mouth, allowing the wreaths of smoke to escape down his nose. 'Now this is what we shall do. If I'm right, if anyone is hiding out up there, their objective will be our gun position number one. If so, they will not be looking in our direction. Their objective will be to take out our gun. We could leave it to the gunners, of course.'

'Yes, sir.'

'But that would hardly be right.' The officer smiled. 'And since we have lost all communication it is only right and proper we go to their defence. So I suggest we quietly make our way forwards to our target—those rocks—and take a damn' good look for ourselves.'

'Sir!' the observer interrupted with a hiss. 'You were right! Two of them, sir!'

'Let me see.'

The officer took a look for himself and saw two British soldiers slowly emerging from the cleft in the rocks, leaning on the back of the huge stones but facing away from them, as if preparatory to making their move.

'Dammit,' the officer whispered. 'Your rifle—quickly! Or we shall be too late!'

The observer had his rifle now, cocked, aimed, and ready.

'In your own time,' the officer said.

The observer fired once. One of the soldiers dropped immediately like a stone as the bullet entered the back of his head.

The second soldier did not even look round. One look would mean his life, so instead he ran round the rocks until he had put them between him and the sniper. Then he kept on running, not caring now whether the machine gunners heard or saw him. He was going to take them out whatever happened.

'Out!' the officer ordered. 'Quick as you can!'

The two Germans scrambled out of their hideout and gave chase, guns at the ready. But Corporal Mickey Todd had more than an adequate head start.

He was ten yards from the gunners' nest with the grenade in his hand and the enemy didn't even know he was there. They were busy non-stop firing, the heavy machine gun clattering its racket out full pelt, drowning out the sound of any approach, helped no little by the general battle thunder of the continuing invasion and now by the scream of aircraft overhead.

They probably were not even aware of the noise of the exploding grenade as it landed right where it should, right in the bull's-eye, right in the middle of the nest, blowing the three German soldiers apart as if they were rag dolls. In a second Mickey was on one knee, sub-machine gun cocked and firing, just in case any of the gunners had survived. Then he was on his feet, running towards the nest to make doubly sure, and once he had seen they were all well and truly dead he turned and ran back, intending to return the way he had come, down the rock pile and back on to the beach—until he saw out of the pale pall of smoke that lay over the cliff two figures running towards him, one firing a rifle and the other an officer with his pistol drawn.

A bullet from the rifle missed his head by inches. Jumping to his right to make himself a more difficult target Mickey shot a fusillade of bullets at the corporal, killing him instantly and knocking him backwards over the side of the cliff. Now there was just himself and the officer, who had stopped no more than six yards from him to take steady aim with his pistol.

Mickey found himself almost grinning. A pistol from that range? Against his sub-machine gun? *Jerry's going to have to be one helluva good shot*, he thought as he directed his snub-nosed weapon at the enemy. *Cheerio, Jerry!*

The officer would much rather not have had to shoot. He would much have preferred it had his target dropped his gun, put up his hands and called it quits. But this was war, and from the look of it his opponent had no intention of dropping his gun and surrendering. *And why should he?* the officer thought. *I have very little chance and he has plenty. So I had better make this one shot tell.*

He had Mickey targeted between the eyes, both hands holding the Lüger steady, feet apart with his right foot slightly behind his left, just as he had been taught by his father. Just as he stood every time he won the regimental pistol shooting tournament. Just as he stood every time he hit bull's-eye after bull's-eye.

He had to kill his enemy before the soldier could raise his weapon to his hip and fire. That was as much time as he had. But still he did not fire, for the soldier's gun seemed to have jammed. He could see the panic in the man as he fiddled with the weapon, as he slapped it with one hand, as he checked the catch and pressed the trigger yet again. But still the gun refused to fire.

The officer kept his Lüger steady and called to the British soldier.

'Please!' he shouted. 'I don't wish to kill you!

Drop your gun and put your hands up!'

'Go to hell!' Mickey yelled back as fiercely as he could, cursing everything and anything he could think of for his faulty weapon.

'No, please!' the German was still calling. 'Just drop your weapon and put your hands up! I don't wish to shoot you!'

Instinctively Mickey knew that whatever had been wrong with his weapon, it was wrong no longer. As if his gun was part of him he swore he could feel its health return and he raised it quickly in the direction of his target and squeezed the trigger.

A line of bullets spewed out from what to Mickey seemed like his own arm, his very being, his own self. He could see them, he swore he could see every bullet as they screamed through the air in a line of death, hitting his target right in the centre of his chest, knocking him upwards and off his feet, killing him instantly in a shower of his own blood, leaving him lying grotesquely splayed on the path, his hands up above his head as if in surrender to death, his blue eyes staring up at the heaven to which he was now headed.

I am the enemy you killed, my friend—that was the line that might have hung in the air above the officer's body. But Mickey did not give his victim another look. Having stopped only to collect the dead man's precious Lüger and the gold cigarette lighter that had fallen from his pocket, he slung his sub-machine gun back over his shoulder and began the climb down to rejoin the battle below, leaving Captain Heinrich Von Hantzen to his death high on the windswept cliffs above the beaches of Normandy.

LONDON, MAY 1945

CHAPTER SEVENTEEN

It was now six days since Hitler had killed himself yet there was still no official announcement of the end of the war in Europe. By Monday 7 May all over the country the tension had become almost unendurable, and as Judy fought her way through the crowds in the street to get to work at WVS headquarters she wondered along with all her fellow citizens when the government was finally going to get itself sufficiently organised to make the declaration of peace everyone knew was already well overdue. By midday, when Judy and some of her colleagues took again to the streets during their lunch break a huge crowd had gathered outside Buckingham Palace shouting *We want the King! We want the King!* Rumours abounded that there was to be a special broadcast at three o'clock that afternoon. Everywhere people were getting out the flags, but three o'clock came and went and there was no broadcast. At six o'clock that evening, when Judy was tidying her desk and preparing to go home, a colleague lugged her old wireless into Judy's room and they all gathered round to hear the news. But all they learned was that the Prime Minister would not be broadcasting that night after all.

By now expectation was fast turning into general aggravation as everyone had to keep their emotions bottled up while they awaited the official sanction to celebrate.

'I don't care,' Judy's colleague said after they had switched off the wireless. 'I've got a ten foot

Union Jack ready to hang out and I'm going straight home to do so. And probably get a bit tight in the process.'

John Tate telephoned Judy as she was about to leave, telling her he had learned unofficially that the following day was to be declared Victory in Europe Day with the day after to be a national holiday as well.

'So we'd better keep the hatch battened down till then,' he said with a laugh. 'All right if I come round about seven thirty and we go out for a drink?'

Before they left Judy's apartment to go out and begin their well-earned celebrations, they learned from a special broadcast at twenty to eight confirmation of the rumour John had reported hearing. The newsreader announced: 'It is understood that, in accordance with arrangements between the three great powers, an official announcement will be broadcast by the Prime Minister at three o'clock tomorrow.'

'If you ask me,' John said as they left the flat, 'the government has done this deliberately. Timed the news of our victory for the convenience of the Yanks and the Russians. It's absolutely ridiculous. We should all have been dancing in the streets days ago.'

Twenty-four hours later the atmosphere could not have been more different. Ever since Churchill had announced on the radio at three o'clock on the Tuesday afternoon that hostilities would officially end one minute after midnight the capital exploded into delirious celebration. Total strangers hugged and kissed each other, danced the hokey-cokey on the pavements and in the middle of the roads, dragged pianos out of front rooms to play for the impromptu street parties that were happening everywhere, climbed lamp posts and statues, hung fairy lights from trees and dolled themselves up in fancy dress or their brightest and best clothes. The noise of the celebrations was tremendous, a cacophony born out of the unspeakable and indescribable relief that the horrors of the last six terrible years were finally at an end.

Judy and John found themselves in the crowd gathered in front of Buckingham Palace just as the floodlighting came on. Everyone gasped, as if some magic had been performed, and broke into spontaneous applause. Even though the Mall was packed with revellers, Judy and John, arm in arm, had found it easy enough to walk through the shifting crowds to a prime position outside the railings with a first class view of the balcony, which had been made ready for the royal family with a rich crimson cloth tasselled in yellow and gold. The mood was much quieter here, a sense more of relief and muted happiness than of outright celebration, yet even so everywhere Judy looked she could see strangers embracing each other, taking each other's hands and arms, walking about and talking as if they were all part of one vast united family.

Without warning rockets shot into the air, spraying the skies with coloured stars and drawing yet more gasps and cries of surprise from the throng. Then, almost simultaneously with the explosion of fireworks, the King and Queen and their two daughters stepped out on to the balcony. Now the shouts came, the yells of delight, the cheers of joy and elation. Everyone waved their arms, their handkerchiefs, their flags, anything they could wave, and in return the royal family waved delightedly back. Judy could hardly hold back her tears as she joined in the chorus of jubilation, before being whisked away by John and caught up in the crowd that was now headed for the park where a huge bonfire was already ablaze.

Again the scene was more like dreamland than reality, particularly when Judy remembered it was only a matter of weeks since London had been reduced to a state of near terror by the avalanche of flying bombs the Germans had directed against it. Yet here were the capital's survivors, linking hands around the bonfire under the twinkling illumination of hundreds of coloured lights hung from the trees and the shrubbery.

'I really think I'm dreaming,' Judy said, laughing as John danced her in his arms around the perimeter of the huge bonfire. 'I really can hardly believe this is all happening!'

Everywhere they went there was the same magical ambience, the great buildings of London that had survived the holocaust of war floodlit once again in soft yellows, with flags and bunting fluttering everywhere. Even the weather had relented, the thunderstorms and heavy showers that had marred the afternoon having cleared to leave a balmy spring night, warm enough for the revellers to celebrate without being encumbered with overcoats.

By now Judy and John had made their way down to the Embankment and along to the Houses of Parliament which were glowing honey-coloured under the battery of lights. The terraces sparkled with lamps, a huge Union Jack underlit by powerful spotlights flew proudly above the House of Lords, and the tower of Big Ben, an edifice that had somehow come to personify the spirit of Britain throughout the war, rose above all else, bathed in light.

Beyond the Houses of Parliament the Thames glowed with the reflections of the thousands of coloured bulbs hung from the ships moored along its reaches, while above the multi-coloured river the sky was lit by the huge beams of rotating searchlights. Since it was now only minutes from midnight, the official end to the fighting in Europe, it seemed everyone was converging on Westminster, to stand and stare up at the famous clock as its hands ticked slowly and majestically around to twelve o'clock. With a minute to go the whole crowd that stood facing the clock fell absolutely silent, waiting for the war to end. Big Ben struck, the sound of the most famous bell in the world chiming sonorously over the city and the airwaves to the millions of people who for the past six years had fought for the survival of the free world.

By the time the last stroke had sounded the big hand of the great clock had swung to one minute past midnight. Europe was once more at peace. At the same time everyone clapped their hands, firecrackers exploded and down the river tugs sounded their whistles and boats blew their steam-horns to celebrate the moment when the world returned to its senses.

The next thing Judy knew was that she was in John's arms and being kissed, but as she stepped back and away from him she realised that—unlike everything else that was happening around them—

their kiss had not set the Thames on fire. Whatever happened, John was still not Walter.

*　　*　　*

Richards burst through the doors of the long sitting room. 'Miss Meggie is coming home to us! Miss Meggie is coming home, Gwen.'

Richards and Gwen from Shelborne had decided to go into business together. They had evolved their plan one evening when sheltering under the stairs during a particularly nasty doodlebug incident, and as a result, while Mrs Tate and young Dauncy had been living with Miss Judy at Owl Cottage, they had become the sole occupants of Cucklington House, while making sure to look after Shelborne for the Tates.

'Mrs Walter Tate will be pleased to have her friend back, won't she? What with her husband missing, and that, she'll have company again.'

Richards nodded, although not quite agreeing. It had already become apparent to him, and others in the village, that the people returning from the war, from whatever occupations, were not the same people who had gone away. Quiet, shy boys returned alcoholic braggarts, restrained young ladies returned chain-smoking neurotics, brave, handsome men came back with their nerves so shattered that the slightest sound made them jump. He doubted very much that Miss Meggie, after all her experiences in the war—and only God and she knew just what they had entailed—would return the same young woman as the one who had volunteered so cheerfully to be sent to *somewhere in Europe*.

*   *   *

After his hero's welcome back to Bexham, Peter had returned to his convalescent home for some months, before being discharged and returning to the village for good. Slowly and carefully setting about putting his garage to rights, and after all the excitement, he suddenly seemed a lonely figure, up on the hill, a new dog at his heels, but both his parents now dead, his father killed in a bombing raid, his mother dying of a heart attack. Not only that but there were really only a handful of cars in the village to service, so trade was slow.

Knowing all this, as soon as she could get herself organised Mattie had asked him round to dinner at Magnolias.

'Just quietly, at home,' she said, trying not to notice the almost pathetic gratitude in Peter's eyes as he accepted, and she quickly pushed Max back down to the village.

Lionel was out, and as Mattie busied herself making the best supper she could muster, she wondered how she was going to tell Peter everything that had happened in his absence, and whether he would even wish to know. She knew she would have to tell him about herself and Michael, she knew she would have to tell him about Rusty, but just how was quite another thing. When he arrived he was carrying a bottle of gin, which boded either well or ill for the evening, depending which way you viewed it, and how much you liked gin.

'Not too strong, Peter.'

Peter ignored her plea, and gaily poured them both two huge gins. Topping them up with only a little bit of water, he sat back.

'Cheers.'

'Cheers.'

There followed the awkward silence that always falls when there have been such great changes in people's lives that they really do not know where to begin, or even whether to begin at all.

'*I*—' They both began with the same word, laughed, and promptly, not knowing how to go on, took far too large sips at their drinks. Then Peter cleared his throat.

'The thing is, Mattie—I wonder if you've seen Rusty Todd, Mattie?'

He had not meant to say 'Mattie' twice, but he had made up his mind, long before the evening arrived, to get straight to the point, and as soon as he could. He could not believe that Rusty had disappeared off the face of the earth or that no one in the village, but no one, knew where she had gone, least of all her parents.

'Not lately,' Mattie lied. 'Why?'

'It's just that I—er—I wanted to see her, but whenever I call at her parents' house they seem most reluctant to even talk about her. Is she—I mean—I *can* take it—is she dead, Mattie? Is Rusty dead?'

'Good gracious no! No, of course not! Why ever would you think that? Dead, Rusty? No, gracious, no, Peter. No, Rusty is far from dead.'

'Thank God for that.' Peter lay back against the sofa, his eyes closed, and then he leaned forward and put a strong hand on Mattie's arm. 'It's just that no one in the village would talk about her—every time I asked after her, whoever I asked, they just turned away. It was as if they could not bring themselves to tell me she was dead.'

'No, Rusty's not dead, Peter, far from it.'

'In that case, Mattie, please, please tell me where she is. Everyone is carrying on as if she has been sent to prison, and they're too ashamed to talk about her, or she has committed suicide, or done something they think shameful.'

'Do you really want to get in touch with Rusty?'

'Want to get in touch with Rusty? I'm in *love* with Rusty, Mattie, and that's not the gin talking, if you don't mind my being so honest. No, I want so much to see her it hurts me to even say her name, and that is still not the gin talking. But—I mean—I think she must know I'm home, if she's still living round here,' he went on awkwardly, 'what with the welcome I got, and all, so I think the reason she hasn't got in touch with me is . . .' He nodded at his missing leg. 'You know. My leg. I mean, girls don't like half men, do they?'

Mattie stared at him, and against her will her eyes suddenly filled with tears. Life had so changed everyone—no, not life—war. The war had so changed everyone.

'Oh no, Peter, your leg is certainly not the reason Rusty has not got in touch with you, I can tell you that for certain. The reason she has not got in touch with you, Peter, is because she's had a baby, and she doesn't want anyone to know, although of course everyone does. You know the village, they don't speak about such things, keep themselves to themselves about such matters. Bexham after all is still Bexham, Peter.'

Peter stared at Mattie. 'She's had a baby.' He paused. 'Oh. I see.'

'Her parents aren't ashamed of her, I mean

they're not like that, the Todds, but they have to respect her wishes. It's Rusty who's ashamed, Peter, that's why she moved villages to have it, to have the baby. And that is why she has stayed where she is, because she doesn't want to face people with her baby. *I* understand, but I'm probably the only person who *does*. You see, I had a baby, as you know, and if my father hadn't been so sweet about it, I dare say I might have run off somewhere else. But also—I happen to know the father of my baby is married, but Rusty—well, I think it's different for her. The father of her baby is *not* married; she just doesn't want him to be put in a position that he might not like—to think that he had to marry her. That would be awful. And I understand that too.'

'Who is the father, Mattie?'

'You'll have to ask her that yourself, Peter.'

* * *

The following day, armed with the address given to him by an understanding Mattie, Peter made his way to the village indicated, found the cottage which Rusty was renting, and slipped in the side gate of the front garden. He was in such a state that he could hardly see, and when he did look down the old brick path, past the innumerable cottage flowers and vegetables set out in traditional style, through to the back garden—a short strip of lawn, its boundary bordered by another cottage—Peter thought his heart might stop.

She was wearing a dress he did not recognise, hanging out the washing on a line filled with nothing but baby clothes. The baby himself, dressed in a pale blue romper suit with yellow ducks embroidered across the front, was sitting up in a smart blue harness looking round at the world with that particular confident look that babies always assume when they know very well that they are not just the delight but the total centre of their mother's lives.

With Rusty's back still turned to him, and with so many napkins still to pin up as she quietly hummed to herself, Peter took courage and limped slowly up to the pram.

As he stared into the little fellow's face, and held one of his hands, he knew that he had no real need to ask Rusty for the name of the father of her baby—their baby. He was not just Peter's son, he was Peter's image, with one notable exception—his vibrantly red curly hair.

* * *

Judy was also hanging out washing in the garden of Owl Cottage, but it was of a very different kind. Her washing was sheets and towels, all of which seemed intent on wrapping themselves around her at the most unexpected moments.

Now that Loopy and Dauncy had gone back to Shelborne, now that she was alone once more in the cottage, now that John had at last realised that not only was there nothing between them, but there never would be, putting out sheets to dry on a sunny day seemed like the most idyllic occupation imaginable. Judy was alone at last, for the first time for what seemed like years, alone to think about Walter, imagine what their life might have been like, had he survived the war. He had been studying law before he joined the Navy. Soon he would have been catching the train to London, going to take up some brief, eating dinners, which barristers and such people always seemed to spend so much time doing, coming back on the train, and telling her all about it, while she set the small oak dining table with some pleasantly light supper, both of them settling down to listen to the wireless afterwards—perhaps a concert, or a comedy half hour.

Judy struggled to subdue a particularly recalcitrant sheet, thinking what a paradise it would have been, and how she would have loved every minute of it. It might be wrong, but now that she was alone again she had taken to hugging this imaginary life of hers to her, their life as it might have been, hers and Walter's, had not the war come between it and them.

* * *

Loopy was getting used to being at Shelborne again. At first she had been afraid that going back to the house would bring back all those agonising memories of life before the war, of Walter saying goodbye, of her going to pieces, of Dauncy striving valiantly to cope with her. And with all that would come the old temptation to lose herself in alcohol, to take to her bed, to shut off from real life and her responsibilities. But, whether because of Dauncy, and the pure unaffected joy he evinced as he burst through the door of his old home, or because of Hugh's evident content on retiring from London, Hugh and Dauncy's enthusiasm carried her through those first, strange days of peace. Besides, she was determined to be positive. She at once made plans. She would change the covers in the sitting room. She would somehow or other obtain paint to redecorate, she would grow vegetables, she would plant flowers if she could get the seeds.

Only the piano remained silent.

It had never been played since Walter had gone missing, and in deference to the intensity of Loopy's feelings Hugh had always imagined he might never play it again. He would definitely never play Gilbert and Sullivan—least of all *HMS Pinafore*. He had long ago resigned himself to the idea that the gaiety of those pre-war days was gone for ever.

Until one afternoon, not long after they had settled back into Shelborne, Loopy, seated alone in the back garden, the sound of the sea not far away, suddenly got up and went back into the house, through the French windows and into the sitting room, calling for her husband.

Hugh, busy clearing out the garage, and making plans to take his car off its blocks, and somehow get it up the hill again to Peter Sykes, called back to his wife, 'Coming, darling! Just coming!'

Loopy's voice had not sounded so happy, so light and filled with something that he could not put his finger on since before the war. Hugh at once stopped what he was doing, and went to her, still wiping his hands on an old striped bathing towel, a towel with a Scottie dog embroidered on it. Standing stock still in the middle of the sitting room, staring at him, Loopy remembered that Walter had always loved to bag that towel after swimming.

Bags I that towel. Bags I Scottie!

But for some reason the memory of the young Walter, shivering from the cold of the sea, his bright eyes looking up into hers as she towelled him, no longer hurt her. She stared at Hugh wordlessly for a second or two, the realisation coming to her that it was as if she herself had been very cold, and now she was getting warm—really warming up; realising that the memory of Walter, of the towel, of bathing off their boat, of picnics held in inlets, of the little boats the boys were always making to float in the bath upstairs, did not hurt her any longer.

'Hugh. Tonight. Will you—do you think you could play the piano for me? Play the piano again tonight, Hugh, for Dauncy especially. I know he would like it.'

Hugh stared back at his wife, realising with shock and delight that standing once more before him was his old Loopy. Gone was the gaunt woman with the strained expression, the suffering woman who had lain for weeks upstairs, the woman who had left their house to go and live with Judy, as if by being near his wife of only a few hours she would be closer to Walter. Here, standing before him once more, was *his* Loopy. She smiled and lit a cigarette.

'Oh, and Hugh—let's make some dry martinis. I found some gin and vermouth I had hidden in the cellars when I was intent on drinking myself to death—and there's quite some left!'

Hugh took her in his arms. Not only was she Loopy again, she was more than that, she was whole again.

That night Hugh played the piano, badly in need of tuning though it was after so much time.

Of course he did not dare to play anything from Gilbert and Sullivan—until, that is, Loopy touched him on the shoulder. Looking up into her kind, expressive eyes, into the face that he so loved, he found her smiling down at him, understanding only too well what he was not playing, and why.

'It's OK, Hugh, you can play Gilbert and Sullivan, you can even play Walter's song.'

'I don't know that I should . . .'

'No, you can. You can play it, because you may not know, but I do. You see, I was sitting in the garden shelling peas, and suddenly, I don't know why, but I knew that it was all right to play Walter's bedtime song again.'

Dauncy, in the kitchen attempting to make a chocolate pudding for dessert out of cocoa, a few eggs and butter that Gwen had managed to scrounge for him, turned.

'Crumbs,' he said to Captain, his new puppy. 'Father's not played that since . . . you know.' He started to hum along with the sound of the piano and his father's voice, once more singing, 'We sail the ocean blue, and our saucy ship's a beauty . . .'

CHAPTER EIGHTEEN

Richards had never been more worried about Miss Meggie than when she asked to borrow his razor. That she had returned from what he now described to Gwen somewhat euphemistically as 'Miss Meggie's foreign experiences' skinny, hollow-eyed and with a chain-smoking habit was hardly surprising.

Knowing that it would be against all the rules if he should try to ask Miss Meggie for any details of the missing years, Richards had promptly set about trying to feed her up, and although she had hardly touched her food to begin with, after the first few days he had found, hearteningly, that he was returning to the pantry with less on the plates than when he had left it, which was, although not much, at least something.

'I went all through this with her grandmother, Mrs Gore-Stewart, after the Great War, believe me. We always had this sympathy for each other, with her saving my leg, and both liking to play the piano, and Chopin, and that. So, right from the start, it was me that was able to tempt her appetite back with little morsels, and chats and things. That and walking, and sea air. In fact that's why she bought this place, for the sea air, doing her so much good after all she had endured at the Front.'

'Oh, it must have.'

Gwen, who was much younger than Richards, looked sympathetic, and attentive, which was one of the many reasons why Richards found her such a boon to have around him. Not just her apple cheeks and comely figure, but her attentive manners, so hard to find nowadays.

'See, it's not at the time that you suffer, Gwen.' Richards breathed on a piece of silver and then rubbed it with his special silver cloth. 'No, there *is* no time for that, not at the time. It's afterwards. That's when I saw what had happened to Madame Gran, but then of course Miss Meggie being left with her, that was nothing but a boon, although it did not appear as such at the beginning, as I am sure you appreciate, what with Miss Meggie being such a firecracker. But a young thing about the place, it's a wonderful distraction, really it is, and so Miss Meggie proved to be to Madame Gran.'

Walks by the sea, walks on the downs, walks to the Three Tuns, walks to the shops, had all been part of Richards's recipe for getting Miss Meggie back to her old self, that and people coming to see them at Cucklington House. Even now there was some talk of Miss Meggie trying to get Miss Mattie together with the eldest Tate boy; all that had seemed as though it might bring Miss Meggie back to the real world.

Endless chat about shortages, and how best to make things like marmalade. Everything was aired with himself and his new business partner Gwen. Everything from the problems of trying to get the hens to lay more eggs to the difficulties of finding new tyres for your motor car. The real, if petty, things that keep most human beings jogging along in some sort of fashion.

But now, after all that, and just when he thought things might be about to come right, here was Miss Meggie demanding a razor off him.

'It's all right, I'll be careful to wipe the blade, Richards, I promise,' Meggie said, trying to reassure him.

Richards nodded, handing it to her, and at the same time glancing round for Gwen, who, over on an afternoon visit from Shelborne, had already zipped upstairs to remove the key from the bathroom door.

Goodness, what a thing it was, to be so nervous about Miss Meggie, but such had been her depression, her blackness, her inability to really respond to anyone who visited, their mutual concern for her was so great, they just could not risk anything untoward, especially not now they were getting a bit of colour into her cheeks, and a bit of food down her.

Minutes later into the bathroom went Miss Meggie with Richards's razor, and at such a strange hour—half past two in the afternoon, just after luncheon, when you really would expect her to be setting out with him for a walk to the shore.

'Water running!' Richards nodded from outside the bathroom where he was stationed looking back at Gwen who was pretending to be dusting.

'Singing!'

'The sound of singing's not exactly what you would expect from a potential suicide, is it?' Gwen whispered, to cheer Richards up.

A few minutes, the sound of water swishing, and more singing.

'Not heard anything like that since she got home, have you?'

'No—that at least is true.'

Finally the door opened again, and Miss Meggie's voice coming with its opening flooded Richards with relief, there was no other expression for it.

'It's all right, Richards, I haven't loused the blade up, at least I don't think so, but really—precious though your razor blade is, I know—I could not put up with French lady's armpits one more minute!'

Richards blushed practically purple. Typical of Miss Meggie to be standing there in nothing but her bath towel, lifting her arms up to show himself and poor Gwen her impeccable clean-shaven armpits.

'Miss Meggie!' he exclaimed, for once truly

shocked by her.

'Well, I know, Richards. Quite. But, I mean to say, of all the things one does for one's country, that was quite the worst! And I mean to say, I can't wear an evening dress with armpits like that, can I?'

* * *

From that moment on, Richards and Meggie seemed able to talk to each other as they had in the old days. It was as if, with the removal of the final, physical vestiges of 'Martine', Meggie could now set her sights on the future, put behind her the long and often terrifying journey she had taken across Germany from Cologne, until she had finally caught up with the Allied army and returned home to England, two stone lighter, older and still unable to quite believe that they had, actually, won, that the war was over. Cologne, Heinrich, his terrifying sister, the Nazis, the Gestapo, they were all over. Not in 'pending', not about to happen all over again, but quite gone, and with them her youth.

'You don't really want to stay on at Cuckers, now Madame Gran has gone, do you, Richards?'

Richards looked first awkward and then relieved.

'It's not that I don't want to stay on at Cucklington House, Miss Meggie, it's just that Gwen and I—well, we were thinking of setting up in business together, taking over the Leaping Hare on the other side of the harbour. That's what we were considering. Light meals and refreshments, that sort of thing. Gwen is a good cook, and has no wish to be married, but she would appreciate a change. She's spoken to Mrs Tate, and she was very amenable. Fresh fields and pastures new, that sort of thing.'

Meggie nodded, all understanding.

'Of course, Richards. I shall be very sad not to see you at Cuckers, but it's only right that you and Gwen should want a change. Goodness, you've been in Bexham all the war, and that is a long time.'

'And you, Miss Meggie?' Richards asked, trying not to look relieved. 'What would your plans be?'

'To live here, at Cuckers, which as you know Madame Gran left me, and to let Brook Street. The lease is up in a few years anyway, but I have no stomach for cities any more, Richards. Not any city, not even London, much as I love it, or did. With this in mind I shall go up to London on the train on Tuesday, stay the night at Brook Street, make sure that everything is as it should be for the new tenant, and come back on Wednesday morning.'

'Will you require any packing done, Miss Meggie?'

Meggie nodded. 'Yes, if you wouldn't mind packing my night things for me, Richards—oh, and my pale green silk evening gown.'

'Shall I put out Madame Gran's emeralds to wear with it?'

'No, thank you, Richards. I was not—I will not be wearing Madame Gran's emeralds on Tuesday evening, just my string of pearls, and my pearl bracelet. That is all.'

Meggie lit a cigarette. Burlington Arcade, the sound of their laughter, walking through the streets that had seemed to be teeming with quietly frightened people, making love at his house in

Cheyne Walk, it would all come back, and leave no room for the intervening years. All that surviving had taken it out of her, all that living a lie, pretending to be someone else, all that hiding from the memory of turning Davey down. Surely it would all go, once she had replaced it with those other, happier memories.

* * *

'Good evening,' the head waiter looked down the list of names on the entries, 'Mrs—Mrs . . .'

'No, it's Miss, Miss Gore-Stewart.'

'Table number six, of course.'

The man, dark, Italianate, his expression oddly sympathetic to a beautiful young woman, dressed in a stunning silk dress, dining alone, led the way to the appropriate table.

He pulled a chair out for Meggie and she sat down. Alas, her silver cigarette case and lighter had long ago been lost in the war, somewhere, somehow; instead she placed Madame Gran's ornate gold cigarette case and slim gold lighter beside her plate.

'Champagne, please, for one.'

'Of course, madame.'

'Mademoiselle.'

She knew that they would have drunk champagne, to celebrate the end of the war. She tried to shut out the noise of the other diners as she remembered his voice, so clear, so vibrant, and imagined how their conversation would run. Davey was always joking but never facetious, not like Meggie. Meggie had always been determinedly facetious, not wanting to commit herself, taking note of Madame Gran's warning of what wars did to people, putting their so great love for each other into 'pending'.

What a fool she had been, a stupid, stupid fool, not realising that love had to be caught in your hands, clasped tightly, held to you, before it went away and the bombs came, and death, and sorrow and horror, and innocent people of all kinds were killed or maimed.

A waiter came to her table and removed the second place setting. She watched him, not really registering his presence, trying to think, trying to arrive at the right choice. What the devil would they have danced to—not 'In The Mood'—no, something more romantic, perhaps. She summoned a waiter.

'Ask the band to play this, would you?' Meggie scribbled the name of her chosen song on a piece of paper.

Some few minutes later, as she sipped at her champagne and stared ahead of her, the strains of her chosen song floated across the dance floor to table six where one beautiful young woman, in a green silk evening dress, sat smoking and drinking while new and different young men took new and different young women in their arms, holding them close as they circled the floor, and she sat watching them, trying to imagine what it might be like to be dancing with them, Davey holding her in his arms, trying to imagine what it would be like if she was not quite alone.

Report from the Sussex Argus

THE MEN RETURN!

With the men returning from the war Sussex housewives everywhere are only too happy to return to home and hearth. After the deprivations of the war there is no doubt that the joys of the kitchen beckon. No more twelve-hour shifts in factories, or any of the other work that was so vital in war. The men are back and ready and willing to fill the jobs previously occupied by women, and the women are only too thankful to return to the kitchen and their making do and mending, to their knitting and sewing and all the other homely crafts that they have been forced to abandon on account of Hitler and his Nazis.

However, true though we know this to be, we did find some dissenting voices.

'Personally I shall miss my years as a ticket inspector on the railway,' Lady Melton of Upper Street, Bexham, told our reporter. 'As a child I was never allowed to play with my brother's trains, and being employed on the railways has been a dream come true. If I am ever called upon again, I shall not hesitate to volunteer. It was the most exciting time of my life, and although I am afraid the admiral is not happy when I tell him this, it is the truth. The admiral meanwhile has learned how to cook an omelette, really quite well, so it all goes to show.'

Of course not everyone feels like Lady Melton. Many are only too glad to get back to their jam making and their kitchens. With this in mind please turn to page six for a new recipe for Turnip and Rhubarb Jam and to page seven for 'Pleasurable Pinnies', a special feature on glamorous aprons for the clever, fashion-conscious housewife. Shoulder frills are going to be all the rage, we hear.

By our reporter.

* * *

Since she had been living alone, Judy's very private and solitary life had become all too firmly based on an imaginary one. She knew it had lately been taking too great a hold on her, becoming too real. She could not have said why, but with summer come, and the fields behind Owl Cottage turning a wonderful golden colour, with the pathway that passed the cottage becoming almost impassable beneath the proliferation of wild flowers and humming bees, she did not care.

Anyone seeing her setting the little oak table for two, making supper for two, talking to Walter's photograph as if it was himself come back to her, would undoubtedly have her taken away in a plain van.

'And quite right too!' she told Walter's photograph, blowing it a kiss.

Living alone again, after the cramped conditions of sharing during the war, was such bliss that she had become quite ashamed of her unadulterated joy in the space that she now had to herself. No one to worry about, just herself. No one to think about, just herself. With Loopy and Dauncy returning to Shelborne, peace had brought with it a sudden oasis, but not a void. A temporary halting of everything, during which Walter and only Walter filled her every waking thought, and many of her dreams too. Walter dancing, Walter laughing, Walter making love, Walter teasing her, Walter singing.

She turned and went to fetch the salad that she had carefully made for two. How ridiculous. She had become so obsessed with her fantasies, her imaginary life, for a second she thought she could actually *hear* Walter singing, instead of just imagining it.

And yet.

She stopped.

She could definitely hear a voice coming from the path that ran down the side of the field. A voice singing what Hugh always said had been the young boy's favourite song from Gilbert and Sullivan.

The song was coming nearer and nearer. Judy sighed to herself as she crossed to the wireless that she always played during meal times to cover the silence of being quite alone. Perhaps the singer was a labourer returning home. It suddenly seemed hard that the voice should sound so like Walter singing his childhood favourite from *HMS Pinafore*.

'We sail the ocean blue, and our saucy ship's a beauty . . .'

The voice came nearer and nearer still, until, just as she was about to turn up the wireless to drown out the memories of those happy days before the war, it seemed to be filling the small back garden, and it was definitely not a labourer. It was the strong voice of a real man coming towards the little French windows of the cottage, coming nearer, and nearer.

Judy's already large brown eyes grew larger and larger until she felt that they must have filled her face, because, of a sudden, there it seemed *was* Walter. And yet it was not Walter either, certainly not as he had been in her lonely dreams and fantasies. This was a broader brown-faced Walter, looking just like a Norwegian sailor in one of those thick navy blue sweaters made of rough, tough, scratchy wool, a black cap on his bonny head, a duffel bag slung on one shoulder.

Judy tried to speak and failed, she tried to walk towards what part of her still thought might be just another of her imaginings, but somehow her feet would not do as she wished. It was only when he reached out and took her in his arms that, feeling only half conscious although wholly alive, she realised that the impossible had happened, that somehow Walter had come back to her. Walter was alive, and holding her in his arms, and they were both laughing and crying at the same time, and kissing, and kissing . . . more kissing than even Judy's dreams had been able to conjure.

Report from the Sussex Argus

MISSING NOW FOUND!

A midsummer shock for the Tate family of Shelborne, Harbour Road, Bexham. Imagine their joyful amazement when their second son Lieutenant Commander Walter Tate, missing believed lost, returned to the bosom of his family last week. Rescued off the coast of Norway where his submarine had sunk, Lieutenant Commander Tate was hidden by the Norwegian Resistance in the mountains, and subsequently worked with them for the rest of the war. Unable to get a message to his wife and family he determined to surprise his wife, Judy, at their home, Owl Cottage, Back Lane, Bexham. Walter's father, Hugh Tate, who has been a resident of Bexham since 1922, told our reporter, 'There is much joy in that household, as you can well imagine. There will be a family celebration at the weekend when Major John Tate will be home on leave.'

By our reporter.

Epilogue

From a speech by Clement Attlee—September 1942

> 'The work women are performing in munitions factories has to be seen to be believed. Precision engineering jobs that would make a skilled turner's hair stand on end are performed with dead accuracy by girls who had no [previous] industrial experience.'

The output in munition production went up from one and a quarter million at the start of the war to eight and a half million by 1943. Forty per cent of this workforce were women. In engineering 35 per cent were women. In chemicals and explosives, the most dangerous type of factory work, women were invaluable, making up 52 per cent of the workforce. Royal Ordnance factory workers at times totalled a female workforce of 80 to 90 per cent.

Chivers Large Print Direct

If you have enjoyed this Large Print book and would like to build up your own collection of Large Print books and have them delivered direct to your door, please contact Chivers Large Print Direct

Chivers Large Print Direct offers you a full service:

* ☆ Created to support your local library
* ☆ Delivery direct to your door
* ☆ Easy-to-read type and attractively bound
* ☆ The very best authors
* ☆ Special low prices

For further details either call Customer Services on 01225 443400 or write to us at